**Praise for the Novels
of Faith Hunter**

Blood Cross

"Readers eager for the next book in Patricia Briggs's Mercy Thompson series may want to give Faith Hunter a try."
—*Library Journal*

"In a genre flooded with strong, sexy females, Jane Yellowrock is unique. . . . Her bold first person narrative shows that she's one tough cookie, but with a likable vulnerability . . . a pulse-pounding, page-turning adventure." —*Romantic Times*

Skinwalker

"Seriously. Best urban fantasy I've read in years, possibly ever." —C. E. Murphy, author of *Walking Dead*

"A fantastic start to the Jane Yellowrock series. Mixing fantasy with a strong mystery story line and a touch of romance, it ticks all the right urban fantasy boxes." —LoveVampires

"Stunning . . . plot and descriptions so vivid, they might as well be pictures or videos. Hunter captures the reader's attention from the first page and doesn't let go." —SF Site

"A fabulous tale with a heroine who clearly has the strength to stand on her own . . . a wonderfully detailed and fast moving adventure that fills the pages with murder, mystery, and fascinating characters." —Darque Reviews

"A promising new series with a strong heroine. . . . Jane is smart, quick, witty, and I look forward to reading more about her as she discovers more about herself." —Fresh Fiction

continued . . .

W9-BMP-093

Host

"Hunter's world continues to expand in this highly original fantasy with lively characters where nothing can ever be taken for granted."
—*Publishers Weekly*

"Hunter has created a remarkable interpretation of the aftermath of Armageddon in which angels and devils once again walk the earth and humans struggle to find a place. Stylish storytelling and gripping drama make this a good addition to most fantasy collections."
—*Library Journal*

"Readers will admire [Thorn's] sacrifice [in] placing others before herself. . . . Fans will enjoy reading about the continuing end of days."
—*Midwest Book Review*

"With fast-paced action and the possibility of more romance, this is an enjoyable read with an alluring magical touch."
—Darque Reviews

Seraphs

"The world [Hunter] has created is unique and bleak . . . [an] exciting science fiction thriller."
—*Midwest Book Review*

"Continuing the story begun in *Bloodring*, Hunter expands on her darkly alluring vision of a future in which the armies of good and evil wage their eternal struggle in the world of flesh and blood. Strong characters and a compelling story."
—*Library Journal*

"This thrilling dark fantasy has elements of danger, adventure, and religious fanaticism, plus sexual overtones. Hunter's impressive narrative skills vividly describe a changed world, and she artfully weaves in social commentary . . . a well-written, exciting novel."
—*Romantic Times*

Bloodring

"A bold interpretation of the what-might-be.... With a delicate weaving of magic and scripture, Faith Hunter left me wondering: What's a woman to do when she falls in love with a seraph's child?"
—Kim Harrison

"Entertaining ... outstanding supporting characters ... the strong cliff-hanger of an ending bodes well for future adventures."
—*Publishers Weekly*

"The cast is incredible.... Fans of postapocalypse fantasies will appreciate this superb interpretation of the endless end of days."
—*Midwest Book Review*

"Hunter's distinctive future vision offers a fresh though dark glimpse into a newly made postapocalyptic world. Bold and imaginative in approach, with appealing characters and a suspense-filled story, this belongs in most fantasy collections."
—*Library Journal*

"It's a pleasure to read this engaging tale about characters connected by strong bonds of friendship and family. Mixes romance, high fantasy, apocalyptic, and postapocalyptic adventure to good effect."
—*Kirkus Reviews*

"Hunter's very professionally executed, tasty blend of dark fantasy, mystery, and romance should please fans of all three genres."
—*Booklist*

"Entertaining ... a promising new series.... Steady pacing, dashes of humor, and a strong story line coupled with a great ending neatly setting up the next adventure make this take on the apocalypse worth checking out."   —*Monsters and Critics*

"Enjoyable ... a tale of magic and secrets in a world gone mad."
—*Romantic Times*

ALSO BY FAITH HUNTER

The Jane Yellowrock Novels

Skinwalker
Blood Cross

The Rogue Mage Novels

Bloodring
Seraphs
Host

MERCY BLADE

A Jane Yellowrock Novel

Faith Hunter

A ROC BOOK

ROC

Published by New American Library, a division of
Penguin Group (USA) Inc., 375 Hudson Street,
New York, New York 10014, USA
Penguin Group (Canada), 90 Eglinton Avenue East, Suite 700, Toronto,
Ontario M4P 2Y3, Canada (a division of Pearson Penguin Canada Inc.)
Penguin Books Ltd., 80 Strand, London WC2R 0RL, England
Penguin Ireland, 25 St. Stephen's Green, Dublin 2,
Ireland (a division of Penguin Books Ltd.)
Penguin Group (Australia), 250 Camberwell Road, Camberwell, Victoria 3124,
Australia (a division of Pearson Australia Group Pty. Ltd.)
Penguin Books India Pvt. Ltd., 11 Community Centre, Panchsheel Park,
New Delhi - 110 017, India
Penguin Group (NZ), 67 Apollo Drive, Rosedale, North Shore 0632,
New Zealand (a division of Pearson New Zealand Ltd.)
Penguin Books (South Africa) (Pty.) Ltd., 24 Sturdee Avenue,
Rosebank, Johannesburg 2196, South Africa

Penguin Books Ltd., Registered Offices:
80 Strand, London WC2R 0RL, England

First published by Roc, an imprint of New American Library,
a division of Penguin Group (USA) Inc.

First Printing, January 2011
10 9 8 7 6 5 4 3 2 1

PUBLISHER'S NOTE
This is a work of fiction. Names, characters, places, and incidents either are the prod-
uct of the author's imagination or are used fictitiously, and any resemblance to actual persons, living or dead, business establishments, events, or locales is entirely
coincidental.

The publisher does not have any control over and does not assume any responsibility for author or third-party Web sites or their content.

If you purchased this book without a cover you should be aware that this book is
stolen property. It was reported as "unsold and destroyed" to the publisher and neither the author nor the publisher has received any payment for this "stripped book."

The scanning, uploading, and distribution of this book via the Internet or via any
other means without the permission of the publisher is illegal and punishable by
law. Please purchase only authorized electronic editions, and do not participate in or
encourage electronic piracy of copyrighted materials. Your support of the author's
rights is appreciated.

To my Renaissance Man,
who plays guitar and sings me to sleep, never says no to a
challenge, and brings me chocolate

ACKNOWLEDGMENTS

(in no order whatsoever)

Mike Pruette, Web guru for www.faithhunter.net and fan.

Rod Hunter, as always, for the right word when my tired brain was stymied, and for making the research trip to Louisiana so much fun.

Joyce Wright, for reading everything I write, no matter how "weird."

Kim Harrison, Misty Massey, David B. Coe, C. E. Murphy, A. J. Hartley, Stuart Jaffe, Tamar Myers, Greg Paxton, Raven Blackwell, Christina Stiles, and all my writer friends, for being our own unofficial writers support group.

My Yahoo! fan group at www.groups.yahoo.com/group/the-enclave/.

The Puddy Tats fan group.

My cowriters at www.magicalwords.net.

Lucienne Diver, for doing what an agent does best, with grace and kindness.

Last but not least—

My editor at Roc, Jessica Wade, who has helped to sculpt the multisouled Beast in Jane.

Y'all ROCK!

CHAPTER 1

I Didn't Know You Had a Brain

I rolled over, taking most of the covers with me as I stretched. I felt like a big, satisfied cat—well fed, well loved, and nearly purring with contentment. Beside me, still snoring softly, was Rick LaFleur, my boyfriend. *Crap.* I had a *boyfriend.* I was still trying to get used to the idea. We'd been together for more than a month, when he wasn't disappearing into the underbelly of New Orleans investigating—well, investigating something he had yet to share with me. Or when I wasn't tied up with vamp HQ security systems. The Master of the City had ordered a total upgrade of the grounds; I was earning my retainer.

Our jobs meant stealing moments when we could.

The relationship with Rick was still new. Still scary. I wasn't yet sure when to push the barriers of conversation, or sharing of info, and when to hold back. Rick is a cop, so some things he can't share; my job means keeping clients' secrets, so ditto on the not sharing. It puts a barrier between us at times.

Worse, part of me was still fighting having him around. It wasn't that I resisted commitment. Really. Part of me just resisted sharing my territory. I mean, I already shared my body with another soul, and having another person around so much had seriously affected my lifestyle, stealing time from the other half of my dual nature. I hadn't shifted into Beast in two weeks, and while she had nothing but good stuff to say about my sex life, my big-cat was pacing unhappily at not being allowed out to hunt.

I sat up on the side of the bed and retied my hip-length hair into a sloppy knot at the back of my head, tucking silver-tipped stakes into the makeshift bun. For a rogue-vamp killer, it was an action similar to a cop carrying his weapon with him to the potty. Overkill, paranoid, but once it had kept him alive, so it became habit. Stakes twenty-four/seven had become my new habit.

I eased out of bed and padded naked—except for the gold-nugget necklace I never took off—to the bathroom of my tiny one-room apartment in the Appalachian Mountains. I had given my landlady notice on the place, and Rick and I had motored up from Louisiana on our bikes—his Kawasaki and my bastard Harley—rented a small truck, and cleared out my stuff. All that was left to load was the TV, the bikes themselves, and the last of my linens and clothes. Even the bed had come with the furnished apartment, and I didn't own much except things I could carry—clothes and weapons. My job usually re-quired a lot of travel, and I wasn't in a position to own or keep a lot of stuff unless it helped me stay alive.

Starting to wake up, moving in the murky light with ease, I put on water for tea and turned on the coffeemaker. As I worked, I checked on the weather through the window to see a very dark, gray dawn, with lowering clouds and intermittent rain. The thermometer on the tiny porch read seventy-two, not bad for summer in the mountains, though it might hit ninety by noon. We had arrived last night, and had only today in the high country before heading back to New Orleans, where I was living for the next six months, thanks to the retainer I had accepted from the Louisiana vamp council. When that gig was over, I'd have to make a decision where to live, but the past few months had been profitable enough to make that much less worrisome than during my once-upon-a-broke-and-destitute time. And with Rick in my life, it was nice to be stick-ing around one place for a while.

I sat in a pink painted chair at the kitchen table, waiting as water burbled in the coffeemaker and the flames hissed under the pot. Pink was my landlady's color, not mine. The shade had never bothered me, as I wasn't here often enough to care one way or another about the decor, but Rick had teased me unmercifully about the frills, ruffles, tucks, buttons, and florals that Old Lady Pierson had thought appropriate for the rental space under the eaves of her house.

I clicked on the TV to check the time, muting the sound. CNN was on, showing a still shot of a good-looking man with fierce eyes, very black skin, and short-cropped hair. The words "Breaking News" lit the bar at the bottom, followed by "BBC claims existence of were-creatures."

"Crap," I whispered. Beast awoke inside me with the instant attentive awareness of the predator, and focused through my eyes at the screen. I eased up the volume one notch and drew on Beast's excellent hearing to listen to the commentator, whose voice-over spoke about the picture of a reporter, blond-haired and fair-skinned, holding a microphone.

"Though no independent confirmation exists, BBC investigator Donald Cooper, seen here in the center of the screen, has released an interview with an African man referred to only as Kemnebi, pictured in the upper portion of the screen. Kemnebi claims to be a were-cat, a black leopard. In the footage that follows we see Kemnebi remove his clothing and shift into a jungle cat. We caution our viewers that the BBC footage is graphic and depicts partial nudity common to his culture."

I leaned toward the screen and watched as footage began to roll. The man from the still shot, who was carefully filmed above the lower hips for decorum's sake, began to remove his clothes, dropping them one by one to the floor. He bent, most of him disappearing from the screen as if to remove his pants, and then crossed the room. He was tall and thin, muscles well defined, his skin stretched over a frame without an ounce of fat. He moved with a lissome grace uncommon in humans other than dancers. Still silent, the man knelt on a cushion on the floor, the camera viewing him from the side, the long, lean length of his body gleaming—a lot of skin for an American cable TV network.

Tension raced through me. It could be a joke. No new supernatural being had appeared on the world stage since the vamps and witches came out of the supernat closet after the Secret Service staked Marilyn Monroe while she was trying to turn the president in the Oval Office. No elves, no pixies, no trolls, no brownies, no nothing. Certainly no weres or skinwalkers—or there wasn't since I killed the only one of my kind I'd ever met. That very old, very nutso skinwalker had stolen the form of a vamp and taken to killing and eating humans and vampires, so it had been a sanctioned kill. Since then, as a shape-shifter in hiding, I was a singularity in the world of humans, vamps, and witches. No longer, if the BBC's claims were real. *If.*

I closed my fingers on the arms of the chair, digging in with my nails. I'm a skinwalker, not a were; I didn't know if the magics would be the same, totally different, or only subtly dissimilar. *If it was real.*

The man began to lose focus. A pale fog seemed to sift from his skin and surround him, blurring him, the mist moving slowly, as if caught in a breeze. Dark lights sparkled through the haze, looking like black crystals on the digital footage. It wasn't exactly the way I looked when I shifted, though a lot of things might affect what I was seeing, from the digital processing software to my cheap TV. But it was familiar. Very achingly familiar.

The black lights surrounding Kemnebi increased as the mist above his skin darkened, deepened. His bones popped, a sickening sound, as they shortened or lengthened and the joints reshaped. He threw back his head, mouth open in what looked like a silent scream, like gut-wrenching pain. Black hair sprouted all over his body. His spine bowed and arched. Canines grew up from his gums, an inch long on the bottom jaw, longer on top. His jaw and skull took on different contours, flowing into a catlike form. I could see the effort and agony as his flesh rippled, stretched, and restructured into something else.

I couldn't look away from the screen. Cold sweat broke out on my body. I could hear my breath, coarse and uneven over the soft patter of rain on the metal roof. My heartbeat raced and stuttered.

Beast placed a clawed paw onto my mind as if to calm me, her gaze intent on the screen before us. *Beast is not prey*, she thought at me. *Will not be afraid.*

Yeah, right, I thought back. I never looked away from the transformation on the television. My eyes burned, hot and scratchy. I shivered, skin prickling. Two minutes passed. The fog that was a man wisped away. A jungle cat sat on the floor where once the man had knelt. It had a black coat, with barely visible muted spots that caught the light. Its paws had retractable claws like my Beast's, but its tail was long and slender, unlike my Beast's heavy, clubbed version. The black leopard looked into the camera. Huffed. And, I swear, it grinned.

Beast trembled deep inside, her coat bristling against my

skin, coarse and almost painful. *Big-cat. Like Beast. But not like Beast.* Beast opened her mouth and chuffed in displeasure, pulling back her lips, showing her fangs deep in my mind, as if the leopard on-screen could see her challenge and her strength. *Beast is better. I/we are better hunter. Stronger.*

"Is it real," said the CNN reporter when the screen flashed back to a still of Donald Cooper, "or is it a hoax? Or maybe it's only special effects for an upcoming British action-adventure blockbuster. Or"—his voice dropped lower—"maybe other supernatural creatures like Kemnebi, the African black were-leopard, have been living among us all along. More on this breaking news as it develops."

I flipped to the BBC, finding only footage of a war zone somewhere, and began flipping cable news stations for more on the were. There was nothing. Not yet. From behind me, I heard the bed squeak and had a moment to school my face as Rick rolled over and glanced at the television, then stared at me, sitting naked in the stark shadows created by the TV's glare. He smiled slowly, his eyes roaming over me in the bluish light, his teeth white against his black two-day beard. Even with the stubble—or maybe in part because of it—he was stunning. Black-eyed, slender, my six feet in height or an inch more, he had the smooth golden olive complexion of his mostly French and American Indian heritage. With his shaggy, bed-head black hair, he was by far the prettiest man I had ever known. Just looking at him could make my heart speed up, dance around, and melt into a puddle of happy hormones. Even this morning, when the world was changing around me. "Morning, babe," he said, voice gravelly with sleep. "What time is it? I smell coffee."

"Morning, yourself. Sorry I woke you. It's five a.m. I put on a pot."

"The rain woke me, not you. How did you live here with the noise?"

The question was rhetorical and I didn't answer. I'd scarcely noticed the rain on the metal roof. As he slid from the sheets, the light from the TV caught the scars on his chest and abdomen, white against his skin, big-cat claws in harsh relief. He'd nearly died fighting the skinwalker in sabertooth lion form that had tried to kill him while he was undercover for the New Orleans Police Department, something he'd half forgotten. He was alive today only because Beast and I had chased off the skinwalker and called the vampire Master of the City of New Orleans to save him.

Rick stretched his way into the bathroom, the flickering light dappling his skin, his tattoos looking dark and menacing—the golden eyes of the crouching mountain lion and the bobcat on one shoulder visible in the gloom, the globes of red on their claws too bright. Seeing them, I shivered again. I didn't believe in fate or karma, but the presence of my two cats painted on his body had always seemed like a sign, a portent, that we should, and one day would, be together. And now we were. When one of us wasn't working.

The bobcat had been the first animal I'd shifted into when I was a child. The mountain lion was my adult beast, and my Beast, the other soul sharing my head. That she was inside with me wasn't skinwalker magic, but something darker. She was there by accident, but even an accident didn't make the black magic any cleaner, purer, or more acceptable.

Beast is amused by my guilt, any guilt, even the guilt I feel about stealing her soul. My Beast goes by many names: cougar, puma, panther, catamount, screamer, devil-cat, silver lion, mountain lion, and even the North American black panther, but they all refer to one beast—the *Puma concolor*, which once was the widest ranging mammal on the North American continent, and is still one of the largest modern-day land predators in the continental U.S. other than humans, bears, a few large wolves, and the vamps.

Rick moved toward the coffeepot like steel to a magnet and found a mug in the dark. My heart did a little pitter-patter and a blood flush touched my skin, evidence of Beast's appreciation of my boyfriend. Since Rick and I had, um, gotten together, my own emotional roller coaster had smoothed out, and her rut had faded. I hadn't had any more peculiar crying jags, and Beast had begun to purr more often. When Beast is happy, everybody—or everyone in my body—is happy. I heard coffee pouring into the mug and the softer sounds of swallowing. Rick sighed in pleasure, a sound I was learning had many different meanings—food, music, and sex each had its own sigh. Coffee, however, was in a category by itself, being as much relief as bliss.

I looked back at the TV, back on CNN, and saw a still shot of a sitting leopard. I gestured with the remote, keeping my voice light, slightly wry. "Big news. Guy claims he's a black were-leopard. I just saw him change shape on BBC footage."

Rick went still, staring at the screen, studying the jungle cat that was sitting with its front paws close, ears pricked forward, preening and purring, making nice with the camera. "Pretty cat," Rick murmured finally, his voice oddly casual. The "pretty cat" comment made me smile and made Beast huff with something like possessive jealousy, which was amusing on all kinds of levels.

Rick's fingertips brushed the cat-claw scars on his chest, an unconscious gesture. "It's got green eyes and a round pupil, like a human. Not cat eyes."

Shock chased the contentment away. The sabertooth lion that had almost killed him had had round pupils. *Rick was remembering.* "Big-cats have a round pupil," I said, my voice sounding calm despite my speeding heart rate. "Housecats and some smaller wildcats have a slit pupil."

Rick grunted, eyes fixed on the screen, his tone mild in counterpoint, as if saying, *Well, how 'bout that.* "Turn it up."

I did as he requested, and flipped to the BBC channel where the were-cat news was on again, and Donald Cooper was saying, "—quite keen on the hunt, he is, when in cat form. Vegetarians and animal protection organizations the world over will likely put out quite a stink at his diet, which is fresh meat on the hoof, and, according to him, tastes better if he brings down his prey with his were-teeth and claws."

Beast agreed with the statement, sending me images of a big-cat bringing down bigger prey. It was graphic and bloody and beastly. Beast huffed with amusement and retreated back into the darker parts of my mind.

Rick took his mug to the bed and sat, patting the mattress. Over coffee-scent, I smelled tea steeping. He'd poured hot water in the pot, over the leaves in the strainer. I smelled a strong black I particularly loved, an organic Darjeeling first flush that I would have all the time if I could, but at a hundred twenty bucks a pound, it was too dear for regular drinking. This pound was a gift from Rick, unexpected and generous and thoughtful.

In the kitchen, I removed the leaves and joined him in bed with my own mug, tea sweetened and topped with a dollop of Cool Whip, and carrying a box of Krispy Kremes that had been Hot 'n Now last night, and were still fresh enough to melt in my mouth. I curled into the crook of his arm, not easy when there was no height disparity, but not impossible for the truly determined. It was cozy and warm and well established, as if we cuddled this way every day instead of only when we could grab the time.

On some level I felt guilty for sleeping with Rick, for being so homey and comfortable with him outside of marriage. My housemother in the Christian children's home where I grew up would have chided me for it. A lot. It was that guilt that pricked me now as I lay against him, watching the flickering screen. And that guilt that I shoved away, deep inside, to worry about later. A lot later.

Overhead, the rain's metallic pattering grew into a drumming roar. Rick turned the TV up another two notches and I snuggled close to him, skin to skin, watching the events unfurl across the globe as America woke to a world quite different from the one they'd left behind in dreams. There was an unconscious tension thrumming through Rick as he watched, and his hand strayed often to his scars.

We had missed the interview with the black were-leopard, but tuned in for an in-depth and politically astute dialogue between Donald Cooper and Raymond Micheika, a rare African were-lion who said he was the leader of the International Association of Weres, and of the Party of African Weres. Rick spelled out the acronym—PAW—and said he thought it was amusing, while I thought it was disingenuous and too cute for the raw power of the man. Raymond Micheika was an alpha predator, bigger than Beast and twice as vicious.

I can be big, she reminded me smugly. *The I/we of Beast can be alpha male sabertooth. Kill any male big-cat in personal challenge.*

"Some cat species run, live, and hunt in packs," I murmured, to Rick as much as to Beast. "Take on one, I bet you take on them all."

Rick said, "Yeah. I'd hate to meet him in a dark alley, especially with his cronies around. 'We need a bigger gun,'" he paraphrased the old *Jaws* movie, his voice tight in contrast to the light words. I turned and watched his face. "If there's cats, then there's gotta be other things," he said, sipping his coffee, his fingers still tracing his scars. "Maybe whatever gorilla-type creature Big Foot is. Maybe that fish thing they see in the Great Lakes. *Werewolves*," Rick said. "The B-grade movie variety." He knew I was watching him, but he kept his gaze on the TV, avoiding my eyes, not letting me in. He took a slow breath and said the words that had been playing around inside his head. "Sabertooth cats." When I didn't reply, he said, "Like the one that got me. You killed it. And it changed back to human."

"Part human," I said, watching his face, my breath tight, "part vamp, part sabertooth."

"If they only change partway back when they die, why haven't we found any half-human skeletons?" His fingers caressed his scars, his eyes glued to the TV, tension buzzing through him, almost singing from him.

"He wasn't a were," I said slowly, knowing we were straying perilously close to the word *skinwalker*.

"He was something else." His hand slid from his scars, his tension softening. That was what I liked most about Rick, other than his sex-on-a-stick smile, his tats, and his ability to let me do my job without being overly protective. He was smart. He didn't overanalyze things. He just . . . accepted what was.

"Yeah."

The thing I liked least about him, however, was job related—the fact that we couldn't share much of our lives. So far, though we'd been sleeping together for weeks, he hadn't talked about the attack that nearly killed him. He'd been undercover at the time, and the story he had been told was that I had followed him in human form, chased off the cat that had mauled him, and later killed it. But his memories had to include two cats, not one. Someday we'd have to address that. Someday we had to address a lot of things, if our relationship was to continue.

I sipped my tea, waiting, giving him a chance to draw whatever conclusions he might be heading toward. He opened his mouth, stopped, closed it. It was like missing a step in a dance. As if something had gone astray, been omitted, and I had no idea what.

A half beat later, Rick indicated the TV with his mug and veered the subject onto a different course, his tone forced, but lighter, his voice the cop-tone he used when he was telling something he knew for fact. "That's a slick bit of video. This wasn't filmed fast and dumped on the airwaves. They spent time with it, which means the BBC's known about weres for a while."

I shifted slightly to see his face better. But he didn't look my way. "And?" I asked, trying to read his body language, recognizing the slight trace of adrenaline leaching from his pores.

"There's no way they could keep it totally under wraps. Word probably got out that it was going to hit the airwaves. And whatever weres we have in the U.S. will have been informed it was going to break and will make a statement. Fast." He said it like a pronouncement rather than just guessing.

When Rick was undercover, he had been investigating the vamps, and though he'd been outed to them, any weres . . . *Crap.* Any weres would never know he was a cop. He could fit in anywhere, which had made him so good undercover. And Rick had been mostly unavailable for the last couple of weeks, appearing for quick breakfast dates, late-night dinners, and for this trip into the mountains to move me to New Orleans. Suddenly I realized why Rick had been working undercover. It had something to do with weres.

My cold chills returned, lifting my skin in tight points as if my pelt rose. Beast rumbled inside, watching Rick, curious, focused, like a kitten watching a fluffy toy twisting on the end of a string, not sure if attack was warranted. I breathed in through my open mouth, Beast-like. The scent of his body was like the color of daffodils, yellow and tart. Rick *did* know something.

He took a donut and ate it in three bites, washing it down with coffee. "This announcement," he said, sounding more certain than prophetic, "will be followed with one of several reactions." He licked the sugar from a finger and held it up. "One. The press will go wild. That's axiomatic, actually." He held up another finger. "Two. More weres'll come out of the closet. Three. The white supremacists and the xenophobic human extremists'll join hands and vow to hunt down and exterminate the nonhumans."

"And they call you a glass-is-half-full kinda guy." I could hear the low timbre of concern in my voice.

"Hey, I'm an optimist, babe," Rick said. But he still hadn't taken his eyes off the TV; he still hadn't looked at me. He chuckled and took another donut, gesturing with it. "It's gonna be a zoo. You know. Wild animals. Zoo."

I made the requisite groan over the humor. "You know something, don't you?"

He lifted a shoulder, noncommittal.

Apprehension started to churn in the pit of my stomach, heavy, bitter tasting, a dark, recirculating whirlpool of possibilities. Wondering what he knew. Wondering if—okay, hoping that—skinwalkers would come out with the weres. Hoping that I finally wouldn't be alone. And worrying what Rick might do when—if—he learned he had been sleeping with one. "*Pretty cat,*" he'd said of the black were-leopard, as if he had liked it. But it was a heck of a lot easier to be blasé about a theory; it might be quite different in a relationship reality. And, last, wondering what he had been doing undercover with weres.

I hadn't smelled anything on him, but his sisters had cats, and there were at least a dozen barn cats at his parents' place. If he'd been with were-cats, I might not have noticed.

Back on the BBC, Donald was chatting with the big-cat, Kemnebi, once again in human form, about how he became a cat, the interview we had missed. The were-cat spoke English, the dialect one of those liquid African accents that flowed like water down stone. "We reproduce much as human do, mating and having baby. But we have litter, some small, some large, some with cat baby that have potential to change to human, some with human baby that have potential to change to cat. Some with both. Potential is there, ready to be awakened."

"You don't bite to make a were-cat?" the anchor asked, clearly surprised.

"No. To bite a human, even in self-defense, is against all of our laws," he said, his black-skinned face compelling. "To bite a human, hoping to turn him into one of us, is a death sentence. We may not mate with human, for fear of passing the contagion. For this crime, there is no mercy."

Rick started to speak and stopped. A broken instant later he said, "Jodi's gonna love adding that to the woo-woo files." Jodi is Rick's boss, in charge of all paranormal investigations in the party city of the South. "Especially the part about a human-shaped mother giving birth to a litter of kittens and humans all at the same time."

I didn't reply. We watched, switching channels between the networks and the cable stations as the sky lightened outside, despite the din of rain. We didn't talk, though I wanted to ask questions, wanted to know what Rick was thinking. I had a feeling that a normal girl would have been pumping him for answers about his were-knowledge. But I had no idea what to ask or how to do it. Unlike most girls, I hadn't spent my early years absorbing the social interactions between humans. Impossible to do while living inside the body of a mountain lion; nearly as hard to do while living in a children's home, the amnesiac outsider with no English and no past. So I sat on the bed, my shoulder under Rick's, snuggled close, with him, but alone.

Near six a.m., Rick changed to FOX, which was running an interview purported to be with one of the leaders of the U.S. werewolves, the Lupus Clan, based in Cheyenne, Wyoming. "What'd I tell you?" Rick said. We'd slid down in the bed, under the covers, mugs replenished and a box of cereal open between us as we ate it, dry. "*Werewolves*. B-grade movie version." The purported wolfman was muscled but slender, strawberry blond, tough-looking, aggressive, angry, gesticulating in a hostile manner, his words being bleeped as he cursed at the reporter.

Rick said, "Bet it'd tick him off to hear this, but he's mean as a pit bull."

It struck me as funny and I chuckled, mostly in relief. Rick slanted me a grin and I snorted, feeling better, though not sure why. On TV, the pit bull/werewolf was still going at it.

"He stands about six feet tall," Rick mused, "and probably one eighty. How big do you think he'd be as a wolf?" There was something odd about his tone, but then there was something odd about Rick today altogether, so I didn't know how to categorize this new odd.

"If the law of conservation of mass and energy holds true," I said, thinking about what happened when I shifted into any animal that genetically might equal my body mass, "then he'd be a wolf weighing in at one eighty." Rick looked at me in surprise. "What?" I asked. "I took physics in high school."

"So did I but I'd never remember the name of a law. I didn't know you had a brain," he said, teasing. I made a fist and mimed socking him. He took my fist and kissed my fingers, one at time, which had my toes curling. I gripped his hand, holding it tightly, as if it might disappear. As if *he* might disappear. "Besides," Rick said, his lips moving against my knuckles, "it's magic. Why would the physical laws hold true?"

"Why wouldn't they? Those black motes that floated around him when he changed looked like sparks of some kind, which is energy." I muted the TV and rolled over so I could look up at him, and so he'd have better access to my fingers and any other parts of me he might want to reach, wanting to touch him, wanting him to touch me. I slid my other hand up his arm, his skin warm against my palm. "When the man became a black were-leopard, the cat looked big enough to weigh one eighty."

"So if a fat guy got turned into a were, he'd be a fat were?"

I laughed at the mental image of a pudgy black leopard, rolls of fat undulating as he walked. Beast showed fangs, not amused. "No. Remember, that Micheika guy said the caloric requirements of shifting were enormous."

"So fat people could get bitten by a were and lose weight every time the moon was full."

"You're a funny guy. Funny, funny guy." But the mundane dull chitchat and the texture of his skin had relaxed me. "They get killed for biting a human. Not a good way to promote weight loss."

"There is that. And they go furry once a month. Hard to hold down a job with that." Rick returned his attention to the TV and switched between news channels to stop on CNN again, where they were playing an early-morning telephone interview with a Texas senator named Jones about the "problem with the supernatural creatures in our midst," as he put it. Jones, his speech pattern stolen from small-town Southern Baptist preachers, said, "In species that live for *cent-u-ries* instead of *decades*, of what use are *stat-utes of lim-i-ta-tion*? And, how long is a *life sentence* for *vampires*, who live decades longer than *real humans*? How will we deal with the *cost to the prison system* in terms of prison cells that will be occupied for *cent-u-ries*? In terms of *feeding* the *bloodsuckers*? Keeping them safe from the sun? In terms of the *confine*-ment *require*-ments to hold a *creature* that is so much stronger than *humans*. How do we control the foul things?"

"For vamps, you hire a vamp-killer," I said to the screen, "and give them true-death, according to Mithran Law. Human law can't apply. Which Congress will figure out sooner or later."

"They haven't so far," Rick said, cynical and disparaging, "and it's playing havoc with the legal system."

Just to round out the hater of nonhumans, Jones added, "And these *witches*. The Holy Scriptures tells us that we 'must not suffer a witch to live.'" He raised a finger toward the sky. "Our *great coun-try* has already fallen far from God's *i-deal* by allowing—"

Rick lowered the volume and switched through the news channels, the TV glare flashing with each channel jump. He said, "Even money says Jones likes small boys, and that he'll propose a law that allows law enforcement officers to shoot first and ask questions later when it comes to weres, vamps, and witches."

"Did you hear that?" I rolled back upright and took the remote, found the channel and raised the volume on the TV to hear the wolfman say, "... killed my grandfather, Henri Molyneux, and stole our hunting territory from us. Murder and grand theft." He snarled, "I can prove Leo Pellissier is guilty of it. And"—he glared into the TV camera—"there's no statute of limitations on murder."

"Oh crap," I muttered, seeing a sidebar photo of Leo, vampire Master of the City of New Orleans, dressed in a tuxedo, looking gorgeous and suave and anything but dangerous. I'd seen him wearing his other face, his vamped-out, creepy, and dangerous as a rabid wolf face. Though the wolf thought may not be politically acceptable now.

Rick laughed, half mocking, slanting his eyes at me. "Vacation's over," he said. "Your boss is accused of murder. You know he'll want his pet rogue-vamp killer at his side." He looked at the time on the screen. "It's ten minutes to dawn. He'll call. Five bucks." He held out his hand to shake on the offered bet.

"You knew all about this," I accused. Rick shrugged, not denying it. "And you offer me awful bets," I grumbled. "No, thanks." Five minutes later, my new cell phone chirped. Rick rolled out of bed, hunting up his clothes.

I answered the phone, which displayed Leo Pellissier's private number.

CHAPTER 2

A Fighting Ring

"Morning, Leo. I'm watching the news and the so-called were-wolf accusing you of murder," I said in my professional, all-business tone.

"Good morning," he said, sounding urbane and wry, the slight hint of French in his tone. "Yes. Such an accusation is unfortunate in several respects."

No kidding, I thought. But I didn't say it.

"Envoys of the IAW arrived in Washington, D.C., two weeks ago, and have been engaged in closed-door talks with the national Council of Mithrans and members of Congress about the changing geopolitical situation. At the same time, a high-level member of the Party of African Weres and his assistant were also sent to New Orleans to parley with me regarding their bid for worldwide recognition."

I narrowed my eyes at Rick, who was watching me, a slight smile playing on his mouth. To Leo and Rick I said, "You didn't think it important to tell me that *were-cats* were in town? For two *weeks*?"

Rick shrugged and mouthed, "Orders. Politics." As he spoke, he reached for his phone vibrating on the cabinet top.

"The applicable phrase was 'Need to know,'" Leo said, "and a vampire hunter had no need to know about weres. This unexpected allegation against me of werewolf murder may, however, significantly complicate matters with the cats, despite the fact that wolves and cats traditionally do not get along."

Which was news to me. Everything about this situation was news to me. I was ticked off because I had been kept totally out of this loop and I shouldn't have been.

"I require your presence to finalize the security upgrade for the Council building and to research what possible evidence the wolves might have against me."

"And how am I going to do that?" I asked, just to yank his chain.

"You have access to certain files. You will use them."

I could almost see his chin jut out in that "don't push me" manner he has. I was pretty sure Leo was talking about the files from the woo-woo room in NOPD. The Master of the City knew the New Orleans Police Department kept files on all the supernats, including him. While he didn't like it, he wasn't averse to using them to his advantage.

"I see that you are still in the mountains near Asheville, North Carolina," Leo said. "Can you be back in New Orleans by dusk?"

I frowned at the phone, which was a top-of-the-line, next generation, mini-electronic marvel, with every available bell and whistle. Leo had given it to me recently, insisting that the GPS location system in it could save my life. It seemed it could tell him where I was when I had it with me too. I didn't like being on Leo's leash, but he was paying me enough to keep me from griping about it too much, though I'd bought a throwaway phone for private calls. "If the rain eases up, and we break all the speed limits, it's possible."

"I'll have George send coordinates, map, directions, and address to your cell," he said. "A persona non grata is encroaching upon my territory and it is likely that he had contact with the werewolves in the past. Meet with him, find out what he knows, and then send him packing."

"Yeah, I'll just walk up to the guy, smile sweetly, and he'll spill his guts," I said, heavy on the sarcasm. I'm not the kinda girl guys go goo-goo eyed over, but I didn't say that part.

"Then obtain his information, and warn him off by whatever means you deem appropriate."

Now, *that* I could do just fine. Breaking vamp heads is a personal and professional specialty. "This guy got a name?"

"Several. You will be provided a description. After you deal with the interloper, you will return to the Council building to assist in security preparations for the diplomatic celebration, which will officially welcome the were-cat envoys. You will also address security concerns for the visiting dignitaries and their accommodations." His words were growing clipped and hurried. Dawn was dangerous to even the most ancient vamps, and Leo would want to be in one of his lairs before the sun rose. "And I expect a report on your investigation into the evidence against me by tomorrow."

"That's not enough time—"

"At dusk." The connection ended.

I looked at the phone and sighed. No one said good-bye anymore.

"Rain's letting up," Rick said, setting his cell back on the table and rolling to his feet, lithe as a cat himself. "Want to see if we can get the bikes loaded? I don't know what your orders were, but mine are to get back to town ASAP. We'll need to cancel breakfast with Molly and her sisters at the café." He pulled on his boxers and jeans, and bent, looking for his shirt. Any hopes I'd had of a long, leisurely morning in bed, followed by a hearty breakfast in the Seven Sisters Café, evaporated. And I liked to eat. A lot.

I sat up and dropped my feet to floor. "I hate vamp politics."

Two hours before dusk, we reached my freebie house, the two-story French Quarter residence where I was living rent free for the duration of my contract with the Master of the City. When we opened the doors and stepped from the rental truck, the heat hit me like a wet, soggy fist. Summer in New Orleans is not for the fainthearted.

Rick wheeled my bike off the truck and I carried my stuff down the narrow two-rut lane beside the house to the side porch and stacked it near the new grill Rick had bought me. The size of the pile surprised me. I didn't like to think of myself as owning much in the way of worldly possessions, but the kitchen utensils, linens, and clothes took up four extra large shopping bags and two cardboard boxes of middling size. For me, it was a lot of belongings, and I hadn't realized how many things I had accumulated in the last few years.

Rick, already looking distracted, his cop-face in place, kissed me on the cheek and walked off, leaving me there, on the porch, alone, with a casual, "I'll drop off the truck. See you at breakfast tomorrow, babe." I stood there, listening to his booted feet as he walked around the house, got in the truck and drove off. No hesitation or uncertainty in his stride.

Breakfast? See you at breakfast tomorrow? That's it? Then I remembered the calls and texts he'd received on the trip back. He was needed, and I'd bet my left big toe he was headed back undercover with the visiting were-cats.

Disgruntled, I locked the side gate, hauled my bags and boxes inside, and put away the clothes and other stuff. Little of what I owned was suitable for the heat of a New Orleans summer, and my linens were thrift store purchases—flannel and rough terrycloth—not the six-hundred-thread-count sheets and plush towels I was using as part of the freebie house. I left most of it in the bags and boxes in the back of my bedroom closet, next to the gun safe, where it took up most of the floor space.

The house was empty—my current roomie was out doing witch council things—which was fine with me. I wasn't happy to have Evangelina Everheart, water witch, professor, and three-star chef, as a guest—except for when she cooked, which made up for a lot of inconvenience—but her sister, Molly, had volunteered my home as a base for the visiting witch. Molly was my best friend, and I had never been able to say no to her about anything.

With the house to myself, there was plenty of time to get weaponed up. Meeting a guest at dusk meant I'd be up against a vamp, and an enemy of Leo's meant he was a master, so I wanted every edge I could get—bladed pun intended. I unlocked my newly installed weapon cabinet, and laid my arsenal out on the bed. I had a lot of weapons—the Benelli M4, several handguns, lots of blades and stakes, both silver and wood. And a vial of holy water I still hadn't tried on a vamp. In two velvet bags I also had a pink diamond witch stone used for black magic and a sliver of the vamp's Blood Cross that hadn't been requested back. Yet. Weapons of steel, silver, wood, and magic. Not that I expected to keep the arcane ones. They weren't mine.

By the time I was dressed in my silk long johns and the black leather fighting gear—modified armored biker garb—I was bristling with weapons, some of them new. The gold nugget on its doubled chain was pinching me under the T-shirt and silver chain-mail collar, so I bent forward and wiggled a bit until it fell into place.

My Benelli M4 shotgun was strapped into a harness on my back and loaded with seven 2.75-inch shells in standard configuration, the shells hand packed with silver fléchette rounds. I had three handguns, the Heckler and Koch 9 mil under my left arm, a .32 six-shooter on my ankle, and a two-shot derringer I'd tuck into my braids when I got there, all loaded with silver. I had my favorite vamp-killer—a specially made knife with an elk-horn hilt, a deep blood groove along the blade length and heavy silver plating except for the sharp, steel, cutting edge—strapped to my waist, and nine other silvered blades in various sheaths and loops. A half dozen silver crosses were around my neck, my waist, and tucked into the clothes. My black hair was tightly braided into a fighting queue and I slid four silver-tipped, ash-wood stakes into the bun like decorative hair sticks. It was way too hot and muggy for the skullcap I had worn a few times. It was also too hot for the silver-studded leather, but nothing protected against vamp claws and fangs like silver and leather.

When the last weapon was in place, I relocked the gun cabinet, securing the three remaining handguns, stakes, the sliver of the Blood Cross, and the pink diamond. I stepped into my newest pair of boots, steel-toed butt-stompers. I like Lucchese Western boots, but the soles were slick and I'd recently made the adjustment to steel-toed combat boots for fighting. I adjusted the hilts in the boot sheathes and tied the laces. Stood and looked in the mirror. I'm not vain, but I always love this sight. Me, dressed for vamp-hunting. I looked good. Scary. An Amazon. The last thing on was the bright red lipstick, the only color on me. Red looked great with my amber-colored eyes and my Cherokee coloring, and with the leathers it looked menacing. Daring. As if I was saying, "Come on. Try me."

Satisfied, I double-checked the info texted to me by Bruiser and left the house. Fired up Bitsa, my only transportation, and headed back out of town. I wanted to get a look at the address before dark.

New Orleans is a big city, spread out in a web of streets, its boundaries and shape determined by the alluvial soil and water on every side, some moving, like the river and bayous, and some more or less still, like the multitude of lakes that were fed by tides and rivers. The place I was going was outside the city limits; way outside.

I crossed the Mississippi River on the Huey Long Bridge,

which felt and looked like something constructed back before modern engineering and had spanned the Mighty Miss for decades. The roadbed of the bridge was coarse gravel asphalt and the sidewalls of the bridge were close, leaving no room for error for the vehicles using it every day.

On the west bank I turned right, upstream and north, and took state road 18, River Road, leaving behind the roar and stink of the city and entering a more industrial part of Louisiana. The architecture here had none of the charm of the inner city, tending more toward one-acre homesites with ranch-style houses, abandoned and run-down horse pasture, a few upscale equestrian barns with practice rings, all cheek-by-jowl with chemical plants, industrial plants, engineering, manufacturing, shipbuilding plants, and, over the levee to my right, huge cranes for moving products onto barges. The river itself wasn't visible unless I took one of the access roads up the levee, and that was frowned upon unless you had a good reason, like a job that took you there.

Despite the country's bleak economic status, a good number of the factories had Help Wanted signs. Few of the industrial plants were abandoned; there were no broken windows, cracked pavement, weather-stained or unpainted metal buildings. But there wasn't a lot of pretty either. The place had an undercurrent stink of industry and barge. Add in the reek of dying vegetation, unknown chemicals drying somewhere out of sight, the pong of skunk and other musk-emitting critters, and the occasional stench of roadkill—often as not, armadillo, surrounded by buzzards—it wasn't a place where I'd want to spend a lot of time. However, this part of Louisiana had survived the wrath of mother nature better than parts of New Orleans. As I rode through the steamy heat, I was struck by the fact that there were no abandoned, storm damaged, roofless houses. No red-Xed signs with a number showing how many had died in the house during Hurricane Katrina. No empty housing units with Keep Out signs warning of black mold. Life appeared untouched by the misery and blight of the storm, while inner-city New Orleans, especially the poorer, eastern part of the city, still looked awful.

I checked the map on my fancy cell and rode on, past a Monsanto plant and what looked like petroleum refineries, and then away from the river into the countryside, into the middle of bottomland and farms. An hour outside of New

Orleans and the city was forgotten. Bayous, a distant stink of swamp, and agricultural equipment had replaced the now-familiar smell of the French Quarter.

The sun was a red ball on the horizon when I finally found the place Leo wanted me to go. It was a biker bar. Go figure. Booger's Scoot, slang for gross stuff and a motorbike, was brand-new, the Grand Opening banner hanging limply in the airless dusk. A former gas station and car repair shop, the place had been remodeled, repainted, replastered, and freshly stuccoed in white with bloodred trim, but the new look kept the original design of a Spanish hacienda, arches at every opening, even the repair bays, which were now filled with window glass and flower-planted window boxes.

The old gas company sign was still up, the ESSO legend faded but legible. A twelve-foot-high chain-link fence was to one side, enclosing bike parking and camping, a place where customers could leave their expensive rides while they drank, played pool, and socialized, and rent one of the tents or the small cabin to stay overnight. The lot was paved, the campground striped with fresh sod, and there was even a shower house in back. I'd stayed in places like it when I traveled. They were cheap, usually safe, and sometimes clean. Booger's was pristine, with signs posting the rules and a warning to clean up after pets. Booger had done a lot of work, and the number of bikes in the fenced area this early said a lot about his service and his food. The bikes were hard-core, chopped, one-of-a-kind beauties with skulls and crossbones, wild animals, and American flags as part of the paint jobs.

I checked the setting sun and knew I had a half hour to reconnoiter before any vamp might show. For safety's sake, I elected to park in front with the pickups and the one car, facing Bitsa toward the road for a quick getaway if needed. Sitting astride, I let Beast rise in my mind, and wasn't surprised when the first thing she noticed was the scent of food: fried fish, fried shellfish, fried chicken, fried potatoes, grilled beef, and onions floated over the scent of gasoline and high performance machines. She approved of the menu and sent me an image of an oyster po'boy on a thick French-bread loaf. She licked her snout happily and I shook my head. I had a feeling I'd better eat first, before my contact arrived, because Booger might not want to serve me in the carnage of after. And with vamps, I always expect carnage.

I strapped my helmet to the bike and adjusted my leathers and weapons. Beast warned me that I wasn't alone, and so I didn't jump when a voice from the shadows said, "Nice ride. What is she?" My radar went up because he didn't step from the dark for a better look. Bike lovers are usually drawn to Bitsa; she's a sweet little lady. But this guy was talking from safety, only his cigarette giving away his position. White smoke drifted on the windless air from the side, near the chain-link fence. Something about the smell of the guy was odd, not clean, as if he hadn't bathed in a couple of days and had a sinus infection or something. I quested with my other senses and didn't see or hear anyone else. It was just the sickly-smelling guy and me, which should have relaxed me, but it didn't.

Without letting him see what I was doing, I tucked the derringer up under my braids and checked the slide of the stakes for easy removal from the bun as I answered. "She's your basic pan/shovel, put together from two old bikes, and updated by a Zen Harley Master up in Charlotte."

"Is that a Mikuni HSR-42 carburetor?"

The guy knew his bikes. I put his accent as a vaguely familiar west Texas, but his scent was unknown, and if he wasn't standing on a ladder, he was a good six feet six. I hummed an affirmative. "And the lifters are updated hydraulics to eliminate maintenance and help keep the noise down."

"Why would you want to do that?" he said, laughter suffusing his words.

I faced his spot in the dark. "Not everyone wants to advertise or annoy."

"Walk softly," he asked, his tone changing from jocular to something else, something with a hint of a growl in it, "and carry a big stick?" He took a drag off the cigarette, the red ember brightening his face for a moment, ruining his night vision. He had slick, freshly shaved cheeks, ruddy skin, hair pulled back from his face, bushy brows, dark eyes. "Or better still, a shotgun and enough weapons to start a small war."

"Way better than a stick," I agreed.

"You gonna start a war in Booger's?" The tone dropped to a basso threat.

"I'm not planning on it. I'm just here to talk to a vamp. Maybe eat a po'boy, drink a beer, and play a game of eight ball."

"And if Booger said to leave the weapons at the door?"

"I'd have to respectfully disagree." I smiled. "Are you Booger?"

"No. Not Booger. Not a vamp. Interested observer. What's the message?"

"The vamp gets to ask me that. No one else."

The man dropped the cigarette. Beast's enhanced night vision picked out his body as the dim light fell. He wasn't on a ladder. He was built like a fire truck, a solid giant of a man. When he ground the butt out, I heard metal on the pavement, steel on the soles of his boots. But when he moved into the darker shadows, it was silently, hard for a big man with metal on his soles. I heard a door open and noise poured out, a country song on a jukebox, voices, the clink of glass and the smell of beer and grease, and something musky and slightly rank underneath it all. The door shut. He was gone.

"That went well," I mused. Full night had fallen. I hadn't gotten inside before dusk. *Drat.* I glanced at my bike, taking in the faint glow of the witchy locks protecting Bitsa from casual interest or more nefarious intent. I opened the door, and went inside.

The no smoking laws had forever changed the face of drinking establishments, and the air inside was clear. The bar was straight ahead, bottles against the obligatory mirror, and the food ordering station was a bar on the left, with a dry board above it listing menu and prices. Between them was the jukebox, new but looking old-fashioned with neon all around and lots of shiny metallic paint. There were tables scattered between the door and the bars, seating people with food and drinks in front of them.

The floor was concrete, painted navy. Easy to clean. Color scheme was navy and red the color of blood, vamps' favorite shade. Ceiling was fifteen feet over my head, with exposed vents, pipes, and wiring, painted black. On the front wall, the bay doors' arches were windowed with seating. To my right was the pool area, with three pool tables. No one was eating or drinking or playing. Everyone was watching me. I took a breath and the musky undertone of the scents raised Beast's hackles. Deep in my mind, she growled, as if recognizing the odor. She crouched close and looked through my eyes, her paws and claws milking my mind, the sensation unpleasant.

I followed the scent to seven guys and a girl standing in the pool area. One of them was the fire truck-sized smoker from outside. But they weren't vamps, so not my target. I moved across the floor to the bar, taking position on the far left of it where no patrons sat on bar seats to obstruct my movements. I angled my body, keeping everyone in sight, leaned one elbow on the bar, and placed one booted foot on the raised footrest that followed the bar's shape. The position looked relaxed but also gave me leverage if I needed to push off fast. I fished a card out of a pocket and slid it to the bartender. He was a little guy, maybe five feet four with a potbelly and tattoos of birds of prey up his arms. His name tag said BOOGER. I hoped it was a nickname and not his mama's idea of a joke. Booger picked up the card and looked at it.

It said JANE YELLOWROCK in small caps, and below that, the motto: HAVE STAKES, WILL TRAVEL. Vamp-hunter humor. He looked from the card to me. "So?"

"Leo Pellissier sent me to chat with a vamp—average height, slender, black hair. Pretty."

Booger tucked the card in his T-shirt pocket. "Can't help you. My place ain't fancy enough for the fangheads."

Which was very true, now that I thought about it. But . . . Leo hadn't actually said I was meeting a vamp. The only term, beyond the general description, was a persona non grata. Crap. I'd *assumed* vamp.

"Course, there's others he mighta sent you to *chat* with." He nodded to the pool area and hit a red button under the bar mirror. Clanking overhead startled me and I stepped away from the bar as a metal wall, shaped like a garage door, but made of short lengths of chain formed in squares, rolled down and hit the floor. It was a security device, like mall stores draw down at night to protect their wares. Another wall did the same in front of the food bar. Two more slid down over the windows in the arched insets. I tensed to sprint into the night, but it wasn't a cage. The doors to Booger's had no obstructions. The people sitting at the tables got up and left, letting the night air in. The jukebox went silent. No. Not a cage. A fighting ring. But with a way out if I wanted to take it.

Beast growled low inside. She sent a thought picture to me. A pack of wolves against a snowfall, a full moon overhead.

And I got a real bad feeling.

CHAPTER 3

She Was Wearing a Red Thong

I recognized the smell now, like wet dog, but rangier, wilder, feral. Them. The pack. All but one of them male. The girl was watching me from the shadows, her bottom lip caught in her teeth, her eyes excited and gleaming and possibly not quite sane. She was a tiny, blond thing with a deep tan, her skin catching the light with a sheen of perspiration. She was loaded down with bling-style jewelry, dressed in a skirt with a tight, spandex waist that left her pierced navel bare, the short skirt belling out around her hips. With it she wore a tight tank and no bra and red platform sandals with four-inch heels. Reaching behind, she gripped the pool table and levered herself up, her feet swinging, sandals flying off and into the darkness. She was wearing a red thong and made sure I knew it. Oh joy.

As the wolf-bitch moved, she stirred the air, and I caught the reek of sex hormones. She was in heat. No wonder she was so demonstrative.

The men I could see all wore jeans and T-shirts. And except for Fire Truck, were barefooted or wore flip-flops. Which was weird until I spotted the boots lining the wall near the side door. I sniffed one last time, scenting them. I had never met a werewolf, but I was meeting them now. Leo hadn't sent me to meet a vamp and send him packing. He'd sent me to meet a pack of wolves. Without warning and without backup.

These guys didn't ride down from Wyoming today, which told me the interview footage from this morning—the one where a wolf had accused Leo of the murder of a man named

Henri—had been taped, suggesting the wolves had been here longer than a few hours. They'd marked territory and were willing to fight for it.

One of the wolves stepped forward, his feet bare and silent on the painted concrete. I recognized the angry werewolf from the TV. The strawberry blond leader who cussed so much. His movements were graceful, feral, deadly. Around him the others fanned out, starting to form a semicircle. Fire Truck stood in the back, pulling off his boots.

"Jane Yellowrock. Rogue-vamp hunter," I said to the leader, loosening my knee joints and adjusting my balance. "I was sent to deliver a message. But none of you matches the description." Pretty wasn't a term anyone would use for a werewolf.

He slowed his advance at the words and his men stopped dead—not quite the dead immobility of vamps, more like the unmoving quiet of hunting predators. "Rogue-vampire hunter? I have hear' of such. Human who are licen' by the bloodsuckers to hunt down those they cannot." His accent was Cajun, a robust version, words full of harsh Rs and shortened or missing Ts, so that when he spoke it came out, "Rrrogue-vampirrre hunterrr." And, "hun' down dose dey canno'." An intriguing, rumbling growl. The taped TV interview this morning had been so full of bleeped cussing that I'd had no clue of an accent.

He smiled and I could see the wolf below his skin, all teeth and canine ferocity. "Roul Molyneux," he said, introducing himself. I had a feeling I was neck deep and sinking fast in vamp politics. Leo had sent me into this, whatever this was. "I am alpha, pack leader of the Lupus Clan of the Cursed of Artemis, of the United States of America."

Roul wasn't a big guy—not like Fire Truck, standing in the back of the room, lighting a cigarette despite the no smoking laws—but he was well built, with that full mane of hair and blue eyes, his looks enhanced by the sensation of power that surrounded him, a charismatic command-mode power, something all his, over and above the wolf magic and pack energies. An alpha wolf.

I took in the others at a glance, various mixtures of humanity—wolfanity?—and I wanted to laugh, but figured I might end up dead real fast if they thought I was making fun of them. There were two black guys, the wolf-bitch, two white guys, Fire Truck, a mixed-race block of muscle who might once have been human, and Roul, who was more gorgeous in person than on TV. Three other men appeared in the side doorway, limned by the security lights outside, and there were likely even more I hadn't seen. Considering the number of bikes parked outside, I was guessing twelve to twenty wolves, all in human form. Not good odds if this went beyond chatting. I had seven shells in the M4, ten rounds in the H&K and one in the chamber, and another six in the ankle holstered gun. The derringer would only make them laugh. I had extra magazines, but if I needed them I was probably dead anyway.

"Vampire hunter don'—" Roul's eyes narrowed and he sniffed in quick bursts, wrinkling his nose, his neck outstretched like a dog on a scent.

"I smell catamount, I do. An' . . . owl." He breathed slowly, his face hardening. "And Leo's blood in your veins. He has fed you to heal, yeah, and his pet shaman too, I'm thinking. You stink of magic, sundry kind." He sniffed again. "You not human. Yet, you not were, no."

Beast tightened, claws out, painful in my mind, her body taut and ready. "Not entirely human," I agreed, controlling the slight shudder of panic in my voice, knowing they would smell any reaction, the faintest fear-sweat. "I don't want a fight."

Roul laughed and, at the sound, his men moved forward again, spreading out. As if they had rehearsed, they kicked off their flops. Started stripping off their clothes, throwing them aside with casual abandon. Instant fear thudded through me; I couldn't catch my breath. There was something primal about a group of men ripping off their clothes, moving toward a woman, no matter how well armed she was. "I just want to deliver my message and go. No blood spilled, no death." Just an order to get out of town. Yeah, that was gonna make me real popular.

An electric frisson of magic danced along my skin, as if the air was suddenly filled with the ozone of a fresh lightning strike. They were going to change, right here. Right now. My lips pulled back from my blunt human teeth. Beast growled and the sound came from my own lips. One of them laughed and I backed away two steps, a chain wall clinking against my butt.

"I fear we don' always get what we want," Roul said.

Great. The guy was a philosopher. Something about the idea of an intellectual werewolf struck me as funny, and, despite the circling wolves, I grinned. Drawing on Beast's speed and strength, I pulled my Benelli and the H&K, covering the males with a swing of the shotgun barrel, and sighting the 9 mil at the wolf-bitch girl. She didn't smell dominant, but as the only female present, she had some kind of power. I assumed.

"No we don't, Roul. So, tell me"—I moved the barrel of the Benelli from one male to the other, pausing on each for a moment before moving on, my emotions settling into battle readiness, cold and empty—"will I get what I want if I fill you all full of silver shot? Is silver deadly to weres, like the myths say? 'Cause I'm loaded for vamp with silver fléchette rounds, and I'm betting they kill your kind like they do the fangheads. Slow, painful poisoning."

The pack-mates halted as one, midmotion, midstrip, midlaugh, which told me the silver myths were true. But the pack was nearly in position to attack, and if they did, there wasn't a dang thing I could do about it until after the fact. I was licensed to kill rogue vampires, not weres. If I killed them, it had to be provable self-defense. I had to have the wounds to back any claim in court. I hadn't seen security cameras, but if I attacked first and someone was filming, I could have legal charges brought against me. Booger had disappeared. Convenient for him. Not so much for me. "Silver poisoning is a nasty way to die," I said.

Thoughts danced behind Roul's eyes like antsy fireflies. He frowned. "I was to meet here for parley, at invitation of . . . another." He jutted with his chin. "You Leo' courier, I'm thinking. Deliver message what he say."

At invitation of another? Another what? "Not much to it. Get out of town. You are persona non grata."

"No." He showed me his teeth, lips pulled back, nose wrinkling in a dominance snarl. His canines were longer than a human's and looked wicked sharp. "No' this time. We not leave. Leo stole much from us when he took our territory. Human law, I'm thinking, give it back to us."

Again the pack began to close in. I had no room to back away unless I could reach the button to open the metal wall and jump onto the bar. I was being herded or circled, and either one was bad news. I fought down a flight reaction and aimed the shotgun at one male who was already naked, his back bowing and breath coming in pants. The sensation of ants crawling on my skin spread, thickened.

"If we don' receive permission to enter the city and retake our hunting grounds," Roul said, "there be a two-pronged consequence, yes?" He watched to see that I was following his words. "As we parley, here and now, in state capital our pack lawyers prepare to file injunction, they do, six, four, t'ree injunction, against Leo and his business concerns. In less than one week, the financial apparatus of all the Mithran' will grind to a halt. Then, our lawyers, they turn over evidence to human law enforcement, provin' that Leo Pellissier kill our former alpha. He will be charge with murder, yes? Brought to justice in a human court of law." He smiled, clearly relishing the thought. "His power base will be destroyed by this pack here, Lupus Pack, utterly, forever. We leave him with nothing."

"Leo might have something to say about that."

Roul threw up his hand and the wolves in human form closed in several steps, others now blocked the door. My heart jumped into my throat. Two naked guys were on their knees, backs hunched, taken by the change. The alpha wolf lifted his head, as if readying himself to howl.

Beast had been eerily silent, not bragging that she could take them. Not a good sign. A dozen possible outcomes flashed through my mind with a single heartbeat, none of them ending well for me. "Wait." I took a chance. "We're still under parley rules."

Roul ducked his chin, his lips back, his teeth all pointed, no longer human. "Shhpeak." I had a feeling that was the only word he could manage at this point, his voice lower and gravelly.

"Since the death of his son, Leo's been deeply in the *dolore*. I don't think he cares what you do to him as long as vampire grief rides him. I'm betting he's spoiling for a fight, not in a courtroom but under a less than full moon, and he'll take a lot of you down with him, if it comes to physical battle. He's powerful." I remembered seeing a hint of the power of the Master of the City, calling his vamps to heel. "He has the might of all the vamps in the city to draw upon. I honestly don't think you'll survive. Even in wolf form."

Roul swallowed, fighting down his beast. I recognized the struggle. He took another breath. "We . . . not go back."

Without a detectable sign from Roul, the pack closed in.
They had spread their attack circle as far as the walls and
chain barriers permitted while I stood here and chatted. I
should have run, hard and fast. *Crap!*

Magic permeated the air, prickling on my skin like electricity. Like fire ants stinging. Like a warning of war. Beast
growled, low and dangerous, the sound of her anger coming
from my mouth.

Three wolves had shifted fully; they stood, ruffs upright
and teeth bared. Others were coated with a mist that hovered
on their skin, darker than the gray mist of my own change; it
was tinted faintly blue, swirling faster than my own change-
energies. Looking angry, somehow. These crouched and threw
back their heads, a human mime of a wolf howl, but silent,
agonized. The three fully changed wolves stepped in front of
them, protective. Wolf magic grew, crackling like flames on dry
tinder. I couldn't catch my breath in the electrified air of the
bar.

Roul stood before the front windows, only his head and
hands changed, wolf claws, doggy-shaped and blunt, but bigger, evolved for grabbing and bringing down big prey. They
were all naked, even the girl, crouched in the shadows, on a
pool table, turned away from me, halfway through her change,
her wolf-bitch-in-heat stench hitting the air like a warning.

I was in big trouble. Thanks to Leo Pellissier, who sent me
here to *talk*.

Six wolves had fully changed and I still didn't know what
to do. There was no getting past them and outside; I couldn't
open fire without it being clear self-defense. *Where is the security camera? This is a setup. Has to be.* But I didn't see a
camera anywhere.

A black wolf lunged, maw open, slavering. Beast shoved
her power into my bloodstream. Adrenaline like fire in my
veins. *Flight or fight.* Time did a little twist and bump. Slowing
like cold honey.

I fired the shotgun one-handed. Beast's strength took
the recoil. As it backlashed through me, I fired the handgun
at the wolf-bitch, the shots overlapping, but a blurred
form dropped from the pool table and was gone. I'd missed her entirely. Closer, the charging wolf yelped, barely heard over the
concussive report. Hit in the chest. He flipped back in midair.
Dead. The mostly human shape behind him curled in on him-

self, keening, his magics disrupted by the pattern of silver shot that peppered him as it spread out.

Beast-fast, I fired the M4 twice more, taking down two wolves.

Fired again at a leaping wolf, freshly changed. This one was bigger, stretched out in midair. He took the shell full face. His jaw, teeth, and brains exploded backward. Silver burst into flame in his blood. He fell in a heap at my feet. The others seemed to sense they faced a more deadly opponent than they had expected, and one hit the lights. The place went black except for light through the windows. I crouched into a shadow, knowing their wolf eyes were better in the dark than my human ones, even if I drew on Beast's vision.

The semiautomatic barked in my hand, hitting and missing as I methodically emptied the magazine at wolves, counting rounds as I fired. The wolves were freaking fast, streaking close and swerving, and I missed most of the time, in the dark. I fired the last two shotgun shells at two wolves silhouetted in the doorways like guards, hoping the silver fléchettes would slow them down. There wasn't time to reload the M4. I set the shotgun at my feet. Digging one-handed in a pocket. My fingers touched a replacement magazine for the nine mil as I fired the last rounds in the H&K. Three wolves leaped at me. Knocked me to my butt. Claws digging at me even through the armored leather. The magazine slipped away, into the deeps of the pocket. Huge teeth and fangs ripped. Tearing at me through the leather armor. Flinching at the taste of silver rivets and studs. Snarling. Growling.

I rolled and got the magazine out, snapped it into the sidearm, the sound lost beneath concussive deafness. I grabbed for the six-shot from my ankle holster. A wolf came out of the dark. Snapped at my face and I dodged. Fired. Teeth snapped on my ear. The pain was distant, my blood hot on my skin. I got the backup gun free. My brain having trouble with the different firing sequences between pistol and semiautomatic. Muscle memory finally won, and I fired with both hands. But I had a feeling I'd missed almost every shot since the lights went out.

Fangs ripped at my hand. Fingers went numb. The H&K clicked, empty again. I dropped the sidearm. Pulled a vamp-killer. Fired the last two shots with the pistol. Pulled and emptied the two shots in the derringer. I was down to blades. I was a goner. The wolves were too fast, too many. My hands were slick with blood, some of it mine. I stabbed upward, cutting into the belly of a red wolf with amber eyes. Sliced the hamstring of another. Both fell away.

A monstrous wolf landed on me. Knocked out my breath in a grunt I couldn't hear over my damaged eardrums. Fire Truck. Had to be. His jaws snapped down. At my throat. And met the silver collar. He yelped in surprise, teeth caught in the chain-mail mesh. Jumped back. Ripping the protective necklace from my neck, the rings and the busted clasp caught on one of his canine teeth.

I sliced across the face of a shaggy wolf with Roul's blue eyes. He danced back out of blade length. And then farther. The movement of the wolves halted, all of them looking up.

I panted, trying to catch my breath. Hurting. And became aware that I wasn't alone. A slender form landed beside me, silhouetted in the window, poised on the balls of his feet as if he'd dropped from the black ceiling. Another opponent. *Crap*.

In an eyeblink, I took him in. He stood bent-kneed, two blades drawn, silvered swords, one long, one shorter, but not Japanese in style. Spanish, maybe. He was dressed all in black, top to toe. Lots of silver. More than I wore. Weird what you think in the heat of trying to stay alive and figuring you aren't going to.

He held the blades in what was clearly a martial position, one blade pointed forward at two o'clock, the other to his left side at his nine o'clock, making small circles, at an angle to the ground. His stance made the wolves his target, not me. I had help. The relief was so sudden that nausea rose up my throat, burning and acidic. *Zorro*, I thought, naming him. I wanted to laugh at the thought, but I didn't have the breath.

"Roul, Roul, leader of the Lupus Clan," he said. I heard him, even over my concussed ears. His voice was like ice cream, cool and rich, melting into a pool of hot caramel. I shivered at the tone, his words in an accent that would have been sexy had I not been bleeding, in pain, and thinking I might die shortly.

"This is not the way—to kill the messenger." He made a little *tsk-tsk* sound. "You knew that Leo would not permit your wolves in his city without a fight. Do you desire to waste all your energies on this, the first round of the game? No, no, no. Think. You have made your point and bloodied your opponent."

And that opponent would be me. I took the opportunity to stand, feeling pain in one knee and ankle. I had landed wrong when they pushed me down. I swallowed and the fang abrasion in my neck and throat pulled and stung. That was gonna hurt until I could change. Bad.

I adjusted my grip on the weapons, and pain zinged up my arm. My fingers were ripped; one, maybe more, wasn't working at all. Someone turned on the lights in the pool area, the illumination like a camera flash, throwing the room into harsh relief.

I spotted the smallest wolf, the bitch, on the fringes of the fight, under the pool table she had been sitting on earlier. She was bleeding, weight on three legs. She was the one I'd hamstrung. I grinned at her, knowing my expression was vicious. I was hurt, but some of them were hurt a lot worse. Not that that would have kept me alive much longer. Sheer numbers would have won in the end.

"Withdraw for now," sword-guy-Zorro said, "and wait. Leo must come to you eventually, one-on-one. That is a battle you may yet win."

Roul threw back his head and howled, throat exposed, the sound not mournful at all, but filled with fury, like nothing nature had ever planned or created. Magic sizzled and hissed through the room. And they attacked.

Zorro stepped in front of me, blades flashing. I turned my back to his. Tried to place my feet for better balance, but the knee was weak. I dropped to my good knee, injured one up, foot on the floor. I cut upward. At the underbelly of a wolf. A second wolf came from my left. Fast. Faster than I could move. Fire Truck. The massive wolf bit down on my elbow. Bones crunched. Mine, unfortunately.

Pain shocked through me, up my arm, down to my fingers, paralyzing. With one arm, I fought off another wolf, but Fire Truck sensed my weakness. His jaws relaxed, left my wounded arm for an instant. Snapped back in, mouth open. Latched on again, just below the injured joint. Growling, he shook me, slinging my entire body left and right, across the blood-slick floor. I gagged with the pain. Stabbed at him. Caught him on the side.

From above, I saw a flash of silver. Fire Truck yelped. Dropped me. Zorro stepped across my form, booted feet to either side. I curled around myself, shivering with shock and pain. Found the H&K under my side, jabbing. One handed, I changed magazines, clumsy and slow.

Around me, the silvered swords sang, the man moving with grace and speed that a dancer would envy. Fast as lightning and nearly as bright. He was faster than anything I had ever seen. Faster than a vamp. Two more wolves went down, blood pooling, looking black on the navy floor. There were more than twenty of them. Seven were dead or too wounded to crawl away.

Roul's wolf leaped from a table and landed on my protector's back. Claws scoured along his cheek, a right paw curved in and tore through his shirt, raking along his side. I couldn't fire without risking hitting Zorro. With my injured hand, I stabbed up. Slicing along the wolf's side, cutting deep. The wolf yelped and flinched. As if anticipating it, Zorro bent, took one step, and twisted; the motion threw Roul across the room. A long blade swung up and scored the wolf's other side as he flew. Wolf blood and the blood of the swordsman flung into the air. Roul landed hard and slid, scattering tables and chairs.

I shot the wolf closest. A gray-black wolf with deep drown eyes. It skittered back, legs flailing, claws losing purchase on the blood-slick floor. I aimed at another.

The wolves drew back. Roul turned, tail down. He limped for the side door, the others racing with him, leaving behind their fallen. Seven lay unmoving. Five more crawled or limped for the exit. Five seemed mostly healthy and scattered, taking up the rear, growling at me and my savior. "My count was off," I said. I caught the hint of movement to my side. An impact over my ear. And blackness closed in around me.

CHAPTER 4

Yeah. Sure. Strip, Zorro.

I came to in the open air, looking up at the stars and the sliver of a *one day moon*, Beast-talk for the first moon after a new moon. I'd have smiled but the pain hit me, an electric agony that tore through me like a red-hot spear. A hand caught my nape and eased me to my side where I threw up on the grass. "Crap, that's bad," I gasped.

"The pain or the regurgitation of stomach contents?"

"Both." We weren't on civilized grass, like the sod near Booger's. Beneath me were rough cut weeds, like the parish might mow on the verge of a secondary road. And the world was dark, no artificial light. Yet I smelled hot pavement and exhaust and heard the pinging of Bitsa's engine, a sound I'd have recognized anywhere. The bike should be cooled off, still parked at Booger's Scoot. The bike should have been impossible to kick-start for anyone but me, what with the witchy locks activated. But Bitsa had been ridden here, wherever here was. And I had to guess that I'd been transported here too. On Bitsa? Over Zorro's shoulder, my boots dragging on the ground? The mental image was farcical and I chuckled, my tone as sour as the taste in my mouth.

"I have healed you as much as I am able," Zorro said from close by. "My magics, they are few in this world. And you are not fully human. Though I have protected you from contagion by the wolf-taint, I dare not try more."

I rolled back, face to the night sky, concentrating on breathing. The *one day moon*, sharp pointed and thin, was perched in a live oak tree, half hidden by the leaves. On the night air was the faint stink of swamp, the vomit, blood—a lot of it mine—and were-stink. *I have protected you from contagion by the wolf-taint,* he'd said. At least I wasn't going to howl at the moon in a couple of weeks.

"Did you hit me? There at the end?"

"No. Regrettably, we both missed one wolf in human form. He hit you. I hit him." Zorro shrugged, the motion looking odd in the moonlight, as if his shoulders didn't work right.

I sat up. Slowly. My body creaked and spasmed with the motion. I was breathing hard, sweating in the heat, even with my jacket unzipped. He offered me a bottle of designer water and opened it when I nodded. My fingers worked to close over the bottle. Huzzah. Fingers worked. I drank. The moisture cleared my head, enough to know I was still hurt, though not quite so badly. I stretched out the arm that Fire Truck had worried like prey. My elbow was in less salutary condition, but it would heal next time I shifted. I cleared my voice to ask him his name and, instead, what came out was, "Where the heck were you? There weren't any rafters."

Zorro chuckled softly and stretched out his legs on the night-dark grass, crossed his feet at the ankles, and leaned back to brace his upper body on locked arms. On the night air I smelled jasmine and pine as he moved, and the commingled scents settled my stomach, but vanished before I could draw another breath. "I was perched on the horizontal ventilation shaft. Dusty." He brushed at his silver-studded clothes.

The ventilation shaft had been twelve, fifteen feet over my head in the old Esso station of Booger's Scoot. That was some drop.

I tried to roll to my feet and pain ricocheted through me, but it was the dull pain of healing, not the fresh pain of new wounds. "Thanks," I said, "for the medical help and the water. But mostly for the fancy sword work. You saved my butt."

"And other parts of you as well." There was humor in his voice, a clean and fresh amusement, nothing dark in it. When most people laugh, there is a wry, insulting, sardonic, or cutting edge, a dark aspect to the humor, or falsity, a polite laugh. Not so with this guy; his laughter was joyful, like a kid in a park, and I found myself smiling with him for no good reason.

"And other parts of me as well," I agreed.

"And you saved me from more serious injury at the end,

when you gutted the large wolf on my back. My thanks returned."

I hadn't gutted Roul, more a surface cut, but I didn't argue. "Jane Yellowrock."

"Yes. The hunter of insane vampires. Have stakes, will travel, à la an old television show, back when everything was black-and-white."

I had a feeling he was alluding to a different world and not just the technology of the day when he said, "everything was black-and-white," but I didn't quite follow.

He held out his hand and said his name. It sounded like Sjheedmeircy, but before I asked he said, "It is a shortened version from Girrard DiMercy," and offered its spelling when I still looked confused. "The first syllable of my first name, Gi, with a French accent?" he prompted as if I was a little slow after being wounded. Which I was. "Mamá was French, and the name was her choice. Papá raised me, and he was Castilian Spanish."

"He taught you to fight? The sword style looked Spanish."

"He did, it is. And your style is American gunslinger combined with street knife fighting. With, perhaps, a bit of mixed martial arts in your background."

"A bit." And though he had insulted my fighting technique as being crude, rough, and inelegant, it didn't feel like an insult. It felt friendly, like his laughter. I tried out his name and settled on a simple Jhee sound, trying to approximate his French-Spanish Gee.

He moved and again I scented jasmine and pine. And I realized it was coming from him. From Gee. Underneath the floral and tree scent I smelled heated copper—blood. I breathed in slowly. He smelled of plants and his blood of odd metal. Weird. "You aren't human," I said.

"I certainly hope not." It was a laughing slur, words that might have sounded insulting had they come from anyone else.

"And you're bleeding."

"I am. When you are well enough, perhaps you would be so kind as to bind my small wounds. My magics do not extend to self-healing here, I am afraid."

"Not in this world," I said, remembering his words as I came to.

"Indeed."

I made it to my feet, wondering what he was. He wasn't vamp, witch, shaman, or werewolf. I was sure he wasn't a were of any kind. I found medical supplies in Bitsa's saddlebags, and took them to where Gee sat. That small activity drained me. I needed to shift and heal, but that would have to wait. There was too much unsettled for the moment, and no privacy at all. "Pull off your shirt."

"Be gentle with me," he said.

I laughed, the sound breathy. "Yeah. Sure. Strip, Zorro."

He unbuttoned his shirt and tossed it aside with much the same abandon as the wolves had shown, but with far more grace. "Pah. Zorro was a lover of young boys and a dancing master. I bested him three times in the rings. He was never my match."

My brows raised at his laughing insult of a national icon—his suggestion that he had lived in the time of, and fought with, the real Zorro—and the sight of his naked chest. In spite of my lingering pain I knew he was beautiful, exquisite, lovely even, in the way of a man who danced a lot, rode horses a lot, worked out a lot, and loved a lot. Smooth skin of a pale very-milky-chocolate color, a V of chest hair framing his torso, and a faint film of pale energies running on and under his skin. Black hair. Pretty. *Crap*. This was the guy Leo had sent me to find. Not the wolves. Unless they had been a lucky bonus. Vamps are sneaky. Everything they do has layers of purpose and meaning.

Leo's enemy had saved my life. And . . . he wasn't human.

Beast pushed me aside and stared out through my eyes. In her vision, his energies looked blue with swirls of pale lavender and pale pink, like watercolors painted on silk. Nope. Definitely not human. And his magics looked odd, like maybe he was wearing a glamour, or even layers of glamour. As I thought that, the perfection of his torso vanished. Blood-clotted lacerations appeared along his ribs, spoiling the effect.

I frowned and looked at his face, speckled by dim moonlight through the leaves overhead. He was bearded with a carefully shaped Vandyke, black hair against the soft chocolate of his face, dark eyes that might have been deep green. I blinked and his right cheek appeared crusted over with dried blood. "Neat trick. They did a number on you, Zorro."

"I will have lovely scars to charm the ladies, no?"

"I have a feeling the ladies will never see them." I tore

open packages and laid them out on the grass: gauze, sterile cleansing wipes, packets of Betadine, pads and bandages, Cling Wrap, and a pair of small scissors. I travel prepared for trouble of all kinds.

I cleaned his wounds, finding them less severe than I first expected, all except one on his side, where a rib was exposed. I smeared the wound with antibacterial ointment. "You'll need stitches," I said, covering it with a sterile pad and wrapping his chest with the Cling Wrap, which was like a combo of rolled gauze, ace bandage, and tape, all in one, holding everything in place.

He shrugged, his frame moving under my hands as I wrapped his chest. The mellow blue, lavender, and pink energies swirled over my skin. In Beast-vision, I saw them crawl over my hands and up my arms. Beast pressed her paw onto me and her retractile claws punched deeply, pulling me out of his glamour. I growled and pinched him, hard. "Stop that."

He flinched away with that mesmeric laughter burbling in his voice. "Forgive me, senorita." He covered my hands with his. "I cannot help myself in the presence of such beauty."

"Cut the crap, *Zorro*, or I'll leave you here to bleed." The energies receded. His glamour might have worked if not for Beast and for the fact that I knew I wasn't a beauty. Interesting, maybe. Not beautiful. And then I realized that *my jacket was unzipped*. He'd unzipped my jacket . . . I held out one zippered side and said, "You unzipped my riding leathers. Just how much were you unable to help yourself in the presence of my *beauty*?"

"I would never take advantage, senorita. Well, not much. I peeked, I admit," he said, his tone roguish and teasing.

I wanted to belt him one, but it seemed ungracious to punish a guy after he'd saved my life. Just for looking. Nothing was unbuttoned or unsnapped or missing. I touched my gold nugget necklace, finding it hanging around my neck just like it was supposed to be. But painful abrasions marred my nape, in the shape of wolf fangs, where Fire Truck had tried to rip out my throat and gotten the silver necklace instead.

"You are lovely all over," Gee whispered. He lifted a hand and smoothed a strand of hair back from my face. "We could have such delightful times together."

"Not gonna happen. What are you? You aren't anything I've ever smelled before."

He breathed out his disappointment. The energies of the spell he wove withdrew as he stood, picking his shirt off the ground and using it to button away all that luscious skin. The glamour faded further when he had himself covered. "Nor I you, though you smell of times long gone and beings long dead."

"You're Leo's persona non grata, yes?" When he didn't answer, I said, "Fine. Why were you in the ceiling, watching, and why did you help me when things got hairy? And for that matter why did you wait *so freaking long* to help me?"

"I was watching to see if Leo would really come to the place he was invited. To see if old loves and old enemies might have lost their hold over him. The enemies have not, it seems. I must wait to determine about the loves."

It clicked into place. Leo had been invited here, alone, to meet Zorro—something he had left out of my orders and explanations and maps and addresses—and Zorro had also invited the weres. As if he was doing an intervention, or something. "Go on."

"I am Girrard DiMercy," he shrugged, "once Leo's misericorde, the blood-servant who brought peace to the clans' long-chained scions when they did not wake from devoveo."

"Peace..." I added that to the foreign word *misericorde*, a picture forming. The word was the name of a weapon, the mercy stroke or mercy blade, a long knife used in medieval times to deliver the death stroke to a knight who had received mortal wounds but would lie dying, in great pain, for a long time. But a mercy blade in conjunction with the devoveo was something new to me.

When first turned, vamps went into a state of prolonged insanity, forcing them to be restrained and imprisoned for years, sometimes decades, until they regained their sanity and self-awareness. It was a mental state from which some did not ever return. "You killed the long-chained," I breathed.

He nodded once, the gesture formal as a bow. "When the decade of devoveo, or sometimes two, had passed for a Mithran scion to regain sanity, the Master of the City would summon me, sending me to the scion-lair of the master whose child would never recover. I would seduce the master to drink of my sweet blood. It has been said"—he splayed a hand over his chest—"to be as intoxicating as the finest wine. And they would sleep while I performed the onerous duty and put the scion out of his misery."

Gee lifted his swords and began to reweapon. That was the first moment I noticed my own were missing. A hot flush of anger and fear shot through me, a painful jolt. And then I saw my weapons lined up neatly on the grass, the blades shining and clean, the shotgun and handguns beside them, even the stakes from my hair that I'd never had time to draw.

Stiffly, I stood and reclawed, putting the blades into their respective sheaths and loops, the stakes into my hair. Several were missing; I wasn't surprised. Beside the weapons was a card. The light was too dim to read, but it felt like a business card, and I tucked it into a pocket. I pulled the Benelli's harness over my jacket, pain lancing up and out from my partially healed elbow. As we both worked, Gee talked.

"Before the last vampire war in 1915, the Master of the City, Amaury Pellissier, who was Leo's uncle in the human flesh, called me to bring peace to Leo's daughter. The girl had not found herself; she had raved for over twenty years. But Leo met me at his scion-lair. He resisted the taste of my blood, resisted the seduction that would have made the loss of his child easier to bear, and he fought me." A trace of surprise flowed beneath the words. "No one had ever fought me before. Begged, yes. Pleaded or raged, yes. But never fought.

"Leo refused the proper dueling tools of swords or pistols, and attacked me with his bare hands." Gee shook his head in wonder. "He wounded me. Rather badly." He cocked his head at me and I felt his magics questing out; I wondered briefly what he looked like beneath the spell that covered him. "Would you care to see my scars?" he asked as if he had read my mind.

"No." I said dryly. I was beginning to sense Gee's magic was all about sex, compulsion, and glamour—in opposition to the job he'd described, which was all about death.

"Pity. I was forced to leave for a time to heal."

"Leave this earth."

"Precisely," he said with that lilt of laughter. But his delight died when he continued, "By the time I returned, the war had begun and ended and Leo was Master of the City, his uncle and most of the previous clan masters dead. The ones who remained were not of the old ways. Like Leo, the new masters did not wish their young brought to true death by the blade of a stranger, at a time chosen by another. They wished to face that mercy-gift alone. The old ways were dying away.

"Leo banished me. He banished the weres. There were many reasons for his enmity," he said. "They sided with the wrong faction in the war. They broke their own were-laws with impunity, as wolves have always done."

I wondered which law they had broken. Maybe the one about biting humans, because they sure had bitten the crap out of me.

"Perhaps it was partly a whim; he had always hated the two-natured and Leo was always the passionate one, sensitive, fervent, full of intense emotions. Perhaps he will never allow them to return."

I gave a half shrug, remembering Leo raving mad after I killed the thing masquerading as his son. But before that he had healed me from a wound that would have maimed a human. I had seen a different kind of passion then. I set my hair-stick stakes in place, the silver tips scraping my scalp. I picked up my cell, checked to see that I had missed three calls and several text messages. Those I ignored for now and brought up my location on the GPS map app and then brought up directions to see me back to a main road. I was only a mile from Booger's. It was a handy little device.

"When I left, Leo's prime blood-servant went with me."

"Uh-huh." I checked my ammo. Not much left.

"Magnolia Sweets. His sweet Magnolia." When I didn't react to the name, he went on, while I changed out empty magazines for full ones. "He loved her to distraction, but she could not stay with him. Within the year, she was gone."

Blood-servants who no longer sip of their master's blood age rapidly. Magnolia would have died of old age soon after leaving. Gee however, a self-proclaimed blood-servant, had lived. Yet, he didn't smell of vamp blood, so his longevity wasn't part of a new vampire relationship. The youth was his alone and not something he had shared with Magnolia to keep her alive. Maybe it didn't work that way. What'd I know?

"Leo brought his daughter to peace some few years later, but he never summoned me back. And since that time, the Mithrans have suffered greatly."

I straddled Bitsa and sat. "How so?"

"To kill their own children? Would it not bring you to the brink of insanity?"

I saw an image from Beast's past, a vision of dead kits. Their bodies had been ripped and torn apart by claws and teeth. I started. She had never shown me this, and at first I thought, *wolves*. But then I saw the prints in the soft soil and pooled blood. Mountain lion. A big one. And I smelled his scent in her memory. Our memories. We had tracked the male. Leaped down upon him from a high rock as he lapped at a river, the roaring water and cold wind hiding our presence from him.

I felt the impact as we landed. Driving the breath from both of us. Felt the fierce delight as our claws dug into his flesh. As our fangs bit into his spinal column just above his shoulders. And shook once, hard. The sound/feel/taste as his spine broke. The body collapsing beneath us falling into the water. The shock of cold as we followed him in and under. Released the kill and swam up through hated cold water to the surface. To the bank. Where we shook. And screamed our conquest to the jagged rocks above.

The memory faded and dispersed like a mist under a hot sun, leaving me with the taste of the kit killer in my mouth and the fury of vengeance in my mind. "Yes," I said softly. "It would." I puffed out a breath, not liking my next words even before they left my mouth. "But Leo isn't ready to ask you back. He sent me to tell you to get out of his territory or face the consequences." I couldn't read his expression, but giving him that message after he saved my life was wrong on every level I could name. "He said to use whatever measures I thought necessary to make sure you left. That part of the message I'm refusing." I tried to smile and couldn't, as something akin to survivor's guilt trapped me. "I'm sorry."

"Until the Master of the City returns me to my rightful place in the clans, there will be no peace for him. None for them. No balance in their souls. No tranquility. I am *necessary* to them." He tilted his head. "But then . . ." He walked around me on the bike, graceful as a flamenco dancer, considering. "I have heard you have killed young rogues caught in devoveo. Perhaps you are the new Mercy Blade of the Mithrans."

Kit killer, Beast hissed deep inside me.

"No," I said to them both. I stood and brought my weight down on the kick start. Bitsa roared to life. "No way." I left him there, on the side of the road. I was miles away, in the city, the lights of vamp headquarters lighting the night, before I remembered several things. Gee had never told me what he was. Gee had started Bitsa as if the witchy locks weren't there at all. Gee had carried me, somehow, from Booger's. And my silver chain-mail collar was still missing. I touched my throat, finding only the gold chain and nugget. Gone. The lacerations were healed, but the protection of the collar was absent. Replacing it was gonna cost me dearly. "Crap."

My official cell rang while I was crossing the bridge and again just as I got to the far side. I pulled over on a patch of worn-out grass and smiled when I saw Molly's number displayed. "Molly-girl, what's cracking?"

"Nothing is cracking, Aunt Jane."

I chuckled and said, "Does your mama know you're using her cell, Angie Baby?" Angelina was my goddaughter, Molly's daughter, a scary-strong witch who had come into her powers a decade too young. She lived with those powers battened and corded down and yet, she still knew things. Could do things. I'd seen her.

"No. I'm bein' a bad girl. But you gots to stay away from the blue man."

Shock thudded through me. "Okay, Angie Baby. I promise."

"Cross your heart?"

I dutifully crossed my heart. "And hope to die."

"No. Don't do that! You be careful! I love you, Aunt Jane."

Tears stung my eyes. "I'll be careful. I promise. I love you too, Angie Baby."

CHAPTER 5

You Can't Blame a Vamp-Killer for Trying

I wove my way through New Orleans city streets to vamp HQ, making a few stops on the way. I had a report to deliver and I had discovered that it was easier to give one in person than to write it out and have it messengered over. Vamps aren't big on the Internet. They want things on vellum or parchment with fancy penmanship and flowery words. I was a modern girl. While my computer skills were only okay, my penmanship stank.

I motored up to the gate at the vamps' official headquarters. For the first time I'd ever known it, the place was locked down. The wrought iron gate was shut, security lights lit up the grounds, and an armed guard walking a big brute of a mastiff was patrolling. The guard smelled like vamp and not blood-servant. Weird. The suckheads never did their own chores when there was a blood-servant around to do it for them.

There was no sign in front of the stone-faced, multistory building—never had been—but the arched windows, the long line of steps up to the door, and the façade were bright with security lights. I spotted new cameras on the eaves and, with Beast-sight, saw laser paths lacing the grounds. My old pal Bruiser had been a busy boy, installing and integrating the hardware I had proposed to upgrade the system. Bruiser was Leo's prime blood-servant, head of security for the vamps in the city of New Orleans, but he'd been a much more laid-back guy until lately. When Leo had cleaned house by killing off his enemies, not all of them had been so easily dispatched.

I sat-walked my bike up to a new intercom with a camera and pushed the little red button. When a voice responded, I said into the speaker, "Jane Yellowrock, with a report."

"Please remove the face mask and present proper picture identification."

I stuck out my tongue, though I had it properly back in my mouth when I pulled off the helmet, but there was nothing I could do about the cheeky grin. Not sure what proper identification might mean to a vamp, from a zippered pocket I dug out my bike license for North Carolina, my Private Investigator ID for the same state, and my official rogue-vamp-hunting card with the cutesy slogan. It was always good for a laugh with the long-lived vamps. This one didn't chuckle when I presented them to the camera, but the gate did swing open.

I was met at the bottom of the long steps by the vamp and the dog. The vamp was an old one, a master himself, one of Leo's loyal scions, though I couldn't remember his name, only that he had a Texas accent. Lot of Texans in my life tonight. I called him Tex, and he didn't seem to mind. The dog growled at me, showing teeth, but I wasn't impressed. I'd been growled at by bigger critters tonight. "Knock it off, doggie. Howdy, Tex. What's kicking?"

The vamp lifted one side of his mouth in a half smile and pulled the dog to heel. The growling subsided. "Evening, Miz Yellowrock. New security protocols set up by the boss, including an air lock inside the front door in the foyer, with an armed guard."

"I hope so. What good is a guard if he isn't carrying?"

Tex let his smile widen. "Couldn't agree more, ma'am. You'll have to remove your weapons there, before being escorted inside to Mr. Pellissier."

Though vamp citizenship was being considered in Congress, at the moment they were treated as aliens, and carrying a weapon beyond the foyer of a council house would merit the same punishment as taking a weapon into a foreign embassy or a federal courtroom. It was a good way to get jumped on and locked up. "He's here tonight?"

Something shuttered behind Tex's eyes. "Mr. Pellissier is here every night, ma'am." He turned away, pulling the mastiff with him. "Take care, you hear?" There was a warning in his tone, not that I needed one. Leo had been worse than unpredictable for weeks. But every night in vamp HQ, and not in his clan home? That was strange.

I made my way up the long steps to the front door, cataloguing the security changes. The front door was opened by a blood-servant flunky with the dead eyes of a burned out soldier—until he recognized me. A huge, gap-toothed grin lit the face of a seriously big guy; tall, well-muscled and bald, he looked like an escapee from the World Wrestling Federation. I grinned in return. "Wrassler," I said. I nicknamed almost everyone I met, and had never asked Wrassler his real name, though his had evolved down from WWF-Guy to WWF, to the current Wrassler. He seemed to like the latest moniker.

"If it isn't little Janie. Come on in."

I shook my head at the name and looked over the air lock. It took up a six-by-six-foot space inside the foyer, and it was much more than it appeared, constructed of bulletproof glass and reinforced titanium bars. It was seriously cool. "Where do you want the weapons?"

"Here," he pointed to a glass-topped table with beveled edges, which looked like a weird place to stack weapons until I saw the black trays. Wrassler looked me over and laid out all six, a grin on his face that said he was making a joke.

"Cute." I felt like I'd been dressing and undressing—weapon wise—all day, but I wasn't about to argue with security precautions, especially as I had been suggesting these for weeks. Vamp-hunting was fun and paid well, but the gigs were hard to come by. Security was my bread and butter.

I pulled the Benelli M4 and placed it across one tray, the barrel longer than any of the black resin platters. Three handguns went in the next, still smelling recently fired. His nose twitched and I knew Wrassler caught the smell. When he raised his brows in question, I shrugged, hiding my grin. His eyes tracked over me, noting my bloody, fang-ripped clothes. He stuck a sausagelike finger into a jagged rip in the leather over my elbow. "Bet that hurt."

I grunted. "Yeah. And I'll be submitting a bill for the repair." Into the third and fourth trays I placed five vamp-killers each, lined up neatly; the crosses filled the fifth, laying them so the chains didn't knot; all but two of my stakes went into the sixth dish. I was hoping the sheer number of weapons would make him overlook the pair of silver hair sticks in my fighting bun as a fashion accessory. It wasn't smart to be unarmed within fang range of a vamp, not when said vamp had tried to kill me already, and may have sent me to die tonight. When Wrassler didn't notice the hair sticks I'd retained, staring at the array of weapons in bemusement, I tapped my cheek with a fingertip as if thinking, made an "aha" gesture, and held out the vial of holy water to him. "You'll want to hold this one."

He laughed and took the vial, setting it with the crosses, which seemed appropriate. "That's my Janie."

"You do know that name annoys me."

"Yep. Assume the position, little girl."

"Even worse."

"I know."

After a thorough but totally professional pat down, I followed Wrassler to the stairs and up one flight. I'd been on most floors of vamp HQ, but the doors were always shut, making it hard to orient myself as to purpose. Wrassler knocked at an interior room, meaning no exterior walls, no windows, not that there wasn't a way out hidden behind a bookshelf or something. *"Entrez."* Leo's voice, speaking French.

Wrassler opened the door, keeping his body between the room and me. "The Rogue Hunter, Mr. Pellissier."

"Weapons?"

"None, sir."

A hint of humor entered Leo's tone. "How many?"

"Filled up all six trays, sir."

"Mmm. Hair sticks?"

Wrassler looked at me and I sighed, pulling the silver stakes/hair sticks out of my bun and setting them on the carpet at my feet. "No hair sticks, Leo," I said. I didn't want to get the big guy in trouble. Wrassler gave me a glare, to which I shrugged back with a "So sue me" expression. You can't blame a vamp-killer for trying.

"You may enter."

The guard closed the door behind me, and I faced Leo's office. Tyler Sullivan, a whip-thin, pale-skinned black man with dark eyes and full, sexy lips, Leo's second in command, stood barring my way. His eyes were empty and blank and cold, his posture military-parade rest, but with something cocky and cruel in his bearing. He looked me over head to foot and made a little twirly gesture with one finger. I turned around and when I was facing him again, he said softly, "Assume the position, Miss Yellowrock."

"I just got a thorough pat down."

"Assume the position, Miss Yellowrock." His voice didn't change inflection, didn't insist, didn't cajole or demand. But it *was* implacable. I assumed the position and was once again body searched, a lot harder and more forcefully than before. And a lot more personally.

When he was done he stepped back, shifting position from one foot to the other without proper body mechanics. Which he would likely not have done had I been a guy. Ticked off at where he had put his hands, I turned, stepped fast into his personal space. Slammed him back with a body shove. The instant he was off balance, I hooked his ankle with one of mine and jerked. And rode him down. Landed with a knee in his gut and fingers at his throat. He grunted before I shut off his air. Too late, his eyes widened with alarm.

I leaned in close and whispered, "You touch me like that again and I'll rip out your throat." I tightened my fingernails into the sides of his trachea and pulled up as the heel of my hand pressed down. "Do you understand? Blink twice for yes." Tyler blinked twice, hard. I flowed to my feet and watched him rise. The takedown had been necessary, in a strictly dominance sense, but he wasn't quite so cocky now. I'd embarrassed him in front of Leo and made an enemy. I'm good at that, though it's not a talent I'm proud of. Tyler left through the door I'd come in, his face flaming.

Leo was standing in front of a fire, dressed in a white lawn shirt, one that would have tied at the throat with a fine ribbon, had the tie not been loose, exposing a swathe of his chest. The sleeves were rolled up, the hem tucked into loose black pants of some woven, nubby material, maybe raw silk. He was holding a teacup, the fire behind him, his eyes opaque in the shadows.

He'd watched the scuffle without a change of expression, and he wasn't breathing, which meant he wasn't scenting all the blood-scent markers on me. Still as a marble statue, he watched me. I glanced around once, fast. Leo's personal business space—as opposed to his council business space, which might be anywhere in the building—was an office in name only. Every inch of wall space was hung with tapestries and heavy drapery and the tile floors were liberally covered with Oriental rugs in every shade. The room was chilly, with the AC blowing hard through overhead vents, working to compensate for the hickory wood fire. The older vamps liked fireplaces, the expensive ambience of their human youths, with no regard for global warming.

There was a lot of burled wood furniture, some painted with gilt designs, several wingback chairs around a small table set with the remains of high tea, a table desk so old it might have been hand carved for a Spanish royal in colonial times, with a laptop open on it, and a modern ergonomic desk chair. I just itched to open and explore the armoires that did double duty as cabinets. Nosy, that's me, an occupational hazard even if I wasn't naturally inquisitive.

There was also a chaise lounge in the back of the office, a fancy one with tufted gold velvet upholstery and a velvet throw covering a girl, her back to me, her pale hair tousled. She was obviously naked beneath the velvet. I flicked a look at Leo, holding a teacup, everything but his eyes still immobile, and looked back at the girl. She was breathing deeply and evenly, asleep. "Hope I'm not interrupting anything important," I said, making sure he heard the sarcasm.

Leo followed my eyes to the girl and smiled, unexpected gentleness on his face. "Not at all. She will sleep another hour or two." He took a breath and looked back at me, his head tilted, puzzled at the scents he found on the air. "You have a report?"

"Yeah, I do. I nearly died tonight, thanks to you." Leo set his cup on the green marble mantel and waited, breathing shallowly as he scent-searched me. "You sent me to negotiate with a persona non grata in your place. Remember that? And he brought a pack of werewolves. I nearly died."

"Wolves?" His face underwent a change and my blood nearly stuttered to a stop. Leo Pellissier, Master of the City, was surprised. I smelled shock and anger boil through his blood and his pulse jumped once at his throat. He sniffed, hard, short breaths, and his nose curled. His fangs snapped down with a little click. "The Lupus Pack has returned," he snarled. I nodded, careful to make no other sudden moves. "How many?"

"Fifteen left alive that I saw, and maybe seven dead at the scene."

His brows rose but his fangs stayed down, two-inch bone-white weapons. And me without my stakes. "You are a capable fighter, Jane Yellowrock, but you are no match for a wolf pack.

You were only supposed to meet and remove from my territory one Girrard DiMercy."

"It might have been nice to know that. Next time give me a name and a species, how 'bout it? But it happens that Gee saved my butt from the wolves. Even killed his share. Saved. My. Butt." I enunciated each word. "So you can deliver your own get-out-of-town message." Leo's eyes blazed at my insolence, but I pressed on, pushing the envelope, because it was what I did best, except kill things. "You want to tell me why he's even still alive? Blood-servants don't generally live for nearly a hundred years after their last sip of vamp blood."

Leo's face hardened. "No. I wish to tell you nothing."

"That figures." Usually it was dang near impossible to read vamps' expressions, but Leo was giving things away willy-nilly. He didn't like Gee; if the guy was on fire, Leo would let him burn to death rather than waste water peeing on him. If vamps peed. Now I was curious, but it wasn't the time to ask. "You're making this a lot harder than it has to be, Leo."

"Girrard DiMercy is not welcome here."

"He told me his story. The one about your daughter. He said you need him."

"I need nothing from the Mercy Blade," Leo snarled.

I almost said, "He claimed he kept you sane," but I kept my mouth shut on that one too. "His blood. He says you need his blood. Like Magnolia Sweets needed *your* blood."

Leo closed his eyes and turned away but not before I saw the raw pain on his face. He gripped the marble of the mantel with both hands and bent his forehead to it. His fangs snicked back into place. Something about his scent changed, growing less peppery, more almond. The rolled sleeves of his white shirt revealed muscular forearms and the flames he faced outlined his body in reddish light, toned and hard, though slender. I wondered if he had fenced with Gee when the man lived in New Orleans. Still facing the fire, he said, "Did he give word of my sweet Magnolia?"

"Yeah." There wasn't any way to sugarcoat it. I sighed and rubbed my sore elbow. "She died. I'm sorry, Leo."

"Kill him," he whispered to the flames. "I will pay you to kill him."

Shock raced through me again, a strange, discordant emotion, as if shock layered on shock, two beasts racing along my nerve endings, separate and distinct. "You want to hire me to kill a man? No."

"He is not a man. He is not human. He took her from me, and he has never been punished."

"He claims he didn't steal her from you. He said"—I thought back and dredged up his exact words—"'He'—meaning you—'loved her to distraction, but she could not stay with him.' Could not, Leo, not would not, not wanted to leave you, but 'could not stay' with you. Maybe you should reconsider killing this guy until you know more."

"He has bewitched you, as he did my Maggie."

"He tried. He failed."

Leo raised his head from the mantel and looked at me. His eyes were dry, which was a relief. I hadn't been sure if he was crying or not, and a teary-eyed Leo wasn't something I felt capable of handling. Still, the raw anguish was hard to take. "She could not stay with me? What in this entire world would have been important enough to keep us apart? What would have been worth dying over?"

"Beats me. Talk to Gee." I had rhymed it. The titter I had been fighting since the "vampire peeing" thought burbled perilously close to the surface before I slammed down on it hard. My sense of humor was gonna get me killed.

A knock sounded at the door. Bruiser stuck his head in and smiled when he saw me, not hiding the relief in his expression. He'd been half afraid that his boss would drink me dry. Had Tyler sent him running here? "I'll be downstairs in the Situation Room," he said. "Get your escort to bring you when you're done here."

I looked back at Leo. "You've got a pack of werewolves in the city. Their lawyers are attempting to freeze all the fang-heads' financial activities, bring murder chargers against you for killing the previous pack leader, and bring the vamps to their knees in the human courts. They still say they have proof. And no, I don't know what."

Leo nodded regally, despite his shock. His eyes traveled from me to the far corner of the room where the girl slept. "You may go."

I bit my tongue and left. I hate it when they do that—dismiss me as if I'm the little scullery maid. But I didn't complain. Another waste of breath. Bruiser closed the door behind me, a finger over his lips. To Wrassler, he said, "We'll be downstairs.

You may relieve John at the front entrance. His shift is over. I'll call you when Miss Yellowrock is ready to leave."

Wrassler gave an offhand salute and strode down the hallway, his shoulders taking up most of the space between walls. I hadn't noticed it before, but walking abreast of the guy would be impossible here. "Good thing I don't mind being the little woman and shuffling along behind."

Bruiser looked at the guard and chuckled, reading my thoughts. "He was hired for his physique as much as his training. This way." He didn't speak again until we were in the elevator, headed for the basement, or maybe the subbasement. Or maybe a sub-subbasement. The elevator was in the back of the hallway, to the left of the entry, and it had no buttons. To get anywhere, Bruiser had to slide his ID card through and then punch a series of numbers on a keypad. He didn't let me watch as he worked the device.

"What? No eye scanners, no palm print scanners?"

"They're on order; they haven't arrived," he said, his mouth showing the tiniest bit of amusement.

"Leo was emotional tonight," I said.

"Yes. I noticed." The elevator began to move.

"Leo was never emotional until that thing masquerading as his son died. How long does the *dolore* last? I thought his grief would be over by now. Or at least a lot better. And I need to know about some guys, a werewolf named Roul Molyneux, and a nonhuman who used to be Leo's Mercy Blade, Girrard DiMercy."

Bruiser dropped his back to the wall and looked down at his hands, fingers interlaced and hanging limply in front of him. He breathed out, sounding gloomy. "I don't know how much I can tell you."

"I hope it's enough to explain why Leo just offered me a hit."

Bruiser raised his eyes to mine. "A hit?"

"A contract to kill Gee DiMercy."

"Gee is still alive?" When I nodded, he asked tonelessly, "And Magnolia Sweets?"

"Dead. What's going on, Bruiser?"

He smiled at the name. Bruiser was really George Dumas, a good-looking guy—not as pretty as Rick, but no one was—who stood six-four and had a great butt and a wonderful nose. That might sound weird, but I have a thing about noses, and

Bruiser's was dang-near perfect. His butt in a tuxedo or a pair of tight jeans won awards in my book too.

He sighed again. "You know about the previous vampire war in this city."

"If you mean the one in the early nineteen hundreds, I know it happened. That's it."

The elevator door opened onto a sterile hallway smelling faintly of floor wax. The overhead lights were dimmed, but brightened as we stepped out. There were only three doors, all of them locked with keypads like the one in the elevator. Bruiser punched in some more numbers and opened one. Inside was a large room centered with an oval table and chairs, a modern bronze light fixture with a single large globe—almost as big around as the table—open side facing up, hanging over it. Closed laptops were placed in front of each chair and computers hummed softly at the back of the room. A huge monitor, maybe five feet across, hung from the ceiling, the screen black. There were papers at the foot of the oval table, and two chairs were pulled a little away, as if we were expected to sit. Bruiser claimed a chair and indicated one for me. I watched as he restrained himself from pulling out my chair like he would for a lady. Controlling my grin, I sat. He sat. I waited as he thought, smelling coffee and tea at the back of the room on a rolling beverage cart, and wishing for a strong cuppa.

"In the early nineteen hundreds, the mayor of New Orleans had been made aware of the"—he steepled his widespread fingers in front of his mouth, thumbs under this chin—"*monsters* in the midst of his populace." As usual, when Bruiser talked of the past, his British accent grew stronger, more pronounced. I settled in for a story.

"When the vampires split into two aggressive factions and went to war, he might have stayed out of it, had not the human body count risen so precipitously." Bruiser studied me over his fingertips. "The human servants did what they could to make the bodies disappear, but it was impossible to hide them all. The mayor charged his assistant, Roland Iveries, to bring an end to the carnage in Storyville and the French Quarter." Behind his fingers, Bruiser's lips twisted in a broken expression, empty and a bit lost.

During my previous hunt, I had learned about Storyville, a district of the city set aside by Sidney Story from 1897 to 1917 for legalized prostitution, houses of ill repute, saloons, gambling hells, honky-tonks, music halls, and similar places catering to the baser side of human desires. The vamp who had done my employment interview had owned one of the whorehouses and still did. Katie's Ladies had operated outside of Storyville during the vamp war, in the house where I currently lived, and was still operating in the house that backed up to mine in the French Quarter. I didn't know what the cops thought about the house of prostitution, but since it was run by a vamp and catered to vamps, maybe it fell under a "don't ask, don't tell" edict.

"Following a particularly vicious clash in late 1914, where several blood-slaves were killed under the eyes of a reporter of the time, Iveries called the clan masters together, the most powerful Mithrans in a thousand square miles. He volunteered to act as ambassador to parley a peace agreement between the factions. His boss, the mayor, had an important port city to run; the deaths were drawing unwanted naval attention. An angry admiral, I believe.

"It's my guess that Iveries coveted the immortality the Mithrans could offer, and was hoping he could trade a service to them worthy of being admitted into their number via blood-rite." Bruiser dropped his hands, meeting my eyes. "Back then, there had been no mention of the decade of madness experienced by new converts."

"Converts?" I asked, mild derision in my tone. "New *rogues*."

Bruiser flipped his fingers to the side in a hand shrug, not disagreeing. "Before the last war, my mother was the main draw in Katie's Ladies."

I blinked; quickly schooled my face to hide my surprise. "I thought your mother was gentry in England."

"Impoverished gentry, in Somerset, before we immigrated here. Far more impoverished after my father's untimely death. Men—vampires—paid twenty dollars to spend an hour with her, a lot of money at that time. She accepted only a *very* few gentlemen callers." Bruiser's muscles went taut, his mouth hard, tight with history. "It was said that her blood tasted of lilacs and roses." I thought of Gee, the floral scent of his skin, the peculiar metallic scent of his blood.

"What's the difference between a place like Katie's and vamps picking up donor meals in bars? Neither one offers a traditional blood-servant relationship."

"True, but with vampire madams, the girls and boys are vetted according to age, general health, drug dependency, willingness, and a comprehensive understanding of a vampire's deeper needs. While not a blood-servant bonding, it offers more than a one-night stand with a sick, stoned, drunken child."

"Okay." I filed that away for later consideration. "Go on with the history lesson."

"The factions were loathe to gather in one place, even under a flag of truce. The werewolves had picked sides, and the balance of power had shifted precariously. The mayor's henchman made certain that my Lady Mother, the Lady Beatrice, would be on hand to *assist with the negotiations*." His voice went toneless, as if the memories were suddenly so weighted that they stole any music from his soul when he said, "Iveries hired a werewolf to kidnap my sister Jacqueline. He raped her, and Iveries sent back the soiled sheets."

I couldn't hide my reaction. Bruiser curled in a shoulder as if to say, *Yeah. That's what I felt about it*, and went on with his tale. "My mother agreed to do whatever Iveries wanted to get Jacqueline back alive—if no longer unharmed. He required her to issue the invitations to a diplomatic parley, and because she would be there, five of the Mithran clan masters agreed to attend. With the balance of power attending, the other clan leaders fell quickly into line.

"The werewolves had been acting as strong-arm security for both sides in the war, and agreed to follow whatever outcome arose from the meeting. The previous Master of the City was not as vehement as Leo in his detestation of the two-natured. The wolves assumed that no matter who won, they would remain welcome.

"At most such human assemblies of the time, wine or champagne was offered. For Mithrans, there was blood. And sex. My mother served as willing donor for both."

I had already schooled myself not to react, but I felt my small flinch. Bruiser gave me a smile, more tired grief than anything else.

"She brought me to the meeting and hid me in the next room. I was to listen and peer through pinholes in the wall, and if one of them mentioned where Jacqueline was being held, I was charged to bring my sister home. And to let my Lady Mother know that her daughter was liberated."

I kept my reactions still this time, but I wanted to kick something. I watched his body language, listening to his breathing, calling on Beast's senses as well as my own. I was sure he didn't tell this story often. Maybe never. It wasn't lighthearted conversation. I swallowed down my reaction to the barren expression in his eyes. He wouldn't have appreciated sympathy.

"I knew what my mother was. I understood how she earned the coin that kept us fed and provided the education that would later keep us both out of the gutter. But I had never ... seen her work. She took them all on, men and women equally, giving of her blood and her body until she was bruised and nearly bloodless, whiter than the linen on their tables, white except where she was stained with her own lifeblood. And Iveries watched and laughed as his 'gift' to the vampires was consumed."

His lips twisted hard, too fast for me to read the expression shuttered within. My own eyes were emotionless, my face carefully blank.

"They thanked Iveries for the gift. They all knew what he had done to secure my Lady Mother's willing participation. But not one of them mentioned, or cared, or perhaps even knew, where Jacqueline was being held or if she would be freed." Bruiser laced his hands on the table, his body language protective, controlled.

"Midway through, a vampire and woman came into the hidey-hole where my Lady Mother had left me. Before I could scream, the vampire clamped a hand over my mouth and set his teeth at my throat. It was Leo." Bruiser studied his hands as if he'd never seen them.

"Leo was one of my mother's lovers, her favorite. He was already powerful, old enough to be a clan master, though he was second in his clan, scion to his own uncle and bloodmaster, the Master of the City, Amaury Pellissier, in the next room.

"Leo and the woman with him had been working to bring an end to the vampire war, and had followed a werewolf, hoping to discover where Jacqueline was being kept. He discovered she was hidden in Saint Louis Cathedral in Jackson Square. He couldn't enter a place with so many religious icons, so he gave me a gun and sent me with the woman to find her."

Bruiser released a faint sigh. "We found the little room in the bowels of the church. We fought and I killed the werewolves watching my sister. We brought her to safety, but it was too late. At some point in the parley between vampire factions, my mother must have given up hope of survival. She imbibed a large amount of medical colloidal silver—with brandy, to hide the flavor of the vampire toxin. Before they realized what she had done, she had poisoned most of the blood-masters in the city." Bruiser smiled, a cold, hard flex of lips with no humor in it.

"When they realized what she had done, they strapped her down to the table where they had come to speak peace, and set her afire. Alive. And when she screamed out the name of Iveries as her cohort, though he was not, they strapped him down with her. The fire spread, and the resultant conflagration burned more than a city block of Storyville's best houses. It was the beginning of the end of the district set aside for legalized prostitution," he said wryly, "and the end of the vampire war of the nineteen hundreds."

I had sat through his recital, awful as it was, but I had no idea why he was telling me all this. So I said, "Um. I'm sorry. That's awful—"

Bruiser held up a hand, stopping me, and said, "My mother's sacrifice put an end to the violence. The heirs took over, reinstituting the Vampire Council, which the previous clan masters had disbanded. Now that Leo was clan master, he sent Gee DiMercy away for having earlier attempted to give the mercy stroke to his daughter. And the werewolves who were complicit in the war and guilty of the rape of my sister were punished in accordance with were-law. The remaining wolves were exiled." He smiled sadly. "They swore vengeance on me and mine for the death of Henri Molyneux."

Henri was Roul's grandfather. Okay. Now it was starting to make sense. That was the problem with vamps. They lived centuries, and everything that happened today had roots in things that happened decades, centuries, or even millennia before. "Your sister. Was she bitten?"

"By the werewolf who raped her? Yes, but she survived, unturned. I never learned how."

I thought about Gee's comment that he had kept me from getting the werewolf "taint." Had Gee helped Bruiser's sister avoid the taint? "And the woman who helped you free her?"

"Magnolia Sweets."

Leo's prime blood-servant of the time. "And Leo and you killed Henri?"

"A small cadre of wolves had bitten a number of women, hoping to turn them so they might have mates. The penalty for attempting to turn a human is death, as stated by were-law, but there was no one to perform that justice in the United States. We carried out the penalty prescribed by were-law on the offenders, four wolves," he said. "Henri, as alpha, was guilty by default."

Which meant that on the surface the new MOC had punished the weres guilty of biting humans. But the reality of that justice was wrapped up in vengeance for the attack on Jacqueline. Gotcha. Vamp politics were often bloody.

"There were some deaths from wolf attacks in and around the city before Leo exiled the weres, and all the women they attempted to turn died. My sister lived into her mid-eighties, and died with her sons and daughters, grandchildren and great-grandchildren at her side." Bruiser made a little tossing motion again, indicating an inconsequential addition. "A very few wolves remained, causing trouble, and refused to abandon their hunting territories until the next full moon, but they were handled."

"So that's why Leo is willing to open diplomatic discussions with the African weres and not the werewolves."

"The most current reason. There are older ones."

There always are. "And Gee?"

"Gee left. And Magnolia Sweets went with him. Her abandonment and betrayal was more than Leo could bear. He was truly inconsolable with her loss. He appointed me his first blood-servant, though I was only twelve at the time, untrained, and not suitable for Leo's other needs."

I interpreted "other needs" to be sexual in nature. "And now Gee and wolves both come home at a time when the vamps are in disarray following another war and coup attempt, and the appearance of were-kind on the world stage. The timing is significant."

"Not a war," he said. "Not a coup. A war goes on a long time, between recognized opponents. A coup d'état means a change of leadership, usually by violence, which didn't happen. It was a . . . corporate reorganization." He seemed happy with the phrase, but most corporate reorganizations don't leave a lot of heads lying around or blood splattered walls. 'And with predators, timing is always significant."

"And the hit Leo asked me to make?"

"You may rest assured that he will not ask such a thing of you again." Bruiser met my gaze and gave a small smile. "There are others who will assist him in such endeavors."

Others. He meant assassins. *Was Bruiser talking about himself?* Once, not long ago, he had suggested that he took care of that kind of problem for Leo.

"Let's turn our attention to security concerns for the party," Bruiser said.

There were always vamp parties. They lived for them. Well, parties, sex, and blood. And conspiracy. And power plays. "Fine. It's what I get paid for."

"The two were-cat envoys have been in the city for two weeks now, living in the Soniat Hotel, engaged in clandestine discussions with Leo and the Vampire Council."

"Two weeks," I said softly. The vamps knew Rick by sight; the were-cats would not. Rick was a handsome guy and would fit in anywhere undercover. Certainty settled in the pit of my stomach. It all fit.

"The worldwide announcement was well handled by the were-cats. It was a wise move, getting the Mithrans on their side, from the beginning. There will be parties on the same night at every major Mithran holding in the U.S., the most prestigious in New York City, to be attended by the New York Council of Mithrans and Raymond Micheika himself. Louisiana's party will be the second largest in the nation," Bruiser said, "the *official* meet and greet between the were-cat envoys and the Louisiana Mithrans, and will take place here, in our ballroom."

"And the wolves?"

"Are not invited." He hesitated. I swiveled my head to him, brows raised. "The wolves and the cats do not treat together. They are mutual enemies, just as in the wild."

"Okeydokey. And what else. You never have just *one* bad thing to tell me."

"The press will be present," Bruiser said, letting a resigned breath out.

My pulse shot up. "The *press*?" I said. If nothing else proved to me that Leo was still crazy, this did.

Bruiser ignored my tone. "All of the networks will be outside and can be handled by NOPD, but we will have local cable inside. They have agreed to three cameras and cameramen, two reporters—one for color and one for interviews—one producer, and a makeup specialist. We have limited them to three grips, for a total of ten."

"You are out of your mind," I said. Bruiser raised his brows in that supercilious, infuriating manner he had to have learned from Leo. Or maybe from his Lady Mother. "If you let the press in here, and all hell breaks loose, Leo will be crucified. And you can't tell me that weres and vamps are best buddies and so there's no chance for problems."

"Crucified?" Laugh lines creased the corners of his eyes.

"This is monumental stupidity. The *press*?" I hissed the word.

"The press. I suggest that you acclimate to the concept. Mithrans the world over are now using the press for information dissemination and propaganda. So are the weres. What is it you *youngsters* say?" he asked, his tone mildly mocking. "Oh, yes." He snapped his fingers in a *got it*, manner. "Deal with it. Leo has decided to bring the press into his inner sanctum. And you are in charge of overseeing my efforts to keep him safe."

I caught it. I understood. Bruiser had been in charge of Leo's safety for over ninety years. Now Leo was asking me, the outsider, to look over his shoulder. A big bash, with the weres and the press and the potential for disaster, it would have been Bruiser's chance to shine, and here I was, the new supernat du jour, looking over his shoulder. And then it hit me. If the were-poop did hit the fan, it would be *my* fault, not Bruiser's. I was so freaking stupid. I should have figured all this out before now. I bet Bruiser himself had suggested I help out.

He swiveled his chair and indicated the papers on the table before us. "Security for the visiting envoy, his female assistant, and for the out-clan visitors who will be staying here at the council house during the negotiations."

I had a lot of thinking to do but now was not the time. I took a slow breath to calm down, order my thoughts, and then took us to safer conversational ground. "Tell me about the envoys. What exactly is an assistant and what does she do?" An assistant would be the easier mark for an undercover operative. Ergo, the assistant was Rick's target.

Bruiser shook his head. "I don't know if she's secretary, lover, spy, or slave. The African weres have seldom been to this continent and, according to Leo, the U.S. wolves operate differently from the were-cats. The big-cats have civilization. A well-refined society. Wolves have only pack."

"Big-cat." The word buzzed at the edges of my consciousness like a bee at a window. I caught myself, holding my reactions under firm control. "Are all weres predators?"

"So far as I know."

"Hmmm. No were-bovines, were-gazelles, were-gerbils, or were-swans?"

Bruiser shook his head. I didn't know what it might mean, but it had to mean something. After all, they were called the Cursed of Artemis, and that goddess had been a huntress herself.

CHAPTER 6

You Get to Dress Me

Two hours later, I yawned and looked at the time. It was two a.m. Thursday, and I hadn't slept since Wednesday morning about this time. "Sorry. I'm not used to vamp hours yet."

"I'd have thought the new boyfriend would be keeping you up late."

I leaned back in my chair. From anyone else those words might have sounded jealous. Bruiser's voice, however, was mild, vaguely curious, faintly amused, as if he knew Rick and I hadn't seen each other much lately. As if he knew Rick was undercover . . . I squashed the desire to ask. "As per our discussion," I stood, stretched, and headed for the door, "I'll talk to my guys about providing security for the soiree. During the negotiations themselves, the safety measures in this conference room are sufficient. I want to see the sleeping quarters for the envoy and the assistant, the ballroom, the entrances and exits for the press, the greenroom, the kitchen, and anything else that grabs my fancy while we walk. Then I'm for home and sleep."

Bruiser didn't argue; he stood and led the way. The rooms for the were-guests were on the second floor, each with an exterior wall and windows: walls two feet thick, built of reinforced poured concrete, bulletproof glass in the windows. Inner walls were soundproofed. The intercom in each room rang directly to security, the kitchen, or housekeeping. New, secure phone lines were being installed, allowing the envoys to make unmonitored calls, as the walls' iron rebar reinforcing made sat phones and cell phones unreliable. Both rooms would be swept for electronic monitoring before the guests' arrival and daily thereafter.

The rooms were really two small suites, one decorated in brown, the other in green. Each suite had a sitting room with love seats, the ubiquitous fireplace, a small table and two chairs, a minuscule desk, and a minirefrigerator filled with drinks of every conceivable kind. The bedrooms were small, the space mostly taken up by queen-sized beds and one upholstered chair. The baths were elegant but not spacious, the closets comfortable but not walk-ins.

There was a sprinkler system in case of fire. An alarm rang if emergency doors were opened, and security cameras monitored them constantly. Static security cameras were set at the ends of all hallways. "Secure Internet for their computers?" I asked.

"Password protected and capable of encryption, if they wish," Bruiser said. "We have a dedicated antenna dish on the roof, installed yesterday. We've tested the alarm system and the intercoms. There are two small rooms across the hall for their bodyguards." He nodded to the rooms across the way.

"When is the last time the sprinkler system was tested?"

Bruiser's face ran through a series of muted expressions as he looked up at the ceiling.

"Never, then," I said. "Get the company who installed it in here to check it out. Make sure the workers are accompanied at all times. Also, electronic monitoring equipment was a lot easier to detect back in the old days. If you have someone who wants to see what's happening in vamp HQ today, they'd use fiber optics, installing a system separate from any audio or electronic information monitoring. Systems could have been installed at any time, with any upgrade, or even yesterday when your dedicated dish was installed."

"They might install multiple separate systems?" When I nodded, Bruiser asked, "And how would they go about that?"

I said, "It's easy to install and hard to locate fiber optics. You just thread the cable conduit through a vent or alongside an existing cable. The conduits can be run quite a distance as long as there aren't many bends. If there *are* too many bends, then surveillance would require junction boxes. The boxes themselves are problematic and much easier to detect than the actual cable, and would likely have to be installed during original construction or remodeling, like when this place was wired for cable or when satellite TV was installed."

Bruiser looked at the flat screen television on the wall of the bedroom. "We had cable until yesterday."

"And no one pulled the old cable out of the walls, because it's too much trouble," I said, making it a statement. Bruiser gave me a nod that said I was correct so I continued. "They just left it in place. Having cables in place for other things makes it difficult to discern what cable is good cable and what cable is spyware. However, fiber optics don't provide audio monitoring, which is usually a lot more effective in terms of info gathering, but if someone managed to get fiber optics installed, then they probably got audio somewhere too."

Bruiser was looking at me in unhappy surprise.

"What? It's what I do, besides hunting and killing rogue vamps. Licensed security expert and PI, remember?"

"I do. And yet, knowing that, I have apparently been underusing your talents and skills. Something I intend to remedy immediately."

There was a double entendre in there but I decided to pretend I hadn't heard it. "Lucky me. But since I'm earning my retainer, walk me through the hallways to the ballroom and the conference rooms and anywhere else your guests might be. I'll talk about the pros and cons of micro-sized audio transmission devices, long distance mikes, heat sensing, and Internet info capture." Bruiser had thought his security measures adequate. I was sure he cursed under his breath, but I pretended not to notice.

Another hour later, I knew twenty times more about the council building than before. I'd seen the ballroom—holy fancy pants, Batman—and gone over the logistics for the press.

Most people thought that blood-servants were smarter and knew more than an average human, due to their increased lifespans and brains kept healthy with vamp blood feedings. But living longer meant more to keep up with, more to learn, all on an adult's brain power—the learning centers already hardened into slow-changing patterns. Most blood-servants were behind the times, no matter how hard they tried to keep up. In terms of security measures, Bruiser was stuck somewhere in the last decade of the twentieth century and the business was changing fast.

"One final thing," I said. "The fixed security cameras installed throughout the building are fine, as long as you map out blind spots and cover them too. If I wanted to disrupt this meeting for political reasons, or kill a were for religious or mental instability reasons, or just make trouble, I'd get the building specs and security specs from whomever installed the system, memorize them, and come in with the guests or the caterers at the party, mill around, and then put an incendiary device in or near the guests' rooms and set it to go off when a door is opened, or a toilet is sat on or something. You got holes in the system, and if I wanted in, I'd get in."

"You are a dangerous woman, Jane Yellowrock," he said, his tone guarded and reserved. "Thank you for the advice and your time."

"Thanks for the paycheck. See you at the big bash." Spotting Wrassler, I waved down my escort and headed for the stairs.

"Wear the dress with the yellow jeweled collar, and whatever armaments you deem appropriate." I looked over my shoulder and Bruiser's eyes fell from my face to my boots and back up, lingering on my butt in the leathers. Okay. That was different. Warmth spun through me and my toes curled. Beast, who had been unusually silent all day, perked up finally. She liked Bruiser. She liked him a lot. His voice dropped to a low vibration that made my blood heat. "I promise I'll let you keep your toys this time."

"You paid for the dresses. I guess you get to dress me." Which was not at all how I meant to say that. I opened my mouth to correct it but everything that came to mind only made things worse. I snapped my mouth closed. Bruiser laughed in that securely masculine way that made a girl's heart race. Wrassler was looking back and forth between us in speculation. I turned tail and headed for the stairs before I said anything more stupid.

From behind me I heard Bruiser say, "I'll be swinging by to pick you up in the limo. Nine o'clock." The last time we had been in Leo's limo we had ended up on the floor in a mad make-out session that had stopped way too late. And way too soon. I lifted my fingers to show I'd heard but I didn't look back. No way. I was a one-man woman, and Rick was that man. Most of the time. When he was available. I remembered the cheek peck and the cavalier *adios* from earlier with a curious dissatisfaction.

By the time I got home, the itchy feeling left from being near Bruiser had blown off in the warm breeze created by riding Bitsa. In deference to my houseguest, I turned the bike off and walked her the last few feet to the side gate of the house. *The* house, not *my* house. It was, by definition and contract, temporary housing. I unlocked the gate, carefully locking it behind me to keep out potential robbers, rapists, or gangbangers looking to make street cred. The paperwork and cleanup after killing a human intruder would be a pain in the butt.

No gates could keep out the really dangerous things; for that I had Molly's, and now Evangelina's, wards. With Beast-vision, the magical shield looked brilliant, electric blue in the night, and it buzzed over me, slightly uncomfortable, as it let me through. And this time it sent a static tingle through my fingers that hurt. I mimed a silent *owwww* and shook my hands. I'd have to ask Evangelina to back off on the power levels. I parked Bitsa against the house on the side porch and went inside. Standing at the bottom of the stairs, I heard Evangelina's steady breathing, and Beast stirred deep inside me.

Hunt?

"Yeah," I breathed. Moments later I was standing in the backyard, naked except for the gold nugget necklace that tied me to the mountains I had left only hours before. The gold wasn't skinwalker magic. It was something darker that my skinwalker forebears would have considered black magic. In an arcane way, the nugget coupled me to Beast, a symbol of the event that had originally bound us together. In ways I didn't understand completely, the gold made my shifts into mountain lion faster, easier, and helped me find my way back home when in beast form, even if it was a temporary home. Without the nugget, I'd be back to shifting only when I had lots of time to meditate my way into the change, or force it, painfully.

I dropped five pounds of steak, slightly heated in the microwave, onto the grass, fastened a small travel pack around my neck, containing clothes, the throwaway cell phone, my IDs, and money. I sat on a boulder that was still more or less in one piece, wrapped a fetish necklace made of the bones and teeth of a mountain lion around my fist, and curled my legs into a half-lotus position on the boulder. I could shift into Beast without the necklace if I had to, but this was easier. Tonight I was doing everything the easy way.

I relaxed, listening to the wind. Felt the pull of the slender sickle moon overhead. I listened to the beat of my own heart. Beast rose in me, silent, predatory, claws digging into my consciousness. I slowed the functions of my body, my breathing, my heart rate, let my blood pressure drop, my muscles relax, as if I were going to sleep, the ritual motions and meditation of the shift bestowing their own power to the change.

Mind clearing, I sank deep inside, my consciousness falling away, all but the excitement of a hunt. I dropped lower, deeper, into the darkness where the lost memories of my first human life swirled, broken and jagged in a gray world of shadow, blood, uncertainty. I heard a distant drum, smelled herbed wood smoke, and the damp heat of the night beaded on my skin. As I dropped deeper, memories began to firm, memories that, at all other times, were submerged, both mine and Beast's, memories that had been brought closer to the surface by time in a sweat lodge with a Cherokee elder and shaman, Aggie One Feather. Guilt struggled with the relaxation of the change. I hadn't been to Aggie's in a long while. Beast dug in with her claws, forcing me back.

As I had been taught by my father so long ago, I sought the inner snake lying inside the bones and teeth of the fetish necklace, the coiled, curled snake, deep in the cells, in the remains of the marrow. Science had given the snake a name. RNA. DNA. Genetic sequences, specific to each species, each creature. For my people, for skinwalkers, it had always simply been the *inner snake*, the phrase one of very few things that was certain in my past.

I sank into the marrow hidden in the fetish bones. I reached into the snake and dropped within. It was like water flowing in a stream, a whirling current. Like snow beginning a slow roll down a mountainside, gaining momentum, a tongue of destruction swallowing everything in its path. Grayness enveloped me, a cloud of energy sparkling with black motes, bright and cold, as the world fell away. I slid into the gray place of the change.

My breathing deepened. Heart rate sped. And my bones . . . slid. Skin rippled. Fur, tawny and gray, brown and tipped with

black, sprouted. Pain, like a knife, slid between muscle and
bone. My nostrils widened, drawing deep.

Jane fell away. Night was rich with wonderful scents, heavy and
heady and speaking of life. I panted, soft hacks of sound in the
back of my throat, and listened, ear tabs twisting left and right.
Hum of cars, notes of music, laughter of humans, animals rustling. Good sights, better with cat eyes, brighter, clearer. Good
smells, better with cat nose. I hopped from rocks. Sniffed at
food. Curled nose and snout. *Old, dead, half-cooked meat.
Dead prey.* Soon would hunt, would tear flesh from bone. But
stomach ached. Shifting took much from us. I ate.

Belly full, I stepped to top of rocks, broken and sharp, and
leaped to top of tall fence, brick warm and high like limb in
sun. Dropped down, into yard. Small dog living there was
asleep and safe. Easy prey, but Jane says no. Only opossum,
deer, nutria, rabbit. Wild prey.

I padded around house to street. Crouched beneath big
leaves of plant, good hiding place. Smelled of Beast spoor.
Stared into street. And saw man. Standing in shadows across
street. Watching Jane house, her den.

Not Rick, though Rick had stood in night and watched Jane
house before they mated. This was man from fight place, man
who was man and not man, man with blue and purple magics
on his skin. Man who smelled *wrong.*

How did he find me? Jane asked.

I sent her mind picture of big-cat sniffing spoor.

*The son of a gun put a find-me amulet or a tracking device
on me or Bitsa. I never even thought to look. I'm getting sloppy.*

I sent her mind picture of blue magic on her hands like mist
moving on ground.

Gee spelled me, Jane growled, *and followed me here.* She
went silent a moment. *The house wards felt it. That was that
odd electric pulse.*

I hacked in agreement and padded back, to alley, over wall,
and up another street. Man-city was never silent or dark, but
night was better than day to run through streets and find truck
to ride, like claws in hump of bison, into the country. Trucks
everywhere, not running in packs like deer or elk cow and
young, but each like solitary hunter, going its own way. I chose
small one that smelled of bread and fried potatoes and leaped
onto top, heading across river.

When I jumped from truck into shadows, I was far from city, and smells were rich and thick as fresh blood, good smells, not man smells. Opossum, wild dog and feral cat, water birds. Wet smell of turtle, frog, rat, dead things stinking. And . . . deer scat.

Mouth watered. *My territory. Hunting grounds I marked as my own. Good place to hunt. Half a moon since I claimed it.* I paced slowly away from street, into woods, marking ground with scent, rubbing musk glands onto brush, scraping bark from trees with killing claws as a sign. *Mine. My hunting grounds.*

Water smell was everywhere, still and stagnant with dead plants, thick with small moving things. Smell of alligator. Wanted to hunt alligator, but didn't want to get in water. Alligators big in water, bigger than Beast. Fast. Pelt hard as bone. Deer better. Followed deer scent into woods, heavy with piney smells, summer flowers, trace of skunk on breeze.

Inside forest, on edge of lake, smelled deer, saw hoof-prints, two-toed, in mud, from empty-moon-night. Last night. Counted smells and scents. Was more-than-five deer, more than Beast could count. Jane used numbers of more-than-five, not Beast.

But deer had not come to drink tonight. *Odd.* I crouched and breathed in feel of wind. Touch of moonlight dim under trees. Stars, many overhead, not like man-cities with man-lights on poles and houses. Water dark and deep, with stars in them too. Remembered when kit tried to catch stars in water. Got wet. Good hunter now, left stars in water and followed deer into night.

Later, hoofprints dug deep into ground. Running. Smell of deer in fear. On top of deer track was new scent. I stopped. Tested air, drawing in scents over tongue and through nose, long scree-sound of tasting-smelling. Growled. Hissed. Knew this scent. *Wolves.* Found prints, wide and big as Beast's, claws digging deep. *Wolves running. Chasing Beast's deer.*

I tightened body, curling shoulders in to protect spine, paws close. Remembered long ago . . . Wolves stole hunting territory, stole prey, making Beast hunger, belly hurting. Wolves and man brought hunger times, killed off good things to eat. Hunger times bad, like deep hole with no way out. Remembered. Hissed in anger. *My territory!* Wolves again hunted on big-cat-spoor-marked ground. Stole Beast-prey. I raised my head and screamed, she-cat sound, echoing back over water, through trees.

Jane was worried, thinking of man-not-man watching her house, her den, and werewolves at Booger's. *You haven't hunted in a while and this is the closest forest to the city*, Jane thought. *Is it the same wolves? Werewolves? Here on your hunting ground?* Asking human questions, like questions of kit.

Same scents. I tried to show Jane traces, parts of one scent, parts of many, but humans are scent-blind, even Jane; deer scents were too many for her to understand, wolves were too many. I raced into the night, deer hunt forgotten, following wolves. Hit new scent. Strong and rancid. Blood. Much blood. Wolves had killed and feasted, the night before attacking Jane in Booger's. I growled, hacking displeasure. *Kill wolves. Wolves die for this.* This *time Beast will not run.*

I padded to kill-site, blood-stink strong on wind. Meat and bones scattered. Half eaten. Blood soaked into ground. Deer wasted. Stolen. Wolf-stink heavy on air. Fury filled chest and lungs. Pounded in blood and heart. I screamed. *My grounds. My deer. Mine!*

Soft sound, like breath drawn. Stopped. Listened. Again, breath of wounded prey. Hunched to ground, senses reaching, smelling, tasting, seeing, hearing, feeling of air. *There.* Padded silently to side of killing ground. Found fawn, injured, laying beside body of doe. Dried blood down haunches. Studied fawn.

She'll be okay, Jane thought. *It's only superficial lacerations.*

Has spots, tiny hooves. Too young to survive alone. Fawn panted in fear and pain. Eyes liquid in dark of night. Anger inside grew. Took fawn throat in killing teeth. Jane hid from death in back of mind. Silly Jane.

I wrenched, tearing fawn throat. Drank hot blood. Ate in fury, tearing meat. *Fawn should have been food for winter hunt. Doe gone. Cannot save. Waste, waste,* waste*! Wolves are* waste. Ate in anger, tearing, ripping with teeth.

When stomach was satisfied, anger died. Padded away from kill-site. Sat. Groomed pelt. Thinking Jane-mind-thoughts.

Stood and padded through night, around kill-site, around and around in widening circles. Like dog, hunting for scent. Hacked in displeasure, pausing, staring around at dark forest. Put head down, padded on. Sniffed. Big-cats do not hunt like stupid *dogs* with nose to ground. Brain not right for scent-hunting like dogs. Big-cats hunt with eye and ear, ambush hunt. But Jane in mind with Beast, made Beast do what other cats cannot.

Found scent of another. Stood, motionless, front paw up. Head to ground, breathed in, drawing air through nose and over scent sacs in mouth, *scree, scree*. Unknown scent, yet familiar. Big-cat scent.

Another mountain lion? Jane thought, startled like bird in bush, rising up.

Big-cat. Not like Beast. I tested wind. Looked up into trees. Saw moss hanging like dead prey in trees. Tasted moss once. Plant. Bad taste.

No big-cat waited to pounce from trees. Found and followed scent. Tracing back through pines in rows, as man plants forest. Paws in mud showing size, showing claws like Beast's.

Paws almost as big as yours, Jane said. *Retractable claws.*

Left prints in wet ground. Not good hunter. I nosed prints, sniffing, thinking. Big-cat had followed wolves. Hidden in trees and scrub, off to side, downwind of wolves. Big-cat was young. Female, like Beast, but not like Beast.

A female cat of another species, Jane thought.

Watching. Tracking wolves. Makes no sense. I followed scent a long way, back along wolf trail to man's road, hot tar and dead things along its sides. Wolf and big-cat scent disappeared. Not on other side of road. Just gone. Smell of magics faint on air, like mist above stream. *Wolves changed into humans here. Got in car or truck. Big-cat maybe travel like Beast, on top of same truck.*

Jane thought, *So the were-cats know where the werewolves hunt.*

Too many predators. Not enough prey, I thought back. I went back to kill-site and sat, looking over dead prey, winter-full-belly wasted to summer wolf-kill. Padded around clearing, smelling, looking. Found more big-cat sign, curls of bark on ground. Looked up, into branches; leaped into tree, smelling cat. High up, was limb good for waiting on prey. Hunched and moved along branch, paw, paw, paw, balanced. Her scent rank and strong here. Downwind of kill-site.

Good place to watch. Smart cat. She marked territory, claws raked along high branch, scent marked on limb, claiming hunting ground. But she let wolves hunt. Cat had watched wolves kill prey she claimed. *Now she is stupid cat. Makes no sense. And after wolves gone, cat had not gone down to eat. Wasted more deer. Left hurt fawn. Stupid kit mistake.*

All predators are trespassers in Beast's hunting ground. Anger burned hot in belly, like grief when kits killed, like anger when Jane first steal self, like hunger times come again.

Dawn was gray in sky when I paced away, under low tree, where pine needles were piled deep, and thought of Jane. Gray fog grew up around Beast. Pain pain pain, cutting self deep. Letting her be alpha.

I came to on the needles, breathing deeply, being pricked all over. I didn't know why, but Beast liked shifting on pine needles, which hurt my much-more-tender skin. As usual, I was starving. I pulled the travel pack off my neck and unrolled the clothes inside. They had been there for two weeks and the wrinkles were set in as if I'd ironed them in. I checked the bars and charge on the cell phone. I hadn't brought Leo's phone for several reasons: I didn't want to ruin it if I had to take a swim (there had been a couple of wet close calls and I'd been lucky), I didn't want Leo to be able to track me via the GPS device in the phone, and I valued my privacy. Leo didn't know this number. No one did. So no one could call me.

I dialed my transport while I dressed, pulled on the cheap, thin-soled shoes and tramped out of the forest. I knew where I was, more or less, and which roads were closest. I'd called for a ride before from Beast's hunting ground.

The sun was just above the horizon when Rinaldo found me, the Blue Bird logo on the yellow cab advertising his part-time job. He pulled over and I got in the front seat. He took in the wrinkled clothes. "There no parties *no*where round *here*," he said, his Cajun accent strong, heavy on the verbs—those he used—missing a lot of final consonants. It was his by heritage, but was something he could turn off and on for effect or friendship. For me, it was friendship. Had to be. I wasn't a tourist, so he got paid the same either way. "No houses, for sure," he said. "You *want* to tell me why you keep *show* up out here in middle of God-forsaken nowhere?"

"Nope." Rinaldo thought I was a big-time party girl, an impression I did nothing to oppose.

He sighed and did a three-point turn, driving out the way he'd come. "That it? Nope?"

I hid a smile and looked out the window. "Yep."

"It one a those limousine parties, right? Where a limo take you everywhere and you *drink* and do some dope and—" He stopped right at the edge of saying we indulged in kinky sex, but I could see the thought in his eyes, appraising, looking over my clothes. "Nope. That don't do it." I shook my head, smiling, my gaze on the world outside. "But I *figure* it out *some* day. Meanwhile, you want food."

It wasn't a question. Shifting required the use of energy, which I replaced with calories, and there was no way to carry enough food with me. I had a surprise for him this time though. "I have a breakfast date. Just drive me by the house for a quick change of clothes and then drop me off at the Royal Street Café. I'll eat there." I could walk to the restaurant—nothing in the French Quarter was far from anything else—but I was hungry and I could start with hot tea and a loaf of French bread about ten minutes quicker if I paid for the ride. Plus, it was mid-tourist season, and parking can be problematic, even for a motorbike. Rinaldo shook his head and merged from the secondary road into traffic heading to the city.

I had never seen Rinaldo outside his taxi, but I figured he was about five-seven, one eighty; he had a paunch and smelled of tobacco and spicy food, and he had a bald spot he was trying to hide under the first swatch of a comb-over.

At the house, Evangelina was in the shower, singing some Irish-y sounding dirge, a pot of tea steeping, coffee gurgling, and something mouthwatering in the oven. I peeked. There was only enough for one, more's the pity, and I had no time for tea. I removed the tea leaves and jotted a note on the magnet-backed fridge pad Evangelina had provided. "No time for tea. Thanks for the thought. I'll be home for supper. Text if you need anything from the market."

In my bedroom, I pulled on freshly ironed, beige cotton slacks and a teal silk tank over a tight body-smoother camisole. I slid my feet into sandals and draped on an amethyst necklace with a chatkalite focal stone that hung just above the gold nugget, and a shorter copper chain with a green aventurine arrowhead that Rick had given me. I figured a girl should wear the guy's gifts on a breakfast date, right? I French braided my hair halfway down and pushed stakes in. Yeah, it was daytime. But I carried the stakes anyway.

Five minutes later I was back in the taxi and Rinaldo

looked me over approvingly. As he pulled away from the curb, he said, "You should *pierce* your ear, wear some nice gold rings in 'em. I got a sister who *pierce* 'em for you. Won't hurt at all. She good."

I just shook my head and didn't offer clarification. The one time I tried holes in my ears, my lobes came back healed after I shifted. No way to explain that, especially to a guy who wouldn't know a skinwalker from Shinola.

He dropped me at Royal Street Café, refusing the additional money I offered through the window. "Nah. You a regular customer, and good for a laugh or two. Complimentary."

I patted the hood and walked into the restaurant. Alan Adcock greeted me, "Jane, it's good to see you. Your regular table? You alone?"

"Rick will be here shortly," I said, climbing the stairs to the second story, and sitting at our usual table, on the balcony where we could people watch.

Alan followed me, silent, and finally said, "I don't think so." His voice faltered and he looked away, a minor veer of his eyes, as if undecided and suddenly anxious. It was a look I recognized and didn't particularly want to see on my favorite waiter's face, not in conjunction with Rick as subject matter. Uncertainly, Alan said, "He ate this morning already."

I waited a beat, took a breath, and said with a steady voice, "He wasn't alone, was he?"

Alan's dark eyes glanced at the walls as if seeking an answer there. "Ah, no. His sister, maybe? A business associate?"

Something weird happened inside me, a sort of shift to the left followed by a quick drop, like an amusement park ride, leaving me feeling a little nauseous. Anger that wasn't all my own flared up behind it, Beast glaring out through my eyes. *Mine*, she hissed at me.

Alan took a quick step back at the sight, and I closed my eyes, put a hand on the metal curlicue railing and gripped it, until Beast settled. I pasted a reassuring smile on my face, opened my eyes, and described all four of Rick's sisters at once, which was exactly like Rick himself, black hair, black eyes, Frenchy-look, and beautiful. Alan shook his head no. I described Rick's boss at the main branch of NOPD, Jodi Richoux, blond and slightly plump.

Alan turned away and busied himself straightening the

utensils and condiments on a nearby table. "No. Uh. Redhead. Sorry."

Beast hissed, but I clamped down on her reaction. It didn't make sense. If Rick was cheating on me why bring a girl *here*? He could have texted me a Dear Jane letter and broken it off if he'd wanted to take the easy way out. Or just not show up for breakfast. But he brought a *girl* to *this* restaurant *this* morning . . .

"Soooo. You want breakfast?"

Alan sounded just a bit jittery, and I smiled to settle his alarm, but wasn't sure my show of teeth had the desired effect. "Sure. Bring me a rasher of pepper bacon cut thick, a half dozen scrambled eggs, and a stack of pancakes with blueberry compote, extra butter, and that blueberry syrup I like. And a whole pot of tea."

Alan covered his surprise at the quantity of food better than he'd covered his dismay. "You bet," he said, backing away from the table.

I stared around the balcony, not seeing anything, ignoring the couple seated two tables down, thinking, trying to let the anger of possible betrayal dissipate until I knew more. Ricky Bo might be sending me a message by breakfasting here, though what significance there was to bringing a date to our favorite breakfast spot, and breaking a breakfast date with me to do it, I didn't know. He wasn't stupid, so it had to be deliberate, which meant that it had to do with his work, something he was trying to say without saying it. But so many things were out of place in my life all at once, it was hard to see only one piece of the bigger picture. I had to wonder how many of the little oddities taking place were really part of a larger, about to be screwed-up whole.

CHAPTER 7

A Lot of Hooey

Hands in pockets, I walked back to my rental house, taking the long way through the Quarter. The smells of New Orleans changed with the time of day, the tides, and the seasons. Early on a summer day, the prevalent scent mélange was composed of the omnipresent exhaust, the smell of the Mississippi flowing on the other side of the levee, flowering plants and vines in the flower boxes and minigardens beside and behind every building, chicory coffee, beignets, cigarettes, the smell of sex, the smell of bars open twenty-four/seven, and last night's beer, wine, and liquor, along with urine and vomit left by revelers, though the business owners and the city did a good job of washing away the worst of that.

Though Beast's sense of smell was far superior to mine, I had a better nose than most humans, probably left over from the years I'd spent solely in Beast-form, and the stench was intense and full flavored. It was something I loved about the city. The incredible heat and humidity were a lot less appreciated, and I started to sweat within a block of the restaurant, perspiration gathering on my arms, torso, legs, trickling down my spine, and oddly enough, beading on my upper lip, which was something new. I'd noticed locals sweating that way. Maybe I was starting to fit in.

As I walked, I thought about all the weird things that had happened, arranging them in a sensible order that might show me the whole picture, something that combined the appearance of weres across the world, werewolves in New Orleans,

Leo sending me to deal with a nonhuman who then saved me from weres. That same nonhuman pulling a bait and switch on Leo with the wolves—which nearly got me killed—and then set a find-me charm on me. Last, wolves and a big-cat on Beast's hunting ground. It was obvious that weres were the key to everything, but did not explain Gee, or why Rick might bring a date to the Royal Street Café. I resisted the urge to call him, but checked my phone. No voice or text messages. Nothing.

I had the house to myself when I got back, and nuked a mug of tea while I called my backup for the night. Derek Lee answered on the first ring. "Yo, Injun Princess. Whatchu need?"

"Duuuude," I said in an affected surfer-girl twang. He laughed. I laughed. Pleasantries were done. I launched in to the night's needs, which were muscle-and-weapon security, and hi-tech electronic security.

Derek knew his business. He was an ex-marine with two tours in Afghanistan and one in Iraq during his time in. About five minutes after meeting him I had realized he was more than a grunt. The man had skills and panache that seemed a lot more specialized than the other guys in his unofficial little army. "Weapons?" he asked.

"Silver rounds, stakes, vamp-killers. Weres seem to have the same kind of silver allergy as vamps."

"How many men?"

"If I was hiring cops, two dozen. With your guys, maybe half that."

"I can get six. Guys I trust. Guys who can each do the work of two or three."

Six guys with the level of training Derek was talking about, on such notice? Alarm stole over me on little kitten feet. Softly, I asked, "You raising an army, Derek Lee?"

"Nothing to worry your pretty little Cherokee head about."

"I wouldn't want to have to fight you, Derek."

"Not to worry, Princess. And not to stick your nose into."

I was silent a moment, then breathed my irritation out into the cell phone. "Don't kill anyone tonight unless you have to." Derek laughed and clicked off. I stared at the phone for a long moment before going back to work.

While the laptop booted up, I pulled out research papers. I had photocopies of one entire file cabinet from the woo-woo room in NOPD, courtesy of the last investigation I'd done.

Cops didn't let civilians have access to their files without very good reasons, and I recognized the honor and the trust that had led Jodi Richoux to send them to me. I kept the papers in boxes, padlocked in the bedroom closet with my weapons and other gear.

The files were from the vampire file and included their histories, wars, clans, and info on individuals, as well as a lot of hooey, better known as information obtained from confidential informants. Jodi had included a few folders from the witch file cabinet containing info on the local witches, but a quick search through the boxes that comprised my filing system revealed nothing about weres.

I updated the file on the vamp war of 1915, including the info from Bruiser about his mother, Lady Beatrice, e-mailed it to Jodi for her records, and Googled weres. There was a lot of stuff on the net in just the last two days. A *lot* of stuff, though at this point, I could find no other types of weres on the Internet—only cats and wolves. I surfed photographs, some of them Hollywood stills, some that might be real, of weres shifting. Found some viral video of the real thing, of a South American were-cat, a male jaguar who looked deadly in either of his forms. There were interviews with were-cats, putting to rest rumors about rabies among the species, discussing mating habits, and a frank discussion of transmission of the were-contagion, one thing that Hollywood got right—a bite. The cats all agreed that biting a human was against their laws and the one crime worthy of a death sentence. Which meant that Leo and Bruiser were probably safe from reprisals for killing Henri and the other wolves, assuming Roul was serious about pursuing Leo only in human courts of law.

Once, while I worked, I felt . . . something. An odd reaction, as if I wasn't alone. I got up and went through the house, stepping silently, a vamp-killer in hand, listening, watching, scenting quietly. But I was alone. Evangelina hadn't come in. No one was there and no unfamiliar scents lingered on the air to mark intruders. The sensation wasn't like my predator senses, alerting me as when something, or someone, hunted me, but it was odd. And it faded quickly.

Back at the laptop, I researched real wolves, and discovered that there were only four kinds in the U.S.—the gray wolf (*Canis lupus*), Mexican gray wolf (*Canis lupus baileyi*), the red wolf (*Canis rufus*), and the coyote (*Canis latrans*). I hadn't even known the coyote was part of the wolf family. I'd thought they were a type of wild dog. Around the world, the species and subspecies of wolves was varied, with the gray wolf the largest, and the only one that might be big enough to shift, mass for mass, from a modern-sized human to a beast. I'd seen them change, and there hadn't been any obvious mass transfer, so I was betting on gray wolf for the weres I'd fought, though the coat color differences seemed more doglike, with a heavy shift toward Siberian husky.

The rest of the morning, I studied the history of weres online, looking into the worldwide mythos while keeping an eye out for anything new that might pertain to skinwalkers, not that I had much hope. I routinely Googled skinwalkers and had never discovered anything about a nonhuman or a sub-species like me. There was a lot of nonsense about weres online, but nothing suggested a skinwalker. As usual.

By noon I was hungry again, tired, and annoyed. Rick still hadn't called. A small part of my brain was whispering that I deserved to be dumped, that I was nowhere near attractive enough to date pretty boy Rick LaFleur. A bigger part of me was whispering that I deserved to be dumped because I'd abandoned my no-sex-until-marriage, Christian-children's-home upbringing. I was sleeping with him, I'd skipped church to be with him, and I'd caught myself cussing without my life being in danger. Oh, and I'd been having erotic thoughts about Bruiser when I was sleeping with Rick. Guilt. Guilt like a heavy wool blanket.

Other women didn't have guilt, I knew that with a certainty. My house backed up to a whorehouse and none of the girls working there seemed to have any guilt at all. But a truckload of guilt was dumped on me for sleeping with one guy. Go figure.

Not able to deal with my own traitorous brain, or thoughts about my possibly traitorous boyfriend, I flopped down on the bed and closed my eyes. And when that made the images in my head worse, I grabbed my gym bag and hopped on Bitsa hoping that a good pummeling at the dojo might help.

My new sensei was a hapkido black belt, second dan, with a black belt in tae kwon do and a third black belt in combat tai chi, though he had given up competition years ago. Everyone who trained with him knew he thought competition was for sissies and martial arts were for fighting and killing. His style was perfect for me, because I studied mixed disciplines and had never gone for any belt. I trained to stay alive, not to look snazzy, all belted up, or to show off a wall full of trophies. My fighting style could best be described as dirty, an aggressive amalgam of styles, geared to the fast and total annihilation of an attacker.

The dojo was in the back room of a jewelry store on St. Louis, open to the public only after store hours, but open to a select few students during the day. I had quickly made it from casual sparring partner to serious student and I had my own key. I parked Bitsa at the curb and turned down the narrow service alley. It was all of thirty inches wide, damp and dim.

I keyed myself in through the small door of the dojo and locked it after me. The long room had wood floors, two white-painted walls, one mirrored wall, and one wall of French doors that looked out over a lush, enclosed garden planted with tropical and semitropical plants. Cats were sunning themselves in the garden, seeming to come and go as they pleased, eating from bowls piled with food pellets, and drinking out of the large fountain shaped like a mountain stream that splashed in one corner. A weak smell of fish suggested that koi or goldfish had once swum in the pool at the bottom of the fountain, but the cats had likely made that an unworkable environment though I had never asked the real reason that the pool contained only plants. The garden was surrounded by two- and three-storied buildings and was overlooked by porches dripping with vines and flowering potted plants. Sensei lived upstairs in one of the upper apartments.

I punched the button that told sensei he had a student, dropped my bag in one corner, and stripped off the jacket and pants hiding my workout clothes—stretchy shorts and T, jogging bra and undies beneath. I unrolled the practice mats and started warming up. Ten minutes later, sensei showed up, though he tried not to let me know he had dropped into the garden from his apartment above.

Most of his students weren't able to tell when the man literally dropped in, but with Beast's acute hearing and sense of smell, I always knew. The smell of Korean cabbage he loved so much was a dead giveaway. Sensei, whose real name was Daniel, attacked when my back was turned. Leaped through the open doors, seeing me smiling at him in the mirrored wall as he hurtled through the air. For an instant he frowned.

Then he was passing through the air where I had been stand-ing and landed cat-footed to sweep out with his leg. I leaped above it. Kicked with the heel of my foot, straight for his nose. He bobbed his head and shifted his body left. Counter-punched with his right. All in about a half second. And the fight was on.

I was still hiding that I wasn't human, or at least not fully human, and pulled my punches and kicks, keeping them al-most human slow, and almost human strength. I was a lot faster and stronger when I drew on Beast's abilities. An hour later, I was sweating, stinky, breathing hard, and felt a lot bet-ter. And if sensei had a few more bruises than usual, well, I blamed it on Rick.

Not ready to head home, I hopped on Bitsa and tooled my way out of the Quarter to the Shooters Club off Tulane Av-enue. I paid my fee and bought regular ammo, as the silver rounds used for hunting vamps was too expensive for prac-tice. Luckily, I had the place to myself because I wasn't in the mood to be with people. I hung my man-shaped targets and hit the button that shoved the target holder out to twenty feet to start. I'd push it back and back until it was finally at fifty feet, though no handgun is worth much at that range, no mat-ter what shooters do on TV.

I blew off a lot more steam working with my H&K 9 mil, go-ing through three boxes of rounds before I was satisfied with my precision. I wasn't a bad shot, and I knew a good gun and well-practiced hand-eye shot coordination was essential for a vamp hunter, but I preferred blades and stakes and martial arts to bullets any day. With them, I *knew* a vamp was dead.

Still, when I was done, I felt better, and bought a new hol-ster at the front of the shop, one made of supple black leather with black sequins, of all things, that might fit with an evening gown. I had a party to attend, and permission to come armed. No one said that I had to look unfeminine just because I was loaded for were and vamp. I had never thought of holsters as sexy, but this one came close.

.   When I left the shooting range, I dropped by Katie's La-dies, the whorehouse run by my landlady—when she wasn't in a coffin filled with vamp blood and healing from a mortal wound. Deon, the three-star chef, answered the door.

The slight, dark-skinned man blocked my way in, one hand on the door, the other on the jamb, his brows raised and mouth pursed. "The help don' use the front door, tartlet," he said, in his lovely island accent.

I crossed my arms and cocked out a hip. "Deon, you do know that I could break you in two with one hand tied behind my back, right?"

"We could have fun while you tried."

I burst out laughing and Deon opened the door for me to enter. Deon was gayer than a San Francisco stripper, but he'd taken a liking to me and recently begun flirting in the most outrageous manner. "Troll in?" I asked.

"No, tartlet. The boss man, as opposed to the mythical vampiric boss woman I hope one day to meet and feed, even if she is a she and not a he, went to buy liquor. I have your laundry ready. Want to play in it? We could dump it on the kitchen island and roll around—"

"Deon."

He shut his mouth and switched his hips with a satisfied air, crooked a finger, and led me to the kitchen. "I got you present, girl. Replace them ugly cotton thing you wear on your Amazonian bottom," he said over his shoulder, "with silk and spandex pretties."

"Forget it," I said, sputtering laughter. "Give it to one of the girls."

He canted his head slyly. "You will like. I have the best of taste in all things fine."

"Not happening, Deon."

He laughed, the sound happy and devious all at once, floating back to me from the dining room. "You will love the way silk feel on that lovely bottom—"

"Stop talking about my bottom," I said, following him through the dining room into the spotless kitchen.

"Shh. You wake the girls and they need beauty sleep. Where was I? Oh." He held up a black wisp that shimmered in the light.

I stopped dead in my tracks. "Oh. Oh my."

Back home, I took a shower to wash off the remaining stink of anger and aggression and flopped on the bed. This time, thanks to releasing my pent-up adrenaline fighting and shooting, and the calming results of chatting with Deon, I was asleep instantly.

* * *

I dreamed, knowing it was a dream, but was unable to wake.
The sound of laughter bounced off the walls of my mind,
the werewolf laughter of Roul Molyneux, though I couldn't
see him. I turned around and around, seeing Booger's place,
though only as my mind saw it, not as it had been. It was dark
and empty, and the chain walls were down, enclosing me. This
time there were no doors. Roul's laughter echoed hollowly,
rattling the chains with soft tinks all around me.

A man dropped from the ceiling to land on the balls of his
feet and his palms, catlike, but his face was a dog face, tongue
lolling and canines gleaming. He stood and his face went from
comical to snarling in a heartbeat. Other men landed beside
and behind him, stood and began to move forward, spreading
out, boxing me in. They were all wolf-faced and naked with
casual unconcern. Naked and erect.

Instant fear shot through me, faster than my heartbeat,
pricking on my nerves. I couldn't breathe, suffocating. I
reached for my vamp-killer. As in the way of dreams, I wasn't
armed.

An electric frisson of magic danced along my skin, as if the
air crackled with lightning. I jerked, trying to wake, knowing
I was dreaming, but I was trapped. Heart pounding, I tried
to back away, but my feet didn't, couldn't, move. One of the
men leaped at me, covering the space between us in an instant.
Fangs bared, long and vicious.

The scene changed, leaving me in a dark room lit by fire.
Confused, I sucked a breath and darted my eyes around. No
wolfmen. I was sitting, my bottom, feet, and one hand on a clay
floor, the room around me dim with dancing shadows. Fear
grabbed me, so intense that I heaved. Stomach contents rising
fast. Choking me. I swallowed hard, eyes wide in the murk.

A low bed with a thin mattress was against the far wall, a
table and overturned stools close by. Windows with moonlight
beyond, cloth curtains that moved in the night breeze. The
walls were made of horizontal logs, mud chinked. Shadows
moved on them, thrown up by the flames in the fireplace.
Clothes and gear hung on hooks on the walls and sat on
shelves. The shadow of a man, bearded, lunged back and forth,
back and forth. *Yunega*. White man. Hurting *etsi*, my mother.
Her sobs were quiet. Louder was the slapslapslap of his body
hitting hers. Another white man stood ready. Waiting his turn.
The smells of the *yunega* suffocated me. Unwashed bodies.

Fried food. The smell of bad teeth and wet feathers. And the smell of man stuff on the air.

Watching the shadows, I curled my hands, one on the clay floor of our house. It was cool and smooth. One on warm cloth. Damp and warm. I didn't want to look. But I turned my head in the dream, and looked beside me. A man lay on the floor, face up. He wore a long woven shirt of many colors, a wide cloth belt holding it closed. Blood covered his shirt, looking black in the dim light.

His eyes were open, staring, as if watching the shadows on the walls and ceiling. Yellow eyes like mine. *Edoda*. My father. They had killed him. *Yunega* shot him. He died. Edoda died, before he could *change*, the change that would have saved him. Only his hands had shifted into his beast, the claws of the *tlvdatsi*.

"My turn. Get off her. My turn."

"When I'm done," he panted. "You can have her when I'm done."

I shuddered. Dry-eyed. Silent. Staring at Edoda. I opened my hand and placed it over the wound on my father's chest, into his blood. *Warm. Still warm.* I lifted it and wiped Edoda's blood down my face, my cold fingers moving slowly. His blood chilled quickly, bringing the coldness of the dead into my skin. Hand back into the blood; it was cooler now. Cooling so fast. I wiped my fingers down my face again, trailing the coolness of death. Placed my hand back into his blood.

"Hey, kid. What the hell are you doing?"

I looked up. Into the face of *yunega*. Blue eyes. Snarled hair. Stink of white man. I lifted my hand from my father's blood, and painted my face. Blood stripes. Holding his eyes. Promising his death.

I hurled myself from the bed. Hit the floor shoulder first. Rolled. Slammed into the wall. And woke up. Disoriented by the dream.

No. Not a dream. A memory.

I made it to the bathroom and threw up everything that was left from breakfast. Threw up. Over and over. Until the dry heaves were all that was left and my gut was wringing with pain. Tears and snot coated my face. I spat the last of the vomit from my mouth and collapsed on the floor by the toilet. Sobbing silently, gasping for breath.

I had forgotten. Forgotten the men who murdered my father. Raped my mother. Forgotten the bloody stripes on my face, cooling and sticky. How had I forgotten? How had I ever forgotten?

The wolves had reminded me. Circling me. Naked and predatory. Like the men who killed my father and raped my mother. Shudders shook through me, rattling my bones. How had I ever forgotten?

Long minutes later, I reached up and flushed the toilet, pulled myself to my feet and into the shower again, taking my toothbrush and paste with me. I stayed there a long time.

Darkness fell while I was dressing. I could smell steak broiling and the tang of whisky beneath it. Evangelina was home, cooking dinner that included something for me, as she didn't eat much meat. I wasn't in the mood for food. Every time I closed my eyes I saw the image of the man moving on the log wall. The blue eyes of the watcher staring down into mine. Smelled gunpowder and semen and sweat and wet feathers. I shivered in the cool house as the air conditioner came on.

I had a hard night ahead of me and I needed calories, needed calm. So I shoved the dream into a dark place in my mind, knowing it would come again, knowing there was nothing I could do to avenge my mother or my father. It had been over a hundred years since my memory had been a reality. I was no longer a child denied vengeance and trapped inside the body of another, stronger creature. This time, I couldn't hide away in Beast-form. I would have to live with it all. Sometimes, not knowing is a good thing.

I shoved stakes into my hair, belted on a robe that had come with the house, and went barefooted to the kitchen. Beneath the robe, I wore the black silk wisps given to me by Deon. I wouldn't have thought the spandex would stay in place or be the slightest bit comfortable, but they were, moving when I moved. I was going to hate admitting that to him. He'd gloat.

Evangelina was in the kitchen, drinking her whisky straight tonight, no ice, and humming a tune, her long red hair unbound and swinging as she danced to soft music, something Celtic and wild, with drums and trilling flute. She had lit scented candles and they fluttered as she moved, uncomfortably like the images in my dream, but much better smelling.

In the candlelight, Evangelina's hair looked darker red

than Molly's, with streaks of rich brown in it, and she seemed to emit a soft reddish glow as she danced through the room, like a warm aura. She usually wore staid business suits but tonight Mol's eldest sister was wearing a loose floral dress that swayed with her dancing and when she looked up at me she grinned and lifted the glass in a silent toast. The grin and the toast were surprising enough, as Evangelina didn't exactly approve of the motorcycle mama her sister liked so much, but when she hooked her arm through mine and pulled me into her dance, I was more than surprised.

In my shock, my feet took their time finding balance and rhythm but three awkward steps later I compensated and stepped into the beat; I didn't have a choice, it was dance or fall down. As soon as I was moving, Evangelina let go and swayed around the rectangular table and chairs. I stopped dancing but a half smile pulled at my face and some of the horror that still clung to me from the dream eased away, pushed back by her joy and her half drunkenness. Maybe it was a spell, an enchantment fashioned out of her laughter and the warm scent of whisky, but whatever it was, it eased the melancholy that was riding deep in my soul, the misery of the dream that was really much more. I didn't like magic not my own, but this I welcomed. It was . . . healing. I said, "It was a good day at the negotiations, I take it?"

When she rocked back her head and raised her arms in what might have been a victory dance, I smiled, seeing this stern, conservative woman so carefree. Evangelina was the eldest of the Everheart sisters, a decade older than I was, never married, fierce as a warrior, like Boadicea, the Celt warrior woman. She was also a businesswoman, logical, determined, judgmental, yet able to see a situation from all sides. I was scared to death of her. But I'd agreed to let her stay here because Molly had asked. I do a lot because Molly asks.

Evangelina and the council of New Orleans witches were in negotiations with a delegation from the vamp council about three things: their rights, safety, and legal compensation for the loss of their young to a nutso vamp who had killed witch children for decades as part of dark magic ceremonies, the same ones that had left me keeping a black magic, pink diamond in my safe. It made me feel good to see her so happy when she had such a dark job.

I opened the fridge and twisted the top from a golden wheat

beer. Evangelina took a long slow mouthful of her whisky and smacked her lips when she finally swallowed. "Things went exceptionally well today. Yes, they did. They went well because George Dumas likes you." I nearly dropped the bottle, a fragile laugh skittering up from my belly. My brittle calm shattering. "And I think you like him too." She laughed at whatever she saw on my face. "A lot. And Molly agrees with me."

But there was something dark in her eyes that said that mutual attraction—no matter that it hadn't been acted upon—was a bad and dangerous thing.

"George is . . ." I stopped, sipped my beer, thinking. "George is good. A great guy. I'd have snapped him up in a heartbeat, once upon a time. But he belongs to Leo, heart and blood, and—" I stopped and sipped again, hiding my grin. I'd almost said "and big-cats don't share well." I settled on, "I don't share." Beast huffed with laughter, rolled over in my mind, paws under her chin, and closed her eyes.

Evangelina pointed to a chair and I sat. She had found some good china, so delicate the light seemed to illuminate the plate from inside, old, if the patina didn't lie. And real silver. The beer looked out of place on the table and I set it aside. She poured me ice water and opened the oven. An oh-my-God scent boiled out, beef and black pepper. Hot potatoes. Broccoli steamed on the stove. My three-star-chef guest put food on my plate worthy of a king. There was sour cream and cheese and bacon bits in the double-baked potatoes, hot bacon dressing on the spinach salad and poured over the broccoli, and I breathed in and sighed with total contentment. Evangelina laughed softly and sat across from me. Murmured a blessing. I didn't think she worshipped the same god I did, but I didn't object. I just added a silent one. And dug in.

About halfway through I looked at Evangelina's plate. It was mostly salad, herbed eggs, and an egg custard. "What are you wearing tonight?" she asked. "I've seen your closet and you only have a few things."

"You've seen my closet?"

"You would rather I hired a housekeeper? Or let Deon clean?"

"Oh, heck no."

Evangelina chuckled and ate some spinach. Without bacon on it. Ick.

"I have orders to wear the one with the sparkly stuff on wide lapels."

We indulged in girl talk over the rest of the meal, a totally weird experience to be so chatty with Molly's dragon-lady sister. She poured a dessert tea, tiramisu flavored, and served little bowls of an iced confection with shaved mint on top. It was heaven. And it settled me some way I hadn't expected, leaving me refreshed and calm for the night's work.

CHAPTER 8

Đie Young Then, Sonny

I was dressed when the limo pulled down the street, its V-8 engine thrumming. Vamps aren't into green in any way at all, and saving the planet by saving gasoline isn't among their priorities. I turned, letting the long dress swirl around my ankles, checking to see how much the skirt would inhibit movement. The sleeveless dress was made of thin black silk crepe with a plunging neckline held to decorum with strips of black silk charmeuse. The neckline's lapels were embroidered with tiny faceted citrines and yellow quartz and black jet beads, which caught the light and mirrored my amber irises. The new sequin-studded leather holster straps were belted on over the waist of the dress and under one lapel, while the holster and H&K were snugged at the small of my back under a short cape that draped from the neckline to my hips.

I didn't want to attend a party. I wanted to stay home and watch movies with Evangelina and maybe eat a bucket of her homemade ice cream, but I had work to do and Leo Pellissier expected me to do it. I turned, watching myself in the mirror.

The dress was designed to hide weapons while making me look like I had a lot more class than I did. The mirror suggested the designer had been successful. Beneath the wide, flowing skirt that belled out as I moved, I had three thin blades and one vamp-killer strapped to my thighs. My hair was braided and twisted into a bun so tight it made my scalp ache, and eight silver-tipped wood stakes acted as hairpins. My only jewelry was the gold nugget necklace and the gemmed collar of the dress. Beast sent a satisfied purr through me at the vision of the weapons and the bare skin of my arms and throat. *Trap*, she thought at me. *Looks like prey but isn't.*

I wasn't adept at putting on makeup, so all I wore was bloodred lipstick. Stark and striking was my best bet. New dancing shoes were strapped to my feet, not club shoes, but real dancing shoes, the kind ballroom dancers wear, with straps across the instep to hold the shoes in place and slightly clunky heels for stability. Wearing them, I was six foot three, and imposing. *Looks like prey but isn't.* Yeah. Exactly. And I might be able to pull it off, after the magic of Evangelina's dance and the dinner she had prepared—mostly meat and carbs, my kinda meal.

She wasn't altruistic by nature and I had to wonder if she intended me to benefit or if I just wandered into her own private spell of happiness. Whatever the reason, I was no longer seeing flashes of nightmares. I took a calming breath, as deep as one that prepared me for a shift. I could do this. I could deal with the dreams later. I spun the lock on the weapons cabinet in my closet, sealing inside everything not in use.

I was moving for the front door before the knock sounded but Evangelina beat me to it, holding the door open wide so that street light and foyer light met and blended and Bruiser's eyes didn't have to adjust. He stood in the doorway, a black tux molding to his frame, taller than I was, even in the dancing shoes, his shoulders boxer wide, and his butt cradled by the expensive cut of the suit. His hair was different tonight, combed straight back and moussed into place, a 1940s style that looked elegant and made his hair seem darker than his normal brown. He nodded to Evangelina without really seeing her as he entered, his eyes on me, moving from the tips of my toes to the tips of the stakes fanned out around the back of my head like a wood and silver halo. His eyes were heated and heavy as they slid over me, and I flushed as if he touched me. It was enough to help push the remnant memories of the dreams far away. Evangelina pushed his shoulder to move him inside; shut the door.

I don't know what I expected him to say, but I wasn't disappointed when he said, "Weapons?" Eyes holding his, I gave him the list and his mouth curled up as I spoke, his gaze searching out the probable location of the blades and gun. "Show me."

I turned around and flipped up the small cape to display
the holster, my right hand on the butt for drawing, and whirled
back around, sliding my legs, one at a time, through the skirt
slits in little dancer kicks. Bruiser was a leg man and his pupils widened at the flash of skin. I was sure the kicks and skin
would have been flirting for most girls, but I had no idea how
to build upon it. And no desire to, I assured myself.

I ducked my head, feeling self-conscious, and picked up my
tiny bag, sliding the long strap over one shoulder. I nodded
good-bye to Evangelina and caught her watching Bruiser. A
quick glance at Bruiser showed him watching back, surprise
and unwelcome speculation on his face, as if he'd just recognized her, standing in my foyer. "Miz Everheart," he said.

"Have fun at the ball, Mr. Dumas." She lifted the nearly
empty glass in the half-drunken salute I'd seen several times
this evening, though this time she seemed stone-cold sober.
"Don't let Cinderella here kill your golden goose."

I flinched at the acerbic tone and the insult, feeling sucker
punched. Bruiser said, "That would make you the ugly stepsis-
ter in your jumbled nursery rhyme."

"More like the wicked witch of the west, sweetie, with a
broom, a gingerbread house, and a big cauldron out back to
cook up curses."

"I was under the impression that you were a white witch,
not a sorceress."

"I walk a fine line during negotiations. And I've been
known to bloody my athame when needed."

"I'll keep that in mind, Miz Everheart."

"You do that, Mis-ta Du-mas," she said, spacing out the
syllables in what sounded like a taunt. Evangelina turned her
back and moved into the kitchen where she turned the music
up, Celtic notes tinkling on the air.

Bruiser's eyes followed her through the doorway and
stayed there for a moment before swerving back to me in
question. I said, "You did know she was my houseguest, right?
Molly's idea, by the way, not mine."

"It must have slipped my mind." As usual, when he was
thoughtful, his English lilt slipped out, though muted by decades in America. It gave him a mixed accent, part British,
part old-guy American, part modern American. He gave me
that half smile, the faint but intense one that had been known

to curl my toes, and raked my body with his eyes again. "You look striking tonight, Jane, lethal and lovely."

Striking. Good choice of words, I thought. "Thanks. You look good yourself." I cocked my head. "Weapons?" I quoted.

Bruiser lifted his coat to the side, exposing a semiautomatic handgun as if it was his only weapon, but Bruiser was security for Leo Pellissier, which meant for the greater Mithran Clan of New Orleans, which meant he was packing big-time tonight. I glanced at his ankle and his smile widened fractionally. "A .32 snub-nosed," he said, his tone final. When I pointed to his waist he breathed out a laugh and said, "Two blades in spine sheaths and a .38." I waggled a finger back and forth from one arm to the other. "One blade on each wrist," he conceded, "no more. All we need are blades in the toes of our shoes to arm us as well as Bond. James Bond," he said, sounding all Sean Connery on me. Connery had always been a hottie, far as I was concerned.

With the talk of weapons, my pulse and breathing had settled; the tension still coiled in my psyche loosened. *Yes. I can do this*. I locked the front door behind me and led the way to the limo, sliding across the seat, the leather soft as butter, and replied, "Let's hope we don't have to kill anyone tonight. I nearly ruined a perfectly good dress at the last vamp party I attended."

"I'll see another is sent to you," Bruiser said, closing the car door and sitting close, with his outer thigh touching mine. The limo pulled away from the curb as the warmth of his thigh passed through the layers of cloth and into mine. I glanced at the floor of the limo, where Bruiser and I had ended up on our last ride to a vamp party.

Crap. I have a boyfriend. Who disappeared after showing up at our *breakfast place with different girl.* My heart thumped hard once, and heat that hadn't been there a moment before whispered through me. It traveled up my thigh to settle low in my belly. A breath later it purled out and through me, giddy and drunken, like the magic of Evangelina's dancing. Like the spell she had woven out of elation and joy. And I remembered her taunt.

I knew that some of the magic she was dancing had affected me. Calmed me, and then upped the intensity of my happier emotions. I had been in the presence of varied magics, all unlike my own, ever since I first arrived in New Orleans. And around a *lot* of magic in the last couple of days: were-change magic, Evangelina's witch magic, and even Gee's blue magic on my skin, any of which might affect Beast's wild influence, and charge my own skinwalker energies. It was a cocktail of magic that could make any girl a little unsteady.

Bruiser shifted on the seat next to me and the heat in my belly did a little somersault. *Stop it*, I commanded myself. But my pulse sped up and I saw a vision of Bruiser and me on a big bed, with the sheets torn, the pillows on the floor, and the mattress skewed. Us panting and sweaty and a little bloody. Beast's idea of good sex. Heat steamed though me, hers more so than mine.

Magic. Yeah. This was magic. Evangelina's magic. And it was powerful. Suddenly, I wondered if the little witch had done it to me on purpose. I couldn't decide what to do with my hands. I folded them together in my lap, which felt all prissy, not like me. But if I put them to my sides, one would be in Bruiser's lap. I strangled the desire to laugh, knowing it would come out as a nervous titter. I was a vampire hunter, for pity's sake. There would be no more mad make-out sessions with Bruiser. Not anywhere. I had a boyfriend now. Rick. Pretty boy Ricky Bo. Who might be cheating on me. At the thought of Rick with another woman, my pulse spiked painfully, my heart twisting inside my chest. *Crap*. What had Evangelina done to me?

Beast placed a paw against my mind, her claws pressing down, exerting enough pressure to almost hurt, but not quite. I saw reddish energies beneath her claws, sparking, sparkling, and curling away. Evangelina's spell fled from Beast's claws, and I could almost see it scatter, like pink motes in the darkness. I closed my eyes and sank back against the seat, breathing too fast, but back in control of myself.

"As Leo's Rogue Hunter," Bruiser said, and I struggled to remember what we were chatting about. Oh, yeah. Bruiser was still talking about a new dress. "—and hired security, you will be expected to attend many such high-priority functions over the course of the next year, and it will not do at all, to have you appear in the same dress. And don't complain," he said, as though I had been about to object to a fitting, which I hated. "You are paid well. Looking beautiful as well as deadly upon occasion is part of your employment requirements, and the dresses come with the job. Madame Melisende will whip up something in her shop to fit your needs, according to your last measurements, deliver the dress, and make any small adjustments. It will take a quarter hour of your time at most. And you do know, don't you, that most women would groan in pleasure at being given designer clothing as part of an employment package."

I couldn't think of anything to gripe about in the scenario he described, especially with him paying, and the unexpected *beautiful* comment. I almost reminded him that I wasn't most women, but I figured he knew that already.

Bruiser poured and handed me a glass of champagne. I took it, sipped. I'm more of a beer girl, but even I could tell this was very good stuff. It further settled my insides, which were still ruffled by the witch magic. "Nice," I said.

Bruiser agreed with a murmured note, a soft *hmm*, but he was staring out the car window. He was preoccupied, and as I watched, seemed to pull into himself and away from me, aloof and reserved, caught up in his own thoughts. Better. Much better. His distance and Beast's paw on my mind cleared the last of Evangelina's spell from me like the sun evaporated rain. We rode the last blocks in silence.

When we reached vamp HQ, the driver drove around to the back of the building, passing a few cars parked on the street, and one panel-sided van, black. Antennae bristled from the roof. "Cops are watching the place," I said.

"Noted," Bruiser said.

The driver parked. Bruiser opened the door and handed me off to his second in command, Tyler Sullivan, with a curt, "Run over the security measures once again with Miz Yellowrock. If she suggests any modifications, make them and inform me of the changes." To me he added, "The envoy and his assistant arrived this afternoon via private car and have been ensconced in their rooms since." His mouth formed a thin line and he added, "They brought their own security, one . . . something. I don't know what it is, but it isn't human. Leo says it isn't a cat; it smells like dead fish and it's fast. It left its rooms once and real-time on the camera is a blur, but it didn't get out of the building. On slow-mo it looks humanoid with green skin."

Slow-mo was digital feed slowed down. I speculated on what creature had green skin and smelled like dead fish as the demands of the job took over. It didn't sound like a were, but any creature charged with security detail had a job that might run in opposition to ours. Someone we had to keep an eye on.

Adding a new species into the mix tonight didn't make me all happy inside. I looked at the men milling in the parking area, armed, dangerous, and smelling like blood-servants. They all looked edgy.

To Tyler, Bruiser said, "Take care of her. Keep her out of trouble." He walked away.

Keep her out of trouble? I had no idea what that meant, but there was a more important question to ask Tyler. "Why is everyone so tense?"

Unexpectedly chatty, Tyler said, "Leo hates weres, but with the attention the national vampire council has given the were-cats, he's had no choice but to deal with the envoy. He isn't happy about it." He studied my face, adding, "Rumor has it that *werewolves* are in the city."

I tilted my head to acknowledge his statement. "They are. And when Leo is unhappy everyone is unhappy. Got it."

Tyler said, "Come. Your guys are here, under guard, and George wants you to vet them."

I'm not sticking a thermometer up anyone's butt, I thought, but I was wise enough to keep the witty, though vulgar, thought to myself.

"My guys" were six ex-marines, not happy being kept in a locked room, their weapons in the hands of vampire blood-servants. I could hear a shouting match between two hot-headed grunts all the way down the hall. From the expression on Wrassler's face as he guarded the doorway, he could hear it too—improved hearing, another benefit I could chalk up for blood-servants getting regular blood sips from a vamp.

Tyler veered off down another hallway and I was left with Wrassler, who looked uncomfortable in a suit, like a bear in black tie, communication headset on, earpiece in his left ear. He opened the door and I sauntered in, Wrassler behind me. I interrupted, "If I wanted you guys dead and I had a loaded Uzi, I could have opened this door and sprayed you all down."

I heard a click from overhead and quickly counted the soldiers in front of me. Five, not the six I expected. I looked up and met Derek Lee's eyes. His full lips were closed as if holding in a laugh, and he was perched in the supports above the dropped-ceiling tiles. Two tiles had been slid out of the way to allow room for his body, and his dark skin and night camos blended with the shadows. He had a nine millimeter aimed at my head, and another one aimed at Wrassler. The argument had been a ruse to keep us from seeing how many were present until someone had the drop on us. Neat and clever. The big guy behind me was frozen into immobility, a gun inches from his nose. Only now did I realize that the room didn't smell of anger pheromones. I started laughing.

"If you'd wanted us all dead," Derek said, "you'd have been leading the way through the pearly gates, Injun Princess. Nice dress, by the way, especially from here." Derek was looking down the front of my dress. I resisted the urge to spread a hand over my chest.

Wrassler asked, "How'd you get a weapon in here?"

"I'm good. Better than your boys." Derek dropped from the ceiling, landed with easy grace, and handed me the weapons. The demonstration was finished, and my position as alpha established by the relinquishing of the guns. It was nicely handled. Vintage Derek.

"Derek Lee, meet Wrassler," I said.

"Good name for you," Derek said.

"How come you don't have a nickname?" Wrassler asked. Derek looked at me.

I didn't have an answer. Some people had nicknames, some didn't. Simple. I wasn't into self-examination to figure out why. "Have you had a look at the grounds?" My question wiped away the last of the effects of Bruiser's thigh against mine, and if a little voice was still making suggestions that I sleep with him, I could blame it on spells and Rick with another girl. It was time to work.

"We got a man in over the back wall near the parking area. Inserted a camera. Saw a funny-looking little guy speeding around."

"Green skin?" I asked.

"Coulda been. Low light camera only showed heat sigs. He's colder than a human, hotter than a vamp."

"You got a man in to the compound?" Wrassler repeated.

"In and out. Slick as owl shit, my man. Like I said. We're way better."

Wrassler's mouth turned down. To stave off the looming pissing contest, I said, "We need to work the grounds and the building. Wrassler, send an electronics tech with one of Derek's men and see if you can find anything the Leprechaun might have planted on cars or the premises."

"I'll go with the ET guy."

I looked at the grunt who was speaking. He had been with Derek and me on two other jobs and survived both, but I'd never been privileged to know his name. This time he was wearing military ID stenciled on his chest pocket that said V. Angel's Tit. My brows rose, and the guy, who was probably a mixed-race kid, with café au lait skin and green eyes, grinned at me. It seemed I was still not worthy of knowing their names. A quick glance around showed me the names, V. Martini, V. Lime Rickey, V. Chi Chi, V. Hi-Fi and V. Sunrise. "V as a first initial with a drink name after. This job's code name is Vodka?"

"Vodka Ball Buster," Derek said.

I assumed a ball buster was another drink. Derek's name was officially V. Lee's Surrender. I didn't know what drink it was, but the Civil War note was cute. "Get 'em their weapons," I said to Wrassler, "assign them each one of your security guys or gals, and let them get to work. If *they* got in over the wall, we have to assume that someone else could have too."

Wrassler nodded and touched his headset, speaking softly into the mike. "What about you?" he said to me when he was done.

"I want to see the security console again and check out the camera placement updates I recommended. I want to look over the press entrance again. And I'm hungry."

"The greenroom is on the third floor, off the ballroom. Snacks and sandwiches, water, colas, and coffee are available. Beer and drinks after, with a real meal, if anyone wants," Wrassler said.

"That's mighty white of you," Vodka Chi Chi said, baiting the bigger man.

Wrassler said, "You want to say thanks, offer a little sip to one of the Mithrans." He grinned and it wasn't intended to convey humor. "They like *fresh meat*."

Chi Chi sneered. "I'm not a blood whore, white boy. None of us are, except to heal combat wounds suffered in the employ of Mr. Pellissier."

Wrassler laughed again. "Die young then, sonny. I'm sixty-four years old." The two men looked one another up and down, while surprise blinked its way through the soldier's dark eyes.

"If y'all are finished sniffing each other," I said, "we have work to do." *Men*.

We split up, me with Wrassler and Derek in the electronic monitoring room, where I got my first glimpse of the green-skinned security guy. He was no Lucky Charms Leprechaun, all stovepipe hat and chin whiskers. He was a little golem of a fellow, Yoda with fangs, about five-two, slender as a reed, with joints that seemed to bend the wrong way, bones that seemed too slender and too knobby. His head was too big for his body, his ears were set too far back on his skull, and when he ran, he seemed to be on his toes, like a dog or cat. His clothes were loose and baggy, hiding a full view of how he was put together, which might have been vaguely froglike.

Beast sat up and peered at him on the monitor, holding me down with a paw. She didn't send me any images or comments, but I got the distinct impression that she wanted to kill the little green guy—yeah, he was pale green, like olive serpentine or some bread molds—and leave him for the buzzards.

I had no idea what he was, but Wrassler got word quickly that Green Moldy Guy had planted a dozen spy-eyes in the parking area and on the grounds, his actions all undetected by the monitors until the footage was viewed slow-mo and the time stamps compared to Derek's visual of the grounds. The envoys weren't playing fair, and clearly had an unannounced, undisclosed goal in New Orleans. It took us the better part of an hour for Derek's IT guy to find and remove the minicameras in the parking area. We got it done just in time for the clans to start arriving.

Two months ago there had been eight clans, divided into two groups according to clan affiliation, and a stable power structure. Then a few vamps wanted more of the pie for themselves and there had been a mini war—short, bloody, and decisive. Now there were four clans: Pellissier, Laurent, Bouvier, and Arceneau. The other vamps had either merged under a surviving clan or they were dead. Or in hiding and plotting a coup, if you believed the gossips, which I did. Only Clan Pellissier had any real power, the others were under Leo's thumb. Or his fang. Pick an analogy.

Wrassler touched his earpiece and handed one to me. "We have guests." The vamps had started to arrive. Without seeming to hurry, but with a lot of speed just the same, Wrassler and I left the electronic security monitoring system in the hands of

V. Angel's Tit and one of Wrassler's ladies, a whip-thin, older woman built like a stiletto and with a tongue just as sharp. I placed my earpiece in and dropped the mike to my chin, hiding the receiver under the little cape next to the handgun as we reached the ballroom.

Neither Bruiser nor Leo was in sight. Right. In vamp politics Leo would be last to arrive, before the were-guests. I checked the ballroom one last time. It was ornate in a style all its own, a sort of colonial Moorish mix, with pointed arches and domed ceilings high overhead, held up with fluted columns painted with gilt. There were stained-glass insets in many of the domes, illuminated by artificial lights. No sunlight had ever been in this room, or in any of the council house rooms used by the vamps themselves.

Underfoot, the carpets were so rich my feet sank into them with each step, and where the carpets stopped was pink marble flooring, smooth as the inside of a pearl. Linen-draped tables and side chairs circled the walls, furniture that belonged in museums. Curio cabinets filled with exquisite objets d'art, interesting historical and archeological items donated by vamps, and the macabre, like the shrunken heads and human-skull drinking cups, handmade items of tribal life: flutes, stone hammers, small pieces of pottery that had been shaped without a potter's wheel and fired in open fires, the unglazed sides charred with smoke in unusual patterns. Bouquets were everywhere, and the smell of roses and aromatic lilies and jasmine pervaded the air.

There was gold-plated serving ware and utensils, nothing silver to harm the vamps or weres. Tables laden with cheeses, fish, a dozen meats, and a boatload of tropical fruit sliced into bouquets were set up for the human servants, with an alcohol bar and a cute bartender blood-servant dressed in a red tux. The food smelled wonderful and my stomach growled. Evangelina's steak was long gone, but I had a lot of work to do before I could get that sandwich waiting for me in the greenroom.

All the servers brought in by the caterer had been vetted and body-searched, and armed blood-servants loyal to Leo were stationed everywhere throughout the building. The media types were in place, cameras in three strategic places in the ballroom. The color girl—a reporter who would gather sound bites from the guests—and the on-air reporter were in place.

The makeup guy—I had expected a girl and it felt odd to recognize my sexist tendencies—had commandeered a corner in the greenroom.

There was no blood bar with willing blood-slaves set up behind a curtain to provide the vamp partygoers their dinners, not with press present. Leo had made the proclamation: feed before you show. There were a thousand things that could go wrong tonight, but the smell of blood in the presence of two predator species wasn't going to be one of them. The place was as safe and secure as I could make it. Still, the blood thrummed through my veins when the doors opened and the first vamps walked in.

Clan Laurent was this first arrival, meaning they got the best places for their scions and blood-servants, but this also put them at the bottom of the pecking order among the clans. That vamp one-upmanship stuff wasn't my department. Bettina, clan master, entered alone, the petite woman standing in the doorway like a runway model. Bettina had once been clan master of Rousseau, but was taken down by rivals within her clan, not according to vamp law, in personal sanctioned combat, but outside proper channels. Gossip claimed that when her clan was disbanded, Bettina survived and called the sire of Clan Laurent to personal combat. She won, and Clan Laurent survived.

Bettina was an exquisite woman with mixed-race heritage, mostly African and European, and once she had been so sensual that lust wafted off her like steam above a volcano. Now, she was colder, more introverted, and when her eyes flashed fire, it was the fire of anger, not sex. Her heir and two other master vamps stepped to her from either side in choreographed pacing. They moved into the room, their blood-servants behind them, two blood-servants per vamp, the number allowed by Leo. The stink of vamp was swept up by the air conditioner and filled the room, smelling like dried herbs and fresh blood, the way an old-fashioned herb shop might smell if someone slit a human's throat in it. The first twelve visitors had arrived.

Next in the pecking order was Arceneau, with four master vampires: Grégoire with his heir Dominique on his arm, both blond with chiseled faces, and two African masters to either side, Kabisa and Karimu, twins, both female, tall and regal, like walking Egyptian statues wearing flowing creations unmistakably made by Madame Melisende, *Modiste des Mithrans*, my dressmaker. Both women were soldiers. I recognized the gait, surefooted and assertive, though nothing in their dossiers suggested battle training. Arceneau's scions and blood-servants fanned out around them and moved into the ballroom. I smelled fresh mint from them, overlaid by a hint of rosemary. It wasn't a scent I'd have associated with a vamp, but vamp pheromones were mutable, like a human's.

I looked at the clock to see 11:27. Two clans to go, then my first look at were-cats up close and personal. My Beast was prowling inside, slow sinuous steps like a lion in a cage. Which she was, in a way, caged inside me.

The third clan was Bouvier, its new co-masters Innara and Jena, who were mind-joined Anamchara, and who had been loyal to Leo during the recent unpleasantness, stood in the entry to the ballroom. They were little things, the tallest standing five-four in heels. Their master had been killed true-dead by the opposing camp and the girls had swept up his power base in their cute but deadly little hands. They were going for the gay twenties look tonight in contrasting teal and aqua silk sheaths embroidered with beads, crystals dangling and catching the light. The silk hems ended at their shins, but the crystals formed pointed Vs that hung lower, accenting the crystal shoes each wore. Which looked really uncomfortable. The outfits were perfect with their bobbed hair, one dark blond and one darker brown. Their clan heir, Roland, who was a big guy by vamp standards, stood behind them, arms crossed, showing muscle through the cloth of his long tunic, which was vaguely Arabian in style. Behind him, another master and all eight blood-servants filled the open doorway. They looked charming and implacable as they moved into the room, blood-servants spreading out and posturing for position. The air took on a vamp stink so strong that my nose itched and stung. I needed to sneeze out the reek, but the next breath would only be worse.

The on-air reporter, who was standing near me, gasped and backed away. I glanced at her and back at the vamps and almost shook my head. She was no twenty-something ditzy girl, but an older woman, a seasoned reporter, likely retired from a bigger network, let go because of age, but that experience was nothing in the face of vamp mesmerism. Her lips hung slightly open, her eyes glued to Roland.

I looked back at the vamps. Yeah. Vamps were gorgeous all

right. Pitcher plants or Venus flytraps, ready for fresh blood and willing flesh—or a victim stupid enough or susceptible enough to fall for them.

The reporter moved toward Roland, her mike in front of her—a shield and a sword. Or an offering. He turned to her and smiled, his face looking almost beatific. And hungry, in spite of the edict to eat before showing up here. He held out an arm and slid it round her when she reached him. She fell back against the iron-band strength of it, her throat exposed. *Prey*, Beast whispered in my mind.

Roland kissed the side of the reporter's neck. Teasing. But his fangs stayed snapped back in his mouth and he released her with a kiss and promise I heard across twenty feet of pink marble floor and Oriental rugs. "Later, my lovely. I'll come to you before dawn." She was toast, but she was a big girl. I had other worries. Like the cameras capturing too much. Not too much of the vamps—that was a job for the spin doctors—but too much about the layout of vamp HQ. It could be dangerous for the security of the place.

Unlike other vamp parties I'd attended, no one went immediately for food or alcohol, but took up positions around the room, as if keeping sharp for trouble. *Crap*. What did they think was gonna happen? I was suddenly conscious of the blades on my thighs and the weight of the H&K at the small of my back. Possible collateral damage was everywhere. My mouth went dry.

Everything was ready for Leo. But seconds passed. Minutes. The vamps were immovable as marble headstones, not bothering to breathe, since they didn't have to talk. The blood-servants mimicked them. Except for the breathing/heart beating part. It was unnerving. But at least the vamped reporter had regained her equilibrium. She was standing in the corner having her makeup touched up, casting confused and nervous glances at Roland, who was ignoring her. Cat and mouse. Literally. A vamp playing with his dinner.

At twelve minutes to twelve, Leo was standing in the entrance, his authority a nimbus around him, crackling with electricity that lifted his shoulder-length black hair on a breeze of power. I hadn't seen him move there. No one had.

CHAPTER 9

He Got a Whiff of Me

The blood-servants' breathing changed. The younger vamps blinked, startled. Leo stood, still as pale marble, his skin glowing with recent feeding, drawing power from all the vamps in the room. His eyes were bright, as if lit from within, with an odd sheen to them, as if they swam with precious oil. The scent pattern in the room changed as Leo stood there, demonstrating his power, siphoning off theirs, his own peppery scent overpowering all the other vamp smells. Every eye in the ballroom was on him.

Leo had no heir, and as MOC, he was entitled to additional scions, so there was no surprise when four master vamps stepped behind him in a semicircle, all males. I wondered if—under different circumstances—my landlady, Katie, who had been Leo's lover in the past, would have stood behind him, a lone woman in the midst of the men.

All of Leo's henchmen were familiar. I'd learned their names after they tried to burn down my house. Alejandro and Estavan, both of Spanish origin, but different centuries; Hildebert, a German guy whose name meant bright battle; and Koun, who claimed to be pure British Celt by birth, though history said his people were destroyed long before the first vamps appeared in the British Isles. Hildebert and Koun were the warriors of Clan Pellissier, and I'd really rather not have to face either one in battle. The fact that Leo brought them with him instead of someone prettier and more delicate was significant. My heart rate sped. Leo moved his eyes across the room until he found me, searching me out as if he could hear my blood pound and place me by the sound of my heartbeat. *Crap. Maybe he could.*

Staring at me, he said, "The Council of the Mithrans is . . . *gathered.*" The word reverberated through the room; shivers raced over my skin, raising to sharp pricks of pain. For the vamps, there was *power* in the word *gather*. When they *gathered*, they joined in some arcane way, cooperating to make decisions and conduct business. It was mystical in ways that I couldn't understand. Leo inhaled and I exhaled, as if sharing with him my breath. Another breath followed. And another. It was intimate and intense, his eyes holding mine, and when Beast again placed a clawed paw on my psyche I caught myself, holding my breath a moment to break the exchange. I hadn't given my blood to him. I hadn't fallen in thrall to him. Which meant that Leo shouldn't be able to draw power from me. Yet, I could feel the strands of his power sucking something from me, even now, even with Beast's intervention. This was freaky, and maybe tied to the magics I'd been exposed to, like radiation poisoning, weakening me.

The Master of the City stared at me for a long moment, assessing my independence and self-containment before sliding his eyes away. When he did, something snapped inside me, like a dried stick breaking, audible and sharp. I put out a hand and caught myself on the nearest doorframe, my balance unsteady for a moment. I glanced around the room to see every vamp and blood-servant staring at Leo, mesmerized. Yeah, freaky.

Leo looked them over, breathing in their scents. His eyes closed and he raised his face in something like ecstasy. He jerked his head to the right and opened his eyes, searching the ceiling and the perimeters of the room. Confusion and anger etched his face for an instant before it melted away to the usual expressionless manifestation of vamp-dom. I had no idea what he had smelled or what his reaction meant. He took a breath, this time so he could speak.

"We will meet and treat with our ancient enemies, the Cursed of Artemis," Leo said. "We will parley and be bound by the treaty that we sign in blood. We will be bound as the fathers of all Mithrans, the Sons of Darkness, are bound, by honor and by duty. By command of the Sons of Darkness, this night begins cooperation between species on this hemisphere, as it has already begun in Europe and elsewhere. The humans

have grown strong, too strong to battle. They have not con-
strained their population growth, and our territory shrinks.
The Cursed of Artemis and the Mithrans have *no choice* but
to parley." The words "no choice," were spoken without inflection, yet still managed to sound forced and unwilling. "Are we
agreed?"

With one voice the vamps murmured, "We are agreed."

Leo stepped into the room, his scions behind him, ten
blood-servants behind them, Bruiser at the forefront. He
looked pale. They all did. Leo had fed well on his most trusted.
I hoped they didn't all pass out from blood loss.

As the group cleared the open doorway, two other forms
stepped into the opening, one from the left, one from the right.
A voice from the back of the room announced, "Sabina Del-
gado y Aguilar, priestess, and Bethany Salazar y Medina. Outclan, keepers of the histories, the Blood Cross, and artifacts of
power."

I watched as the two women, who studiously ignored one
another, stepped into the room. I mentally filed away the sur-
names of Bethany, as they weren't in any dossier the cops had
on her. Once again, I had to wonder, as I had over the last few
weeks, how and where the women had gotten the last names,
as neither was from a Spanish region, and neither surname
had likely been around a fraction of the centuries they had.

The women walked with heads high and feet soundless
into the reception room. They were as different as two women
could be, Sabina looking matronly but starved, chaste, and set
apart in her white, nun-style dress and wimple, her skin the
pale olive of her Mediterranean origins. Bethany was dressed
in African splendor with ivory and gold necklaces, earrings,
rings, and bracelets. Her body was swathed in a billowing red
silk shawl over a full, apple-green silk skirt and a tight matching top that seemed to make her dark skin glow. She was barefooted and gold rings were on her toes. She flowed to Leo and
kissed his cheeks, holding his face between her palms. Sabina
came behind her and kissed Leo as well, murmuring, "The
outclan honor the Master of the City."

Leo kissed the women in the same fashion and said, "The
Mithrans honor the outclan." More softly he said, "Let us welcome our guests."

Two lesser blood-servants stepped to a different doorway
and unlatched the double doors; they swung inward, heavy

and stately on silent hinges. On the other side stood Kemnebi, the black were-leopard I'd seen change on TV. He was ebony black with the sculpted features of an ancient Egyptian sarcophagus. His lips were full, his tip-tilted eyes were blacker than a moonless night. He was dressed in the flowing white outer robe of an Arabian prince; beneath it, a full black silk shirt was gathered into black trousers. Black boots polished to a sheen threw back the light. His head was uncovered, black hair shaved close. He wore a gold torque around his neck centered with an image of a falcon. I was sure the falcon was the Egyptian god Horus, which was confusing, because the goddess, who had supposedly cursed the weres, was Greek.

Behind him stood a woman, wearing a long full coat woven of shimmering cloth of gold, that hung open from her midriff to reveal a white silk skirt and tunic. Hair—blue-black, lustrous, and glistening—hung from either side of her white headdress to her thighs. I had long hair, but this girl had me beat. Her skin and features looked Mediterranean, not African, and her bare feet showed in raffia sandals, toenails polished deep purple. She had henna tattoos on the backs of her hands and up her feet, disappearing beneath her clothing. The smell of cat, perfume, and faintly of dead fish wafted from her.

I felt Beast rise from deep inside me and stare out at the weres, curious, questing. *Like Beast?* she thought. I didn't know, but my attention held to them with a laserlike focus. They were the closest thing to a skinwalker I had encountered since the insane liver-eater skinwalker who had been masquerading as Leo's son. And him, I had killed.

"The International Association of Weres and the Party of African Weres greets the Louisiana Council of Mithrans. I am Kemnebi; this is my assistant Safia. We are black were-leopards from the African Congo, of the country of humans called Gabon, from the region of the Rapides Mabila, and from the tribe of the leopards who reside there. We come to parley with you."

Leo started in with his names and titles. "Leonard Eugène Zacharie Pellissier, Master of Clan Pellissier, Master of the City of New Orleans ..." I blanked him out. Heard it all before. When he finished, he started in on the names and titles of Sabina and Bethany.

"Names are important to weres," Bruiser said softly beside me. He had maneuvered close while Kemnebi spoke and I slid my eyes to him and back to the action on the floor, where Leo and the black were-leopard were shaking hands and sizing each other up. And both were sniffing the air, as if scenting was part of their recognition process.

"Is that so?" I murmured.

"Kemnebi is Egyptian for black leopard. Safia means lion's share."

On the ballroom floor, the vamps were forming a formal reception line, to pass in front of the were-guests and the vamp VIPs. Sabina and Bethany stood first, Leo next, with Kemnebi and Safia last. The female were's head was down, her eyes on her hands clasped in front of her.

"Titles instead of personal names, maybe? And the woman—what?—belongs to him?" I had strong antislavery beliefs, but knew it still took place in many countries, parts of Africa included.

"Probably to both questions." He changed the subject. "Leo wants you in the line, behind the Mithrans of Clan Arceneau, and in front of their blood-servants."

I couldn't keep the surprise out of my voice when I said, "I'm the hired help, not a guest."

"As I explained to him," Bruiser said, his voice tight. "Leo has his reasons."

I thought about that. Leo knew I wasn't human, though he didn't know what I was. He thought I smelled like sex candy and a challenge all at once, something the vamps had a hard time resisting, though it hadn't always been that way. Until Leo accepted me, the vamps had thought I smelled like an encroaching predator. I was betting Leo wanted to see what Kem did when the were-cat got a whiff of me. While I let that thought simmer, I said, "Where's the little green guy?"

"In his room. Unless he found a way out past your men and the heat signature cameras they set up. They are exceptionally well trained."

"They're independents, mercenaries. I just get to pay for their services from time to time," I said.

"Now," Bruiser said. He touched the small of my back, just below the holster and just above my buttocks, and gave me a gentle push.

I wasn't willing to be Leo's experiment, but I didn't feel like I could say no either. This might fall under the heading of security, to know how a were-cat reacted to me, and if so, that made it part of my job description. Leo was a bastard but he was a smart bastard.

I slid into place in the line just after Karimu, offering apologies to the blood-servant behind her, who would have objected, by saying, "Mr. Pellissier wants me here." Then I added, to salve the man's pride, "He wanted his Rogue Hunter in line with you and your clan as a . . . sign of approval," I improvised quickly. I felt brilliant when the man nodded and stepped back a half step out of my personal space. I usually stank at social situations, but his reaction was an indication that I hadn't trespassed on blood-servant sensibilities. Karimu's only response was a twitch of his lips. A vamp with a sense of humor.

I shook Bethany's hand, and she didn't react to my being in the receiving line, almost as if she didn't recognize me, which made me all kinds of happy. I'd rather not be on her radar. Sabina took my hand, and hers was cold with the exact flaccid, loss-of-elasticity flesh of the dead, which made my skin crawl, but I shoved down on the reaction. She raised her eyes to mine. "You still retain possession of the sliver of the weapon?" she asked, referring to the sliver of the vamps' Blood Cross she had lent me to kill a dangerous vamp. I had tried to return the artifact but found her gone from her chapel-lair in the vamp graveyard. I nodded, and saw from the corner of my eye, Leo look my way in surprise. "You will bring it to me. Soon." She slipped her hand from mine, looking away.

Leo, next in line, took my hand. His was warm with another's blood. "Leo," I said. It should have been "Mr. Pellissier" in a formal receiving line and in the line of duty, but I was halfway ticked off with the MOC, and didn't mind him knowing it. He showed me a lot of tooth and fang by way of reply and handed me off to Kemnebi. "Our fearsome Rogue Hunter," he said, by way of introduction.

The visiting dignitary took my hand, looked into my face, inhaled, and froze. It wasn't vamp immobility, but it was dang close. He spoiled it when his pupils widened and nostrils fluttered just a bit. And when he took a second breath, he inhaled through nose and parted lips with a scree of sound, flehmen behavior, the way I do when scenting someone.

"What is this woman?" he asked Leo. "What is she?" When Leo didn't answer, Kemnebi tightened his grip on my wrist and yanked me to him. One arm went around my waist, hard as iron. His open mouth was at my throat. His breath hot and moist. His magic sought and quested at me like a big-cat twining around my body, but this was deeper, sharper, more intimate. Hot prickles of power sparked against my skin, painful and electric. Beast hunched down, pelt rising with alarm. She showed teeth and hissed.

"A beautiful woman," Leo said, "one worthy of your bed."

"What?" I tried to step back but were-cats are strong. Kemnebi resisted. A growl snarled out of me. I felt claws in my mind, piercing. Power leaped into my consciousness. Strength flooded my system as my Beast poured adrenaline into me. *"Beast is not prey."*

In an instant I was three steps back; the visiting envoy was staring at me wide-eyed. The room had fallen silent. That dead silence of terrible affront. *Crap. I had spoken aloud.*

Some silent, logical part of me played back over what I had done to break free. Basic moves. Stepped to my right. Twisting, dropping motion of my left arm to break his grip, the strength of my arm against the comparative weakness of his fingertips. Simple. But Kemnebi had not been expecting me to resist or to be armed. When his encircling arm had encountered the H&K at my back, he had reacted with broken hesitation.

Leo had just offered me to Kemmy-boy as a bedmate. I glared at Leo, remembering his Dark Right of Kings, which he employed to sleep with any vamp or blood-servant he wanted. Not me. I wasn't a blood-servant or blood-slave he could order around. I wasn't his to use or to give away. And he wasn't going to pimp me out. Not gonna happen.

"My Rogue Hunter is, indeed, not prey," Leo said smoothly. "As to what she is, I think, and my shamans think, that she herself does not know."

It might have been nice to know that one, I thought. And then I smelled blood. Strange and pungent. The odor filled my scent receptors, big-cat and human, intermixed and prickly. I looked at Kemnebi's wrist. There were claw marks across the inside of his wrist. Big-cat claw marks, bleeding. And I had no idea how I had given them to him. I glanced at my hands. Human. Perfectly human.

Kemnebi lifted his wrist and sniffed it, his eyes widening further. The woman beside him was staring at me, her lips parted in shock, her nose wrinkled back like a cat. Scenting me. "I do not like the way this woman smells," Kemmy said.

He is dangerous. He is my enemy, Beast spat at me. But I

kept it inside, silent and contained. I didn't answer his comment with the insulting rejoinder on the tip of my tongue, "*You stink too, dude.*" It would have been a childish insult, on top of drawing his blood.

On the periphery of my vision I caught movement, a slight shift of darkness, and glanced that way, to see Bruiser. He had deliberately moved to attract my attention in the room of immobile bloodsuckers. His hand made a "move along" gesture toward the woman last in line, like an usher in a movie house. I shoved down Beast's volatile reactions to Kemmy and held out a hand to Safia. I said something inane before moving away and to the safety of wallflower status, my mind whirling, figuring things out.

Leo had wanted me in the reception line to see how Kemnebi would react to me. Bruiser had known and not warned me. Leo had planned to offer me as a sex toy to the werecat. Knowing Leo, he might have just been curious how Kem would react, but if the were-cat had agreed, Leo would have expected me to follow through just on his say-so. Bruiser had known and not warned me. Leo was an ass with the worldview of a feudal lord of the fourteenth century and felt that people were his to do with and give away as he pleased. Bruiser was an ass of a different sort, and I intended to see that his nickname was a description of his skin tone. Soon.

I spent the next two hours avoiding the prime blood-servant, doing my job. I made sure there was plenty of food and drink for the humans. I ordered coffee brewed as a secondary choice to the alcohol being served. I assisted in finding chairs and bringing them in from the rooms off the hallway when the vamps wanted to sit and chat with one another. I kept two vamps from coming to blows over protocol, which I didn't understand anyway, offering to knock heads together and stake them, in order of importance, and let them choose who died first. They behaved thereafter. I went back and forth to the security room, checking the monitors and getting firsthand views of anything untoward. All the while, I took security reports on the earpiece of the headset, which was making my job much easier.

I touched the mouthpiece and said, "The green security guy. Update."

"Still contained in his room," Angel's Tit said, satisfied.

I made another circuit of the ballroom. When Sabina stepped in front of me—make that, appeared like a magician's trick and I nearly fell over her—I kept in the girlie scream but it was a near miss. We hadn't spoken in weeks, and now I was the target of her attention, twice, which didn't give me a warm and fuzzy feeling at all. She reached up and cut off my mike with one hand, her other a band around my nape, pulling me down to her. Her flesh was cold and hard as marble, and as always she smelled of old blood, like an ancient crime scene.

Her mouth at my ear, she said, "I have smelled such creatures before. When the Eldest Son of Darkness visited, a century ago, he failed to rise one night. Leo sent for me, and together we entered his lair. The premises stank of blood and violence, of injury and pain; his holy lifeblood, and the blood of another was splattered against the walls. Though it was inconceivable for a single being to defeat a Son in battle, even by day, the lair scented of two combatants only. His attacker was an African cat, perhaps a lion. Or a leopard. Leo told no one. Now, *you* have allowed such a beast into this domain. If there is death, let it rest upon you."

She released my neck and I jerked away from her threat, or her curse, whichever it was. She was gone; the place where she had stood and held me was vacant, filled only with swirling air and the reek of old blood. Real old blood. The stench curdled in my nasal passages. I didn't know when the priestess had last fed, but she needed another dose. Cold prickles raced across my skin, as much a reaction to her words as to her touch and her strength. I hadn't gone for a weapon. Hadn't even tried. Not normal. Not good.

I shook like a cat after a dunking in a winter-cold stream and blinked away my fear. I could deal with my reactions to the priestess later, since I had lived through the experience. I touched my neck, missing the silver collar the wolf Fire Truck had broken in the fight where I first met Gee. For a moment I thought I smelled the peculiar pine and floral scent of him. My pulse pounded beneath my fingertips and I sucked a deep draught of air. Turned left and right, searching. The scent was gone. Had never been there at all.

I imposed calm on my system, and forced my thoughts to the info the priestess had given me as part of her threat. A Son of Darkness—one of the first vamps—had possibly been killed by a big-cat. By Leo's own son, maybe, a skinwalker who had access to big-cat fetishes. Or maybe by another were-cat, here without the MOC's permission. Was that what she was hinting? As usual, Leo hadn't found it pertinent to share that information with me. I checked my mike and stepped to the doorway of the ballroom, scanning for trouble.

Everything was okay. Hunky-dory. Music was playing on the loudspeakers, a big band swing number, lots of horns and a funky sounding bass. I had a mental image of a vamp DJ spinning tunes somewhere out of sight. Or a Wolfman Jack. Definitely appropriate for tonight. Titters rose in my throat and I swallowed them back down, concentrating on the ballroom. Four couples were dancing, including Bruiser, who was spinning a master vamp through a series of complicated moves. He looked good with Dominique, her blond elegance against his dark sophistication. Humans were gathered around the food and drink tables. I glanced up at the nearest security camera and flashed an OK sign, knowing that Vodka Angel's Tit would see it.

A half minute later, I heard breaking glass. From above. It fell like stained sleet, tinkling toward the floor, the colors of blood and sapphire, narrowly missing two vamps who leaped away with vision-stealing speed. I looked up. Caught a whiff. Pulled my H&K and a vamp-killer even before I identified the scent. *Wolves* . . . The glass landed, nearly silent on the rugs.

Werewolves dropped into the room, plummeting from the ceiling . . . *like my dream*. It was like my dream. But the three were in human form, falling from the broken stained-glass windows in the high arches, spinning down on zip lines, two males and one female. *Clothed. Not naked. Not my dream.*

"Werewolves in the ballroom," I said into the mike, taking in the room. Leo was vamped out, fanged and clawed, Kemnebi stood beside him, scenting, his human lips wrinkled back, his hands black-furred and clawed. He turned to Leo, as his snout began to reform in a shower of blue-black sparks. "Backup. Now!"

The female wolf wore Middle Eastern dress much like the were-cat assistant, and her skirts belled out as she slowly descended, showing tanned leg and lace undies. The males landed first, on pointed toes like dancers and unhooking their harnesses as they landed; one guy turned and caught the wolf-bitch. It was graceful and balletic and dangerous on every level I could imagine. Wolves had gotten in. My security measures had failed. *I* had failed.

I took aim at Roul Molyneux. Before I could fire, three weres raced into the hallway behind me in wolf form, claws clicking on the marble floor.

CHAPTER 10

You Want Me to Shoot Him, Boss?

Holding aim on Roul, I turned so the werewolves faced my vamp-killer, which protected my side. An additional three weres showed in the open doorway across from me, the door the vamps had come through at the start of the party. And behind them was the little green guy. Had he let them in? It was the only thing that made any sense. I gave a fast update into the mike, location of the bogies and their numbers. I ended with, "The head were-cat grew front paws and claws." *Like Roul had done when I met him.* But I didn't say that part. The wolves to my side had stopped. Muzzles down, snarling, snouts wrinkled, ears pinned, they closed on me, steps careful and slow. They had fought me once before or they would have attacked without a second thought. With a sliding snick of sound, I chambered a round and took careful aim on the closest wolf. A human woman stood behind him, a hand to her mouth. My guns were loaded with silver, but if I missed, a human or a vamp would die just as easily. There were too many of both in the ballroom and collateral damage was unacceptable.

Hard breathing, running footsteps, and Derek issuing commands filled my earpiece. He and a Vodka boy appeared on either side of the weres behind me, boxing them in. At the sight of them, the wolves stopped. They sat in the hallway, tongues lolling, looking proud and happy; they'd gotten into vamp HQ. "The dog learned a new trick," I muttered. One growled at me, ears going flat, looking less doggy and more wolfish. Before I could decide how to respond, Derek's other soldiers raced up,

covering the doorways and the ballroom. And Tyler stalked
into the room, a compact selective-firing shoulder weapon—a
submachine gun—held in both hands, supported high on his
chest. With it, he took aim at the were-cat envoy, Kemnebi.
"You want me to shoot him, boss?" In less than eight seconds.
Everything had gone FUBAR.

Behind me, Derek and Vodka Hi-Fi had weapons on the
weres. Knowing my flank was covered, I stepped into the
room, moving my gun hand from target to target, catching
a quick look at Bruiser. He was standing much like me, but
holding two sidearms, his body poised to cover two segments
of the room, presenting a smaller target to two different ad-
versaries. His feet were spread and knees slightly bent, ready
for either shot. His jacket was shoved back, one pant cuff was
hitched up, showing sock and a bit of leather. His face was
white, mouth a thin line.

Dominique stood to his left, her cheeks bright red in a
paper-white face. Fangs out and holding a wicked-looking
knife. Leo had been shoved behind her, the sclera of his eyes
bloodred, pupils fully dilated. Ten razor-sharp claws and more
than two inches of bone-hard canines ready to fight. Vamped-
out and pissed. *Crap.* This was gonna get messy.

"We were not told that *wolves* were to attend," Kemmy
said, disdain in every syllable. "We do not treat with wolves."

"Yeah? Well, I got a feeling that your little green guy didn't
stop them," I said. "Maybe when he ran around the backyard,
wolves were coming over the walls and up to the roof without
ever touching the ground." I didn't add that it was a rookie
mistake. I didn't even have a camera pointed up. Could werewolves jump twenty feet in a single bound? Mentally castigat-
ing myself, I repositioned myself and my weapons between
Leo and the were-cats. *Cat.* The female was gone. My panic-
o-meter shot back into the stratosphere. I took in the entire
room. Placed every vamp and were. No girl were-cat. When
had she disappeared?

Leo shot a look at me, vamped but in control. Relief
slammed through me with my blood. At least one thing was
okay, then. He turned to the were-cat. "The wolves are not
here at your command?" Leo asked, his words only slightly
distorted by his state.

"My kind killed the last werewolf in Europe during Charlemagne's reign. They are the *lesser* were. Their females do not survive. They cannot breed true. We do not treat with *dogs*."

Charlemagne's reign was in the eight hundreds. During the time that vamps lived in Rome as Mithrans. Had that been part of what caused the vamps to disperse? Some kind of supernatural war?

"We are no' dogs. We are wolves, *predators* like you." Roul turned to the nearest camera. *Crap, crap,* crap*! I forgot about the media.* His natural charisma hitched up a notch, and his accent practically made love to the cameras. "Leo Pellissier is murderer and thief. And I have proof, I do." Roul looked like a GQ fashion plate, strawberry blond–streaked hair fanning out in a mane, wearing pants, boots, and a white shirt rolled up at the arms, the neck open. He stepped away from his two cohorts, head back, striking a pose, rakish and theatrical. The cameras were all trained on him, loving him.

I glanced at his companions. The man with him was dressed similarly but in dark brown, and the woman was swathed in silk styled like the were-cat's dress, but hers was pale blue; she was dressed so much like the missing female were-cat that the skirt, top, and head scarf outfit had to be required dress. Blond hair fanned out from her veiled face; only her eyes showed, heavily shadowed, and her lids sparkled with something that looked like gold dust. Her skin glowed, darkly tanned. The smell of rut filled the air, wolf in heat, and vamps and weres alike stared at her. The were-bitch walked without a limp, proof that her kind healed from nonmortal wounds as fast as I did, because I remembered hamstringing her. But I'd used a silvered blade, so she probably had an ugly scar, not that I'd noticed one when she displayed her legs on the way down.

The reporters were eating it up with a spoon. Careers would get made tonight.

"The Lupus Clan have file legal writ against Mithrans, yes," Roul said. "We will see justice in court of human law." The werewolf bitch placed a hand on Roul's shoulder, but she was looking at Bruiser and Leo. Mostly at Leo, I thought, but I couldn't be sure.

Leo's fangs clicked back into the roof of his mouth and he closed his eyes. When he opened them a moment later, he looked like the Leo the media loved, urbane and debonair, a sophisticated Frenchman in contrast to the rougher, action-adventure character presented by Roul. But what Leo said wasn't going to help put a good spin on anything that had happened so far tonight. "We will not treat with the wolves that we drove away, wolves who broke were-law, who have returned against our will and against our proclamation. Any charges they bring are specious and without merit and not binding unto us.

"We are not bound unto the system of law of these United States of America . . ."—he hesitated, then added—"at this time. We are Mithrans, a separate nation, bound only by the Vampira Carta. We treat and parley as separate peoples." He sounded suspiciously above the law in his comments, which wasn't going to go over well in the court of public opinion, but when looked at from a legal perspective, it might have been dang near perfect.

Jodi Richoux was gonna hate that. So was the U.S. justice system—which was already having kittens over the thought of having to confine a vamp—in total darkness during daylight hours, bars far stronger than those needed to detain a human, not to mention the whole "must drink human blood" dietary requirements problem. And I had to wonder if this was the decision of all the international vamps, or if Leo was swimming in dangerous waters. The little disclaimer "at this time" might not be enough to save him if the vamps at large took umbrage with his high-handedness.

I looked from Leo to Bruiser, who was watching me. When he caught my eye he looked around the room as if telling me to do the same. The wolves had padded into the center of the room, surrounding their human-form buddies. The security types were all in the room with us, except for Vodka Angel's Tit, the only security type guarding the perimeter. Not good. I had to wonder if the weres planned it this way, and if so, was it a cover for something else?

Before I could key my mike to speak to Angel, I heard him say, "Bloody female vamp just appeared in the building, second floor, moving downstairs fast. Approaching ballroom."

Murphy's Law was working overtime.

The smell of blood hit me just as she appeared in the reception room, lots of blood, with mixed scent signatures. Like the top-note in a really bad perfume, was cat blood. Below it, overriding the cat smell, was vamp blood—the reek old and rotted. That was the only clue who had come visiting, and it identified the unrecognizable female better than a calling card. Katie of Katie's Ladies. Risen from the vamp grave that had healed her from a mortal wound. But cat blood, fresh and potent, said something else had gone seriously wrong tonight. Kemnebi turned to her and hissed.

Katie was caked in dried blood; it fell from her in flakes and granules, shifting down from her stiff dress with little shushing sounds, like reeds in a slow breeze. Hair, skin, clothes all were coated with the blood and it stank with a rotted meat smell. Back hunched, arms bent and out to her sides, her feet bare and slender, she turned slowly, taking in the room. Her magics snapped and sparked like carnelian flames, visible to Beast-vision. Powerful. Eerily potent.

She growled and Beast slammed into me at the sound, filling my limbs with strength. My lips peeled back from human teeth, and the blade felt good, like a steel claw in my hand.

Katie pivoted slowly, and as she turned, she took in a deep breath. And pulled power from every vamp in the place, feeding from them. With Beast so close to the surface, I could see the power drain shifting in the air, a bloody-reddish wind, and when she turned to me, her fangs were three inches long and stained bloody red. Her eyes were vamped out so big the entire orbs were black, leaving no trace of the grayish hazel of her irises, and only a tinge of bloody sclera.

The draw of her magic punched through the room like fangs into an artery, sucking at magic, at the life force itself. Vamps began to fall to the floor where they lay writhing, gagging. The magic pressed against the weres. Drawing on their power, draining off their control like the moon at her fullest. The wolfman with Roul grunted and fell to the floor, his back arching, starting to change against his will. The wolf-bitch sank to the floor shivering, resisting, hiding beneath her robes. Roul bared his teeth, revealing fangs, no longer fully human. Kemnebi lifted clawed paws and growled low, cat-anger. The humans were having trouble getting breaths, some fell like the vamps, and lay as if dead. One cameraman hit the floor, camera first, shattering the expensive gadget.

I felt the bite of Katie's power, siphoning at my own, nips of electric teeth. It hurt. Beast resisted, claws digging deep in my psyche. Katie moved around the room. Fresh blood coated her lower jaw. A single drip landed on her crusted breast, glowing like a ruby on her dried-blood flesh. She had fed. She smelled like she-cat blood. I looked around. Safia was still missing.

Katie found Leo in the throng. Everyone in the ballroom felt the moment their eyes met. Sparks flew and danced on the air. It was Fourth of July and Mardi Gras and New Year's all at once and even the humans in the room could see it, feel it, erotic and sexual and primal, like battle and sex all at once. I felt the tug deep in my belly. Instantly, I remembered a photo I had once seen of Leo and Katie, her skirts tossed high, him servicing her with his mouth, her head thrown back in ecstasy.

"Katherine, do you challenge me?" Leo asked. Bruiser tried to stop him, but Leo stepped away, out onto the center of the ballroom floor. Behind him, Kemnebi watched, his black eyes full of anger and disdain for the wolf changing and for the vamps and blood-servants who had no resistance to vamp power. His claws and paws began to reform into human. It was clear ol' Kemmy was no longer having trouble fending off the power grab.

"Leo?" Katie whispered. Her voice was rough and coarse, not the liquid velvet it once had been. "My Leo?"

Leo reached Katie, one hand following the length of her crusted hair, blond beneath the dark stain of old blood. He cupped her face, a look of joy in his eyes. He encircled her waist with an arm and pulled her gently to him, embracing her. Leo breathed out, his breath like a caress. Katie relaxed, resting against him. The dance of power in the room slowed. And Leo's fangs pierced her throat so fast even I didn't see the strike.

Katie screamed and hit him in a scissor motion, bringing both arms up and back down. The blow drove them to the floor. But Leo kept his fangs buried. His arms imprisoned her, his legs wrapped around her as they rolled across the floor. Everyone still standing scattered. Fights broke out as they moved.

Bruiser reached my side, holstering his weapons. "Katie has the blood of eight clans," he said. "She isn't sane just now, but she's powerful as hell. Leo can't let her take over." He was gone and I was left putting sense to the words.

Katie was back, unexpectedly, from the grave that healed her. An unexpected rising meant she was likely not sane yet, as vamps had a tenuous hold on that particular mental state. She'd been buried with the blood of *eight* clans mixed into her coffin, absorbed into her very flesh. She was like a fully charged battery, designed to draw even more. At the moment, she was power incarnate, insane and hungry, unless Leo could defeat her and drink down her power. Thanks to the recent mini war, there were fewer total vamps and only *four* clans in the city, for the Master of the City to draw on to seal his power base. Leo's four to Katie's eight.

He'd asked her if she challenged him. *Crap*. He'd made it a legal duel. She hadn't replied, too nutso to make a rational response, but she hadn't stopped stealing power that was his by right either, making it a legal challenge for the position of Master of the City. I couldn't think of a better way for Leo to keep his people safe—all the alternatives meant another war. If an insane master vamp as powerful as Katie divided the clans or took them over, things were gonna get *really* bad, *really* fast. So Leo threw himself onto the pyre as sacrifice like a good leader—who wanted to stay in power—would. I wasn't gonna be happy having to admire Leo for that.

My thoughts took an eyeblink of time, but in that moment, the power draw stopped. Carnage began. Across the room, vamps shook themselves awake and stood. Wolves attacked. Fights broke out between species. Blood-servants raced to their masters, offering throats so the vamps could function again and maybe get them all out alive.

Roul shook like a dog and looked around, his humanity restored but not his temper. He was a mad dog. *No. Don't say it.* I swallowed back a crazy laugh. Roul put his head down and bulled into a pack of fighting wolves and vamps just as the group rammed into a table of meats, sending food flying. The place reeked of blood—vamp, were, and human. In a corner, two vamps from clans no longer in existence, and always hated enemies, tore into one another. Other fights broke out and blood-servants joined in. It was a free-for-all. And I wasn't dressed for it, as usual. Kem stood all alone, observing, his mouth in a snarl. Looking around the room. Looking for Safia.

I keyed my mike. "Angel, give me some good news."

"Got none, Legs," he said into my ear. "The little green guy got out, the cops have showed up at the front gate, decked out in paramilitary gear. They have ladders and they're coming over the walls. They've got every unit in the city headed your way. Oh. And the wolves are loose. Who! Who let the dogs out?"

"Not funny, Angel," Derek said, reaching my side.

"Sorry, Sarge." He didn't sound sorry, but he instantly started giving updates on the location of the wolves loose in vamp HQ. Not all of them had stayed in the ballroom.

Derek and I met eyes. I said, "We need to find the female were-cat. Katie fed off her."

He gave me a chin-jut of understanding. "You take care of the MOC. I'll get the premises locked down and the wolves contained."

"How?"

"Trank guns. All my guys got 'em."

I should have thought of that. But who would have expected werewolves to attack? And if not wolves, then who had he been planning to tranquilize? Q and A for later. Job now.

We spun in opposite directions, Derek trotting through the doors issuing orders, me wading through the vamps after Leo and Katie, caught in a mortal embrace.

I was stopped by Dominique, heir to Arceneau, and Bettina, master of Laurent. They were facing off, the energies between them cracking with fury. Both had blood-splattered clothes and bloody mouths; both had flushed skin and smelled warm-blooded. They had fed. Fully.

I grabbed an arm on each and shook them hard. "You can challenge each other tomorrow night. Get your vamps and servants together and follow me." I was as surprised as anyone when they looked from each other to me and nodded.

Dominique called aloud to Grégoire. Bettina closed her eyes. Shaun Mac Lochlainn, her heir, and her other two vamps raced through the melee to her side, all three with torn clothes and bloodied bodies. The summoning was impressive, and so were the men who responded to her call. It made me wonder if she had mind-joined with Shaun. More to think about later. More slowly, Dominique and her clan *gathered*. The human blood-servants followed, surrounding their masters. The clan leaders had gone from mortal enemies to allies in a human heartbeat.

"Wall off Leo and Katie from the rest of the room," I said to the vamps, "and then give Leo what support you can. If Katie wins, this night will be a bloodbath."

"I like bloodbaths," Dominique said. I didn't want to inspect that line too closely, especially as her eyes were alight and she looked so cheerful all of a sudden. They all did. The smell of blood and fighting was like drugs to vamps.

Mac Lochlainn and his pals moved in front of us and started clearing a path between the fighting vamps and humans, some by asking, others, those too belligerent or out cold, by simply tossing. We moved forward with an awful efficiency. I heard bones break as the vamp warriors cleared the way. A lot of people were gonna be sore tomorrow. If they lived through the night.

Kabisa and Karimu, Arceneau's soldier twins, worked to the side, holding off four wolves, using blades with ruthless efficiency. Sending the wolves yelping, bleeding, limping away, where "my guys" tranked them. They fell so fast that they maintained wolf form. *Ooh rah.*

I spotted Leo and Katie in a corner of the room, bodies wrapped around each other seemingly melded together. Fangs and claws were embedded in flesh and they held each other still, like two wrestlers, evenly matched. But Katie had her fangs in Leo's throat and Leo had his buried just below Katie's right collarbone. Not a good site for draining a victim.

Katie lifted a hand and smoothed Leo's hair, like she might soothe a pet, her hand steady and controlling. I didn't like that one bit. Leo was splashed with blood, his clothes ripped and showing pale skin. Very pale skin. Katie was harder to judge under the garish blood-based body makeup, but I was thinking she had a well-fed, rosy hue.

"Dominique, how do we separate them when we get there?"

The blond woman turned to me, blood on her chin. Surprised, she said, "We feed him."

"Ah. Right."

Moments later, we reached Leo and Katie. Dominique held out her hand and Karimu, eyes fierce and intent, placed a clean blade in it. Dominique sliced her own wrist and held it near Leo's face. He opened his eyes and slid his fangs from Katie's chest. He sank them into Dominique and sucked hard. She hissed. Fell to her knees beside Leo. A moment later, Leo released her; Dominique fell over and was carried away by her blood-servants as Grégoire knelt in her place, rolling up his sleeve. The two men held glances a moment, Leo's vamped-out, Grégoire's calm and still.

Grégoire said, "My pledge to you. My pledge to Pellissier. My pledge to the Master of the City."

"You will be rewarded and recompensed."

Grégoire chuckled, the tone dismissive. "Drink, my friend. And win." Leo sank his fangs into Grégoire's arm at the elbow.

Over my earpiece I heard, "Sarge, cops are at the door. And ... I'm seeing blood in a hallway on one of my monitors. No one's been fighting there."

"Location?"

"Outside Leo Pellissier's office."

Ruse. Opportunity. Battle and mayhem in the vamp-camp would be a great opportunity to accomplish a goal if one were prepared and willing to take a chance. I saw an image of a big-cat lying on a tree limb over a path to a watering hole. Waiting for the opportunity to attack the unwary. Or a great place to take a nap.

Both, Beast assured me. There was something smug in her tone.

"Let's see about the blood. Meet you at Leo's office," I said into the mike. I raced for the stairs and was third to arrive. The door was open, the stink of blood searing my nose, overwhelming my senses. A Vodka Boy was scanning the nooks and crannies, weapon ready for firing. Derek stood over the body. Lying on blood-soaked rugs was the petite, diplomatic assistant. Safia. What was left of her. Derek was cursing fluently and nonstop under his breath.

Beast shoved her way to the forepart of my brain and studied the scene. *Not a human kill. Claws and killing-teeth brought her down. But not for meat. Wasted meat, wasted blood.* Beast drew in a breath over my nose and tongue. *Gun fired here.*

I processed and shared her comments but with a few sophistications of language tossed in. "No vamp would have wasted her blood. No wolf would have wasted her meat. Katie was seen on a security camera in this hallway. She had fresh blood on her face when she appeared in the ballroom."

"Katie killed her?" Derek asked. "Old rogue?"

"Don't know. We're gonna need the cops, who happen to be at our door—lucky us." I looked from the body to Derek and added, "I don't believe in coincidences. Make copies of all the camera and TV footage. We need one for us. If any of your guys are wanted by law enforcement, get them out of here."

"We're clean. You let the cops in. They've brought in a ram to take down the front door. A white chick in an evening gown will settle the cops faster than a brother with guns."

I'd have laughed except for the body at my feet. Instead, I said, "You get to the ballroom and tell them the cops are here. See if Leo has Katie under control. If not, stake her."

His eyebrows went to his hairline. "You sure about that?"

"No, but what choice do we have? Katie may have killed the were-cat. Whatever she may be tomorrow, right now, Katie's rogue. I'm the Rogue Hunter. My order."

"Yes, ma'am. You are that."

I didn't take the time to inspect his comment. I raced for the front entrance, set my visible weapons on the glass table near the air-lock door, and checked over the foyer of vamp HQ. Empty. Silent. I entered the air lock. Taking a deep breath, I opened the front door.

There were cops at the entrance, Jodi Richoux at their head. Jodi in tactical gear was something to behold. Pert, a lot shorter than I am, blond hair tucked under a helmet, cinched into body armor never intended to mold to the body of a curvy woman. Ugly but efficient attire. Someone needs to talk to armor designers about female body shapes and style.

Beside her was Sloan Rosen, her second in command. He looked like a fashion plate in his armor. Just wasn't fair. Behind them were more cops, two holding a battering ram. Jodi recognized me and said something coarse and vulgar, which I ignored. "We need you," I said. "We have a dead body."

It took a while to assure Jodi that the violence was contained. Based on the two species' proximity, she had been expecting ongoing hostile behavior and vamp aggression problems. She and her team had been primed and ready, watching the live media coverage from the unmarked van just in case, and had gone into action when the first bodies hit the floor.

The cops spread out in vamp HQ, a few to prowl the hallways, a few to the ballroom, a few joined Angel's Tit to look over camera footage, and Jodi came with me back to the body. Oh joy. Because the status of vamps had yet to be decided in terms of U.S. citizenry, and because Leo had formally declared vamps to be a separate nation, all on TV, recorded for history, Jodi passed the legal hot potato up the chain of command. Her bosses agreed to send her a CSI unit to work up the crime scene, and ordered her to seal off the building. They were sending for the Bureau of Diplomatic Security. The bureau, also known as DS, was the law enforcement and security arm of the U.S. Department of State. It would take them hours to get from Washington, D.C. to New Orleans. Dawn. Maybe later.

All I could do at the moment was play freaking-dang-hostess and hope Leo and Katie had been separated by the other vamps.

The mess was gonna get interesting—or harder, deeper, and stinkier—and fast.

CHAPTER 11

Don't Beat Yourself up over It

While I was dealing with the cops, the press had regained consciousness en masse and discovered that cameras were still capable of filming. They caught footage of werewolves trotting away, or being carried out like dead dogs. Of wounded humans and well-fed vamps. They garnered half a dozen impromptu interviews, sending the feed out live again, before Leo—who had managed to subdue Katie—shut them down. The feed had been picked up by FOX and had gone out to the nation, but it was after two a.m. and the hullabaloo was less than it might have been. So far. After dawn things would change. After dawn, everything would change.

To keep fallout to a minimum, Bruiser ushered the press to the greenroom with promises of medical treatment for their bumps and cuts, with assurances of interviews with cops, vamps, any were-creature who was willing to chat, and blood-servants. He'd have promised them most anything to get them away from the ballroom and its blood splatters, blood pools, and evidence of chaos. Like sheep, they followed him and settled in the greenroom—not that it was green—paying no attention to the lock on the door that was designed to keep them safe. The fact that the lock was on the outside to keep them in wasn't discussed or discovered until after it clicked shut.

They made a ruckus and there would be hell to pay later, but the short-term benefits seemed worth it to Leo and Bruiser. I'd been confined in the greenroom before and it was comfortable, as much as a temporary lockup can be, with couches, a TV, and food humans can consume. They were also given a nurse, as promised, two vamps to chat with, Innara and Jena, and an armed guard for their own protection. Uh-huh, right. It wasn't my decision, but it *was* easier to get things done without the constant interference.

I told Roul and his were-bitch—whose face was still covered—to gather their wolves, and picked out a room for them to wait in. I had a police videographer take digital footage of them as they entered for verification of cuts, injuries, and bloodied muzzles—which they all had. I told Roul to keep them all in wolf form until the cops got to them for collection of physical evidence, but watched them change back to their human forms almost as soon as the words were out of my mouth. I was glad I'd chosen a room with a security camera to document which wolf was whom. I found them some clothes, and made a call to the kitchen for a dozen meat trays. Much like me, weres needed calories to make the change and they were ravenously hungry. I left them when they started looking at me like I was dinner.

It was clear that there were things going on under the surface of the political tug-of-war, beneath the bloodletting and the personal combat, things that I had no clue about, things that would pose bigger problems later if I didn't handle them properly now. And I was surely messing up from lack of knowledge, an unclear vision of vamp and were history, and my own shortcomings. But I kept at it. The job was my responsibility.

One of the Vodka boys took a camera to get pics of the ballroom, and moments after he got the first shots, the cops ran him off and stationed a guard there, labeling it a crime scene.

The little green guy turned out to be missing. I made a run to the security room to have the techs pull footage of the hallway near Leo's office and the carnage in the ballroom and the hallway near the green guy's room. I hoped that by slowing down the digital feed, we might see him come and go. Within seconds of isolating that footage and slowing the speed down, we saw the green ... whatever it was ... exiting his room. Angel had missed it. I caught an expression of self-loathing cross his face. "Don't beat yourself up over it. Yoda with fangs can *move*. Like, faster than human eyes can follow." Angel just shook his head and cursed under his breath. "Keep scanning

footage. Make sure we have copies of *everything*. I'll be back,"
I said.

I answered so many questions and dealt with so many
problems in the half hour after the cops arrived that I starting
feeling befuddled; I retired to the nearest ladies' room for a
break, where I saw to my personal comfort, and then leaned
against the wall at the sink, closed my eyes, and rested for just
a moment. When I opened my eyes a few minutes later, I felt
a little better. It wasn't exactly a minivacation, but it was an
oasis of calm in a frenzied night.

I checked my phone, feeling a stab of disappointment when
there were no calls from Rick. Stupid, to miss a guy who had
only been in my life a few weeks and might be cheating. The
thought pierced. Rick might be cheating on me with the were-
cat female while undercover. I shoved the pain down hard.
Later. Thoughts for much later.

To brighten my night, I had a voice mail from Molly, telling
me a joke she'd heard about "puddy tats" that had sent her
into hysterics. She was giggling so hard I couldn't understand
a word she said, but her laughter lightened my heart. I saved
the message for a future smile.

Putting the cell away, I caught sight of myself in the full-
length mirror. I looked tired, pale, and hungry, like some
cheap blood-junkie. I needed color and food. I'd managed to
hang on to the tiny purse during the clash and freshened my
mouth with red lipstick.

Much like the way I'd decorated my face with my father's
blood. The thought stabbed up from the deeps of my mind
and twisted, tearing like the killing strike of a barbed blade. I
hadn't mourned Edoda, my father. I hadn't avenged his death.

I swore softly, the sound sibilant in the bright room. I would
mourn and worry later. The job was what counted at this moment. I smoothed my hair back again and scratched my scalp,
which was starting to ache, and adjusted the bun and the stakes
thrust through it. "The job. Right," I whispered to myself.

Since the sandwiches were locked in with the press, I
slipped out of the restroom and made a quick trip through the
kitchen, where I picked up a serving tray of cold shrimp and
another one of cheese, which I ate on the way back through
the foyer, gulping fast. I dumped the empty platters on a small
table and followed the newest arrival to Leo's office, where all
the action was. The guy I followed was the coroner.

It looked to me like Safia had been mauled to death, but the coroner had to make an official pronouncement before the legal investigation could proceed. Louisiana, like a lot of states, has a coroner system in place instead of a medical examiner system. A coroner is an elected official—a person winning the job in a popularity contest, who may, or may not, be as well trained as the job requires. A medical examiner is fully certified, usually a pathologist with training in the related fields of law enforcement, anthropology, and forensics, and is appointed by a politician. We got lucky. The New Orleans assistant coroner who showed up was both—a pathologist with a degree and a vote-winning smile who was being groomed for the office of head coroner. He was also part witch. And Jodie's cousin, Peter Richoux.

Jodi and I stood in a small crowd in the hallway outside Leo's office as Peter worked. The reek of blood, buckets of it, starting to go bad, was sickly sweet. Leo stared at the dead woman, Kemnebi at his side. There was no sign of Katie, but Leo looked wan and drained—pun fully intended.

Peter at work consisted of standing and studying the body. For the first time, I allowed my eyes to linger on Safia and catalogue her injuries. Safia was golden skinned, black haired, dark eyed, a small woman but with long legs and delicate fingers. The henna tats on her hands and feet swirled up her limbs to stop at her knees and midway between her elbow and shoulder. If weres shifted like I did, then they lost all body paint in a shift, making the tats expensive in terms of time. If the paradigm held true, the tats also proved that she hadn't shifted tonight.

Kemnebi was staring at her, grief and horror on his face. He closed his eyes and his body went still for a moment, hunting-predator still, and when he opened them, all emotion was gone from his face. He stared at the scene as if he looked over the corpse of a stranger. But I had seen the vulnerability and anguish.

Her clothes were bloody. She lay on blood-soaked carpet, saturated and squishy beneath her. Her throat was gone, ripped away in three-claw tears, revealing her cervical spine and more about tendons and vessels and muscles than I needed to know. There were puncture marks on her chest between breast and shoulder. Defensive wounds showed on her knuckles; her fingernails were stained with blood and tissue.

Hair was caught in the wound, blond like Katie's. Or maybe my assumption that Katie killed her was faulty. Maybe a human had done the dirty deed, or a vamp, or werewolf. And Katie came upon the scene later. But it didn't look good for Katie.

Safia's abdomen at her waist had been gored, ripped into, the descending aorta pulled free, and savaged. It was the work of a large, fanged predator. Likely Katie. I parted my lips and breathed in through my open mouth. The stink of blood and big-cat was overwhelming. The coroner opened his bag at his side, set a plastic sheet under his knees, and bent over Safia.

Peter Richoux had light brown hair and fair skin with a smattering of freckles across his nose that made him look much younger than his actual age, and the perplexity on his face as he studied the corpse subtracted several more years, making him look all of twelve.

He pulled a digital pocket recorder and murmured into it the location, time, date, and the condition of the body when he found it. Kneeling beside Safia, the recorder on a thong around his neck, he opened a black bag and removed a small temperature and humidity monitor that he set on the floor. He took out a cylinder, screwed open its top, removed a long, slender thermometer with a metal tip on the end. He made a tiny cut on Safia's side, over her liver, with a scalpel, and inserted the thermometer several inches into the cut, checked his watch, again noted the time. He began checking for signs of lividity or rigor. I had seen forensics workups a number of times in my years as a PI and a vamp hunter, but never on a human-looking girl who had been transformed into meat and blood.

He was about five minutes into his practiced routine when Peter stopped and looked around. "Anybody know what the normal body temperature of a were-cat is? When she's human? And do they form rigor like a human? This is my first were, here, y'all. And it's not like there are manuals on this species yet."

Leo turned toward his were-cat guest, his demeanor stating that Kemnebi was the only one capable of providing an answer, and distancing himself from the questioning. The cops in the room looked the African man over, taking in his robes, checking for signs of blood spatter, and calculating his relationship with the deceased. Tension almost crackled in the air,

though Kemnebi had no emotion on his face and nothing in
his voice when he said, "We stiffen in death just as humans do.
Her normal resting temperature is thirty-nine degrees."

I figured he meant Celsius. Peter pulled out a fancy electronic device like a PDA, only with more bells and whistles,
punched some numbers on the keypad and said, "One oh two
resting temp." He looked at the thermometer and his other
equipment, punched in some more numbers, and said, "Current temp indicates victim has been dead approximately two
hours. Give or take a half hour."

I spoke into my mike. "Angel. Focus on footage from one
hundred fifty-five minutes ago. Find out where everyone was.
Make a chart. Note where everyone is at ninety minutes ago.
Pull the feed focused on the doors of private rooms and bath-
rooms. Whoever did this got bloody and needed to shower
and change."

"On it, Legs."

At least until the DS arrived, which was going to be a good
four more hours, meaning after sunrise, Jodi was in charge.
She stared at me hard, her cop face on, irritated and anything
but deferent, even when she transferred the look to Leo.
"There's a blood trail from the body, and if your people," she
shot a look to me and back, "hadn't trampled it and contami-
nated the crime scene, we might be able to pinpoint the killer
tonight. As it is, this is going to take a long time to process."

Leo nodded once, inscrutable and royal, as if giving her
permission to continue. I just shrugged. I wasn't a cop. She
had her job; I had mine. My body language must have communicated my thoughts because Jodi's eyes narrowed and she
said, "According to the guys looking over the security footage, Katie was seen running down the hallway on this floor.
She was the only person—including the vic, so far—caught on
film in this hallway the entire night. Until we know different, I
want Katie downtown, under wraps, for questioning."

"That will not be possible," Leo said. He looked elegant and
urbane and . . . clean. Leo was blood free. He'd found a place
to wash up before the cops arrived. Contamination of a prime
witness was gonna tick Jodi off when she figured that out.

"It's not up to you," she said.

The tension in the room went up a notch, a shivery, almost
painful proof of Leo's power. His head rocked to the side in
that oddly reptilian motion, the vamp-gesture that always

made my skin crawl. "Do you have a place devoid of even the merest hint of sunlight? Do you have chains capable of controlling a Mithran? Do you have ways to meet the dietary needs of a Mithran?"

Jodi swore again. Leo smiled, the expression not remotely human.

"Y'all keep tripping over the same old argument," I said, annoyed. "Can't you folks get over the logistics for a minute? Leo, where is Katie? Is she secure, protected, and how long will she be whacko? Can we get a CSI tech to her safely to collect samples and her clothing? Oh. And will she remember anything about tonight when she does get her head on straight?"

"Katie is shackled in a subbasement, under guard, and being fed in such a way that she is unable to harm the donor, despite her mental state," Leo said. "She will likely regain her sanity over the course of the next moon, and will remember nothing about tonight. I will collect any samples from her that are needed, under the direction of, and witnessed by, law enforcement." Surprisingly, he went on, offering unrequested information. "Her rising was supposed to be another thirty days from now, enough time to process the blood that healed her and find herself sane amongst the madness." He looked at me. "Her head has never been on twisted."

That was debatable, and I let a small smile curve my lips, but Jodi spoke before I could refute his claim. "What was the victim doing in this office?"

"I have no idea," Leo said. "It was not by invitation."

Jodi looked at Kem. "Was she sent to steal something?"

Kemnebi smiled. "To my knowledge, the Mithrans have nothing of value to us." Which sounded like so much insult. He swiveled his head and made a small bow to Leo. "Except the prospect of peace and political alliance in the world of humans."

This was why I was never gonna make it as a politico. Slap, insult, kiss and make up, tease, bait and switch.

Leo bowed back, matching the bow for depth and duration. "The Mithrans of the Louisiana Territory are honored to work with the were-cats of Africa." I figured it was part of the diplomatic stuff until another possible meaning sank in. It might have been two conspirators agreeing to cover each other's backs. I analyzed the words as the others talked, not liking the ambiguities at all.

"What do you keep in this office?" Jodi asked.

"My personal and clan records: financial, historical, and diplomatic, current and cached."

Jodi looked around the room and I could see the avarice in her eyes. It was like a treasure trove to a cop who catalogued such information, and Jodi's team did. "Did Katie do this?" she asked, gesturing to the body.

"Traditionally, Masters of the City have handled Mithran lawbreakers," Leo said. "Until our status is clarified with Congress, there is no legal reason to change that."

"That isn't what I asked," she said.

"No. It isn't." He stood there, looking superior and dazzling and the tension in the room went up another notch.

"He won't incriminate her," I said. I looked at Kemnebi. "Kemmy, baby, how's your nose?" His brows went up, whether at the meaning, the nickname, or just being addressed by a woman, I didn't know, so I pushed. " 'Cause if you can smell the attacker, it'd be a big help."

"I am not a dog to sniff out murderers."

Jodi's eyes narrowed. "You calling cops dogs?"

"I think he's talking about the wolves. Seems big-cats and wolves aren't best buddies." My earpiece crackled and I said, "Angel has the footage pulled up and the monitors ready."

Jodi looked at the coroner, her cousin. "Peter, you okay here? Need anything?" Peter didn't look up, but grunted and made a little shooing motion with one hand. I took that as a desire to be alone and led the way to the stairs. On the way I heard that the little green guy had been found swimming in the fountain in the back yard. "Looks like the backstroke," the voice said over the ear-com system. "The water's bloody." I heard the sounds of water splashing and soldiers cursing, and the voice said, "His clothes show traces of blood and he doesn't seem to understand English. He's gibbering at us."

I dropped back to Kem and said, "What species is the green guy you brought with you?"

"He is a grindylow," Kem said, "from Britain."

"Grindylow, like in Harry Potter?" Jodi asked.

"Harry Potter? No." There was no mistaking the expression on Kem's face as anything except contempt. Harry wasn't his favorite fictional character.

"What's a grindylow, then?" Jodi asked.

"They are . . . pets. Most of the time. Guardians, occasionally. Less often, the enforcers of were-law. They are of limited intelligence, similar to a small child, or a chimpanzee." He looked up, as if trying to remember something. Or as if taking time to concoct a lie. "They like water and prefer cold climes. But they will stay with their . . . master, no matter the climate change."

"Right. Uh-huh." There was something in his tone that set my teeth on edge.

"Is there any way he gutted Safia?" Jodi asked, deliberately crude, watching his reactions.

Kem's face contorted for an instant, twisted by the grief he was keeping so tightly bound. Then his face smoothed again. "The grindy is much like—*was* much like—Safia's puppy, devoted to her in every way. I can think of few reasons that he would harm her."

Few reasons, not none. It wasn't a denial. I shot a look at Jodi, who nodded. She was playing bad cop. "The grindy was swimming in the back fountain," I said. "Blood on his clothes, but well washed off. A couple of our guys yanked him out and have him in custody."

"I'll send CSI to bag his clothes." She looked around at the hallway, shaking her head. "This whole place is a maze of areas we need to contain. We don't have enough men."

"Well, let's see if the security footage lets us narrow it down some," I said.

The large security-conference room was an assault on my senses. The room was filled with people. The bronze light fixture and track lights I hadn't noticed before were lit up like torches. The oval table was cluttered with papers, laptops, cell phones, and electronic devices. The air was heavy with smells and noise: a stink of sweat, stress pheromones, the acrid reek of anger, the tang of old tobacco and coffee, the greasy scent from a plate of food that had been picked over and left on the table; a cacophony of voices, phones ringing, electronic beeps, miscellaneous clatter, and coffee was gurgling in the back of the room. The huge monitor hanging from the ceiling was lit up, showing twenty camera angles. It was chaotic and Beast sent me a sleepy vision of rats running across the ground in panic before she closed herself off from me again. I was relieved that she was at least watching. Beast often noted things I missed.

A thin, mid-sixties woman—who had geek written all over her—and Angel looked up as we entered. Angel swiveled his chair and gave me a small nod, as if glad to see me. "Miz Yellowrock, the CSI lady tech and I have narrowed the pertinent camera angles down."

He looked at the woman and she shrugged. "I'm no lady. *Sonny*."

He snorted softly. "You got to stop calling me that, *Gramma*." They both chuckled and Angel pointed to the right side of the big monitor. "This one shows the hallway outside Mr. Pellissier's office, these show the ballroom from three angles, this revolving sequence shows the victim exiting the ballroom and making her way to the office, these two show the wolves exiting unmonitored rooms as their counterparts jumped through the ceiling in the ballroom, the rest show the grounds, the room Yoda with fangs was in, and several shots of him in various areas of the compound. He only appears for a moment or two at a time, easy to miss." He looked at me. "No excuses, ma'am, just the facts."

I had a feeling the gramma had helped restore his equanimity. They were an unlikely team, the young, black, ex-marine communications/ET tech and the middle-aged, white CSI tech, but their partnership seemed to be working.

He returned his attention to the screen. "The views showing the hallways that connect the ballroom to the office are over to the left. We're dealing with two hours of digital feed from over seventy cameras, so there's a lot still to go through and a lot more that might be found, but so far these are the pertinent ones, bookmarked for easy retrieval.

"I also took the liberty of going through the camera footage of the walls and the back courtyard trying to narrow down the time the wolves came over, if they came that way," Angel said. He tapped a camera. "A chef gathering herbs looks up, right here, as if he heard something overhead. Four thirty-two this afternoon. Then, at five seventeen, a guard hears something and looks up. It might give you a timeline for interrogation."

"Police don't interrogate. We question," Jodi murmured, but there wasn't any heat behind the disputation. Angel's Tit cocked a brow in disbelief.

We watched silently, the little group gathered behind Angel's chair, and we proved one thing. Unless she had been moving at warp speed and had done a time jump, Katie didn't kill Safia. We had a time stamp of the little assistant entering Leo's office at twelve forty-seven. It might not stand up in court, being only the flare of her dress from her left hip down and one raffia sandaled left foot as she entered the office, but she moved like Safia.

Nearly an hour later, just before she appeared in the ballroom, Katie raced through the front door, unseen by the guards, and all but flew up the hallway and into the office, moving fast. Even with the feed slowed down, she was a blur, but it was her, no doubt. The dried blood was a dead giveaway, even from behind. Exactly twenty-six seconds later she exited. There was fresh blood on her face, but according to the coroner, Safia had been dead nearly an hour by then. So . . . maybe Katie had some leftovers?

I wanted to smile at my whimsy, but my face was frozen with exhaustion. Beast was bored with the investigation. She was sleeping somewhere inside me and the lack of her conscious awareness was enervating.

We went through the footage several times at various speeds. Found two things. The most important one was—an intruder had been in the ballroom.

The unidentified person was hard to see, and his position was unlikely at best. The toe of a boot was visible in one of the ballroom's ceiling-mounted cameras. A booted person had literally hung around in the arched ceilings, unseen, for hours before the party started, and then, when the wolves made their dramatic appearance, had disappeared. No unidentified person had appeared in any other footage, not so far.

Leo seemed to stop several times in the evening, motion arrested as if he smelled something, and look around the room and up in the ceiling, much as he had when he first entered the ballroom. But he never seemed to discover the source of whatever—or whomever—it was he smelled. I was guessing it was the booted person in the arches. The boot and Leo's scent searches reminded me of Gee, but I kept my suspicions to myself.

The second interesting thing was a little conspiracy brewing. The vamps were passing a little note around, small enough to be cupped into a hand. Every vamp it came into contact with stared at the note for a long moment, looked grim, and passed it on. That footage appeared to interest Leo but was likely unrelated to the murder. When a being is potentially

immortal, life has to become terribly boring. What is there
to do but suck blood, have sex, and conspire? But Leo had
just won a bloody war; he didn't need another; neither did the
city of New Orleans. So Leo followed the activity and note
around the ballroom, reviewing the footage several times, taking names and looking dour. I asked for some footage sections
to be bookmarked and a list kept so we could find everything
easily when needed.

It became apparent that the note originated with Amitee
Marchand, formally of the Rochefort clan in France, and her
brother Fernand. The fiancée of Leo's deceased son was plotting behind his back and I bet myself that they were not planning a surprise birthday party for their master. Leo, grimly
satisfied, was clearly memorizing all the players in the little
conspiracy, whatever it might be. When he rotated his hand
in a little *go ahead* gesture, Angel spun around in his chair,
his hands dangling off the chair arms, his posture relaxed and
confident. "The next part is Gramma's," Angel said.

"Cheeky kid," the older tech said. "There's a lot of things
that don't add up, but this one might—or might not—be
one of the most important." She keyed up a final monitor. It
showed Tyler, Bruiser's second in command, talking to two
of the weres, Roul and the woman, in a hallway after the fi-
asco in the ballroom. And there was something in his body
language that suggested agitation.

Leo asked, "Where is Tyler now?"

"In the back garden," Gramma said, "with the leader of the
armed children."

"She means he's with Derek," Angel said.

"Miss Yellowrock, please see that Tyler is escorted directly
here." Leo's voice hadn't changed, his still-as-death body language hadn't shifted. But I knew he was ticked off. I could
smell anger pheromones coming off him. He added, "By two
of your men."

Two? Oookaaay. I keyed my mike, the action repeated so
many times tonight it was second nature. "Derek, please escort Tyler to the security room. One of your men to each side,
one behind." If Leo thought Tyler needed two humans to keep
him under control, I figured overkill might be wise.

There was a slight pause while Derek interpreted my
words, then said, "Will do."

*   *   *

Tyler looked like a well-coiffed, twenty-something, disingenuous kid, but he moved like a trained soldier. And he was smart.
He knew he hadn't been summoned for drinks and hors
d'oeuvres. As soon as the men pushed through the doors, he
took the initiative and said, "What'd I do, boss?"

Leo nodded to a chair, and Tyler took it. "Remove your
weapons, please." Tyler did, like a well-trained soldier, removing the clip from the semiautomatic handgun and ejecting the
round in the chamber, lining up two additional clips beside
it, and setting two knives beside the weapon. Leo said nothing, just watched and breathed. And I realized he was smelling changes in Tyler's body chemistry. I took a shallow breath
through nose and mouth and caught the smell of sweat, manly,
not rank, soap, antiperspirant, beef and mayo. No worry, no
fear.

"Please observe your actions in the footage and explain."

Tyler nodded once, faced the monitor, laced his fingers together across his lap, and waited. Angel pointed to the specific
camera image and set it in motion. Tyler moved across the
screen and I heard a single hard heartbeat from his chest as
he watching himself engage the werewolves in conversation.
Then Tyler smiled at the monitor. "She looked gorgeous, boss,
what I could see of her. And you said to be nice to the guests.
I figured that included the uninvited ones. I took the opportunity to see if she was available. Hey," he placed an open palm
on his chest and grinned widely, his eyes twinkling, "I'm just a
guy. You can't fault me talking to a good-looking lady."

Leo watched him for a long moment, evaluating. Tyler just
sat there, relaxed and waiting. "You may go," Leo said, "but
leave your weapons here, and do not leave the compound."

"Got nowhere else to go, boss." Tyler stood and left the
room.

Leo's eyes followed him, barren and remote. Softly, he said,
"I have never fed from him. Who feeds my second?"

Bruiser said, "Alejandro, boss."

Leo nodded, his face empty, his eyes distant. "Alejandro
has been with me for more than a hundred years. He has my
blood."

It sounded arcane and archaic, a feudal lord claiming one
of his own.

CHAPTER 12

Katie Ate Dead Meat

An hour before dawn, Peter Richoux had a preliminary ruling on cause of death and it wasn't what any of us expected. He entered the security room, where we were going over more digital camera footage, this time from Derek's low-light cameras, where we were trying to trace the movements of the grindy, who seemed to appear and disappear on different floors like magic. So far as we knew, teleportation wasn't possible, so that left speed, and the grindy had that in spades. Derek froze the footage and we turned our attention to Peter.

He looked as tired as the rest of us, with dark circles under his eyes and his hair mussed, as if he'd rubbed his hands through his hair and not smoothed it back down. As if to prove the point, he ran one hand from his nape, over his skull, and with the other hand, pinched his temples between thumb and fingers. When he dropped his hands, he leaned forward and placed his fingertips on the table like ten body stabilizers and focused on Jodi. "I've done as much as I can here. We'll move the body to the morgue where I'll do a full PM, though not until after I've had some sleep. For now—"

"No," Kemnebi said. "There will be no postmortem, no desecration of the body. Such is not permitted by my people or by our religion."

"Sorry, sir, but the police department will require a forensic autopsy to pursue a murder investigation. The Department of State isn't likely to disagree," Peter said. "And justice can't be done without one." When he spoke, I felt the pull of weak magic. Peter Richoux was not a sorcerer, but he had natural gifts of persuasion that were all his own.

"No," Kemnebi said, implacable. And then I got it. Scientists had been trying to get their hands on a dead vamp to dissect for years. Marilyn Monroe's body had mysteriously disappeared prior to hers, and no other research-based autopsy had ever been accomplished. The bodies of supernats always disappear before a single scalpel can be applied.

"Sir," Peter said respectfully, casting his cousin a hooded glance that I wasn't able to interpret, "I'll have to leave that decision between you and DS. For now, I've collected a few samples from the bod—the scene, and we'll get preliminary results back in a few days. Final results when all the tox screens are done. This isn't TV, so we're talking a couple of weeks. But I can give you a preliminary, presumptive COD now."

Jodi pushed a rolling desk chair to him with her foot. He sat hard, and the chair cushion sighed, faster and harder than the matching sigh of exhaustion that Peter gave. "Anyone got coffee? I smell coffee." Jodi signaled; a guy in technician blues went to a coffeepot in the corner and poured a cup of the three-hour-old brew. It smelled scorched and toxic, but it wasn't my stomach. I watched as the man poured, something in his obsequious demeanor that drew my attention and repelled it at the same time.

Peter spoke and it pulled my eyes back to him. "The victim took two wounds and each appear to be equally mortal." He lifted a finger. "One. A single bullet wound to the left front chest, midclavicular, ascending between the third and fourth intercostals. Maybe a nine mil or .385. The trajectory suggests that she was in the air or her attacker was kneeling. The bullet nicked either the ascending aorta or the subclavian artery. I won't know until or *if* I get to open her up," he glanced at Kemmy and back to Jodi.

"Though there should be an exit wound, there isn't." He took a sip of coffee, nodded gratefully to the man who brought the cup. "And so we should be able to get the bullet for comparison." He lifted a second finger. "Two. Triple parallel wounds—maybe a blade, maybe a claw, severed her carotid arteries, external jugulars, her trachea, and esophagus, delivered from left to right, the killing strike likely delivered with the attacker behind her, though I may change that when I get a better look. It's also possible that she was on her hands and knees and the attacker was over her."

I instantly pictured a shape-changer trying to change forms, as if after a nearly mortal wound. Safia, in my imagination, had been shot and was bent over, kneeling on the floor as she tried to force a change to save her life. Kemnebi closed his eyes, his dark face ashen. His breath was slow, uneven; he shouldn't have to hear this, but I could think of no way to exclude him.

"Barring anything on further analysis," Peter said, "COD is likely to be from exsanguination from the throat wound. She probably bled out in a matter of seconds. Prior to that, she fought an attacker and displays several premortem defensive wounds and abrasions. Postmortem, she was mauled in what looks like an animal attack, similar to a scavenger. But I'll have to verify all this back at the morgue. Again assuming I get the chance," he said. I thought of Katie and the fresh blood that had fallen on her chest. *Crap. Katie ate dead meat. Would that make her nutso longer?*

"I've collected physical evidence, including fibers, dust, hair, and saliva from her postmortem attacker, and particulate matter, all of which already went back to HQ. I figure the DS techs, if they bring any, will want some sent to Quantico, so I collected a matching set for them, everything in duplicate, where possible. Jodi, I know that the crime-scene techs will take a lot longer at the scene. When they're done, I'd like the rugs from the area around the victim."

Jodi drummed her fingers on the table. "I'll see they're sent to you once CSI has a chance to go over them. And we'll keep the room sealed until further notice. Thanks, Peter."

The coroner stood and left the room, his empty coffee cup on the table. I had a feeling the caffeine wouldn't keep him awake once he got home. A CSI tech poked her head in the room and located Jodi, a big grin on her face. "We found a shell casing in the office. It might be a match for that other case we've been working on." The two women held gazes and my radar perked up. I didn't know about another case, but if it intersected with this one, I wanted to know. "And Detective? We found another way into and out of the office. A doorway hidden behind an armoire. It has an antiquated locking system—lever and bolt—and there's blood on it."

Jodi spun her chair to Leo and leaned forward, forearms on her knees, her head jutted forward and her expression totally focused. If she'd been a wolf, she would have been hunting. "Mr. Pellissier, you didn't think it relevant to mention that there's another exit from the room where a murder took place?"

"Many rooms in Mithran institutions and abodes contain additional, concealed egress. We have needed such for two thousand years, to protect us from Christians and from vampire hunters." He slanted a glance my way but I didn't react to the barb. I had wondered if the room had a second outlet when I first saw it. Leo turned back to Jodi, who looked like she was trying to digest something noxious. Maybe the coffee. Leo went on, "I will not allow you access based on diplomatic security considerations."

"I'll find a judge who will grant me access," Jodi ground out. "And until then, you stay out of the office." Leo just smiled at her order, showing a hint of teeth, but no fang. Unless Jodi left an armed guard on the place twenty-four/seven, Leo would go where he wanted when he wanted. And with his ability to mesmerize humans, even an armed guard might not keep him out.

Someone set a ceramic mug beside me and I drank, noticing that it was tea, green and smooth with a floral top note. Good tea. Helped me think. I was trying to arrange the threads of the case and make a coherent picture, but nothing was fitting together. Which might make sense if it was more than one case, overlapping in time but not really a part of one another. That wasn't likely, but that didn't make it impossible.

The last hour of the night went by quickly with nothing much accomplished in terms of apprehending a suspect. I did find a moment to pull Jodi to the side to ask a few questions, leading with, "Your people found a shell casing in the office. What other case are you working on?"

Jodi had no reason to answer; most cops don't share information. However, Jodi had been agreeable about info sharing from the moment I met her. She nodded to the nearest hot coffee, this pot set up by the staff in a hallway, on a small, white-draped table. She poured one for herself and sipped. I was nursing a second cup of tea and I sipped with her, my movements a mirror image. "I don't know how you live without this stuff," she said.

"It's nasty. I like tea." I lifted my mug to her.

"I know. It's weird to see the vamps cater to your tastes."

"Yeah. I kill them for a living. You'd think it would make them less likely to serve me."

"And why hire you? I mean, it doesn't make any sense."

"Either they think that since I can kill them I must be good, and they might as well use my talents, or they're keeping me close to the chest."

"Keep your friends close and your enemies closer?" Jodi asked. "Like that?"

I gave a could-be shrug. "So. What case?"

"Orleans County has some cold cases on file from the sixties that my unit has been looking into since an anonymous tip a few weeks back."

The phrase "a few weeks back" echoed inside me. I'm not an adherent to the religion of coincidence. I wondered if the cold cases were related to the wolves' evidence against Leo, evidence I hadn't had a chance to investigate. Had the wolves called in the "tips"?

"The victims were chest shots, execution style, people who were close to the vamp population about the time they came out of the closet. The only evidence recovered from the kill sites were .385 rounds and shell casings, fired from the same semiautomatic weapon. The casings have the same set of prints on them, prints not listed in AFIS."

AFIS—the nation's Automated Fingerprint Identification System—stored and compared fingerprints and was responsible for matching up a lot of felons with crimes. I dipped my chin to show I was listening.

"There's not a lot of evidence left after Katrina came through—all the paperwork was ruined in the storage units— and I know we may never make an arrest in the cold cases, but if we can tie the shell casings and bullets to a current murder, then we can at least close the old ones." Jodi was watching me, gauging my reaction. This wasn't idle chitchat or information sharing. This was leading me by the nose to some place she wanted me to go.

I said, "And the rounds?"

"The ones from the cold cases have a score mark along them, visible to the naked eye. Any gun leaving that kind of scoring would have been useless at any distance, but perfect for close-in work."

"Like a lucky gun, kept around for special kills?"

"Exactly. We're running the prints on the casing in the office to see if they match the old ones. As soon as we have a bullet to compare to, we'll be able to open a new case file and merge all the old, cold ones in."

"And who do you suspect in the old murders?" I asked. Knowing. Just knowing.

"George Dumas or Leo Pellissier."

I hadn't known I had feelings beyond desire for Bruiser until she said his name. And I hadn't realized I felt protective about Leo either. Stupid. Just plain stupid to feel anything about either one of them, protective of the monster or . . . whatever it was I felt for his blood meal. But there you have it. Feelings aren't logical or sensible.

"You got any problems with that?" Jodi asked.

"No. No problems at all," I lied with a straight face, hoping I was pulling it off. "Why haven't you asked Bruiser and Leo to give prints for matching in the cold cases?"

"Politics," Jodi spat, as if it were an ugly word. "After I get enough to make an arrest, and prove it beyond a reasonable doubt, *then, maybe,* I'll get to haul them in and chat with them and hopefully fingerprint them."

"Have you checked their clothes for GSR?"

"They're bagged and on the way to the lab. There was just too much to work with here."

"Okay," I said, thinking of Leo's clean clothes. Thinking that whistle-blowers in a vamp organization might get drained and dead instead of just fired. Thinking that Leo hadn't left the ballroom while Safia was being killed. I pulled my cell and saw that it was after eight a.m. on Friday. "Jodi." Staring at the face of the cell that Leo had provided, I said, "Leo changed clothes. And Bruiser has access to every locking system in the HQ." She didn't answer and I stared at the cell's face, not wanting to look up. "I'm going home to bed. Call me if you need me."

"Jane."

I shifted my eyes to hers.

"Thanks. If he's guilty then he should be behind bars."

I didn't know which *he* she was referring to. Jodi was a law-and-order, by-the-book kinda girl, so either man, if he looked guilty, would get the benefit of her legal teeth in his leg. She'd be like a rat terrier shaking a buffalo. "I know." I turned and left the building, taking the stairs down from vamp central, into the morning, my dress swinging and swishing against my legs. As I walked, I called Rinaldo; he was in the Quarter, just finishing breakfast, and promised he'd be with me in ten minutes. I walked on, knowing moving would make me harder to find, but needing the push of heart and lungs, the feel of blood pumping and muscles stretching and contracting.

Rinaldo pulled up beside me shortly and idled his cab, keeping up with my pace as he looked me over. "You *look* a million bucks, yes? Janie-girl all *dolled* up, *walking* from direction of the bloodsucker's biiiig pa'tay last night?" I ignored him and got in the front seat, closing the door after me. "You *look* good with knife in one hand, gun in the other. *Sexy*." I looked at him, deadpan, and he said, "I *work* graveyard shift. We keep TV on all night. *Saw* you on the TV, I did. Some pa-tay girl you are."

I'd been outted to Rinaldo. If he didn't know I was the vamp hunter before, he did now. I laid my head back on the seat and closed my eyes. "Yeah. I was there. Take me home, Rinaldo."

"No trip to the nearest fast food place?"

"No. Thanks." I kept my eyes closed for the rest of the drive and Rinaldo didn't pester me, even when we drew up in front of my house. I paid my usual fee, got out, and went inside. The house was silent, chill, with the AC on full blast. I stripped, placed my weapons where I could reach them quickly, showered, and fell into bed. The last thing I did before I fell asleep was check my cell phone.

No call from Rick. No text. No nothing.

I half woke to three quick taps on the front door, rolled over, and pulled the covers over my head. But whoever it was didn't go away; he kept knocking in three-burst rounds like a machine gun on the wood door. It was 2:22 Friday afternoon when I came awake, with a rush, thinking, *Rick*! I rolled out of bed and picked up my robe in a single motion, flung my hair out of the way and raced to the door, shoving my arms into the sleeves. I looked out through a clear pane in the stained-glass door window. And saw Bruiser, still knocking.

All the eagerness went out of me and I closed my eyes, leaned my head against the wall beside the door, and blew out a breath. Anger started to build in a quiet, still part of my soul, anger at Rick. *He could have called. Even deep undercover, he could have found a way to call. One lousy freaking phone call.*

I finished tying the robe's belt with a yank and opened the door. "You're lucky the house wards weren't up, or you'd have singed your knuckles."

Bruiser met my eyes, his dark with exhaustion, black rings under them. The skin on his face and jaw looked worn and slack, as if he'd aged in the last few hours. His clothes showed the fine wrinkles and relaxed hand of high humidity. I looked at the street. There was no car in sight. And there was a large suitcase at his feet. "May I come in?" he asked, his voice weary.

I stared at the suitcase as myriad thoughts and possibilities fluttered through me like ravens' wings, none of them happy ones. On their heels came a workable answer. "The cops found a reason to get prints from you. It was your prints on the shell casing in the office and on the cold case brass." My eyes narrowed. "Leo kicked you out."

"Yes," he said, his fatigue more pronounced. "My lawyer and I spent two hours with them, fending off thinly veiled accusations and allegations posed as questions. When they let me go, a police acquaintance slipped me word that the press is staking out my residence." He seemed to slump as he stood in the muggy heat, and put a hand on the door jamb as if to support himself. "I went to the clan home to find my suitcase packed and waiting for me at the front door. Tyler suggested that I come here. It seemed like a good idea. At the time."

I stared at the suitcase. It was a big one, the kind on wheels with a handle. It would hold a lot of clothes. "You want to stay *here*?" My voice didn't squeak, but it was a near thing. And I was suddenly aware that I was naked under my robe. I pulled my lapels together. "You can't stay at a hotel?"

"They'll find me. No one will look here for a day or so." He closed his eyes as he said the next word. "Please."

It was the "please" that did it. It was one of those forlorn words that a man asks when he's down and out and been kicked around a bit. "Did you kill Safia?"

He met my eyes, so I could read the truth in them. "No. But I may not be able to prove it. The tapes indicate that I was away from the ballroom when Safia first disappeared. There isn't enough evidence just now to charge me."

"Did you kill the people in the cold case files?"

"I don't know. There was a time . . ." He stopped and swallowed, wavering slightly. I could smell his sweat and his fatigue. Beast was awake and watching through my eyes. "There was a time, decades really, after my mother died, when my anger was so great that I killed anyone Leo wanted dead." His voice was flat, and he closed his eyes again, hiding the bleak darkness in them. "Some of the locations in the photographs they showed me looked familiar. I would need access to more in the police files to know if I was . . . responsible." He opened his eyes and held mine, a wry honesty in them. "However, even at my most angry, I have never been stupid enough to leave my spent brass beside a body."

Which sounded like the truth. Not knowing why, I pushed the door open and stood to the side. A grudging tone in my voice, I said, "Guest rooms are upstairs. Evangelina is in one. If you take a room across the hall, you can have your own bath. Sheets are in the linen closet."

A faint smile tugged his lips as he stepped over the threshold and pulled his suitcase after with two bass wheel-thumps. "I can't share your bed?"

Unexpected heat ignited in my belly and began to grow. Beast wrinkled her lips, showing teeth, interested. I gripped my lapels tighter, shoving her away. "No."

"Why not?"

"I have a boyfriend."

Beast sent me a mental picture of her claw raking the rump of a mate who displeased her. I knew she meant Rick, for not calling. *Big-cats do not mate for life*, she thought at me. I drew in a slow breath.

"A *boy friend*," Bruiser said, making it two words. His smile widened and his eyes warmed slightly with amusement. "A *child* in the art of lovemaking."

I breathed past the warmth and crushed down a laugh that was burbling in my chest, let my eyebrows rise, and managed an unsympathetic, half-bored expression. "Upstairs, Romeo. And if you try to move in to my bed, I'll toss you to the curb."

"Yes, ma'am. I'll be the soul of propriety. But you'll regret that decision."

Deliberately misunderstanding him I said, "I agree that you'll be a pain in the butt. But go on up anyway. You look like you're about to fall asleep on your feet."

"Thank you, Jane. A nap would be appreciated."

"Yeah, well, you ruined mine," I said ungraciously, closing the door behind him. "You do your own laundry, your own sheets, and clean your own bathroom. Food is by our resident three-star chef. Dinner is at seven, usually, breakfast between seven and eight on the days she has time to fix any. Cold cereal

whenever you want it on the days she doesn't. Lunch is whatever you want to fix. I don't cook for you."

"Right now, just a bed," he said, climbing the stairs, the suitcase bumping along after him. He was halfway up the stairs
when I went back to my bed, threw myself on top of the sheets
and lay there, looking up at the ceiling. For a gal who didn't
have a family and liked her privacy, I had an awful lot of people in my life and depending on me, lately.

I checked my cell again and found a voice mail from Deon
wanting to know all the gossip from the party. I called him back
and got his voice mail. Communications, twenty-first-century
style. I tried to find sleep but it eluded me, energy racing under
my skin like ants on the prowl, seeing again the teasing look in
Bruiser's tired eyes. He *had* been teasing. I was sure of it. Sorta
sure of it. But then there was that heat that stirred between us,
like electric sparks melded with taffy, heating and stinging, a
tugging, pulling sweetness. And Rick still hadn't called.

When I couldn't keep my eyes closed, I rose and dressed,
braided my hair and pulled out my notes. I came across Girrard DiMercy's calling card. Not a business card, but a heavy
linen, embossed, gilt-edged calling card. I held it to my nose
and caught his scent, jasmine and pine. And realized that I
had smelled it today already. At vamp HQ. I drew in the scent,
remembering it mixed with the bouquets. Gee had been the
guy who served me tea. He had been around a few other times
too, a glamour hiding him, or making him seem unimportant,
socially invisible.

I cursed once and pulled my cell, dialing the number under his name. I was shunted directly to voice mail and greeted
by a mechanical voice. When the beep sounded, I said, "You
spelled me again, spelled us all, and hung around for the police investigation. Call me, you little creep." I hung up, checked
again for a call from Rick and snapped the cell down with
more force than the action warranted. *Men . . .*

Anger scoring the sides of my mind, I dialed Rick's number.
I was shunted directly to voice mail and hung up without leaving a message. He knew my number. He'd call if he wanted to.
Madder than I'd been in a long time, I left the house, hopped
on Bitsa, tearing out of the Quarter and to the firing range
where I blew off a head of steam, shooting my way through
three boxes of shells and shredding four man-shaped targets
before I quit, one target for each man I was mad at: Bruiser,

Leo, Gee, and Rick. I put most of the bullets into the target called Rick, thinking, *call me, call me*, with every shot.

When I was done I stripped and cleaned my weapons at the counter, a nice pile of discarded brass at my feet, bright on the dark-painted floor; solvents, lubricants, and spent gunpowder stung my nose, my eyes unfocused, hands moving through the necessary procedures by memory and feel. One spent cartridge near my boot rocked slightly, catching my attention. I studied the shiny brass as I cleaned, my mind empty and quiet in the aftermath of preparatory and nonlethal violence. My casings were the only ones, the floor having been thoroughly cleaned since any previous shooters.

If someone wanted to frame me, all he would need was my spent brass, with my fingerprints all over them, and my gun. Gather the brass, steal the gun, shoot a few people, police the brass used to make the kill, and toss down the ones with my prints on them. And in Bruiser's case, any blood-servant or blood-slave who had been around for fifty years or more could have set the thing up. Bruiser had to know this. And like he'd said, he wasn't stupid enough to leave his spent brass at a crime scene.

I was packing up my weapons when my cell rang. Once again, hope shot through me like wildfire and died just as quickly. Not Rick. Gee's number. I didn't bother to say hello. "Did you kill Safia?"

"No. I did not."

"Then why were you hanging around the party and the investigation?"

"I followed the werewolves when they entered the compound. I saw the envoy and his small entourage arrive, with the little grindylow. I have not seen one here in . . . quite some time. And never so far from Britain. And never, ever, away from a cold lake, stream, or river. They like cool temperatures. I was curious." He chuckled, the sound as musical as flute notes. "So I invited myself to the party."

"Where you hung around in the ceiling." I propped on the counter at the back of the shooting gallery, my gear beside me, thinking. *There was no scaffolding. Nothing to hold on to in the ceiling*. "Glamoured, right? So we wouldn't see you if we looked up."

"I am clever."

I remembered Bruiser's eyes on my front porch, haunted.

Yeah. That was the word. He'd looked haunted. It was a look that made me want to help, to prove him innocent, and that was not part of my job, not part of my contract, not something that would earn me one red cent. But I was going to do it anyway. "Did you see where Bruiser went when he left the ballroom?" I asked. "Can you prove he didn't kill the girl? Were-cat. Whatever. Did you see who killed Safia?"

"I saw many things last night but little that will help you."

That stopped me. "Why are you here, Gee? What do you want?"

"Good-bye, little goddess." He ended the call with a faint click, and when I called him back, it went directly to voice mail again.

I hung up, irritated and confused; stuck the cell into an ammo pouch in my gear. There were too many things going on to get a handle on it, to see any kind of big picture. "Goddess, my vamp-kicking butt. Give me a straight-out hunt with fanged prey and blood anytime," I grumbled.

"Me too, sister," a voice said. It came from a guy coming in the door of the indoor range, a mean looking little guy with a gun case big enough to hold a cannon. Penis envy? I was nearly mad enough to say it aloud but managed to hold it in. I grabbed the broom and swept up my brass, dumping it into the half-full brass barrel in the corner. Then I stirred my casings into the mix, losing them in the discards of others, very aware of the little guy's eyes on me. Paranoid? Me? Starting to be.

Outside, I kicked Bitsa on and eased into traffic, the air like a hot wet blanket against me.

I made a stop by the main offices of NOPD, telling myself that it wasn't to see Rick, but to look at some files in the woo-woo room. And I believed it, sorta. The guard at the desk was one I had seen before and he slid the sign-in pad to me, tossed me a temp ID badge, and waved me on through. It was shoddy security, but I wasn't about to complain. I made my way up the stairs, Rick's desk drawing me like a magnet. It was vacant. No papers on the surface, no old coffee cup, even the computer was off. There was a layer of dust on top of everything. The layer of dust told me clearer than words that he was, indeed, undercover. Again.

Relief warred with anger. He could have told me. I swerved away and made my way through the room, ignored by everyone and returning the favor, to Jodi's office. I knew where it was, though I'd never been invited in. Which might be a good thing. Jodi and her right-hand man, Sloan Rosen, were bent over reports, Jodi sounding tired, angry, and slightly hoarse. And she was still wearing the same clothes she had worn the night before. I tapped on the door and she looked up, irritation creasing the skin beside her eyes. "What do you want?"

I started to be cute, but instead said, "I'd like to get at the files in the woo-woo room." I felt weird saying the words, as if my own subconscious was surprised. But it faded instantly. "If it's okay."

"Sure." She tossed me a set of three keys and I caught them. Nodded my head and backed away. "Jane," she called. I stopped. "I hear George Dumas is staying in your house." I wasn't quite sure what to make of her tone so I just nodded. "He's a person of interest," she said, "in the death of the diplomatic assistant."

I nodded again. "I just came from the shooting range, where I left a lot of spent brass on the floor. Every single casing had my fingerprints on them. If someone stole my gun and swept up my brass, they could frame me easily." I tossed the keys lightly and caught them. "I'll have these back in an hour." I turned and left the office, feeling Jodi's eyes boring a hole in my back. I wondered if I had a target painted on it. I had lost the chance to hear anything about the case, but I had also lost the chance to be questioned by my friend or asked to spy on another friend and houseguest. I figured I had won.

The woo-woo room had changed since I first saw it, from a utilitarian storage room containing paper copies of all the city's paranormal case files to a storage room with a computer, a dry board, a copier-scanner combo, a table, and more comfortable chairs. I eyed the computer, thinking about trying to log on, but passwords were surely not something I could guess at, and getting caught spying was a surefire way to get kicked out of the room forever. I turned to the hard-copy files and started digging.

I stayed in the woo-woo room for nearly an hour and photocopied a dozen files, most without taking the time to read thoroughly, and carried them back out with me when I left. Jodi wasn't in her office, and I didn't look for her, leaving her keys on a blotter in plain sight. I had a feeling that this case might put a lot of stress on a relationship that wasn't that strong to begin with.

CHAPTER 13

I Intend to Make You Regret That Decision

I wove through rush hour traffic on Bitsa, rush hour actually being more like rush afternoon, one huge snarl of traffic and exhaust fumes and boiling, wet heat. On the way home, I stopped for a few groceries that Evangelina had texted me that we needed, and managed to get a half gallon of milk and five pounds of flour into the saddlebags, fruit and veggies piled on top of the files I'd copied. Even with the traffic, I got back home just after seven. Evangelina's rental car wasn't parked in front, and the house was dark, no wonderful smells of cooking food greeted me when I parked Bitsa beside the back stairs and opened the door. After unloading the groceries, I slid two stakes into my hair and opened a Snickers bar to meet my caloric needs, eating standing in the dusk-dimmed room at the kitchen sink.

"I thought I heard someone."

I identified Bruiser's voice before I tried to draw a weapon, but my heart jumped painfully. He was standing in the opening between the kitchen and sitting room, the space dim, the houses close on each side keeping out the last rays of the sun. Now that I knew he was there, I could smell him, freshly showered; his aftershave, a citrusy scent that was all man, lay faintly on the air. I could tell he had been sitting alone in the silence, which seemed like a not-so-smart decision when one was under so much strain. It seemed like an act that might lead to depression or drinking or something even worse. "You said there would be dinner. A three-star chef." His tone wasn't accusatory, but he did sound oddly detached, almost despondent.

"She's her own woman. Comes and goes as she wants." I crushed the Snickers wrapper and dropped it in the trash. "There's steak in the fridge."

"You know how to cook steak?" he asked, his voice warming slightly.

"Light a match under it. If it doesn't kick, it's dead and done. Toss it on a plate, put a baked potato to the side with sour cream, toss a spinach salad for the vegetable lovers, and pour a beer."

"I'd like my steak with at least a pretence of brown on the outside."

"Wimp."

Bruiser laughed, the sound startled. When it passed he said, "Thank you. I needed that."

"You're welcome. Question. Did you know that Leo was . . . let's call it playing pimp with Kemnebi and me?" A bit of Beast growled out with the words *playing pimp*.

Bruiser stilled at the sound. He breathed out a soft, "No. I didn't." He shifted in the dark, an uneasy sound, edgy and brooding. His pheromones smelled of annoyance, which was a peculiar blend of uncertainty and anger. "I knew he was curious how Kemnebi would react to your scent." His words grew stilted as he added, "That is bloody well all."

I let that hang between us for a moment and said, "Grill's on the side porch. Take it into the back yard to light it so we don't burn down the upper porch. I'll bring out the steaks and some beer."

"I don't suppose you'd like to retire to your bedroom first, for some R and R? It would be"—he thought a moment—"healthy and healing for both of us."

Healthy and healing? "First off, your timing sucks. And second, as pickup lines go that one is at the very bottom of awful. *Rick* bought me the grill. It was a one month anniversary gift." *Yet he hadn't called.*

Bruiser walked to me through the early evening shadows, a murky shape that undulated like a form seen through a rain-runneled window. My heart did a bebop move; I gripped the cabinet at the sink to steady myself, half ready to dart away, though I never ran—not ever. "I'm a one-man woman," I said. "I don't play around."

"Neither do I," he said. "Not with you."

Beast reared up fast, seeing the man through my eyes. She purred once, the vibration in my mind so strong I thought it must have escaped, but Bruiser didn't react. Beast breathed in through my mouth and nostrils, smelling, tasting, wanting him. *Good mate*, she thought, *strong, powerful*. She gathered herself, holding me down and distant. Bruiser stopped so close I could feel his body heat through our clothes. He paused, watching me, his eyes looking down at me, and it felt so odd to be small beside a man. I could feel his breath on my neck and chest, an unfamiliar sensation. I managed the word, "No." It came out breathy and uncertain. I firmed my voice and said again, "No."

Beast raised my head and breathed in his scent, holding me firm and steady. I couldn't step away or run, and when I stood there, like an offering, Bruiser lifted a hand and slid it around my nape, holding me gently, his palm warm and calloused from weapon use. He raised his other hand, cradling my face, his fingers long and elegant and strong. His voice a burr of sound, he said, "I intend to make you regret that decision." Slowly, he brought his face down to mine, the motion disorienting. I could hit him. Knock him out. Throw him out of the house.

Beast laughed. *Good mate. Rick gone. Want this one.*

And then his lips touched mine. Slowly. Gently. Sliding back and forth on my mouth. I could taste him, his breath warm on my skin. I closed my eyes and sighed. Parted my mouth. Rested my face in his hand. And he pulled away, just as slowly. "I'll get the grill going."

Beast released me, stepped back, and I propped myself on the counter. "I'll bring the food." My voice sounded normal, not breathy and aroused, which was a surprise. *I intend to make you regret that decision. Crap.* I was in trouble. Beast huffed with laughter and withdrew, but I could still feel her claws in my mind, pressing and withdrawing, and the breath-stealing sensation of Beast in control of my body. I watched Bruiser as he left the house, his image still wavering and shadowy through the window.

I could have run. Could have locked myself in my room. Instead I pulled my cell and looked for a call from Rick. Nothing. Nada. Not a voice mail, not a text, zero, zip, zilch. I hit his number on speed dial and listened to the ring. Again, I was shunted to voice mail and hesitated a moment after the beep. "It's Jane. Call me. Please." Short, polite, not whiny. And I broke the connection. Through the window, I saw a gout of flame as Bruiser started the charcoal.

I dug out a half dozen small Idaho potatoes from among Evangelina's supplies, wrapped them in damp paper towels, and put them in the microwave. Spinach; tomato; pickles; sliced pickled onion; cold, crumbled bacon from a container in the fridge; some fresh sliced mushrooms I had picked up at the market; and goat cheese. I tossed it all together, with Evangelina's vinaigrette dressing to the side. When the potatoes were hot, though still not fully cooked, I took them from the microwave and wrapped them in aluminum foil. I twisted the tops off two beers, put four more into a cool pack with ice, took two steaks out of the fridge and dropped them into a ziplock baggie with some salt and a few pinches of Evangelina's premixed meat spices, set them into a separate cool pack, and set everything on a large platter. After a moment's thought, I added a third steak and an additional salad bowl in case Evangelina came home in time. Preparing dinner felt homey, settled, and far too comfortable after the kiss. I carried the raw steaks, potatoes, salads, and the beer outside. To Bruiser.

The sun was still above the horizon, casting long shadows, the day still humid and heavy with summer. Bruiser had lit citronella candles to fight off mosquitoes, and had rearranged the furniture from the side porches, bringing down a table from the second floor, moving deck chairs around to suit him. I had lived in the house for months and had never used the furniture.

Standing beside the flaming grill, he was watching me. Like a predator. Focused and alert, his body a silhouette against the brick wall enclosing the garden and the leafy plants thriving there. He turned away from me and his movements were economical, smooth as a dancer's. That was one of the gifts of vamp-blood sips—to live over a hundred years and still have the lithe body of a young man. He glanced over his shoulder once as I approached, holding my gaze.

I shouldn't be here. I should run. But I never ran, not from anything. Running from Bruiser would be . . . stupid. This was my house, my den, my territory. Bruiser wasn't a wild animal wanting to kill me or steal my hunting territory.

I set the potatoes to the side, in the grill's cooler coals, and

handed him a beer, our fingers brushing, mine cold, his hot
from the coals. Standing a foot apart, we sipped in silence, the
sun now a bright ball on the tops of the ancient buildings of
the Quarter. Bruiser leaned to the side and turned on a CD
player, a fusion of swing, Latin, and soul, and the mixed percussion of island influences, a number that thrummed into my
blood, making me want to move. But he sat in a deck chair,
and though my feet said, *dance*, I sat in the chair beside him,
both of us facing the setting sun as the music lazed its heated
way into the dusk and coals grew hot. Fixing supper with a
man wasn't something new. I did it all the time with Ricky Bo.
But this was different. This was Bruiser. And Rick, for whatever reason, had deserted me.

Discomfort wormed under my skin. I had no idea what to do
or say. There were things I wanted to know about Bruiser and
hadn't found the opportunity to ask, but he beat me to an opening conversational gambit, with, "Why do you have boulders in
the garden? Why were they so necessary that you included them
in your contract?" When I didn't answer, he added, "And why
are they broken? I saw the landscaper's bill and I know they
were whole, river-rounded boulders when they were put in."

Secrets. Things I couldn't say. So much for conversation.
Possible lies ran through my head, but I'm not good at keeping lies in order; I always make mistakes when I lie. So I had
to find a version of the truth I could share. When the silence
beneath the music built, Bruiser turned his head my way, waiting patiently.

I said, "There's a spell on them called *hedge of thorns*."
Truth. "The spell works best with boulders." Lie, but acceptable. "I meditate. The stones help me to slide into the proper
state easily." Truth. "If a client agrees to put in boulders, then
it's an indication that he's serious about fulfilling his part of
the contract and about paying me. I've been stiffed for the
bill in the past." Truth but stupid. Okay, I could live with it.
So far. I sipped, and wished, for the hundredth time, that my
skinwalker metabolism didn't burn alcohol out of my system
so fast. I could use some chemical relaxation right now.

"And the broken stones? You don't beat them with a
sledgehammer while meditating."

"The spell breaks them." Lie. Total lie. But better than *I
break them when I shift mass into and out of the stone when I
change into a larger or smaller creature.* Much better.

But I'd begun to wonder if calcite or aragonite might be better, easier to use than granite, being composed of calcium carbonate, which seemed structurally closer to human composition. Calcium carbonate was the most common mineral in caves with stalactites and stalagmites, and my earliest memories of shifting had begun in a cave with those formations—

"Jane?"

I jerked my gaze to him. "Sorry. Woolgathering." His quizzical look suggested that I was lying, or at least not telling a complete truth. "*Hedge of thorns* is a powerful spell. That black ring"—I pointed to the grass—"all around the stones is from one use. The stones contribute to the efficacy of the spell. Molly tried to explain it to me once, but I didn't follow." A mixture of truth and lies. I hated this. Bruiser studied my face, a half smile on his, seeming content to let a silence build between us. Which made me nervous for reasons that had less to do with lying than with the amused heat in his gaze.

Mentally, I floundered through the list of things I wanted to know about him and blurted out, "How old were you when you first drank vamp blood?"

Bruiser raised his head and hooted with laughter. "Good Lord, you do know how to cut to the heart of the matter, don't you, Jane Yellowrock? Why not ask me at what age I gave up my virginity?"

Before I could think, I said, "What age?" *Oh crap*. I felt Beast chuff a laugh as she twisted around my control in a lithe S-shape and stared at Bruiser with my eyes. As if he saw something different in me, Bruiser focused on me like a laser. I/ we/Beast stared back. *Look away is loss of dominance*, she thought at Bruiser. *I will not submit*. I scrabbled at control, reaching for Beast. For a moment it seemed I felt pelt and ribs beneath my palms. The sensation rocked me.

"I was sixteen," he said. "They were female vampires with a predilection for young boys." Beast chuffed with silent delight. "Do you want to know more? There will be a price if you do."

"No," I said, holding Beast silent. "I don't bargain blind."

Bruiser tilted his bottle back and drained the beer, his throat catching the evening light. Lifting the bottle away from his lips, he smiled at the sky and he said, "I'll tell you more. But I'll require a . . . dance as payment."

"Done." Bruiser laughed, and I shivered inside at the sound. My big mouth would be the death of me. But both

Beast and I loved to dance. "But the choice of the dance is mine." The words came from my mouth, sounding sensual and warm and . . . something that was not me. Not at all. Beast was close to the surface, powerful, aroused, and curious. *Curiosity killed the cat*, I thought at her.

Greater than five lives, she thought back at me. And I could feel her heat, her desire. Beast liked Bruiser. A lot. But I wasn't going to play around on Ricky Bo. With a mental move better attributed to the dojo than to conversation, I flipped Beast over and kicked. Though my body hadn't moved, I felt my foot impact her. She spat, spun, and raced out of reach, but I could feel her claws in me, painful, piercing.

Bruiser settled back, a smile on his face every bit as predatory as any expression Beast had ever worn. Dangerous. This was dangerous. And the worst part was that more than half of me didn't mind it at all.

He opened two more beers and handed one to me. I took it. "I was nearly seventeen. Bethany and Katie and Leo were living together most of the time, sharing a lair." He smiled at the sky, and the lower rim of sun slid below the tops of the buildings, throwing darkness over us, cloaking his expression in shadow, but not before I saw the memory of desire there. Potent. Strong. Even after nearly a hundred years. He glanced at me. "We danced there once, you and I." His voice was hot coals and brandy, warming and volatile when mixed together.

Something new blossomed deep in my belly, heating me, radiating outward, warming my skin. Electric sparks danced just beneath the surface of my flesh, pricking and sharp. This wasn't Beast. This was me, all me, half angry and brutal, half needy and lonely. Fear rolled through on top of the need, icy and tingling, mixing with the heat to make something I had no name for. "I remember," I said, not looking away from him. I remembered every step, every move, every undulation. *Crap, crap*, crap. *I'm in* such *big trouble.*

"Bethany and Katie thought a boy of sixteen and still a virgin was abnormal, but then, they come from more primitive times, violent by today's standards; boys became men much earlier in the past. And though it was the twentieth century, and the sexual development of males was very different from their time, they fancied me," he said, sounding very British in that moment. He drank down the beer, leaving only a few inches in the bottom.

"They made plans, they did. They got Leo's favorite female blood-servant drunk—deeply drunk—on brandy and gave her to him. He drank from her and when he was finished with her they brought me in to him. And he drank from me." Bruiser finished off the beer and opened a third. The sun caught on his skin, on the sheen of perspiration, glistening rosy and gold. When he offered me another beer I held up my full bottle, refusing. "The first time a Mithran mesmerizes and drinks from a human is . . . electric. An experience that can only be compared to a state of drunken euphoria. Drunk on champagne, the finest brandy, the best liquors, and joy and laughter and . . . desire. For a boy, not yet a man, it was overwhelming.

"When Leo finished, he gave me a sip of his blood." Bruiser swiveled his head to me, his eyes bright in the drawing night. Shadows crossed his face, stark and discordant against the reddish light thrown by the coals, and by the gold and vermilion sky overhead. "And he swore to protect me and keep me safe for as long as I lived." His mouth curled down, and I knew he was thinking that Leo was foresworn. His master had thrown him out.

His voice was amazed and impotent and empty when he ground out, "I have never since felt anything similar to that first taste. It was like lightning made alive. Like stars made liquid. Like the moon made into air to be breathed into my lungs to give me life." He took a breath, his chest moving as if with pain. "It was like riding a wild, icy river beneath a full moon." Bruiser finished off his third beer, staring at the evening sky.

"And the women took me from him." There was something in his tone when he said, "the women took me from him." It matched the melancholy mood I'd noted already. He slanted a look at me, the alcohol riding him hard, consumed so quickly on an empty stomach. "Do you want details?" he asked, his mouth turning up, his mood mercurial, a wicked gleam in his eyes.

"No," I said. I rotated my bottle, spinning it slowly in my fingers. Leo let them take him. Just like he let the cops accuse him today. Then he kicked Bruiser out. Leo was a son of a bitch. And even Beast knew this experience of Bruiser's was something painful and sexual and wicked and wrong. She didn't press for particulars, but hunched out of sight, letting me be alpha without a fight. Finally. "The coals are ready," I said, my eyes on the bottle, not looking his way.

"There is something about the sight of you that makes me want to tell you anyway." The threat hung between us as if balanced on the blade of a knife. "But I'm hungry." Bruiser stood and put two of the steaks on the grill. They sizzled and spat and my mouth started to water. The moment, whatever it was, was broken.

Relief and disappointment in equal measure flooded through me. I should have made him go to a hotel. This was such a mistake, letting him stay here, preparing dinner under the setting sun. Everything, a mistake. I finished my beer and Bruiser went back inside for more while the meat cooked. I wasn't so sure that letting him get rip-roaring drunk was a good idea, but I wasn't sure that stopping him would be any smarter. There were many ways to mourn, and Bruiser was mourning Leo, mourning a way of life currently, and perhaps forever lost to him. In which case he would age and die in a matter of years.

I still had to mourn my own past, the death of my father, and I had no idea how to go about grieving that ancient loss. So who was I to make suggestions? I kept my mouth shut.

Beast settled to her haunches deep inside me and groomed her claws, her tongue cleaning the curved, sharp edges. When Bruiser dished up the food, five minutes later, she withdrew in disgust, hissing, *Cooked dead meat.* I let her go, feeling relief at her departure.

The sky above was deep shades of vermilion, cerise, and plum when we cut into the steaks. The lights of the city blazed into the night, and the music grew torpid and languorous as Bruiser's selections changed, and we ate. And Beast crept back, like a big-cat through tall grasses, peering for prey, wanting . . . something. Something more.

When we were both done eating, the sky was plum, cerulean, and indigo, and Bruiser gathered up our plates, carrying them to the dark house. When he returned, he said, "I apologize for becoming maudlin." He turned up the music, lit more citronella candles to fight off the insects, and held out a hand. "Will it make up for my faux pas to offer you that dance I promised?"

My lips twitched. Bruiser wasn't one to wallow in his misery. I appreciated that. The mood between us lightened once again, and Beast hunched, tail twitching. I said, "My choice. Merengue, ballroom style."

Bruiser let a half smile show. "Club merengue is more fun, more relaxed." It was also much more sensual, erotic, and suggestive. Beast tightened all over at the thought, but no way was I dancing club merengue with Bruiser. When I shook my head, he sighed melodramatically and changed the CD to a four beat Latin dance number, something fast and sophisticated. He had a great collection of music and I wondered how much of his big suitcase had been packed with CDs. "Come, little girl," he said.

I started to dispute the *little girl* comment, but then, he *was* taller than I. I stood and placed my right hand into his left out to the side at eye level, his right went on my waist. He pulled me closer, his knee between my legs, our right hips touching. I started to protest, but, knees slightly bent, he led me into the merengue, our hips moving, swaying left and right in the closed position of the dance. "Not quite ballroom style," I murmured into his ear.

"No. Not quite." We stepped side to side for several measures, creating a wind, candle flames juddering and stuttering as we moved, our faces so close we might have kissed, eyes meeting in the dark. "Better. Much better than classical." Bruiser pushed me gently into a turn, and another, and another more intricate pretzel as we found our balance and rhythm. "The merengue was always a dance of the masses," he said, his words matching the beat, "of mating and loving and drums beating a wildness into the air, into the blood. It has always been hot island nights under the stars and firelight and the spiced liquor of love." He took my free hand so we were swirling around each other and under our arms, releasing one hand when needed, retaking it when a move was completed.

Beast liked the dance, panting into my mind, her breath warm as the music. Content to be beta, seeming content to be led. "No stars here," I said as he turned me, his mouth at my ear.

"But mating and loving . . ." He slid both hands to my hips, the sensual rocking of hips up and down and around in a figure eight. ". . . we play at that with every step, every move."

The rhythm was constant but the pace of the moves sped and slowed, our hips meeting and withdrawing, meeting and withdrawing in a dance that shouldn't have been this sensual, this intense. Beast nudged my hips, pressing forward against Bruiser's pelvis, easing back. Rocking left and right, followed by a rotating gyre. Not something I had ever done with a partner, but only when dancing alone on a crowded dance floor.

Beast hummed in my ear, *"Mine . . ."*

Bruiser pulled me closer, the suggestion pure sex, a physical demanding. "There is so much more between us than play, Jane."

I should have tucked tail and run. But I didn't. And it wasn't Beast holding me here, but Bruiser's hands low on my hips. One hand rose, sliding up my side, slowly, so slowly, just missing the outside of my breast, which sent electric pulses through me. My breath sped. My heart raced.

A century of seduction teased his hand along my collarbone and shoulder, down my arm to my hand, which he clasped, holding me with his eyes all the way. Challenging me. The look a dare. The hand on my hip slid around, pulled me closer, resting low on my back at the top of my buttocks, massaging with every step.

"No. Play is all there is," I whispered back. "I have Rick."

Bruiser's eyes came alight and he showed teeth in a wicked smile. My blood pounded, following the percussive beat of the music. Our skin was slick with sweat from the humid night and the glowing coals, our hands sliding through perspiration, flesh heated beneath. "But he is gone. And I am here." There was an overt anger in the words, and I heard what he didn't say. Leo was gone too. And Bruiser had no one else.

His hands tilted my pelvis up against him, leading me to a sudden stop. We stood, poised, chest to chest, our breaths matched and rapid, a single beat of immobility, then, slowly, slower than the fast-paced beat of the song, he stepped to the formal, closed position where he held me, his breath on my mouth, my chest to his, our pelvises melded together, his thigh pressing intimately against me.

"I'm here and I want you. And you want me." My eyes were locked to his in the dim light of the candles, close and intense. Bruiser dipped his head as if to kiss me, his mouth a breath away, taunting, teasing, and then stepped to the side, resuming the dance.

He led us into a series of turns as the music built, rose, and fell. Our pelvises thrust and withdrew, curling closer and away. The urgency of our movements increased as the musical number drew to a close, the drums rising to a fever pitch. He thrust me away and under one arm and back, his lead demanding

as the beat. Twirled me hard, slinging my hair around us, and
slammed me back. And we ended the dance with my spine
against the front of his body, his arms and mine all wrapped
around me. Prisoning me. His hands on the flat of my stomach,
under my tee, skin to skin.

We were breathing hard, our hearts beating harder. Bruiser's face was near my ear, his breath moving my hair back and
forth. My braid had come partly undone, the wisps and longer
strands wrapped around us, sticking to our skin, hot and damp
with sweat.

Beast purred deep within me. Satisfied yet wanting more of
this potent music, this powerful dance. *It is alive, like the hunt,
like the play with prey*, she thought.

Cat and mouse, I thought back. *But which of us is the
mouse?* I was afraid it was me.

The music changed, a slower number beginning. I tried to
step away, but Bruiser held us still for the first two beats of
the measure and then stepped to the side. Pivoted my body
around and led me into the steps, to the side, slowly, then back
and forth in a quick-quick pattern.

I recognized a bolero, danced to a slow rumba rhythm, a
conga and bongos providing percussion. The bolero was a deliberate, measured, romantic dance, always performed staring
into the partner's eyes. The heat of the merengue began to
segue into a different kind of heat, deeper, more intense, more
hungry. *Rick is not here*, Beast thought. *Rick no longer pro-
tects his territory. We find another, stronger predator/mate*. She
kicked out, slamming me away, and undulated against Bruiser.

I needed to stop this. I needed to get away. But Beast
wanted more. Much more. Damn Ricky Bo. Why hadn't he
called? He could have called. . . . And damn Beast for reminding me that big-cats don't mate for life.

Bruiser's hand moved against my back, along my spine
with each slow belly ripple, each slow turn, and I could feel
the pressure and heat and texture of it. I couldn't pull away.
"I want you," he murmured. "I want you in my bed, under me.
Moving like this. I want you with me forever."

Rick had never said that. Rick had never said the *forever*
word. Rick never said the *love* word. Inside, something in me
broke, silent and wounded. *Only a month*, I thought back at
the broken part. *We've been together only a month. And Bruiser's had a century to perfect the art of seduction. To learn the*

moves to make and the words to say to get inside a girl's pants. He's looking for a place to be, searching for a new den to claim. Deserted and alone, just like me. But he's a blood-servant. I can't forget that. His allegiance is to Leo, even after Leo kicked him out.

The emptiness in his eyes called to me. Lost and lonely, it sank its teeth into me, hooked its claws into me, and claimed a small place inside my soul. And I let him lead me, knowing it was dangerous, knowing it was foolish, knowing this might be taking me where I didn't want to go. And inside me, something else wept and raged.

The turns of the bolero were almost stately, but the position and movement of our bodies was sensual, sinuous, supple. And he never released my gaze, holding me, holding Beast, with his eyes as firmly as his hands.

The darkness grew, the moon below the horizon, the candles flickering as a slow wind rose. The steps pulled us together and away, only millimeters apart but it seemed so much farther until we met again in a clench that bespoke sexual, teasing, unsatisfied need. My back to his chest again, his hands moved to my abdomen, caressing, leaving aching need in the wake of his hands. As the song drew to a close, he turned me to face him and his hand lifted, cupped my jaw, sliding along my neck, shoulder, down my waist to my hip. He cupped my bottom and drew me closer. In, up against him. Against his hardness.

And the lights went on in the house behind us. "Jane?"

I jerked away. Breaking his hold on me. The heat between us throbbed once with need. Evangelina was home. *Crap.* And, *Thank God . . .*

"Back here," I called. "Streak's on the grill." Shaking, I opened the cool pack and laid the last steak over the dying coals, pushed the last potato over so it would be heated evenly, and tossed the leftover salad. It was wilted but the night was dark. Maybe she wouldn't notice.

"Jane," Bruiser said, his voice close. I stiffened and the coals flared up again in front of me, the heat searing. I stepped back from it quickly. Into his arms. He closed them around me, trapping me. "This is not over, between us." When I didn't reply, he said, "Nod if you understand."

I nodded and he stepped away just as Evangelina opened the door and walked out onto the porch; someone was behind her. It was Tyler. Tyler stopped on the porch, as if surprised, and the two men measured one another for a moment. "We only marinated three steaks," Bruiser said. "We'll need to get another from the fridge."

"I've eaten," Tyler said, his voice betraying no emotion.

"Well I haven't," Evangelina said. "I'm starved. Beer?" She wrinkled her nose. "I'll get a bottle of wine. Beer or wine, red or white, Tyler?"

"Wine, please. Red."

"I have a lovely Spanish Garnacha that will do nicely with steak," she said as she whirled and returned to the house, leaving us three outside.

"I wondered if you came here," Tyler said in his careful, noncommittal tone.

"Safe port in a storm." Bruiser gave a negligent shrug. "Isn't that what you called it? How are the negotiations going? Anything I can help with?"

"Negotiations?" I asked, not happy being compared to a safe body of water.

Beast is not safe, she said to me, insulted.

To me, Bruiser said, "Tyler has taken over security measures at the council house and at Leo's clan home. And all other of my duties, I would imagine." Bruiser gave a slight smile, cool and collected. "I imagine security concerns have been pushed into the background with the police investigation and the arrival of the DipSec people."

DipSec. Diplomatic Security. Got it.

"Not at all. I spoke with Leo only a half hour ago. He wants *you* to handle the witch negotiations, and to move ahead briskly. His words." The tone was scornful, mocking, and though I didn't know what was going on exactly, it was clear that there was bad blood between the two men. Grudgingly, Tyler added, "Katie is being cared for by Sabina in the protective custody of the clan home. She is well, though still in the devoveo of healing." That sounded like Leo's message too, though Tyler didn't specify so.

Bruiser inclined his head with a falsely pleasant air, but I could feel the satisfaction in him. He took the job as some kind of affirmation from Leo, and maybe it was. Tyler seemed unhappy about it. "Has Leo fed from you yet, or are you still second to me?"

Tyler almost snarled, "Your prime place is still secure."

I had thought the men friends, or, if not pals, at least good

coworkers, comfortable acquaintances. I was wrong. Tyler
turned his cold stare to me and I recalled the body search that
had ended with Tyler on the ground and his windpipe in my
hands. Tyler was remembering it too, and he wasn't someone
who forgot a disgrace or a slight no matter how minor. His
gaze dropped to my breasts and along my body, an insulting
perusal, and back to my eyes, promising that a rematch would
end differently. We understood one another perfectly, like two
junkyard dogs understand one another without a bark or a
snarl being exchanged. I had embarrassed him in front of Leo,
so he wanted me dead. Simple as a dogfight. I laughed softly
and said, "Get in line, Sugar. Get in line." Rage, icy as a mountain stream seemed to roil from him. Beast hissed, close in my
mind.

Tyler's eyes sparkled with hate and a promise of retribu-
tion, but before he could act on it, Evangelina opened the
door and stepped out, carrying a wine carafe and two glasses,
a plate, utensils, and a happy, chatty attitude that shut down
the malicious emotional tides. They swirled like undercurrents
through the next hour of chitchat but never resurfaced, and
Tyler left before ten, pleading a busy day working for Leo. It
was a last jibe at Bruiser, who smiled and lifted his fifth—or
was it his sixth?—bottle of beer in drunken good humor. As
soon as Tyler's car roared off, Bruiser excused himself and
went up the stairs. Evangelina looked at me, perplexed. "Was
it something I said?"

"No. They're just being pissant men." And with that I went
to bed too, locking my bedroom door against a possible return of Bruiser's amorous interest. I stood under the shower
as the cold water sluiced off the sweat of the dance and my
arousal, and I wished for icy mountain well water to stand
under instead of the South's tepid version. Feeling better, I
pulled on shorts and a tee. Having guests was a pain, I thought,
as I threw myself across my bed and closed my eyes. Maybe I
should invest in some pj's.

It was after two a.m. Saturday morning when I woke with a
start, realizing that I had left the dishes for Evangelina. And
then I heard the sound that had woken me.

CHAPTER 14

And He Ripped off My Shirt

Something had scratched at the front door. I rolled, taking up a vamp-killer from the bedside table, shoved stakes into my hair, and palmed my nine mil as I slid my toes through a pair of flops. I moved through the house in darkness, drawing on Beast's night vision to make my way. I heard a creak from the top of the stairs and, even though it was probable that no one could see me in the dark, I held up a hand. "Wait," I whispered.

"My wards went off," Evangelina whispered back. "Something got in through the delivery slot in the front door, where I left a passageway for mail."

I had never paid attention to the mail delivery slot, the old metal painted to match the wood. I sidled that way, placing my feet carefully, and saw a flat envelope, the size I might use to send a birthday card. Placing my head against the wall where I could see out through a clear pane in the stained-glass window of the door, I saw a running form down the street. Beast woke with a start. *Hunt!*

"Don't touch the envelope. I'll be back." I ripped open the door and raced up the middle of the well-lit street. There was no keeping to the shadows. No hiding. If the prey looked back and saw me, so what? I lost the flops and took to the sidewalk, my bare soles blistering. Three blocks later I had Jackson Square in my sights, the old cathedral lit up like Disneyland. I puffed to a stop. I had lost him. Or her. Some women run like men. Some Olympic runners. Some college runners. I bent over, hands on knees, breathing hard. The runner's scent lost beneath New Orleans's potent sensory brew.

I had hurt my bare feet, what might be a stone bruise on the left heel and a shallow cut on the ball of the right. Ignoring a covey of businessmen coming out of a bar, I scent-searched, mouth open, drawing air in over my tongue and the roof of my mouth and through my nose, the way cats do. Parsing the scents. But there were too many, new and familiar, strong like gasoline and exhaust and vomit and urine and weaker scents like rats, feral cats, and . . . Leo Pellissier.

I whirled, seeing only a blur as he attacked. Threw up my left arm, catching both of his. Knocking them high. Ducked under. Stabbed up with the vamp-killer, a clean, swift stroke. The blade passed through his clothing and scored his side. He grunted with surprise. I pivoted on my right foot, smelling his blood, cold and potent on the night air.

Belated adrenaline thudded through me. Beast roared up through my subconscious. Lending me strength, speed. Damping my pain.

Lamplight caught Leo's face, gleamed on his fangs. Two inches of killing ivory. He brought up a hand, stabbing claws at my side. I slid left, avoiding injury, my body a fluid motion, making a C shape. The knife whipped toward his abdomen.

Leo bent forward. Throwing his midsection back. Avoiding the blade, shimmering silver in the night. My knee came up as I slid past, spinning. Slammed into his face. *A sucker move and he fell for it.*

Bone and cartilage crunched against my knee. A fang nicked me as I pivoted away. Blood splattered over me, thick and viscous, stinging where it touched me. He whipped around, eyes catching the light, pupils inhumanly wide, vamped out, black in scarlet sclera.

Head back, he screamed. And I smelled the blood that was on his clothes. Old and dried, fresh and still damp. Katie's blood. A lot of Katie's blood.

Then he was gone. I whirled around, seeing and discounting the businessmen, standing mouths agape, like so much stupid prey. Seeing the cop standing at the corner, trying to draw his gun. Fumbling. I spun again and leaped over a gate into a narrow, cobblestone passageway between buildings. It stank of kerosene and fertilizer. I raced along it, slipping on moss growing between the stones, pain shooting up from both feet.

I slid through huge-leafed banana plants and marijuana plants growing in pots in the tiny garden in back. And out a wider passageway, bounding over the gate, one palm on top, supporting the leap. Within minutes I was racing down the street in front of the house, which was lit inside and out. And I smelled Leo. He had been nearby when I raced from the front door. He had been watching the house, watching me. Or watching Bruiser. And, full of crazy-Katie's blood, the half-nutso predator had followed the moving target. Which might have been the letter deliveryman, had I not gotten in the way. *Crap.*

Breath heaving, I sucked warm, moist air, bent over, the H&K still in one fist. I had never taken the safety off, which was a good thing, or I might have loosed a shot during the run. In my other hand was the vamp-killer, the silver plating stinking slightly from contact with vamp blood.

Leo had fed from or fought Katie again. Whatever had happened between them tonight, it had pushed him over the edge. Again. I tracked his scent to the house across the street. It had a convenient, low, brick wall, where someone could sit in the shadows, loitering undetected. Leo wasn't the only one who had used it to keep an eye on the house.

I didn't have a key to my side gate, so I limped to the front door and knocked, feeling the house wards buzz against me, recognizing me. My skin glistened with sweat and blood had trailed down my side, soaking my clothes, and down my leg, to puddle on the ground. The door opened. Bruiser stood there wearing sweatpants riding low on his hips and a lose tank with huge armholes. His arms were bare, revealing well-cut musculature, which would have been a nice sight, if I hadn't been hurting. He was scowling, which wasn't so nice. But the envelope was still in front of the door, untouched as well as I could see.

"You're bleeding," he spat.

I limped in the door and closed it behind me. "Get something to wash away the blood outside. Turn off the lights. A cop saw me fighting and I'm too recognizable. I'd rather not answer questions."

Evangelina, her eyes wide, was standing at the kitchen doorway holding a serving platter with mugs; I smelled hot tea, raw sugar, and real cream. "Son of a witch on a stick." She set the tray onto the bottom step that led to the second floor, asking, "What got you?"

"Leo," I said. Bruiser swore foully and raced to the front door. "Don't worry. I didn't stake him."

"I'll get my first-aid kit," Evangelina said. A witch who traveled with her own first-aid kit struck me as hilarious. I couldn't help the laughter that escaped, hysterical and wild, as adrenaline broke down into toxins and flooded my system with the biological equivalent of poison. She checked her wards, asking, "Vampire blood?"

I looked down at myself and saw the blood. There was an awful lot of it. "Some. I think most of it's mine," I managed, huffing between guffaws that seemed to be getting worse.

"Take her to her shower," Evangelina ordered. "I'll take care of the blood." She took the vamp-killer from my hand and held it to the side. Seeing the witch holding the blade in two fingers brought my laughter up harder and Evangelina shook her head in worry. "Hot water. Not all vampire blood is acidic and poisonous but some is."

"Humans drink it," Bruiser said in surprise.

"And some blood-servants don't thrive. And some vampires can't reproduce except with the bite. And some scions don't wake up sane. Ever."

"Leo drank from Katie," he said, thinking. "Dead blood can make unstable vamps more unstable."

There was something important in the words, but before I could make sense of it, Bruiser picked me up, his body heated and dry against my cooling sweat. My chuckles stopped as if cut off with a knife. The touch of his skin sent my mind skittering and skipping, like a rock spun out over still water. He carried me through my bedroom to my bath and set me on the shower seat. He tossed a huge bath towel over the door, up high, out of the way of the spray, and turned on the water, holding his hand under the flow while I watched, silent, breathless. From my run. Not from the sight of him. No way.

Bruiser turned the hot water on me and steam burst up from the stall floor and walls, beating me. Drenching me. Heating me from the outside in. Pressing my clothes against my body. Stinging in the deeper cuts and making them bleed afresh, especially the one on my knee. The fang wound. And the one on my side. Claw marks, not deep but long and tearing and bleeding profusely. My left side, above my collarbone. He'd been aiming to rip out my throat. I shivered in delayed response. The Master of the City had tried to kill me. Again.

But this time it wasn't personal. Simply a predator-prey response. He saw me run, and gave chase. I threw back my head and laughed again.

Blood swirled and flowed around my bare feet and Bruiser's, thick and scarlet, then thinner, weakened by the water flow. I shivered harder, looking up from our feet as Bruiser knelt in front of me, his face on a level with mine. Eyes piercing as blades. Hair and clothes plastered to his skin. Water running over his body like caressing hands.

He traced my limbs, looking for injuries, raised my arms, pulled me forward, so he could see my back, lifted my shirt to check my stomach and studied the lacerations from Leo's claws. Methodical. Careful. Asexual as a medical technician or nurse. He sat back and held up my feet to see the black asphalt stains and cuts. He winced and took up a bar of soap. And washed my feet.

My laughter stopped abruptly. Tears he couldn't see because of the shower water gathered and fell as shock replaced the last vestiges of hysteria. *He's washing my feet.* His hands moved the soap over my arches, toes, heels and up my calves, massaging and stroking, bubbles rinsing away as soon as they formed. When he was done, he cleaned the fang wound in my thigh, knowing what it was. He had to know what it was. He'd had plenty.

He shook his head as something flashed through his eyes and was gone. "Are you all right?" he asked, his lips moving, his voice lost beneath the roar of the pounding water, his eyes holding mine, requiring an answer. I nodded. "Can you get your clothes off, or do you need my help?" Still no seduction to his words or his tone. Worry. Fear. Anger beneath the surface of that. But no seduction.

But he had washed my feet. And his hands had been . . . not casual. Not at all. "I can do it," I murmured, water pouring into my mouth as I spoke. Bruiser nodded once, the approval of a master sergeant to a trooper. He started to stand and my eyes followed him up. He stopped, midmotion. Becoming as still as the vampire who gave him prolonged life. Slowly, Bruiser leaned forward, gripped my head in both hands. And lowered his face to mine.

He kissed me. Heat arced between us. Sizzling like lightning. A breath left my lungs empty, wanting. I groaned, the sound lost beneath the roar of the water. He yanked me to him, my back arching, his mouth punishing. A bonfire of need exploded within me. I reached for him, his arms and neck slick with water. A rosy glow seemed to envelop me. He leaned into me where I sat, crushing me against the stall wall. I dug in with my fingers and nails, holding him against me. Shower water poured over our faces, our lips.

Liquid and burning, heat flared between us, wet as the shower, intense, building like the steam that billowed around us. He lifted me, one hand sliding under my bottom and taking my place on the shower seat. Pulling me to his lap, my legs around him.

And he ripped off my shirt. Tossed it to the floor. His hands and mouth were everywhere, sucking, pulling, stroking, biting. I arched harder to him, hearing my voice in the distance, buried beneath the roar of the water, "Yes, yes. Please."

I don't know how I heard the bathroom door open, but I did. *Evangelina!* Beast fast, I pushed away from Bruiser and grabbed the towel, covering myself. I pushed open the shower door and stepped out in a cloud of steam, shutting it behind me.

Unable to meet Evangelina's eyes, I said, "Let me get dried off. I'll meet you in the kitchen." I don't know what she saw in my face, but she left the room without speaking, the door clicking shut softly behind her as bloody water drained off me to the clean floor.

I dropped to the toilet seat and sat. In the shower stall, the water went off. A long silent moment later, Bruiser opened the stall door and stepped out. Dripping, he stared down at me as water sluiced down his face and body, puddling on the tile floor. "This *will* happen," he said, a roil of anger beneath his tone.

I shook my head, breaking his stare. He said, "*It will.*" And he left the bath, wet footprints trailing him, his clothes molded to his body.

I shut the door and removed my shorts, tossing them and the now bloody towel both into the stall on top of my T-shirt. I held a folded washcloth to the wound in my knee and another to my collarbone. The bleeding soaked through the wash-cloths and I added another, pressing to stop the flow, knowing that the terrycloth would give the blood plenty of surface to clot on.

I could shift to heal the wounds, and shift back, but there

was no way to explain it to my visitors. Ten minutes later, the flow had stopped. And my heartbeat had slowed and steadied. In the bedroom, I pulled on a pair of shorts, a tee, and my robe. Tightened the belt ruthlessly.

Embarrassed but not willing to show it, I marched to the kitchen and plopped onto a chair at the table, one hand holding each cloth. It was an ungainly march but it was all the pride I had left at the moment.

Bruiser was nowhere to be seen. Evangelina didn't look up when I entered, as if allowing me the privacy I needed, though I'd never thought her capable of such delicacy of feeling. She pushed away the cloth on my knee, murmuring, "Let me see." She prodded and pushed at the wound, which welled with blood. She replaced the cloth and worked my leg, as if checking the joint and tendons. "Does this hurt? This? How about this?" I said no to each query and she opened a sterile packet to remove a long metallic probe. Which she inserted into the wound.

I hissed and gripped the chair seat with my free hand to keep myself from slapping her, holding my chest wound tight enough to hurt myself. "Do you have the faintest idea what you're doing?" I asked.

"Not really," she lied with a small smile. "I just like hurting you. It's deep, but it feels like it missed bone and tendon. It needs some stitches."

"No," I said, ungraciously. "Put some of that antibiotic stuff on it and tape it." I didn't want to worry about stitches when I shifted next. And it was starting to really hurt. And I was mortified about the shower with Bruiser. Could I be any more lewd? Or stupid? I had a bad feeling I could. "No stitches. No doctor." I pulled the robe open and removed the pad.

Evangelina shrugged and said, "Let me see the ribs."

Evangelina hissed and said something under her breath. I thought it was a witch curse, a bad one I'd heard Molly use once. I tended to bring out the foul language in my friends. At the thought of *friend*, I looked up to see Evangelina staring at the parallel, slashing tears on my chest. There were two above the collarbone and two below, angling up, as if Leo had tried to reposition his hand midstrike to take out my throat. He'd come mighty close.

"Don't bite my head off," she said gently, "but you've

got a lot of scars here. And no signs of surgical or medical intervention."

The scars of previous vamp attacks were fine lines, the scaring all that was left of what would have been fatal attacks. The nonmortal ones hadn't scarred at all. I pressed the pad back over the wound. "I heal fast. I've got extra large sterile bandages in my own first-aid kit." I pointed to a drawer. "If you'll get me a large one and smear antibiotic on the cuts, I'll be fine."

"*I* won't," she blew out a frustrated breath. "But you are a stubborn . . . woman."

The pause said that Evangelina knew I wasn't human, but wasn't certain what form of supernat I was. When she didn't pursue the get-thee-to-a-doctor-y comment or the you-are-not-human train of thought, and went instead to find my bandages, I relaxed. "You're okay," I said, "for a ballsy witch."

"And you're okay too, for an ornery whatever-you-are." She peeled the backing from an adhesive bandage and squirted antibiotic ointment onto my wounds. Carefully, she laid the bandage over them, pressing the edges to seal against my skin. "It's still bleeding," she said, and lifted my hand, placing it over the wound, applying pressure. When she took her hand away, I continued the pressure so she could bandage my foot. When she was done, Evangelina washed her hands at the sink, her back to me. "I used to worry about Molly being friends with you. I still do. But more because of the lifestyle and the danger you seem to attract than because of who you are, intrinsically." She turned back to me, surveying me in the kitchen chair, in my borrowed white robe that came with the house. "Yes. You'll do."

I warmed from the comments and smiled at her, a small, uncertain smile.

"Shall we see what the envelope holds?" When I nodded once, she asked, "Why didn't you want us to touch it?"

"Explosives. Poisons. Anthrax." I stood. "Let me get dressed."

Evangelina's eyebrows went up. "Explosives. Poisons. Anthrax," she quoted. "My, my. I'll look it over for signs of magical tampering. From a distance, of course."

"Good idea," I said, though I hadn't smelled any magic either. When I was dressed in jeans, a sweatshirt, and a bra—

protective clothing—I met Evangelina at the door. Bruiser, dressed in jeans and a loose tee was squatting before the envelope, studying it. Not looking at him, I knelt beside him and bent as if to see it up close, but I was scent-searching. I breathed in, through mouth and nose. And was surprised when I smelled Girrard DiMercy.

I sat back. "No explosives, no chemicals. I'll take it into the yard to open it." Neither of them asked how I knew it was explosive-free, and I didn't volunteer enlightenment. I carefully lifted the envelope and carried it to the side door and into the yard. Behind me, the porch light came on and I was aware of them standing side by side behind the closed door. Angling my body so the prevailing wind would carry anything within away from me and away from the house, I opened the flap. Three photographs were inside. "It's okay," I said without looking up. "I'll be inside in a minute."

The photos were originals, one black and white and two in color; one color shot arrested my attention. The tints were wasted by time and sunlight, the oranges, yellows, and reds bright and glaring, the blues and greens muted. It was a picture of Bruiser and a blurred form, maybe Leo, both dressed in clothing from the early sixties, standing over the body of an animal. Or, not an animal. A werewolf. It was caught in half human, half wolf form, and from the distortion, it was changing, or trying to. From the blood, it was dead or dying. Leo and Bruiser were both holding hunting rifles.

The background was not south Louisiana, but a hilly locale. A Land Rover stood in the background, dust covered, rock formations behind it. The photograph wasn't proof of murder, but it was suggestive of some kind of crime.

The black and white photograph was even older, a posed shot of a woman, probably mixed race, with sparkling eyes, full lips, high cheeks, and tip-tilted eyes. Her black hair was piled up in waves and curls that looked artless and had probably taken a maidservant hours to accomplish, and tresses draped to her shoulders as if accidentally fallen there from the touch of a careless but loving hand. She wore a dress from another time, all white lace and silks and a bow under her breasts. She was beautiful in a way I'd never be. I often wanted to hate women like that, but she looked so happy, so in love, it was impossible to dredge up negative emotion. I turned the photo over and read the faint handwriting on the back. "From Magnolia Sweets to Leo, my love."

The third photo was actually four digital shots, printed out together on computer paper. They were of Rick. In one, he was standing in the breezeway of a hotel, a thin slice of the cityscape in the background. He was dressed in biker gear, one hand braced high on a wall, one knee bent, in a negligent, masculine pose. He was with a girl, his hand on her nape, as if pulling her into a kiss. She was wearing a short skirt and gold, six-inch stilettos, her upper body hidden. In another, he was kissing her, his back to the camera, only her legs showing. In another, he was following her into a hotel room. She was redheaded, petite, delicate, sexy, and feminine. All the things I'd never be. And this woman I did hate with a spear of pain that stabbed through my chest.

The fourth shot was Rick with a woman in a setting with a trellis and window basket of flowers. In this one, long black hair hung to her thighs, her arms up and twined around him, languorous. Safia. He was kissing her. Distantly, I noted that the woman's body size and skin tones matched in all four photos. Safia had worn a red wig to meet Rick at a hotel?

My breath ached when I drew it in, belatedly, painfully. A reasonable voice in my head said, *He's undercover. He has a job to do. It's only a job.* A less reasonable voice that had angry Beast-overtones said, *Mine.* And clawed at my heart. But I'd just narrowly avoided sex in the shower with Bruiser. I had no reason or right to feel pain or betrayal.

I folded the paper carefully, so the photos didn't crease, and tucked it into my jeans pocket. I stuffed my feelings away too, without looking at them, and shoved the voices, the reasonable one and the angry one, deeper. I had a job to do.

I went back into the house and placed the black and white photograph in front of Bruiser, who was sitting with Evangelina at the table, sipping tea. I added sugar and cream to the third prepared mug and sat across from them.

Bruiser studied the photo and his lips turned up in a winsome smile, the kind people give when presented with a remembrance of an enchanted time. "I remember the day this was taken. There was this photographer, Ernest something."

"Ernest J. Bellocq?" I asked. I'd seen his work before. He took photos of Storyville and other neighborhoods in New

Orleans for years, and had been the first, and so far as I knew, the only, photographer to capture vamp images on film until digital photography became common. Vamps had never imaged well on silver used in the photographic process.

"Yes, that's the name. Maggie was the sweetest thing I'd ever seen. I was half in love with her when I was a young lad." I laid the color photo in front of him, and Bruiser's face changed. He swore and looked at me, his face closed off, thinking. Calculating? Concocting a story? Maybe.

"No one was with Leo and me when we made this kill." He made it sound like a legitimate hunt, not a murder, but I kept my mouth shut on the comment. "So who took this and why did he bring it to you?"

"Someone with an agenda. Someone who knows most of what's going on and wants me to figure out the rest for him."

"Without giving himself away," Evangelina said.

CHAPTER 15

Good Nose on Ugly Dog

I looked at the sky out the window and judged that it was several hours until dawn on Saturday. I hadn't slept a full eight hours in days and my eyes felt gritty and dry, my body jumpy and strained, my mind fuzzy and overloaded. I needed a good sleep or a good hunt. I needed to inspect Safia's body in the morgue with animal senses to see/smell what I'd missed in human form. I needed to scout vamp HQ with better than human senses too, but with the security cameras on twenty-four/seven that was going to be impossible. And I needed to get away from Evangelina and Bruiser. Far away.

Ignoring my guests, I booted up the laptop, pulled up a city map, and found the location of the morgue. I finished off my tea, closed the laptop, and stood, the chair barking across the floor. "I'm going out. See you in the morning." I intercepted the look my two houseguests exchanged but decided to pretend it hadn't happened. In my bedroom, I grabbed a fetish necklace, made sure the gold nugget necklace was in place, repacked Beast's travel bag, and added a handwritten note with Molly's phone number on it in case I ended up in the pound.

Beast growled once and put her head on her paws, shutting her eyes, not interested in what I was doing. Maybe a little miffed. She could be part of this excursion if she wanted, but Beast was jealous of any time I spent in an animal form other than her own.

The two visitors were still sitting at the kitchen table, talking softly, when I walked back through, which meant that taking a stack of my own steaks from the fridge and a bag of Snickers wasn't going to happen, which just brought home to me the fact that my life wasn't my own anymore. Which really sucked the red off all my candy. I frowned at them, hoping they would take the hint that they were being pains in the butt, but they just sat silent and watched me. I was proud when I didn't slam the door, and the murmur of their voices picked up when I was outside.

I was grouchy and irritated and acting like an idiot. I knew it would pass, but for now I rode the annoyance, letting it power me as I helmeted up and took off on Bitsa, leaving behind the itchy, uncomfortable feelings left over from taking a shower with Bruiser. I wove over to Langenstein's on Arabella Street for meat, forgetting it wasn't open all night, and, even more frustrated, drove around for half an hour, finally stopping at a twenty-four-hour fast-food place and buying a bucket of chicken. Cooked. But they might have called the cops if I'd ordered it raw. I strapped it to my bike, stopped for gasoline, bottled water, and candy bars, and wove around until I found the morgue.

The New Orleans Coroner's Office and Forensic Center was on Martin Luther King Boulevard, in a busy, well-traveled part of town. The building was three stories of new, post-Katrina construction, well lighted, and patrolled by cops. And for the moment, a van was parked at a loading bay in the back, the doors of the van open, the loading bay brightly lit. Two cops stood near a corner stealing a smoke.

There was no wooded place to shift nearby, which wasn't helpful; I needed privacy and calm to call on my magics. I located a private home with a recently planted flower and ornamental tree garden and pulled Bitsa off the street into the shadows under a short Japanese maple tree. I knew that she would be okay where I left her—one good thing about having a police presence nearby and a witchy locking system on the bike was that Bitsa wouldn't get stolen. Standing in the shadows, I listened, scented, and watched for people, security cameras, and anything else that might cause me trouble. Satisfied that I was alone and unobserved, I strapped on the travel bag, opened the bucket of chicken, undressed, and pulled the fetish necklace out. The bones and teeth of a female bloodhound clacked and rattled.

I had acquired the bones from a taxidermist I frequented in the mountains. I had asked him to keep an eye out for any large mammal carcass he might find, and he had called me several times over the years, having acquired dead animals he thought I might like. He had stripped the flesh from the bones and teeth and strung them onto necklaces for me, believing that I was into some strange voudon practice. I had never set him straight. Someday the strange things people believed about me were gonna come back and bite me. Hard. I set the bloodhound necklace around my neck and sat in the midst of ferns, protected from eyes on the street by azaleas and big-leafed hostas. And I ripped off the bandages Evangelina had so carefully applied.

I had never tried the bloodhound form before, but I needed a really good nose right now. I closed my eyes and blew out hard, searching for a calm center, which eluded me for a number of reasons: Beast didn't like it when I shifted into any creature other than big-cat, my emotions were ragged and on edge because of Bruiser, I was angry because Rick hadn't called, and seeing the stupid photos. And getting naked in my own walled garden was one thing, but getting naked in a private yard was very different. It took too long, but eventually I was calm enough to feel my skinwalker energies rise.

I held the necklace and relaxed, listening to the night breezes, feeling the pull of the three-day, sharp-pointed moon, still thin, far overhead. I felt the beat of my heart in my throat, in the palms of my hands, and the soles of my feet as I slowed the functions of my body, slowed my heart rate, let my blood pressure drop, my muscles relax, as if I were going to sleep. I lay on the ground beneath the trees in the humid air, leafy ferns a cushion.

Mind slowing, I sank inside, my consciousness falling away, all but the purpose of this hunt. As always, I set that purpose into the lining of my skin, into the depths of my brain, so I wouldn't lose it when I *shifted*, when I *changed*. I dropped deeper. Lower. Into the darkness inside where broken, painful memories danced in a gray world of shadow, blood, and doubt. I heard a drum beating a measured beat, steady and slow, smelled herbs and the scent of fresh smoke. The night wind seemed to cool and freshen. As I dropped deeper, I sought the fetish and the memory of form and structure hidden in the inner snake lying inside the bones and teeth of the necklace, the coiled, curled snake, resting deep in the cells, in the remains of the marrow.

I took up the snake and I dropped within, like water flowing across a sandy streambed, like sleet peppering the ground with a bitter icy *shush* of sound. Grayness enveloped me, sparkling and cold as the world fell away. And I was in the gray place of the change.

Beast was sulking far out of sight, and my mind was empty and private and alone.

My breathing deepened. Heart rate sped up. And my bones . . . slid. Skin rippled. Hair, brown and black and sleek, sprouted. Pain slid like a knife between muscle and bone. My nose and jaw compressed and grew forward. My nostrils drew deep. My shoulders and hips ground and scraped as bone flowed into new shapes.

Minutes passed until I came to myself, panting, tongue hanging out, hot belly on the cool dirt. *Hungry*, I thought. I stood and shook, ears and loose skin slapping, rippling, and sliding over deeper tissue. I huffed a breath and the smells of the city hit my scent receptors. It was like being blindsided by an odoriferous Mack truck. Ten seconds later the scents and chemical compounds were categorized and compartmentalized by the newly expanded olfactory center in my brain in a way that was unique to this canine species. Ten seconds after that, they had been recognized and identified by my normal human mental abilities, and grouped by similarities. Dogscatsrats, menwomenchildren, overworked toilets and unwashed bodies, oilexhaustgasoline, cigarettemarijuana, beerliquor, antsroachesfleas. Instantly I began to itch and raised a back paw to scratch the side of my neck. Dang fleas.

Unexpectedly, Beast rose from the depths of my consciousness and peered out through my eyes. *Ugly dog*, she thought contemptuously. *Bad eyes.* She was right. Bloodhounds weren't bred to depend on sight. She sniffed through the elongated nose of the bloodhound and crept a little closer to the forefront of my brain, which was odd for her. *Good smells*, she thought at me. *Good nose on ugly dog*, she amended with reluctance.

Not ugly, I though back. *Just not feline*. Beast huffed back in disdain.

I looked around and, satisfied that I was alone, began rooting in the chicken carton. I pulled out legs and breasts and wings and crunched down. One good thing about being a shape-shifter, if I got bone splinters, they were gone as soon as I shifted back. I ate the entire box of extra crispy chicken and biscuits, leaving the mangled paper bucket scattered in the garden.

Stomach satisfied, I trotted through the shadows and into the street, to the open bay door of the morgue. I swerved out of sight of the two uniformed cops standing at the back of the building; they were smoking and discussing wives with the I-can-tell-you-a-better-story tone that men use for women they have been with a long time. I caught a strong scent of newly dead body and blood, some of it in the van beside me, most of it on the air and inside the building. Underneath that was an older scent of big-cat-human-female. Safia.

I slinked around the van and sat hidden behind a wheel and tire, looking for and spotting static video cameras. I judged the limits of their field of view and knew there was no way to avoid them all, but I was betting that the camera feeds went directly to digital storage and were not monitored by a human who might raise an alarm that a dog had gotten in. Considering I could end up in the dog pound if caught, I was betting a lot. I heard the two cops grind out butts and walk out into the night, stretching their legs. I slipped in and, just like that, I was inside.

To call it a morgue was not quite sufficient, not descriptive enough. There were offices and storage rooms with files. There was a room marked REC. EQUIP., which I guessed held photographic, video, and audio recording gear. There was a chapel that could have been used for any religion or none, where I guessed they stashed grieving families. There was an autoclave room that was unlit, and a laboratory area staffed by two lab techs who worked to music blasting through a CD player. To my now-supersensitive nose, the place reeked of cleaning supplies, chemicals, solvents, and bodies in various stages of decomposition.

At the end of the hallway, I rose up and touched my paw to a steel plate on the wall. The door opened with a whoosh. I'd found the area of the morgue that was similar to what I might see on TV and in movies: an evidence collection room, an autopsy room, and a body storage area that hummed with individual refrigeration units and a larger walk-in, multiple-body fridge at the back. To my new nose, the place reeked.

No one was in sight, and it was easy enough to follow the

scent path to the body storage unit where Safia was, in the middle row of drawers. Though I no longer had hands to open the refrigerated unit, my paws were strong. I raised up on my hind legs, hooked the latch with a paw, and pulled. Icy air and the stench of death roiled into the room. The tray began to slide out. Balancing myself on the drawer, I walked on my hind paws, following its movement. When the tray was fully extended, I pressed a red arrow with a V shape below it, and slowly the tray began to drop. It seemed like a nifty device to keep employee back injuries to a minimum in a day and age of fatter, heavier Americans—which meant fatter, heavier corpses.

When the tray was down fully, I was able to drop to all fours and study the girl. Bloodhound eyes aren't the best, and the poor vision is obscured by folds of skin; ears flop down over the ear canal, affecting hearing; but the nose is so sensitive that it beats any other dog in the canine kingdom. I sniffed and snuffed, pulling the scents in over the olfactory receptors in my nose, the blend rich, textured, layered, and intense. Smelling so many scents at once seemed to affect my pleasure centers, because I didn't want to stop breathing in the heady mixture. While I drew in the new scents, I began to separate them into their individual components and categories.

Because she hadn't been autopsied, as I stood over Safia I smelled blood and internal organs, water that had been used to wash the body, hair products, harsh and floral soaps, gunpowder, an unusual fishy smell that might have been her supper, and in her sweat, the pheromones of fear. The cat had been terrified when she died.

I confirmed Safia as the big-cat who had followed the werewolves when they hunted on Beast's territory. The one who watched them kill without killing any deer herself. I should have parsed her scent when I met her and shook her hand, but with all the vamp- and were-smells in the ballroom, I'd missed it.

Safia had seen the wolves hunt before I'd met them in Booger's Scoot. It was unlikely she had *happened* upon the hunt; therefore, she had been . . . invited to watch? I found a plastic bag with Safia's clothes at the bottom of the tray. With my teeth, I tore a hole in the bag and sniffed with short, hard breaths. On her dress, I scented the wolf-bitch. Safia *had* known the wolves. Known and not told Kemnebi; I didn't think his disgust upon first seeing and smelling the wolves had been feigned.

I trailed my nose down her limbs, scenting nail polish remover and polish, the henna of her tattoos, and oddly, a pine and floral scent that was Gee. I snuffed. What had Safia been doing with the Mercy Blade? Curious. I smelled dozens of other scents on her hands, where she had greeted guests at the party the night she died.

Kemnebi's scent was all over her, everywhere, the scent of his skin cells caught under her nails and his semen strong between her legs. The bloodhound nose was giving me information I really didn't need or want.

Over everything was the scent of Katie. The whacked-out vamp had come upon the were-cat within an hour after death, according to the coroner, and had savaged her, searching for blood. There were punctures at chest, groin, and elbow, and she had licked the body free of spilled blood, Katie's vamp saliva strong on the girl where she had ripped open Safia's abdomen and sucked her descending aorta dry. Thanks to the timetable and the video footage, Katie wouldn't be accused of murder, but she *had* drunk dead blood. And Leo had drunk from her.

Beast sent me an image of a young, dead buck, days old, kept safe in a tree for when she got hungry again. And then a vision of steaks bought in a store, wrapped in plastic. Days old. *Okay. Got it*, I thought at her. I eat old meat. *But still . . . Ick.* So far, I wasn't liking the things I learned while in bloodhound form. They were too personal, too intimate. Deep inside, Beast sniffed with a self-satisfied air.

I was about to stop when I found one final scent. Around her mouth, as if she had kissed him just before she died, I smelled Rick. Pretty boy Rick LaFleur. My breath stopped, suspended. Had he been at the party where she died? No. Had he been there, I would have smelled Rick, even in my human form. I was certain. Well . . . almost certain.

I heard voices down the hall and quickly tried to raise the tray. It moved, but far too slowly. Panic thudded into my chest with my heartbeat and I looked around for a place to hide, my dim eyesight a disability and my keen sense of smell no help at all. I could sit under a desk, but even there my feet, tail, and haunches would be visible. Better places were nada. Zilch. So I raced to the door and pressed my side against the wall, hoping the sight of the refrigerator open and the body pulled out to knee level would distract them from me. Two people entered. I couldn't see much from the glare through the open door, but from the smells that pushed into the room with them, one was female, ovulating, wore way too much stinky perfume, hair spray, gel, and body lotion, and one was a male who smoked. A lot. They stopped just inside the opening, the door braced open.

"Did you leave the were-cat's unit open?" the woman asked.

"No. I looked my fill when we unloaded her."

"Maybe she's starting to stink. Do you smell that?"

"Smells like wet dog. My roommate's dog has this skin condition and it stinks like that."

They moved into the room and I scooted out the door as it closed, whipping my tail up and out of the way of the door. I followed my own scent up the hall and back outside, narrowly missing two techs who were standing in front of a vending area, dropping coins and zipping dollar bills into machines that stank of sugar and rancid fats. I had no idea how humans could eat that stuff.

I came to under the shadow of a house, the smell of fried chicken and grease the strongest scent to my nose. The world was brighter, louder, but dull and void, and I sniffed instinctively as if to restore the scent smorgasbord. Nothing happened and shock hit me like a fist. It was like being sighted and waking up blind, and I *was* head-blind, scent-blind. Bloodhounds had a different view of the world from humans or even big-cats. They could experience and know so much more about the world than we ever could. And then I remembered the smell of Rick on Safia's body. He had kissed her. Soon before she died.

Though I was starving from the calorie loss of shifting, I didn't raid the saddlebags yet. I stood, pulled the pack off my neck, and dressed in my jeans, tee, and boots. I felt immensely better fully clothed—a strictly human reaction that Beast had never understood. After putting the remaining gnawed bones into the torn chicken bucket, I ate half a bag of Snickers bars and washed them down with bottled water, adding the wrappers to the garbage.

Stomach no longer cramping from hunger, I pushed Bitsa

out into the street and looked up at the sky. With Beast's time sense, I judged that it was an hour from dawn. If Molly was here, I would have changed back to bloodhound and had her walk me on a leash around vamp HQ to discover what smells I might find, but that wasn't going to happen.

Frustrated, I kicked Bitsa alive and scooted down Martin Luther King Boulevard, away from the coroner's morgue. Every time I discovered something new, it seemed to push me further from any possible unifying truth. I had a lot of thinking to do.

Back home, I found the house dark and silent. I killed Bitsa's engine before I arrived, walked her to her parking space, and pulled off my boots to enter the house. I carried a mug of microwaved tea back to my bedroom, closed the door and riffled through my files again, spending a lot of time arranging and studying the new files I'd photocopied from the woo-woo room. There was one file I had never seen before, signed in by Jodi less than a week ago. In it was a photocopy that wasn't a police report. It read like scientific speculation on the history, mythos, and possibilities presented by the appearance of shifters. It also contained suggestions on how weres or shifters might be located and studied.

Meaning trapped and dissected. I wasn't stupid. Sections were brutal in their analyses, as if psychos had gone to med and postgraduate school and then become animal trappers and taxidermists.

A less bloody section followed, compiled by geneticists and virologists, consisting of explanations of the way that viruses affect genetic structure, followed by some calculations I didn't understand about how physics might allow a shape transformation, and how shape transformation might in turn affect the understanding of physics. Large portions had been whited out and photocopied with the changes intact, not that reading the scientific particulars would have made a lot of sense to me anyway.

I ignored all the technical stuff and turned to the last section where the words CURRENT SUMMARY OF GEO-POLITICAL HISTORY attracted my eyes. There was a copied e-mail—addresses whited out, of course—whose author noted that no were, walker, or shifter of any kind had come out of the closet in Europe, Asia, or parts of the Middle East, or at least not yet.

He posited that there were several possible reasons: that they were fearful of exposure due to cultural stigma, that there had never been weres or shifters in those parts of the globe, or that any weres, walkers, or shifters had become extinct in those parts of the globe. According to the writer, shifters had possibly been a big part of the settling, growth, and expansion of Middle Eastern, Asian, and European culture. No surprise there, guesswork disguised as logic.

I read, "This raises tantalizing hints about the brothers Romulus and Remus, who were raised by a wolf-bitch, and who settled Rome. It suggests the possibility that the satyrs and centaurs of ancient Greece, who were half-man, half-animal creatures, might have been shape-shifters. We might consider the tales of Celtic selkies, pre- and post-Columbian American Indian skinwalkers. The Egyptian god Ra had a falcon's head, Sekhmet the head of a lion—"

It was all guesswork. Educated guesswork, but still just guesswork. I set it down and went online to discover that the writer was correct. To date, no European shape-shifters, no Middle Eastern shifters, and no Asian shifters had come out of the closet. And Kemnebi claimed that his kind had killed the last European werewolf during Charlemagne's reign. Maybe he had been declaring a truth; if so, the weres knew their own history, which meant that they might know about shifters like me, if only in theory.

I found something in the file that looked like parts of a photocopied journal. It was handwritten with that lovely script that people used to learn and use in school, that had been the mark of a well-educated person. The photocopied pages had been highlighted here and there with names, some of whom I recognized: Leonard Pellissier, Lady Beatrice Stonehaven, Grégoire, master of Clan Arceneau, Ming Mearkanis, who was true dead now. I flipped through and nothing else caught my eye until a name popped out at me. The section read:

Magnolia Sweets, Leo's primo blood-servant, is gone. Her son, though young, was groomed as secundo, to take over her duties should she be unable to perform them. But yesterday Magnolia left, and with her his Blade. She abandoned her son and her vampire, impossible as it seems. Leo seems unable to maintain his previous stability and slides into devoveo; this morn, in a rage, he banished his secundo. Terrance has lost mother, position, and clan. He is only a child, angry and lost.

I have prepared a letter to the Rochefort clan, and purchased the child a berth. He goes to France, to sign in blood and servitude there. I hope I do not live to regret my decision, but it seems the right and proper decision, and the action of one who was once Christian.

The words "who was once Christian," bothered me, though I didn't want to look too closely at why. I flipped through the pages but found no indication of the original writer, and whoever had made the photocopies had not been interested in the bit of history. Nothing else caught my attention.

I stretched out on my mattress, staring up at the ceiling, the laptop open on the floor at the foot of the bed.

The ceiling was dusty. It hadn't been dusty when I moved in. I wondered if I was supposed to clean it. Not that I would.

Woolgathering wouldn't help me solve this case, and so far, my search had found nothing that jumped up and squealed, "This guy is the murderer of Safia!" I couldn't see how it all fit together, not yet, but I was certain that it did.

Back online, I did a quick search on the Cursed of Artemis, the proper name for weres. There was a host of info on the goddess Artemis and not much on the cursed. I marked several sites to go back to if needed and studied the dusty ceiling some more, my eyes on a cobweb draping a corner.

Kem had also claimed that all weres were predators. But I was pretty sure skinwalkers could take on forms other than predator. Beast growled at me. *Beast is not prey.*

"I know," I murmured to her. "You're not a dog either, but I appreciate the willingness to let me shift into one."

Good nose, she said, without adding *ugly dog*. From Beast, that was excellent praise.

I rolled over, went offline and placed the report on the floor next to the computer, finishing the summary. There were multiple authors, most of whom disagreed on pretty much every issue. But based on an extensive knowledge of myth and the information gained since the weres were revealed, they agreed on several conclusions: weres were one-creature-only shifters; they were bound by the moon in ways not yet made public; initially, weres had been made, not born, originally created from a human who survived a near-lethal bite by an infected human or animal; there was evidence that some weres could now breed true, suggesting that they had become a human subspecies; and the weres themselves had outlawed turning a human into one of them. Skinwalkers, if they had ever existed, were possibly weres' forebears; and, last, skinwalkers might be extinct.

A shaft of pain pierced me and I closed my eyes against the knowledge that I may have killed the only one like me on the planet. *Later. I can deal with it later*, I thought. Yeah. Me and that gal from *Gone with the Wind*, the one in the green drapes with a plantation to run. I forced my mind back to the problem at hand—weres, skinwalkers, vamps, Gee, Rick, and what they all had to do with killing Safia.

Rick had been undercover and after the were-cats, going after what he would think of as the weakest link, the were-female, that much was clear from his scent on Safia's mouth. Not that I had any way of proving it. Jodi wouldn't tell me and I didn't have passwords for the police computer system.

I tapped the page with a fingertip, remembering the way the werewolves smelled. Sick. And early in the past century, they were breaking their own laws, trying to turn human females, all of whom had died. And the wolf-bitch had seemed crazy as a loon.

The were-cats, however, hadn't smelled sick. Important differences between weres and me—I was born, not made, and I couldn't make another skinwalker via a bite, at least I didn't think I could, which put me into a very different category from a were.

There was more blacked out near the bottom of the report, but the writer closed with one further conjecture, and this one caught and held my attention. "Perhaps the weres, who are all predators, grew in numbers faster than their shape-shifter forebears, or skinwalkers. With both blended into human society, there could have been war between them, with the weres victorious, killing off all other kinds of shifters."

If that was so, it made the werewolves and the were-cats my enemies. Kemnebi had said he didn't like the way I smelled. And Leo had made sure he got a good whiff of me. Ergo, Leo knew more than he was telling about the weres. And about me.

CHAPTER 16

You Like the Boy Toy

I got a few hours of sleep after dawn and before my cell phone rang. I didn't recognize the number and nearly didn't answer, but at the last moment, I flipped the cell open. "Jane Yellowrock."

"Sloan Rosen," he said. I looked at the number and filed it to memory. "Jodi would have my balls if she knew I was calling you. But have you heard from Rick?"

"No. Not since . . . Tuesday? Wednesday? The day he went back undercover, if I'm guessing right, which also requires an underlying guess—that he was undercover with the were-cats in the first place. Not that I was informed."

"You didn't hear that from me. And you didn't hear this either. He was supposed to check in twice a day and it's been well over twenty-four hours. If you hear from him, make sure he checks in. I'm starting to worry."

I sat up in bed and pushed hair back from my face. "I will." "No connection" appeared on the screen and I stared at the phone for a moment, dread growing in my chest. Sloan Rosen had no reason to call me. We weren't buddies. And his excuse, "If you hear from him, make sure he checks in," was specious. For a cop to step out of the established cop fraternity and talk to an outsider, even a wife or parent, about a cop who was undercover, was really odd.

And then I knew. Sloan wanted me to look for Rick. Rick was in trouble, Sloan knew it, and he couldn't help him, not without blowing Rick's cover or making things worse for him.

So, obliquely, he asked the gun-toting vamp-killer to do it—which meant Rick was under the control of a supernat, and they needed someone involved who was capable of handling a supe outside the law. Cops are sneaky. And Rick was in trouble.

I pulled out the sheet of paper and unfolded the printed photos of Rick and Safia. I studied them without letting emotions rise and interfere with reason and observation, looking for details, hints as to where and when the shots were taken. The trellis shot was the Soniat Hotel in the Quarter. The other hotel looked run-down, cheap; the slice of New Orleans cityscape seen through the breezeway might be a way to locate it. With my cell phone, I took several pics of the photo sheet to compare with the New Orleans skyline.

I geared up for a hunt, which meant carrying all the weapons I legally could, and as many as I could carry that weren't strictly legal. And I dressed in silk long johns and leathers, despite the wet and hellacious Louisiana heat.

I was outside in the street, straddling Bitsa, when the cell rang again. I looked at the display and thought about tossing the cell into the bushes. I took a breath to keep from cussing and picked up. "What do you want?"

"Is that any way for a servant to reply to her master's call?" Leo asked.

Servant? Master? "I'm a contract employee," I ground out, my molars tight, "not your servant. And you are, no way, no how, my master."

Leo decided to ignore my emancipation proclamation, and said, "Your Department of State has elected not to require that a postmortem autopsy be performed upon the body of the deceased were-cat, this in keeping with the demands of the Party of African Weres. Their investigative arm is at a standstill, stymied by the demands of Kemnebi. Your Jodi Richoux—"

"She isn't mine."

"—is unable to take control and unwilling to follow my orders."

"Go figure."

"You will discover who killed Safia. And you will bring him to me." The phone clicked off. I noted that the sun was well above the horizon. Leo's lair had to be so deeply underground that no sunlight could penetrate in order for him to be active during the day. I'd seen vamps active by day once before, in a cave deep underground. And I'd seen a very old vamp, stinking of sunscreen, strolling the city streets once, just at sunset, when the last rays of the sun still cast a soft gray light. Could all old vamps day-walk? Was the ability to day-walk something only some bloodlines had? I remembered Evangelina's comment about some vamp blood being poisonous and some not. I was getting the feeling that not all vamps were equal, and lack of knowledge was biting me in the butt again.

And Rick was in trouble. Maybe big trouble.

From memory, I dialed a number in Boone, North Carolina. Maybe I'd say my cell phone bill was a business expense and try to get Leo to pay it. Before now, I'd only e-mailed Reach with personal status and professional kill info; I'd never called him. Reach ran several independent Web sites for PIs and others in the specialized community of security professionals. One site was dedicated to vamp-hunts and hunters, a free, public site where he posted stats, kills, and hunters' professional information. But if one needed his other skills, they came at a price.

He was a shadow in the world of PIs. If you needed something hacked or tracked, and if you were independently wealthy—like oil-sheikh rich—and if you had even a smidgen of digital info to give him, you could hire his services. But there was no guarantee of success, and he had ways to make sure you paid, success or failure. I took a breath and my financial future in my hands as Reach answered.

"If it was anybody but you," Reach said, his voice hoarse and granular with sleep, "I'd send a virus to fry your cell, laptop, and brain, in that order. What are you doing up so freaking early, Jane Yellowrock?"

I felt like I'd been slapped. So I got mouthy, which always seemed to work when I was playing with the big dogs. "Late, Reach, not early. No rest for the wicked. I need some help."

"Not wicked. You're one of those God-lovers. What do you want? And it'll cost you double for getting me up so early. You're with Bank of America, right?" He read me my account number and named his fee. My heart dropped at the amount, but I didn't dicker. Reach could reach anywhere and do anything, and with Rick in trouble, that was what I needed. "I'll start a money transfer, if you approve."

"Yeah, whatever. I need a location of a cell phone, a GPS

tracking of its whereabouts for the last seventy-two hours, in-coming and outgoing numbers and triangulation of any cells he contacted, the addresses and info on any landlines that he communicated with, and any texts that were sent to and from the number in that time period. If the cell is off, then I need everything until it went off. And if you can reach out like the hand of God and turn it on, I need you to do that too." Reach started to interrupt. "Yeah, I know it's gonna cost me big. Take it from the account. And I need a photo location." With my thumb, I sent the photos to Reach. "Check your e-mail."

Keys clacked in the background. "I see the number and a sucky-quality photo. The number is registered to Rick La-Fleur, who happens to be . . . well, well, well. An NOPD cop."

"You got a problem with that?"

"Not me. Who's the babe?"

"I don't know."

"You say that like she's on your shit list. You like the boy toy, right?"

I took a breath to keep from telling him to mind his own business. Once you contract with Reach, you and everything in your life *is* his business. "The cityscape is New Orleans. Using it, you ought to be able to give me a search grid for the hotel; even better if you save me time and just tell me the address."

"What. You want me to do *all* your work for you? I'm not psychic."

I was beginning to wonder. "See if you can estimate if any of the incoming or outgoing cell calls triangulate with the grid of the hotel address."

"Dayum girl, you are loaded. What you been dealing in—drugs or sex slaves?" I figured he had just seen my savings account balance. He answered himself, "Never mind. I don't want to know. This job sounds like fun." I heard sounds in the background as Reach finished pulling up his arsenal of hacking and tracking systems. "Maybe I'll only charge you the usual fee instead of double."

"You sweet-talking devil, you." I closed the cell and tucked it into a pocket, kicked Bitsa on, and roared off.

I made it to vamp HQ in time for breakfast—human blood-servant breakfast, not vamp breakfast, which prob-ably took place at dusk, involved fangs, and did not require cooking. The headquarters' chef put on quite a spread, with a dozen meats, eggs, pancakes, beignets dusted with powdered sugar, biscuits, waffles, pastries, crepes filled with whipped confections, and chicory coffee with cream. I wasn't much of a coffee drinker but I poured a mug and filled a plate and sat with Wrassler, who looked at my plate, looked at my stomach, and chuckled.

I ate in silence for a while, pausing with a forkful of bacon and egg casserole halfway to my mouth when Wrassler said, "You know what I like about you, Legs?"

I grunted and took the bite. I had a feeling that the moniker, Legs, was gonna stick to me.

"You eat like a man, fight like a man, and think like a man. But you still manage to have woman stamped across your chest. Figuratively speaking. I love the leather look."

I accepted a coffee refill from the waiter, topped the cup off with cream, and drank down half a mug. It was smoother than I had anticipated. "Thanks. I want to see the security video of the outside grounds the night of the party."

Wrassler pushed back his chair. "Bring your plate."

I started to stand and caught a faint whiff of pine to my left. Still rising, knees bent, I whirled. Caught the waiter with my left forearm against his throat. Slammed my right fist into his middle. He flew five feet and hit the wall. Before he finished his *oof* of pain, I was on him, yanking him to the floor and dropping onto him, a vamp-killer at his throat. Shock flashed through me when I focused on the man I had just assaulted. He was blond and green-eyed. Then I caught a second whiff of pine, this time suffused with jasmine, and I shook off the fear that I had grabbed a real waiter. "Howdy, Gee. Thought I smelled you."

He sucked a breath and I saw a flash of blue at the edges of my vision. I pressed the vamp-killer against his throat and a thin line of blood welled. "If I get even a hint you might be spelling me, I'll cut your throat." The blue faded and I instantly felt clearer headed. "Drop the glamour."

"Jane? What's with you and Gerald?" Wrassler asked, his voice behind me.

"He's hiding behind a glamour. His name is Girrard DiMercy, and he used to be Leo's Mercy Blade. He's been hanging around the place for a few days now, glamoured."

"I've heard of him," Wrassler said. "Some of the older ones talk about him. And not in a good way."

Older ones... Older blood-servants. Got it. I shook the waiter, letting the blade mark him a bit. Blood trailed around his neck, looking thin in the light. "I said, 'drop the glamour.'"

"All of them?"

That sounded scary. I wasn't sure I wanted to see what was really underneath his charming façades. "How about leaving the one of you as a wolf-killer in place. But keep your magics to yourself while you alter your appearance. Any trace of it on my skin is gonna hurt you." I twisted my fist in his clothes to secure him. His eyes laughed at me, as if he found the hold amusing.

His skin blued for a moment and his features seemed to flatten out. I felt the electric discharge of magic under the flesh of my hands, and something seemed to coil beneath my knee on his stomach. I bared my human teeth at him, just in case he was getting ready to try something. The face I knew as Girrard DiMercy appeared, still laughing at me.

I didn't know if the old tales of supernatural creatures being unable to break their word was true or not. The myth was likely European and I wasn't part of that tradition—I could lie, though not well. I took a chance. "Your word that you will not change or alter shape during our conversation, will not attempt to harm or spell me or any others here, that you will not attempt to change your glamour, and that you will not attempt to escape. Repeat it."

Girrard smiled, a guileless, winsome smile that made me want to release him. So I tightened my fist in his clothes. He sighed and repeated my promise, which was as lieproof as I could make it. Then he added, "For the next ten minutes."

"Thirty," I bargained.

"Thirty," he agreed. "Now please get off my *torse*." It was close enough to torso and I stood, bringing him to his feet with me.

Wrassler was standing to the side of my field of view, frowning, menacing in his bulk. "What is he and how did he get in here?"

I looked at Gee, who upturned a palm, as if to say that the question was foolish and not deserving of an answer. I should have forced a promise from him to answer all questions. "I don't know what kind of supernat he is, but I can guess." Gee looked at me in surprise. "Elf."

Gee brushed his hand along his clothes as if to smooth out

any wrinkles. "Such a plebian, mundane name for a being such as I." Which could mean he was an elf, or not.

"He spells people to not see him, and he can change his face to look like others. Even when he's caught on film."

"Shape-shifter?" Wrassler asked.

"No. Spells. And not witch magic. I don't know what he is, but I have a feeling that he's been playing with my memory, and that I've seen him or smelled him a few times already." At Wrassler's confused look, I said, "He smells like pine and flowers. Like toilet bowl cleaner and cheap perfume."

Gee wrenched against my hold, insult on his face. And I laughed, baiting him, hoping ire might show me what was going on inside his head. But Gee calmed immediately. "You play games. Beware playing games with one such as I."

"I'm just playing the game you already started. Do you know who killed Safia?"

"No. Boring question."

"Do you know who didn't kill her?"

Gee laughed, the sound carefree and childlike. "Much better question. Leo Pellissier did not. George Dumas did not." When I didn't reply, didn't react outwardly, he said, "I know that Safia was shot before her throat was torn out. I know that a man was with her, before anyone else, even the unfortunate Katherine."

"Did you put photos into my mail slot?"

"Why would I do such a thing?"

Not a no. Not a yes. "Because you want to see the vamps and weres be good buddies." He didn't reply. Frustrated, I said, "I want to see the security footage, Wrassler, and I want him close by. You got a secure room with one of the big multiscreen monitors?"

"Yeah. Tyler might not want you to know about it, but he can skewer me later."

"May I watch this skewering?" Gee asked, making it sound lascivious.

I rolled my eyes and hauled Gee next to me. He was shorter than I was, slimmer than I was. And as well armed as I was; I could feel blades sheathed in his clothing. I figured I'd better add to his pledge. "One more guarantee, Gee. If you promise to raise no weapons against me, neither magical, physical, bladed, nor explosive-based, during the thirty-minute time frame already agreed upon, I'll promise the same to you."

"Done."

"Let's go to the movies," I said to Wrassler.

We sat through forty minutes of digital security footage, twelve screens running simultaneously. The room we were in was near the kitchen, cramped, with poor ventilation; it would have caused panic attacks in a claustrophobe, but was suitable for our needs. It had three chairs in a space built for one, a small table, and the monitor. I got refills on my breakfast—a rasher of bacon and crepes filled with some vanilla-flavored whipped cream stuff that was to die for. Gee got some fancy French wine he wanted, and Wrassler had biscuits and sausage. Good breakfast. Better footage. Midway through, the footage from an outdoor camera caught my eye. I said, "Stop screen number eight. Back it up. Stop. Right there. Play."

On the screen, a man in dark clothing had been filmed walking along the perimeter of the outer wall. When a woman appeared, as if by magic, he stopped. They chatted. Then they both disappeared. Neither of my companions said anything, but the room seemed to grow warmer and the air heavier. "Again," I said. When it finished the replay, I said, "Again. Slower. Half time." And on the fourth go round, I said, "Quarter time. And when the girl appears, I want you to back up frame-by-frame until we see her appear, then a frame-by-frame forward progression." No one argued.

The digital footage progressed at quarter time. "Now," I said, sitting forward in my seat, hands laced, food forgotten. The camera shot was of an outer wall, a side street running along vamp HQ. The man walked. The girl appeared. It was Safia. Frame by frame, we watched as the digital footage was backed up. She had seemed to appear out of thin air, but actually stepped from a doorway in the outer brick wall, a section of the wall that slid open and closed faster than a human eye could follow. Only a supe could have made it through the opening in the time it was ajar. Anyone else would have been chopped in two when it closed, or at least trapped in the crack and squeezed. Safia had exited a hidden entrance in the vamp council house's outer wall, and when the couple disappeared, they went back through it, the man pulled along at warp speed. According to the time stamp on the footage, that man had been with Safia after she disappeared, but before she was killed. The progression was stopped on one frame that displayed both faces.

Safia. And Rick LaFleur.

Gee hummed a soft note. Wrassler said, "Maybe we just found catwoman's killer."

I stood and left the room. I said nothing on the way out. My mind was in some strange sort of stasis, not really aware of what I was doing, but moving by rote. I left the compound, strode into the sunlight, and found my bike. There was an envelope on the seat and I tucked it into the saddlebag unopened, uninspected, which was stupid but I didn't care. I kicked it on the bike, and roared out of vamp HQ.

I rode by instinct, the scorching, wet wind in my face. All I could think was, *Rick is missing. I smelled his scent on Safia's face and mouth when I bent over her in the morgue. As of now, he was the last person known to be with Safia, which makes him a person of interest in her death. And I have no idea what is going on.*

I drove back to my house, found it silent and empty, went inside, and stripped; dressed in capris and a tee. And stopped. My fingers were tingling, my breath coming short and shallowly. Feeling strange and lost in my freebie house. I had dropped my lease on my mountain apartment. Packed up my stuff. Brought it to New Orleans with me. Not just because I had extended my contract with Leo. No. But because I was sleeping with a guy I really liked and I hoped, deep down, that there was something special between us. I had chosen him over Bruiser because he was human, and because he might put me first, while George Dumas was, now and always, Leo's creature.

Rick, however, was undercover, sent to watch the weres, at the beck and call of the NOPD. And if he had to sleep with a girl or two to keep his cover, he would. He had before. I'd once listened in on pillow talk from a hotel balcony, heard and smelled and imagined the scene in the room beside me.

Rick hadn't bothered to warn me. Much like Leo owned Bruiser, NOPD owned Ricky Bo. Who had disappeared off the radar, and might now be in trouble with his own people. The cops had a copy of this footage. They would see it eventually and would recognize Rick—who was missing and in trouble.

I had to find him. No matter what happened later with us.

I went to the kitchen, stakes in my hair, a vamp-killer strapped to my thigh over my capris, and a 9 mil over the tee in a shoulder holster that was starting to chafe at the unaccustomed hours of wear. I set the gun on the table. I always feel better with weapons close at hand.

I had brought in the envelope that had been propped on my bike. While water heated for tea, I sniffed the paper, found nothing fresh on the envelope except a faint smell of chemical, like latex or nitrile gloves, and opened it. Inside were more photos and papers. Usually I had to drag clues out of people, and now someone was just itching to give them to me, which made everything they gave me suspect. Evidence handed to me would surely point only in one direction, when there were multiple sides to this investigation.

I spread out the pages on the kitchen table. On top was a shot of Roul Molyneux, dressed in jungle hunting gear, khakis and boots and a jacket with lots of pockets, a high-powered rifle in his hands. He was standing over the body of an African were-lion. What was it about the supernats and hunting one another?

Next was a photocopy of what looked like a legal writ. It was signed by Leonard Eugène Zacharie Pellissier, Master of the City, and was dated March 17, 1916. It was an edict stating that all werewolves who remained in the city after April first would be hunted down and killed. I didn't think it was a gruesome April Fools' joke. Leo hated the weres, and I had to wonder how much that hatred extended to the big-cats. Could Leo have orchestrated this whole thing, the death of Safia, the discord between the wolves and the cats? Maybe even the return of the wolves just at this time. Could he be that Machiavellian? Yeah. He could. He was a master vamp, a bloodsucking monster, with centuries of plotting under his belt. But if so, why? To what end?

There were other photos, none dated, and every one of them contained some image of a were, most of them dead and not of natural causes. Near the bottom was the image of Safia bending over a big basket of spotted kittens, maybe a day old, followed by a photo of a child in a bassinet, followed by a still shot of a black leopard in the basket with the kittens and the human baby. Beast reared up in my eyes and stared at the photograph. *Kits*, she murmured to me, longing in her thoughts like a deep pond, still and cold.

Yeah, I thought back. But I didn't know if Safia's offspring were were-cats. The cop info from the woo-woo room had suggested that the human baby would be able to change into cat form, and the kittens would grow up able to change into human form. But if so, would they really be human in any way, or cats with no . . . soul wasn't the right word. Humanity, maybe. The were-kits were orphans now, whatever they might grow up to be.

I set the photos aside and poured near-boiling water over the tea leaves and left them to steep. I had to focus on the death of Safia and finding Rick. Nothing else was important right now. I took a breath. And smelled pine and jasmine.

I looked up from the papers to find Gee in the room with me. A naked sword in his hand.

CHAPTER 17

You Belong to Me

Beast roared up through me. My breath came hot. My heart thumped a hard, painful beat. Slammed adrenaline into me. I pushed off the floor. Leaped. Up, over the table edge. Midair, I slid my hands over the weapons and closed my grips. Time slid sideways and stuttered. I landed on the table, crouched. Leaped again. Slid the safety off in midair. Aimed. Gee was gone.

I landed, knees absorbing the energy of the jump. Whirled. To find Gee sitting in my chair, his sword resting across the table. "Impressive," he said. "Inhuman." He breathed deeply and smiled, holding my gaze. "You smell wonderful. Like animal, but not like were. You smell like . . . like the old tales of Lolandes. She too smelled of predator and the hunt."

I swallowed down my fight-or-flight response, forced my breathing to slow. Stood straight. But I didn't put the weapons away. Lolandes? A shape-shifter, like me? "Pot, Kettle."

"Too true. I should like to spar with you. With naked blades," he added almost as an afterthought. "But I have no time. What do you make of my photographs?" he indicated the pages. "Good, yes?"

Spar? With naked blades? No freaking way. "If they're not manufactured," I said.

"And why would I do such a thing?" Gee looked honestly curious, as if he wanted to hear my thought processes and conclusions. When I didn't answer, he sat back in my chair, crossed his arms over his chest in a posture that left him looking harmless and small, and waited.

Annoyed, I said, "I don't know. But it's mighty convenient for the wolves to come back to New Orleans just now. Convenient that you just *happen* to be here at the same time. It's also convenient that you have photographs and put them together for me. Call me paranoid, but I stopped believing in true coincidence a long time ago."

"Mercy Blades are fine thieves. I am a fine Mercy Blade." He cocked his head, the motion weirdly birdlike. "There was no Mercy Blade after I left."

I frowned at his right angle topic turn. "Repetition is boring."

"Every Master of the City has a Mercy Blade to do what he cannot. There is a reason for us. A"—he seemed to think a moment, staring up at the ceiling—"a symbiotic relationship. They need us, we need them."

Us. As if he meant more than it might appear. I kept my face impassive, slightly bored. "You kill their children for them. I got that."

"We take the blood and the life force of the rogues for our sustenance. In turn, our blood keeps the Mithrans sane through *dolore* after a scion dies. It is our blood that mends their minds and bodies when they are sent to earth for healing. The relationship was parleyed by the Sons of Darkness, when they realized their scions were ravening and could not be made sane. You have seen Katherine. She is an example of what happens when Mercy Blades are not part of a healing *gather*."

I had seen Katie put to earth to heal from a mortal wound, her body in a coffin filled with vamp blood offered by almost every member of the New Orleans vampires—a healing *gather*. And I had seen her after, loony tunes, raving, nutso. She had drunk from the dead were-cat, Safia. Not normal or healthy vamp behavior. She had attacked Leo. Not smart vamp behavior. I dipped my chin to show I was listening.

"I have visited little Katherine. A single sip of our blood gives assurance of sanity and good health, and one sip can last them decades. The weakest of us can provide emotional well-being for several clans; the strongest of us for an entire region of Mithrans." He said it with pride, and I knew where he fit in. Gee was strong enough to satisfy bunches of vamps.

"Besides a good meal when you kill the rogues, what do you get out of the relationship?"

"Being in their presence allows us to easily open a passage-way from this world into our own. They enrich us. They fulfill us. They bring us joy."

That was what I'd been waiting to hear. All Mercy Blades were . . . whatever Gee was. Not human. Not vamp. They were *other*. "How many of you are there?"

"Four in this hemisphere at this time." He closed his mouth firmly, and I knew that was all I'd get about his kind.

"Why are you telling me this?"

Gee took a slow breath and closed his eyes as if to keep me from seeing what was in them, but his scent increased, the jasmine growing stronger. He opened his eyes and watched me as he spoke. "George Dumas did not kill Safia."

That was what I had been thinking too. Bruiser had been set up.

"I believe that the were-cat's clandestine lover witnessed her murder, when she allowed him into Leo's private office in the council chamber, through the outer wall."

My heart stuttered. He meant that Rick had seen her killed. I didn't react, though my heart squeezed down painfully on the probability.

"If I am correct, then he saw her die, and escaped from the killer by great luck. If I am right, then he would know why she was killed. He would know who used the gun and who tore through her throat. He and he alone would know."

I answered, my voice calm and reasoned. "It's a possibility. But the lov—the guy is missing at the moment."

Gee's eyes stared into mine. I wondered what he saw in the instant before he leaned close and breathed in my scent. His lips were open, his tongue touching the roof of his mouth. I froze, holding still. His tongue was pointed like a hawk's, deep red in color. Not human. "You are goddess born," he whispered. "Ask one of the old ones what this means." Without another word, he left the house, the door opening and closing behind him as it hadn't when he entered. The ward, which shouldn't have admitted him in the first place, didn't buzz.

I closed my eyes with the sudden release of tension. And with pain. *Rick* had *been sleeping with Safia*, according to Gee, who had no obvious reason to lie to me. I looked at the photos Gee had provided and wondered what else I'd need to bring this case to a close. Finding the guilty parties was worth what I was spending minute-by-minute for Reach to find Rick—who knew more than anyone alive what had happened in Leo's office.

I stared down at the photos as I dialed Bruiser's cell. When he answered, I asked, "Of the cold case files, how many of the victims were Leo's enemies?"

"All of them. Hello, Jane. How are you today?"

I didn't answer his pleasantry. "Had they been his enemies for a long time?"

"Likely. The humans were all blood-slaves of his uncle Amaury, and they became Leo's enemies after his uncle's demise. The Mithrans were Amaury's scions as well."

"So anyone who had been part of the clan back before 1915 would know who had needed to be killed to make it look like Leo was cleaning house. That's a lot of blood-servants, -slaves, and vamps."

"Yes." His voice deepened. "Have lunch with me."

"No." I clicked off the phone, but not before I heard him laugh.

I couldn't do anything for Rick, and nothing else came to mind, so I made a call to the Pellissier clan home to set the stage, then dressed in jeans and a denim jacket, packed a small bag, and left the house. I was about to play a hunch, go with my gut, and unlike in TV-land, guts were notoriously unreliable. But . . . someone was trying to prove that Bruiser had been Leo's hired gun. Which he had been. And someone was trying to prove Leo was guilty of murder. Which surely he was. Bloodsucking fangheads didn't live centuries without killing *some*body. I didn't mind if the guilty went to jail for crimes they committed, but I did mind that someone might be planting and manipulating evidence to force the issue.

Tyler was the only player in the game who had tried to tick me off. Tyler was trying to take Bruiser's position, which gave him motive to help whoever was trying to frame the big guy. Or at least turn a blind eye. Tyler lived in the clan home, with access to info and all the older vamps and vamp-blood-enhanced humans. I had a feeling that Tyler could tell me something. Or his belongings could.

Leo's house stood at the end of a well-paved but little-used road, no other houses within sight, and farm and fallow land lining the road for miles. It was on a bend of the Mississippi River, the levee visible in the distance in the daylight, a tug boat hooting, sounding lonely. The clan home was built on high ground, the artificial hillock rounded and smooth, some twenty feet above sea level, higher than the levees. Curling-limbed live oaks arched over the long drive, standing like sentinels on the rising ground.

The white-painted, two-story brick house was a mixed architectural style, half plantation home, half something vaguely European, with dormers in the tall slate roof and gables at each corner, and with turret rooms on the second floor.

Porches wrapped around both stories, interrupted by and incorporating the turrets. It was originally built in the nineteenth century, and to me had always screamed construction by slave labor. Slave labor currently kept Leo's clan home painted and pristine, but by willing blood-slaves, not by humans bought and transported wearing chains.

Slinging the strap of the bag I had packed around my shoulders, I climbed the front stairs and knocked on the door. The woman who opened it was pretty, wearing a conservative, gray housemaid's dress and apron. She smiled at me with recognition, and her eyes twinkled; she had once served me breakfast on the house porch. A lot of breakfast. I handed her my card anyway, and said, "Nettie, I called ahead and spoke with the . . . butler, I guess? I need access to Tyler Sullivan's rooms. And any of Magnolia Sweets' belongings she left behind."

"Miss Yellowrock, Grayson told me that the vampire hunter was due. Come in." She opened the door wider and stepped back. "Grayson told me to assist you in any way I can. Mr. Sullivan is still not here, and is not expected back until nightfall."

My phone call had assured me that Tyler did indeed have a room on the estate, and had paved the way for me to root around in other people's stuff. Sometimes my job was just too cool.

Inside, the AC was turned up to max and the house was freezing. The sweat on my skin chilled fast and goose bumps rose, but I had learned early on that most New Orleans homes, businesses, and offices were kept icy, as much to lower the humidity as the temperature.

The foyer was as big as my living room, floored in white marble with a black, white, gray, and maroon marble mosaic heraldic emblem in front of the door, depicting a griffin with drops of blood spraying from his claws, a battle-axe, shield, and banner. A stone fountain splashed near the crest, and a round table stood in the center of the foyer with a huge aromatic bouquet in its center.

There were two sets of stairs, one on each side of the foyer, curving up and around to a small space at the top, like a stage, with another hallway extending back. I wondered if they had gotten all the blood out of the carpet where Immanuel and two witches died, but it was only a passing thought. I wasn't interested in the suites of the house's occupants. I was more interested in the rooms of the blood-servants. The maid led me through the foyer, down to a formal reception room beneath the upper floor. The furniture was done in shades of charcoal, gray, and soft whites with color in the paintings lining the walls and the pillows on the couches. Rich rugs were scattered all over the marble floors, looking freshly vacuumed.

She led me through a connecting doorway, past the two-storied library, and to a wing of the house not visible from the front. It was a single, beige-painted hallway with doors to either side, bland and boring, and vaguely like a hotel corridor. The maid stopped in front of one, pulled a batch of keys on a retractable cord, and unlocked the door.

I said, "This is not to be discussed with Tyler."

Nettie pursed her lips and lifted her nose in disapproval. "No ma'am. Rest assured, *Mr.* Sullivan and I do not see eye to eye on anything, including the way that women in this house are to be treated," she said. "*With respect*, I hope you find something to fry his . . . his behind."

"I'll do my best," I said.

"In that case, be sure to look into his musical preferences."

"Yeah. Thanks." *Note to self: Never tick off the help.* Inside, it was colder than the rest of the house, the air conditioner turned down to freezing, I was sure. I closed the door and tugged on a pair of nitrile gloves. I went through the closet, which was neat, almost OC in its order, clothing and shoes lined up by color and season. Expensive European-style suits in black, gray, and charcoal, dress shirts in matching shades and starched white, a few casual button-down shirts, workout clothes, two tuxedoes, and jeans all were on hangers. Nothing was in any of the pockets or hidden in the hems. He had a shoe fetish as bad as Molly's younger sisters. I counted fifteen pairs of boots as I checked the shaft of each for hidden contraband, three pairs of running shoes, two pairs of sandals, well-worn hiking boots, four pairs of dress shoes, three pairs of loafers, and three sets of slippers.

Why did anyone need so many shoes? He couldn't wear but one pair at a time anyway. Personally, I owned three pairs of boots, my dancing shoes, running shoes, three pairs of sandals, and flip-flops, half bought here in the city.

T-shirts were neatly stacked on shelves, his tighty whities were actually all dove gray, as were his socks and undershirts. There were several hats on the shelf above the hanging clothes, and a portable gun case that contained three handguns, nothing older than twenty years, and nothing that would fire .385 rounds, like the ones that killed the cold case corpses and Safia. I returned everything to its proper place, glad that the room was dust free. It was much harder to rifle a dusty place and not leave evidence behind.

In the shelving unit were novels in French and German, very few in English, and none familiar to me. One shelf held gun manuals and books on paramilitary and police procedures. Two on forensic practices were interesting, but why would he need them? A drop-down desk was dropped flat against the shelving unit, a laptop to one side. I turned it on and found it was password protected. Tyler wasn't dumb. I turned it back off and hoped he couldn't tell it had been touched. I'm not a computer whiz and today's units could do stuff that seemed nearly impossible.

A big-screen TV and sound system faced the bed. I turned on the sound and heard a left-wing radio personality who sounded as if he threw spittle with each word. I touched the remote once and Rush Limbaugh's bombastic tones reverberated in the room. I returned it to the leftie politico and shut it off. Tyler was a well-rounded political junkie.

An MP3 player was beside the TV, and I set the earpieces in my ears and hit play. After a minute of rifling through his playlist, I turned it off. His musical preferences, the maid had said. The guy liked German and French stuff, but there was nothing incriminating there.

The bed had military-precise sheets, nothing under the mattress or the pillows. Both bedside tables were vacant, no photographs, no little plate with change and gum wrappers, only the remote device, a landline phone, a pad, and two pens lined up perfectly. Nothing was written on the pad, and

I couldn't tell that it had ever been used. A sitting area with two comfy-looking upholstered chairs and a small round table were in front of the windows.

I checked the bathroom. Dull, dull, dull, our boy was dull. But sexually active, if the half-empty packet of condoms indicated correctly.

I stood in the bathroom doorway and surveyed the room, looking for anything out of place. A guitar case was propped in the corner, half hidden behind a chair. I knelt and checked its position so I could put it back perfectly, pulled it to the floor and opened the case. Inside was a guitar. Big surprise. But there were two storage areas with small tops, maybe to be used for picks and extra strings. Inside one was a smudged, sealed baggie filled with brass shell casings. "Bingo," I whispered. In the other compartment was an old but well kept Smith and Wesson 9 mil semiautomatic weapon, which I bet was loaded with .385 ammo. "Got you, you little twerp." I was relatively certain that this was the evidence the cops were using in their investigation against Bruiser in the cold case murders. The cops could find motive, if they searched hard enough, but I had none, except for Tyler to become prime. Maybe that was enough for an upwardly mobile blood-servant.

I felt a compulsive urge to take the gun and the shells: If Tyler learned I'd searched his room, he would move the evidence. If he wanted to move up the case against Bruiser, he had plenty of evidence right here to do so. And, I just plain ol' wanted to be in charge of it all. But that would destroy any case that human law enforcement might make against him. The only other recourse was to turn him over to Leo. Who would likely kill him, probably before I could put it all together, sniff out the person behind it all. Vamp justice was swift and merciless. And the vamp behind it all? Tyler drank from Alejandro. Alejandro had been with Leo for over a hundred years, which predated the vamp war of 1915. Could it be that simple?

Without touching anything, I sniffed the gun; it had been cleaned recently. Kneeling on the floor, indecisive, I chickened out about taking anything. I unslung the small bag I'd packed and took pictures of the casings, the gun, the guitar case, the room. Using my cell phone, I e-mailed them to myself and to Jodi with the texted caption, "Tyler Sullivan's room at Leo's. Used to frame GD. Fingerprints on baggie."

After I replaced everything and closed the guitar case, I set it back exactly where I had found it and repacked my bag. I stood and removed my gloves, tucked them into a pocket and looked around the room one last time. Everything looked unchanged, as if I had never been here. I never wore scent, so even the sensitive nose of a blood-servant shouldn't be able to detect my presence. I hoped.

I stepped from the room into the hallway where Nettie was waiting, pretending to dust, and her eyes flew to my hands as I approached. "I didn't take anything," I said. "But I have a few questions. One: Where did Tyler come from?"

"From France, with Immanuel's fiancée, Amitee. He was head of security for the Rochefort clan."

That stopped me. Rochefort clan. I had seen that name recently. Amitee Marchand had been a blood-servant to the Rochefort clan in the south of France before catching the eye of Immanuel Pellissier. She was also a vamp who had been passing notes at the big vamp-were soirée, something that looked a lot like high school pranks—except when high jinks involved high-level predators, it stopped being cute. It might have nothing to do with the death of Safia or the disappearance of Rick. But I didn't like it.

"Two. The cops will want to see Tyler's musical preferences too." Her face fell. "You be up front with them about how you found the hidden gun and the casings. If you touched anything, you tell them. Don't hold anything back, including me being here today. Okay?" She nodded, but I could see that something still bothered her. "Blame it on me if Leo gets his panties in a wad about anything."

Her laugh was involuntary and musical. She looked down quickly to keep me from seeing her expression, but I got a glimpse. Nettie had a crush on Leo, not surprising in a blood-servant, but I figured she was more amused at the thought of Leo with his panties in a wad.

"Three. If you had to guess, which of Leo's closest scions would either like to see him dead or take his place?"

"Mr. Leo drinks from his most confidential scions, and has for the last few months. They couldn't hide anything from him."

The last few months. She meant since the recent cleansing and reduction of the clans. I remembered Leo saying that Alejandro had his blood. All of which might mean that vamps can read the intentions of the vamps they drink from. Interesting. "Can vamps read the minds of the humans they drink from?"

Nettie blushed a deep red. "Sometimes."

"Ah. Of course." They could read when they rolled their marks. Sexual attraction had a scent all its own. "Four. Any idea where Tyler Sullivan hangs out when he's off duty?"

She rattled off the names of four dance clubs. "The chest you wanted is in the foyer," she added. "You could take it with you, but with the motorcycle . . ." Her words trailed off.

"Right. No trunk. Any way that someone could deliver it to me?"

"Horace will be heading into town later this afternoon for gardening supplies. Give me directions and I'll see that he drops it off at the right place."

I gave her the address, and because it was in the Quarter, no directions were needed. I made my way back to the main house through the long shadows of the early Saturday evening, and back to my bike. When I got home, I dialed Sloan Rosen and asked, "Any word?"

"No," he said. "But Jodi got your message. Don't touch anything. She has plans."

The connection ended. I was left out of the loop. As usual.

It was a summer Saturday night in the French Quarter, hot, steamy, sultry, and packed with tourists. I was dressed in dancing clothes, which meant a flowing aqua print skirt, a tight cami under a matching top, dancing shoes, and my hair up, out of the way. It also meant stakes in the French braid, two knives strapped to my thighs, three crosses under my shirt, and my tiny derringer buried under the hair, loaded for vamp or were with silver rounds. I was going to party, but any party where I spotted Tyler Sullivan might be a dangerous one.

Going dancing in the middle of an investigation, and with Rick missing, felt stupid on the surface. But there was one bar, owned by Leo Pellissier, where Ricky Bo played with his band, and Tyler hung out, and I could kill several birds with the one club. I also needed a release from the tension between Bruiser and me and a diversion from Evangelina, who was acting downright weird—dancing all around the house, singing and drinking a lot more than I thought she usually did. I left Leo's cell-gift on the table by my bed and carried my throwaway phone when I locked the door behind me and headed out walking to RMBC.

I took a deep breath of the night air and my head started to clear the instant I left the house, my worries spilling away as my dancing shoes tapped on the old sidewalks, and my skirts swung against my thighs and knees. It was hot out, and wet, the air feeling like it weighed a hundred pounds. But my breathing still felt freer than it had since Rick took off.

The night was redolent of bug spray, hot grease, cooking seafood, and the water that surrounds and passes through New Orleans. Most people think of the city as being along the Mississippi River, but there's a lot more water than that, with Lake Pontchartrain spreading wide, and bayous winding through it; salty, silty, stagnant smells are everywhere. And the music. Jazzy, bluesy, Southern rock, pop-country heaven. I worked my shoulders back, rolling them to loosen up.

The crowds thickened with both tourists and locals out for the food and music and shopping, and street artists were everywhere. A four-person band played on one corner, trombone, banjo, percussion, and a guitar, a stack of CDs with the name MamaMamba in front of them. They were playing an old Negro spiritual with all the pathos of slavery and pain, and it was spectacular, the woman guitarist tearing up the vocals. I made a mental note to look them up on the Internet and buy a CD or download something.

Across the street from them was a guy in carpenter clothing, carrying a hammer and screwdriver in one hand, a length of two-by-four balancing, wobbling with the slight breeze, on one shoulder. He was perched on a ladder at an angle. Not a stepladder, not a folding ladder, but a fireman-type ladder, one length of wood. Except for the slowly moving two-by-four, he was immobile as a statue. I had no idea how he could stay so still. I dropped a five in his carpenter's bucket and moved on.

Royal Mojo Blues Company was a thirty-something-year-old restaurant and dance hall that had an outside dining area, a bar, a grill that served great food, and a dance floor I knew as well as I knew my own house. I had danced here several times, a few for Rick as he played sax. And maybe some small part of me hoped he would be here tonight.

The smell of fried food, beer, and faintly of Leo, and

the sound of live music blasted its way into the street, an Alabama-style band rocking the house. When I stepped inside, the scents were momentarily overpowering: old and new beer, fried grease, fish, beef, spices and peppers, cleansers, human and vamp scents, marijuana, sweat, and sex pheromones. The place was packed, shouted conversations merging into a background roar, and overpowered by the band.

An ethnically indeterminate, dark-skinned man crooned, shouted, and sang with a smoky voice, eyes closed, swaying his head, mike, and dreadlocks back and forth, one hand at his thigh shaking a tambourine. He was backed up by four musicians on drums, keyboard, bass, and guitar. I waved to Bascomb, the bartender tonight, ignored three men who looked my way with a sexual, predatory interest, and flowed onto the floor, into the crowd, and up to the band. As I moved, I sight-searched for Tyler or Rick. Saw neither.

Dancing alone was never frowned on at RMBC, and couples and singles were pressed together, a writhing mass of dancers. Into the heat and the beat I raised my arms over my head and started to move. One of the courses I took between children's home/high school/teenaged misery and the freedom of adult life was a year of belly dance classes. The best thing about belly dancing was the freestyle moves it added to my repertoire. I opened with hip pops and shifted into a series of *mayas*, remembering Bruiser's hands on my hips as we danced. I threw back my head and shoulders and moved with the beat. Segued into a series of circular figure eights, dropping my arms slowly in front of me, hands moving in opposing, mirrored, wavelike motions from above my head to below my hips.

I watched and sniffed for the men I was hunting, but it was vamp I smelled first, up close. The tang was sharp and astringent as wormwood and dusty like dried sage, remembered from the first time I saw her in her office. I knew who she was even before I heard the silky laugh that her kind can give, low and erotic, like vocal sex. She was close, her vamp power cutting like razors against my skin.

I tensed and whirled, facing away from the stage, grabbing the ends of stakes in my hair, searching with eyes and nose and band-blasted ears. Katie of Katie's Ladies was in the crowd behind me. Watching me. I stepped her way and stopped. Taking her in. Dropping my hands from the stakes. This was a totally different Katie from the mad, zombielike, flesh-eating monster.

Her fangs were snapped back into the roof of her mouth. Her blond hair was clean and brushed, falling like a thick, solid sheet of gold around her as she undulated to the beat. She was wearing a short, teal silk sheath, so tight there was no question that she was naked beneath it. And she was sane, not vamped out, not a nutso killing machine. Her eyes glittered, holding mine, her irises a grayish hazel as she swiveled up beside me, giving that caramel liqueur, sex-on-a-stick laugh. My Beast purred. She liked the sound, she always had, and she liked Katie, in a predator-fascination kinda way. The way a big-cat reacted to cobras, staring and entranced.

Katie's skin was flawless, pale as alabaster, but with a faint blood blush on her cheeks, indicating that she had fed well and recently. She danced her way around the men from the bar, who had found me, whooped, whistling as she matched her moves to mine. I watched her, leery of this woman, this vamp-predator-woman, being here.

I caught a whiff of Gee. And I understood. Gee had, as he said, found and fed Katie, restoring her to sanity far faster than she would have without his blood. *What the heck* is *that guy?* I nodded to the bar and mouthed over the pulsing music, "Buy you a drink?"

She mouthed back, "I'd rather drink from you." She did a full body slither, snakelike, ending up with her chest inches from me. Power sparkled off her, electric and cutting, scalding and icy. The three men hooted and hollered.

I had stopped dancing and I shook my head, no. "Bar."

Katie pouted, her mouth making a little moue and, vamp-fast, moved off the dance floor. I followed Beast-fast, not caring that the men saw my speed.

At the bar, I took the stool Katie indicated, noticing the couple who stood and stepped away, looking confused, their drinks still in front of our confiscated seats. Stifling a sigh, I handed them their drinks and a ten for their trouble, said, "Thanks," as if they had given up their seats voluntarily, and waved to Bascomb. The noise level was marginally lower here and when he came over I could hear his comment, "Missed you around here, Janie. Good to see you dancing. Miss Katie, a pleasure to see you here tonight. Your usual gin martini?"

The drink sounded perfectly hideous to Beast, but Katie cooed a yes. I asked for a Coke, something sugared and caffeinated. With a vamp—recently insane—near, I might need the kick.

We were silent until our drinks came, and Katie tasted hers, which was bluish green and smelled toxic, delivered in a stemmed glass with an onion on a toothpick in the liquid. She nodded to Bascomb, who moved away for another customer. I cut to the chase. "You drank from Gee DiMercy."

"I did." Katie looked at me from under her lashes, flirtatious. "You can smell him on me?" I nodded and she said, "With the taste of his blood on my tongue, I began to awaken, as if from a long sleep filled with dark dreams. And for a delicious, delirious moment I remembered." She closed her eyes as an expression resembling ecstasy claimed her face. "I remembered the *power*. So very much power. Until Leo drank my power away, my magic was great enough that I might have taken the entire city, might have drunk from every throat I encountered." She opened her eyes, and in them I could see her emotions as easily I might a human's. She was grieving, in pain, and though she was sane, there was something frantic, something ecstatic and manic in her eyes that held me still and ready inside, prepared to ward off an attack.

Her fingers fluttered up her throat and down, across her chest and down to her décolletage, resting on the V of her low neckline. "I might have grown fat and content on the blood of this city, not starved as I am, as we always are." I started to ask what she meant when her face hardened. "But Leo drank from me, drained me, and took it all away."

I tried to understand what had happened, but my knowledge of vamp physiology and culture was based on killing the crazy ones, and my experience with the sane ones was still limited. Before I could put it into some kind of order, Katie said, "I wish to hire you to kill Leo Pellissier, the Master of the City. How much money will you require?"

I put my Coke on the counter, too surprised to hold the icy glass without spilling it. *Cripes*, she was *serious*. "Um, Katie, I work for the council, for Leo. He pays me."

Katie said something in French and slammed her martini glass on the bar. The stem broke. Gin, bluish and harsh smelling, splashed over the counter. Her power spat over me like burning sleet, and out across the room. Even the humans flinched, as the air went suddenly arid and electric. The band stopped playing midsong and stood on the small stage, holding their instruments awkwardly. "I hired you. I!" she said in English, her words ringing into the silent room. "You belong to me."

Belong to . . . My first instinct to quiet her vanished, and I spoke in a low rush of whispered words. "I don't belong to anybody. You hired me to do a *job*, which I did. And then Leo extended my contract. I'm not a hired killer, Katie."

"Of course you are. It is what you do, what you are. It is what all vampire hunters are, *murderers* of my kind."

Deep inside, Beast growled, exposing killing teeth. She murmured, *Jane is killer. Killer only*. I ignored her. Beast and I'd had this conversation before. I disagreed with her opinion, but there are times for internal debates, and when faced with an unhappy vamp wasn't one.

Katie glanced up the bar and called out into the odd silence, "Barkeep. Another drink!"

Her words broke a spell over the crowd; on the stage, the players seemed to shake themselves and put down their instruments, announcing a short break. Canned music came over the loudspeaker system, Aaron Neville singing "Jailhouse." The humans in the place started to move again, recuperating from the blast of vampire energies, and I spotted the ones still unmoving in the crowd. Vamps, three of them. Each of them focused on Katie.

"Katie, why do you want Leo dead?" I asked, keeping an eye on the vamps.

"He buried me with the blood of all the clans," she said, surprised. When I made a little, *so what*, gesture, she said, "He gave me the power of them all, and then he took it away. He drained me near unto true death. I would still be chained with the scions had not the Mercy Blade found me and set my mind free. It isn't . . ." She struggled for the right word. "It isn't *fair*."

I grinned and picked up my Coke again, draining it to exchange the glass for the fresh one Bascomb brought. The concept of fairness from a vamp was amusing, but I had a feeling that laughing would win me nothing but a battle I wasn't dressed for. And my momentary concern that Katie might be the vamp trying to get Leo and Bruiser arrested for murder eased. She was too nutso to have arranged the scenario. Bascomb wiped up the mess of Katie's spilled drink.

When he left, I said, "So, challenge him to personal combat."

"He has *my* blood, *my* power," she spat. "I will not win."

"He challenged you to personal combat when you were unable to fight back at full strength due to the *dolore*, which by vamp law isn't an issue. But he won and didn't kill you, which means he respects you and wants you alive." Katie looked up at that, her drink poised halfway to her mouth, her exquisite eyes opened wide in surprise. "He drank from you against your will, right?" Katie nodded and sipped, her face puzzled. "I don't know much about vamp law, but I *think* you're number two in the city, now. Ask him to make you his heir."

Katie pulled in a harsh breath and met my eyes again, hers going half vampy. "His heir," she whispered. "Yes." And suddenly, in a snap of imploding air, she was gone. Katie, pulling the vamp gift for speed that only the old, powerful ones have. And I got stiffed for her drink bill. Figures. Dang vampires.

CHAPTER 18

Woad

I danced another set, accepting a drink from Tex, the vamp who had been patrolling the compound with the huge dog, letting him lead me into a bump and grind dance to one of the band's original country songs, the music too loud and the crowd too boisterous to converse. Beast watched him through my eyes with an intensity that was always surprising to me. She was too interested in vamps for her own good. I scent-searched while we danced, but never caught a whiff of Tyler, Rick, or anyone else I hoped I might find.

When the dance was over, I left the bar, walking through the night, the air like a sauna, my skin glistening with perspiration, my mind free and clear and open. Dancing did that to me—driving away the demons, letting me think. My dancing shoes made soft clips of sound. My dress moved with the barest caress across my heated flesh. My muscles felt relaxed and supple. And with the night breezes blowing a rainstorm in off the Gulf of Mexico, I let my mind float free.

And narrowed the focus of the events of the last few days, starting with the Mercy Blade. He had spelled me the first time we met, with that weird bluish spell that crawled up my flesh. Beast had stopped his enchantment, but I hadn't been thinking like myself since then; I hadn't been thinking about Girrard DiMercy at all, and his scent had been on Safia's body.

Kemnebi's scent had been there too, and in a far more personal way, but he didn't strike me as stupid. Not stupid enough to murder his girlfriend in the business office of the most powerful vamp in the Southern states. Strike Kem off my list.

But then there was Tyler Sullivan. The Mercy Blade and Tyler. The two men were the keys to everything. Whatever the heck it all was.

The front porch lights and the living room lights were lit when I reached the house, and I unbuckled and removed my dancing shoes on the front porch before entering, feet silent on the wood floors. Bruiser and Evangelina were sitting in the living room, a Parcheesi Royal Edition game board on the table between them. Evangelina was dressed in some silky pale pink top, which should have contrasted poorly with her red hair but didn't, and skintight jeans. She looked svelte and toned and oddly younger than I'd noticed, which was strange. Evangelina had always struck me as a Valkyrie warrior woman, brusque and demanding and in charge, riding roughshod over all opposition. But lately she was looking softer, more feminine, far sweeter than I remembered, with a glow to her skin.

When I stopped inside the front door, she was looking up at Bruiser with a teasing expression. *Crap.* She was wearing lipstick. And eye shadow. The sexual tension in the room was heavy enough to stub my bare toes on. Evangelina was flirting with Bruiser, leaning so close the pink of her silk shirt covered them in a pinkish glow.

Beast roared up into my eyes. *Mine*, she thought at me. And in the same instant, I remembered Rick. My heart did a little dump and splat. *Rick*. "Not really," I said aloud to my alter ego. "Not now."

Evangelina and Bruiser looked up at the sound of my voice and Bruiser stood in a motion that looked ingrained, old world charm left over from his early years in England and reinforced by living with a feudal-lord vamp-master. He looked great, his hair shoved back, jeans cupping that great-looking butt, a crisp white shirt tucked into the waist, the sleeves rolled up to expose corded arms. He looked good enough to scoop up on a spoon and lick all over. I smiled at the mental image as Beast growled unhappily and slunk away again, muttering, *Mine. Mine.*

"Evening," I said, aware that I was interrupting much more than a board game. "I need a spell to counteract a spell."

"What kind?" Evangelina asked.

"One somebody put on me to keep me from thinking about

him, or being able to analyze his plans, or even remember that
he was around."

"A sorcerer? The Witch Council would punish him for using spells against . . . well against humans. I don't know what
they'd do about spelling *you*."

"Not a sorcerer. Something else, not human, not vamp, not
witch. He smells like pine and jasmine and . . ." I thought back.
Remembered my own surprise when I had visited the woo-
woo room at NOPD. And the weird feeling, when I was in
my freebie house, doing research, a sensation as if I wasn't
alone. Maybe . . . "Maybe a spell to watch me," I whispered,
"put there by Girrard DiMercy, Leo's Mercy Blade."

Bruiser's eyes tightened on me. "I'm having trouble remembering what Gee did to me, but I recall a blue, misty spell
flowing up over my skin, and the smell of pine and jasmine.
But I don't think he got to finish laying it."

"It's not an egg," Evangelina said.

"Casting it, then. Whatever. Can you take it off?"

"If I can see it, especially if it's unfinished or frayed. Sit
down. Let me get some things from my room."

"Let me grab a shower," I said, fleeing the room. Okay, I
was fleeing Bruiser but no way could I say that. I took a fast
shower, pulled on the clean pants and tee I'd worn earlier, and
braided my hair out of the way.

Evangelina was sitting in a wingback chair when I reen-
tered the room, and the Parcheesi game had been put away,
replaced by two feathers, three candles, a small silver knife, a
silver bell, and a gold cross on a gold chain. I took the seat she
indicated, a pillow on the floor at her feet. Beast didn't like
the submissive position, but I overrode her, sat in a half lotus,
and relaxed.

"You say the spell was blue, so I assume that you can see
magic," she said as she lit the candles. The smell of matches
and flame scorched the air. I took a fast breath. I had given
that away. But neither Evangelina nor Bruiser looked surprised or accusatory or even curious, so I managed a nod, my
heart in my throat. Beast was crouched close to the surface
where she could see, silent, shoulders hunched, her four paws
close together, positioned so she could leap away if needed.
Evangelina turned off the lamps, throwing the room into
semidarkness, flames dancing on the pale wall.

Evangelina said, "You meditate, yes?" At my nod, she went

on. "And you are a practicing Christian." There was an odd note of distaste in her voice, and I remembered Evangelina practiced some other religion. I nodded and she placed the gold necklace over my head, rested it on my chest near the gold nugget. The metal was cold but warmed immediately. "I want you to watch the flame of the white candle. Breathe in its scent. Relax." She drew out the word "relax." The scent of conifers rose on the air, surprising somehow. I'd expected vanilla or some froufrou scent. I stared at the flame, bright in the dusky light.

"Close your eyes and think about the candle flame, vivid, alive in a dark room." Her voice dropped in volume, deeper in tone, like a hypnotist, going for the deep, unconscious mind. I held the image of the flame in my mind and closed my eyes.

"The flame is white and yellow, warm and steady. The flame lights the darkness, throwing back the night. Can you see it?" I nodded. Her words slowed, softened as she spoke, "Good. The wick. It's visible through the flame, rising up through the body of the candle from its base. It's like your spine, rising from the center of you, strong and vital and filled with potential. Your mind and spirit are nestled at the tip of the candle, bright with power and energy. You are the candle. You are the wick. You are the flame."

I nodded and relaxed my shoulders, letting each vertebra settle and loosen, slipping easily into the relaxation and meditation technique. A candle flame is used by many different religious and secular groups to begin the trek into the deepest mind. I breathed steadily, the pine scent now mixing with jasmine from another candle. *Gee*. It reminded me of Gee ... Evangelina had chosen well. My facial muscles relaxed into an almost smile.

"The candle has no purpose without the flame. The flame has no home, no power, without the candle. Yet, the flame consumes that which gives it life," she said, her voice falling lower, "in a cycle of fuel and energy, of matter and mass." Her words filled the softness of the night, slow. Mellifluous. "Watch as the candle is burned by the flame. As the wick is consumed, it gives us light. It gives us warmth. It is a symbol of life and eternity. Yet, even the wick of life burns low, quivers, and dies."

Evangelina was talking about the circle of life, the birth and death of all things, and the rebirth of some new thing from the ashes of the old. "Dust to dust, ashes to ashes," she said. I let my breath go slowly out, sighing, accepting what cannot be truly understood.

"Yet, for now, the soul of the candle burns, bright and steady, lighting your darkness."

"Yessss," I whispered, understanding. This wasn't Cherokee meditation. This was the magic of the white man. But as always, there were similarities, connections, parallels. I watched the candle flame, pure and perfect.

"You are now in a tranquil place, calm, dark, and peaceful. It is the refuge where your soul resides. The home of your spirit. You are protected here in this place of darkness and light and peace. Safer than any place you have ever been. You are warm and sheltered. This is your soul place. Your secret haven." I nodded, smiling fully. I knew this place.

"Open your eyes," she said, softly. "Look around you. The candle burning in this sanctuary is your soul, your life. There is no one here but you. You are alone and secure."

"Yes," I nodded. "Alone. Safe." I breathed in and let my breath flow from my lungs in a long steady exhalation, feeling all the tension fade away. Drums started beating, quietly, peacefully, a four beat rhythm, hard-soft-soft-soft, hard-soft-soft-soft. In the dark, in the fluttering shadows, misty fingers and ghostly hands slid against deer skin drums, tightly stretched. Herbs burned on a fire. Wood smoke crackled, dry and aromatic. I knew this place.

I focused on the candle flame, but it was wrong. The wrong shape, the wrong size. Wrong. "Not a candle," I murmured. My soul would never be a candle. "Fire. In a pit. Coals . . ." I saw them, glowing and hot, fed by forest deadwood, the heat in the embers moving as if alive. No, I would never be a candle, but I could be a fire, potent with possibility and restrained violence. I licked my lips. They were dry from the heat of the coals, yet, around me, a cool, wet wind moved through the darkness, breathing up from the deeps of the heart of the world. I burned and shivered, balanced between the flame's light and warmth, and the dark, chill night.

"Turn your eyes," a voice murmured in the darkness. "Search out the far corners of the place where you are. What do you see in the light of your soul?"

I turned slowly. Seeing the place of my soul. "The heart of the world," I said.

"Describe it to me."

"It is the heart of the world." What more was there to say? A woman of the People would have understood, but the white woman . . . no. Yet, I could try to describe the vision, the image. "Walls rise up to the rounded roof." I tried to lift my hands to show her the shape, but they were heavy, as if tied to the earth. "The roof melts down. The floor of the earth rises up. And melts again, puddling like fat, rich from an autumn bear. Dripping like your white man's candle."

"Caves? With stalagmites and stalactites?"

I dipped my head. "Water drips everywhere. Little splats. Like the blood of the earth falling, sacrificed. The tears of the heart of the world. A drum beats, like a heartbeat. And on the breath of the dark there is sage and mint and"—I took a slow breath and relaxed totally—"sweetgrass. They burn on the fire. Flames light the walls." I smiled. "And there is pine and jasmine. But only a little. A hint of them, buried under the perfume that burns in the heart of the world." I fell silent.

"There is someone there," the soft voice said. "That person is you. Do you see her?" I nodded. "Tell me what she looks like."

And with the command, a trace of worry curled around me, faint and wispy, like a finger of smoke, questioning. *Why would Evangelina ask about my soul home? Ask about my shadow self?* But the worry escaped, like smoke through a longhouse smoke hole.

"I see my shadow on the walls. I see Dalonige'i Digadoli. A girl. She is four, maybe five. Or twelve. I can't tell. She . . . shifts and flickers." I smiled. "And the shadow of *tlvdatsi* sits facing her. Staring at her in the darkness. Like two . . ." I forced up my hands, lifting them from the floor despite their extraordinary weight. I spread my fingers, turned my hands toward each other, fingertips touching. "Like this." I let my fingers slide together, interlacing, until my palms touched and my fingers curled around, making a two-handed fist.

"Till dot si?" She mangled the word.

Beast thought at me, *All yunega are foolish about spirits of animals. Foolish about spirits of Earth.* I repeated the word properly, so the white woman would not insult the spirit of my Beast. "*Tlvdatsi.* It sounds whispered, almost. The People do not shout their words like the white man."

"There are two of you in this heart of the world?"

"Yes. Always two of us."

Her voice changed. Her scent changed. "No. There is only one. One of you. Look again. See the girl."

"Two," I said.

She paused a moment, as if uncertain, before saying, "This *tlvdatsi*. It is always with you? Part of you?"

"V v." Yes, in the tongue of the People.

She spoke softly again, as if to another. "It may be some Cherokee archetype, something I don't understand. She needs a Cherokee shaman."

"*Egini Agayvlge i*," I said. I struggled to find her white man name. "Aggie One Feather. She knows."

"I see. She is your shaman?"

"Elder. Elder of the People. Of *Tsalagi*."

"She's seeing someone, I think, a counselor. That's good, Jane. That's very good. I want you to relax. There's no need to struggle or feel worried or anxious. This heart of the world is your soul home. The place where you envision your soul to be. It's safe and warm and all yours."

I nodded, relaxing once again. On the cave wall, Beast's shadow flicked an ear tab. I put out a hand and stroked her pelt along her neck, down across her shoulder. Her muscles and sinews were strong. Her breath smoothed, and she purred softly.

"Jane, tell me what you are."

"Evie, no!"

"Shut up. Tell me what you are."

The worry rose again, like smoke from old coals. My shadow self tilted its head, ear tabs flicking, snout wrinkling to show killing teeth, sharply pointed. "No," I said. It came out hoarse, chuffed. A warning.

"Stop it, Evangelina." Bruiser's voice. "This is wrong."

"Fine," the woman snapped. A long moment later she spoke, her voice again calm, soothing. "Jane. I want you to re-member the last time you looked into this place. I want you to compare it to now. I want you to layer one vision over the other."

"Yes."

I/we are Beast. Better than Jane. Better than big-cat, Beast thought. *We are* more.

"Yes." My voice dropped, a low growl of sound. *My place. My den.* Mine. This was the cave from *before*. Long before. The rounded, damp roof of stone, the walls melting like wax. The pillars reaching up and down. Light glinting through the darkness. The scent of burned herbs and wood smoke. The drums. The smell of blood and fat and earth and the sweat of the People.

"Search out the differences, Jane. Tell me what you see. Tell me what you remember."

I stood on four legs and two. The shadows on the wall merged into one, a form with no certain shape, both cat and human, furred and skinned, four pawed and two footed. A shadow shimmering with black motes of light.

I turned slowly, walking in a circle. My breath a pant. Seeing. On one wall were circles and swirls painted in soot and fat and crushed pigments. Carved into the stone were arrows pointing to the right. Lines parallel. Lines like waves—the symbols of the People. And there were paw prints. They padded across the rounded stone roof of the world, big-cat paws in the red of old blood. Human footprints walked beside the paw prints, up and over the roof of the world. Side by side.

I reached out a hand/paw and touched them. They were cool to my touch. The paw and footprints had not been here, the last time I was here in the flesh, as a child of four or five. This was the cave of my being. Evidence of my life. There were also white man symbols, brought here since Jane had been alpha, diamonds and stars, signs and ciphers, and an image of a cross that burned.

My eyes followed the paw prints up across the walls, onto the roof, and into the far corners, where the light did not burn so brightly, where shadows crouched like spiders and hung like bats. And there I saw the hands. Hands did not belong in this place. The Cherokee did not mark rites of passage or lay claim to the caves, not as the ancient white man did. They did not make handprints on cave walls. The hands were not of Jane or of cat. They were *other*.

"Hands," I whispered. "Hands on the roof of the world." I tilted my head to see them. Blue hands in circles of white. White hands in circles of blue. Pigments, signs of ownership applied to the walls of my soul house. I growled low, pulling back lips to show killing teeth.

I could see how it had been done, how each kind of handprint had been made. For the blue handprints, pigments had been crushed and mixed with fat or spit. The paste had been applied to the hand and the blue prints pressed against the walls. For the white handprints in circles of blue, the pigments had been crushed and sucked up into a reed. A hand had been placed on the cave wall, and the pigments had been blown over it, leaving the un-pigmented print. It was as if to say, *I have been here. This is my place.*

"Woad," I said. "Woad." And I struggled upward from the darkness as I understood. Woad. Yes. *Woad*. Woad was a European herb, an invasive herb that took over gardens, an herb used to make blue dye. *Gee did this. Gee used woad to mark my soul house.*

I fought the pull of the heart of the world. I tried to stand, but the weight of the world was great, holding me down. "He came *here*. He marked *my place*." I growled, exposing killing teeth, my tongue finding them blunt and human. Hands fisted, blunt nails pressing into palms.

"Relax, Jane. It's okay, Jane. You are safe in your soul room. You are safe here. And we can make him go away."

I looked up, seeing the handprints. And beside one was a pink flower. A rose. It hadn't been there a moment past. I tilted my head, studying the rose, considering its meaning in this place of my soul. It smelled of roses and wormwood, sweet and bitter both. And it was put there with magic—witch magic. Evangelina had set her spell on me, tracing the lines of the Mercy Blade's magic. Beast snorted, a hacking blend of anger and amusement. "Fire," I whispered. "*I* can make them both go away. With my fire. The fire in my soul home."

"Fire is dangerous, Jane. Let's think of another way." She sounded fearful.

Beast is not afraid. Beast is strong. "Fire," the word was growled.

"No, Jane," she crooned, "I want you to step away from the place of the soul. From the place where the hands are printed on the ceiling. I want you to come back to me, to us, to yourself, here in your house."

"House is not mine," I said. "Cave in the heart of the world is mine. Is ours."

"I know," she soothed.

In the cave at the heart of the world, I/we stood, the weight of the world heavy and thick against us. Our shadows rose with us. And they merged, merged, part *tlvdatsi*, part Dalonige'i

Digadoli, part cat, part human. Our shadow was beautiful. Fearful. Deadly. The flames in the fire pit danced and rose. Water dripped. Drums beat faster, deeper, the beating heart of the world. *The I/we of Beast,* we whispered. *Together we are more than big-cat and Jane.*

We bent to the fire.

"Jane don't—" White woman spoke, and I/we closed her voice out. Pushed it out of the cave. We bent over the fire, the scent rich and herbal and warm, and breathed in the sage and sweetgrass. We reached to the side and chose a thick sliver of wood, pointed on one end, sawn smooth on the other, one side wild and splintered, one side shaped by man's hand. A stake. It was dry heartwood, its cedar scent resinous and tart. *Heart wood to destroy the vampires we hunt and kill.* Our hand closed over it, *tlvdatsi* claws at the ends of human fingers. Pelt, tawny and thick rose up over the bones of our arms. We hefted it and placed the splintered, sharp end of the stake into the flame. It took light. And we rose into the shadows.

The roof at the heart of the world reached down to us. With one hand, killing claws exposed, we scraped an eye from the cold stone. It glittered, lid closed as if sleeping, on our palm. With the other hand, we held the flame to the woad-made handprints. The fire from our torch blazed up, burning the woad, burning the handprints that had taken root. And in the center of each palm, a blue eye appeared, opened, and focused on us. Gee's eyes, shocked. I stabbed at the eye in the center of a palm and it blinked away, but not before I drew blood. It splashed down onto my hand, copper and jasmine-scented. The flames blackened the stone of the roof and the woad lit, sizzling and hot. I stepped away as the flames roared up hot and cleansing. All the handprints took flame, all but the one I had stolen with my killing claws. "Mine," I growled. "My place."

I crouched on the stone floor and watched as the ceiling at the heart of the world flamed and burned. And was cleansed. It took a long time. And no time at all. And when it was done, I sat at my small fire pit and fed the stake into the coals, letting it too burn away. When the smoke cleared, the ceiling was clean again, only the soot above my small fire blacking the smooth rock. I lay down, folding my body, paws beneath me. And I closed my eyes.

*   *   *

I breathed out, and the movement of my chest, the contracting of my ribs, woke me. As the breath left me, I lay unmoving, as if still asleep, yet cracked open my eyes, seeing through my lashes. I focused on the ceiling twelve feet above me. It was smooth and painted white; shadows crouched in the corners, unmoving and without purpose, unlike the shadows of my vision, which had seemed alive and filled with evil intent. I was lying on my back with my head on a cushion, my body on a hardwood floor. I hadn't started out in this pose, but had been moved, positioned so I could breathe easily. My clothes were intact, so I hadn't shifted.

I inhaled, and the harsh chemicals of the white man's world assaulted me. Wax, smoke, cleansers, dyes in the fabric beneath my head, exhaust, mold and sour water, old wood, paint, human sweat. The smell of witch and blood-servant. Vamp-stink from Bruiser's skin, fading now. Riding over it all was the stink of scorched flesh and pain pheromones. Mentally, I catalogued my body, and found nothing wrong, no pain, no injuries. Not my burned flesh, then.

Finding nothing to defend against in the scents or the silence of the room, I relaxed. Despite the reek, I felt . . . okay. Not sleepy. Not unhappy. But calm, full. Satisfied, as if I'd eaten a big meal and then taken a nap. And I felt like myself, which was a thought for later, when I had time to analyze the vision, maybe with Aggie One Feather as my guide.

Movement caught my eye through my lashes, and I saw Evangelina bending over, only feet away, a cloth and a spatula in her hands as she scraped at a tabletop. Her hair hung down in a heavy red tangle, a splendor of curls that caught the lamplight, longer and thicker than I remembered it. A rosy halo surrounded her, an aura in shades of ruby, maybe the aftereffects of using her power. White gauze bandages circled both forearms, six inches wide, heavily padded from elbow to wrist. They were new. They were defensive wounds. The sight of them made me want to laugh.

Evangelina had tried to take advantage of me when I asked her for help. She had tried some kind of witch-spell-empowered hypnosis on me, trying to learn what I was. Possibly trying to set a watch-me spell into my soul, tracing it in over Gee's spell, so she could influence me in some way. *Tricky-witch.* But she paid the price. Savage victory swept through me like a cold wind. She had tried something magical on me, just as Gee had. And Beast and I had won.

Bruiser was sitting on the couch, watching Evangelina, his eyes hooded and intense. They were talking about me, and he asked, "How did she melt the candles?"

"Stop asking me that," Evangelina snapped. "I didn't know an hour ago, and I don't know now."

"So speculate."

"Jane isn't human. She isn't witch or shaman or vampire," she said, her irritated tone suggesting that this was repetition. "She isn't anything associated with the Dark or anything of the Light. She isn't an angel, a demon, or a ghost—not that I've ever seen any of those things, but she doesn't fit the archetypes. She has no intrinsic magic that I can see or feel, but she *did* magic. Low level, but intense. She has some strange Cherokee magic, which is probably how she healed the wounds I bandaged after she fought Leo in the street." Evangelina stood and wiped the spatula off into a paper bag. Softened wax fell into it with a soft thump. "It was magic," she said, surprise in her tone. "We'll know more when Molly calls me back."

I had forgotten about the wounds that had healed when I shifted. *Foolish kit mistake*, Beast growled.

"Is she going to be all right?"

"I. Don't. Know. Stop asking. But I'm sure she'll be fine"— she hissed in pain as her wounded arm bumped her side— "whatever she is." Evangelina left the room, her bare feet padding on the floor. Bruiser stood; I closed my eyes as he came into my field of vision, but not before I saw the ruby aura that surrounded him. It was the exact hue of Evangelina's aura. I remembered the pinkish glow on Bruiser's skin in the shower. I remembered their postures when I interrupted them earlier. Romantic. Rosy. I had thought it was her shirt . . . *Crap*. She was spelling him. Now why would Evangelina love-spell the prime blood-servant of the Master of the City, during negotiations between their races? I breathed out a sigh. Just one more worry.

They still didn't know I was awake. Bruiser followed Evangelina out of the living room into the kitchen and I rolled soundlessly to my knees and up to my feet. Looked around the room. Huh. I had made a mess. All three white candles had melted to a sooty mass, dripped all over the end table and onto the floor. The two feathers, the small silver knife, and bell, were caught in the softened wax. The feathers were ruined, but the other things would be okay after a good cleaning. There was a small gray spot on the ceiling that looked like a shadow, but wasn't. It was soot and wax from the fire that had melted the candles. Cushions were everywhere. A pillow had several scorched holes in it, as if ashes had fallen across it. A cup of tea I hadn't noticed before had turned over, the reddish liquid splashed and the cup handle broken.

It looked like I had tried to burn up everything around me. I nearly snorted with disgust at the mess. I needed Aggie One Feather if I wanted to take a trip deep inside my psyche or into my past. But one thing was clear. Gee had been watching me, following me, with his spell. It had been a good one. Nearly perfect.

Drawing on Beast's stealth attributes, I pulled the gold cross off and dropped it on the pillow, slipped to my bedroom, grabbed my go bag, slung my H&K holster over my shoulder, took up a single vamp-killer blade, a hand full of stakes, and a pair of sandals. I was out the front door before Evangelina and Bruiser were any the wiser. Up the canyon of the street, a heated mist rose from the asphalt on the night-cooled air. The quarter moon hung between the buildings, casting dim shadows. The buildings were ghostly and monochromatic, windows like jack-o'-lantern eyes, lit from within, bright with life, or prison eyes, barred and lit from without, reflective and empty and soulless. The night was oddly silent, the music of countless bars and dance halls and blues palaces a throttled, distant blurred sound. Overhead, storm clouds moved in from the gulf, obscuring half the stars. Rain was coming. Soon and hard.

Standing across the street, I weaponed up, watching in the windows of my own house; Bruiser and Evangelina had just noticed I wasn't on the living room floor anymore. Bruiser raced up the stairs. Evangelina pushed aside the lacy curtains and looked out into the street. I stepped behind a car parked at the curb and stood where she couldn't see me. Watching her, I flipped open the throwaway cell phone and dialed Molly.

She answered on the first ring. "What are doing to my big sister?" She nearly snarled. "And what took you so long to call me. I got three weird messages from her in the last half hour."

I laughed, feeling free and lighthearted. "Evangelina is up to no good all on her own, Molly-girl."

"I was afraid of that. Her message didn't sound like her."

"You mean not all stuffy and uptight and rigid? More like a regular person?"

"Play nice. That's my sister we're talking about."

"We are playing nice. Beast didn't eat her. But your stuffy big sister was trying to figure out what I am, and I think I burned her in the process."

"Tell me."

I left nothing out since our last chat, and it took several minutes. When I was done, Molly was quiet for a long moment, before she said, "Son of a witch on a stick. Okay. I'll handle my sis. But you need to be ready, big-cat."

Something tightened deep inside me. "For what?"

"For what you are to come out. Too many people have noticed you down there in the City of Mardi Gras, powerful people and powerful beings. Discovery of a skinwalker, of the Cherokee variety, would ride the news channels for days. You'd be the subject of speculation by TV and radio personalities and panel discussions by knowledgeable idiots. You're something that no one really knows about, Jane, not anymore, maybe not for centuries. A magical creature of unknown properties, one with a dark and mystical and violent potential. And it's only a matter of time before it comes out."

I closed my eyes against her words. "You're saying I'll have trouble if . . . when I come out. That people will get in my way, in my face, chase me down, cause me problems."

"Capture and dissect you if they can. Just like they would my . . . situations." She meant her children, a sorcerer who had, so far, survived the usual childhood cancers that claimed most male witches, and a witch daughter with two witch genes. A powerful tool in the hands of, well, almost anyone. "Next time you come home, I'll load you down with protection."

Home. The mountains. An image of the moon hanging in the cleft of a mountain gorge, so alike, and so very different from, the vision of the moon over the French Quarter tonight. There, a breeze would be stirring the branches of oak and maple and evergreen, the moon shining on a slow-moving river as the mountain angled up sharply, cracked rock on either side. Mist rose from the black water, still warm from the day. A night bird called, a long trilling tweet. The image gripped me in a desperate, lonely fist. *Home.* I needed to be home, deep in the hills, not in this stinky city surrounded by cars and streetlights and thousands of humans.

But that was Beast talking. I had a job to do. I gripped the phone and opened my eyes on the nightscape of the city of New Orleans. "Okay. So what happened to me tonight and what should I do about it?"

"I think you have a natural protection woven about you from the cave where you first shifted into a bobcat, when you were a kid. Maybe some kind of Cherokee mystical something or other put over you there, put over your soul by your father and your grandmother to keep you safe. Maybe even some latent magic, or a spell to offset the skinwalker natural proclivity to violence and dark arts."

I raised my head at that. It was the first good news I'd heard about me and my kind in a while. *Yeah ... Why not?* Just because most—okay, all—skinwalkers eventually went nutso and ate humans, didn't mean that we were *supposed* to do that. The white man brought many contagions. Why not one that changed skinwalkers? Maybe my father and grandmother had come up with something special, some unique and now forgotten ritual that would keep me from that fate. Forever. And maybe the magic of that ritual just burned Evangelina, and stabbed Gee in the eye for interfering. *Yeah.* A grin spread across my face. *Fire magic!*

"Because Gee's magic is bluish," she went on, "I agree it's European or Celtic based, which means iron will break it better than silver. The handprints suggest that his magic is something more intrinsic and less ritual-based than my own gift. Meaning that he'll have defensives built into his skin. If he has skin."

"What do you mean, 'If he has skin'?"

"He might have scales or a chitinous shell for all I know. There are all sorts of things that go bump in the night. Questions. One: do you still have his eye on your palm?"

Surprised, I opened my left hand and there, on my palm, was the faint tracing of an eyelid, closed as in sleep. "Yes. Sleeping."

Molly chuckled, the sound grim. "That's not low-level magic, to steal part of a spell and make it your own. You can probably track him with it, but if he figures out that you have his eye, he can turn it back on and use it against you. If he comes at you, physically or magically, you'll need to be fast. Hit him and hit him hard." Before I could respond, she said,

"Your cave. Is it a real place? If so, maybe you should try to find it when you come home again."

"Maybe," I said. But if I was honest with myself, it was better than *maybe*. I *could* try to find the cave of my beginnings. I had found a few places from my long-forgotten past already. Excitement zinged along my nerves at the thought. "Thanks Mol. I owe you."

"No, you don't. Now say good night to your godchild so I can put her back to bed."

I heard shifting on the other end of the connection and Angelina said, "Hey, Aunt Jane." Her voice was heavy with sleep and the natural peacefulness of the very young raised in a loving and safe place. "You beat the blue man. But he's watchin' you and you gots to be careful. You gots to watch out for Bruiser and Ricky Bo and the man big-cat. Okay?"

Crap. The kid knew too much. Even with her parents binding them down, her powerful witch genes were expressing themselves in ways most witch genes never did. She was seeing the possibilities of the future. Of *my* future, which was weird. The girl was scary powerful.

"I'll be careful. You keep safe and listen to your parents, okay? Be a good girl."

"Will you bring me a new doll when you come back? A pretty one?"

I chuckled and said, "Yeah. I'll do that. I love you, Angie Baby. Good night."

"I love you too, Aunt Jane. Night."

"Later, big-cat," Molly said. And she was gone.

I closed the phone, stuffed it into a pocket, and studied the blue eye on the palm of my hand. It looked like an old tattoo, worn, faded, ink dispersing into my skin. I was pretty sure it was fainter than before, as it was evaporating away. If I was going to use it to track . . . I raised my hand and sniffed. Lifted my head and sniffed again. The reek of Girrard DiMercy's blood filled my nostrils. But it came from close by, not from my hand.

I looked up. And spotted Girrard DiMercy. He was cloaked in the blue mist of a hide-me spell, sitting on a brick abutment just up the block, in a small nook, the minialcove where other men had spied on my house before. What *was* it with that doorway?

The spell clinging to him wavered and shifted, and other things seemed to be hidden beneath it, as if the layers of his glamours had separated and softened, allowing me glimpses of the visions beneath. He hadn't seen me. I glanced back down at my palm, to see that the blue lines were even fainter.

I slid out of my loose shoes, leaving them on the sidewalk, and stalked silently toward him.

CHAPTER 19

A Fashionista's Closet Full of Falling Stilettos

Girrard DiMercy was sitting with his eyes closed, face tight and intent, his head back. The blue mist cloak spell wasn't strong enough to keep me from seeing him; it was too late to hide himself from me. Way too late. I'd seen his handprints on the roof of my soul, marking me as his. And I'd blasted them away. Now, his hands were relaxed, the outer edges of his palms and little fingers resting on his lap, his fingers and thumbs curled toward one another, as if he held a ball loosely. Except for the blue hide-me mist, he wasn't concealing himself. There was nothing defensive or dangerous about his posture, which made me figure that Gee thought he was invisible, or at least cloaked in night shadows. And one eye was swollen, caked with blood. I'd hurt him for real, just like the wolves had hurt him back in Booger's Scoot.

I pulled on Beast's hunting attributes, moving up the street, my bare feet silent on the sidewalk. As I moved, I considered weapons, should I need one. There wasn't a round in the 9 mil's chamber and Gee would hear if I readied the weapon for firing. And the H&K was loaded with silver shot. Molly had said steel would probably disrupt Gee's magic better than silver, so I pulled the vamp-killer. Though the back and the flat of the blade were coated with heavy silver plating, the cutting edge itself was high quality steel.

I stood three feet in front of Gee and I might as well have

been in Mexico for all the notice he paid me. He seemed som-
nolent, his breathing easy, as if he was sleeping, sitting, his
body relaxed. The blue mist lay thick on his skin and seemed
to swirl slowly with the energies of his spell, growing thin and
gossamer away from his body, denser, and tight between his
cupped hands. The mist was shaped like a sphere, dissipating
entirely beyond the borders of his body, and I realized that the
energies themselves formed a working circle that covered his
whole physical form. I didn't know a whole lot about magic,
but I did know that most forms used circles to contain the
energies, kinda like a force field, to keep anything nasty from
escaping, and to hold the energies in place. I wondered what
he looked like under his glamours.

I hefted the vamp-killer, moonlight glinting on the silver
and steel. I positioned my feet, left foot forward, right foot
back, pointed at ninety degrees. Knees bent, my weight evenly
distributed, I held the blade point forward and slashed down
with a single hard, fast cut, through blue mist. Down toward
the stone on which he sat, breaking the circle of his spell.

Time dilated and slowed. I could see the passage of the
blade through the mist. The way the steel parted the strands
and swirls of the spell. The way they fell away, as if recoiling
from cold iron. Light exploded out around the blade. Blue and
downy, soft and bright, like sparklers in the night. And still the
blade descended. The mist had weight and texture. *Like flesh*,
the thought popped into my mind. Heat billowed up my arm,
warm and moist. And the smell of cauterized blood. The reek
of burned evergreen. The stink of charred jasmine. *Oh* crap.
The spell hid his body. I'd cut Gee himself instead of his spell.

The mist retreated, almost a flinch, and snapped back hard.
A punch of power hit me. Electric and solid. Muscle, claws,
and something soft, hit me, like a bronze, spiked fist in a down
glove, the fist supercharged with electricity. I felt/heard a
sharp, sizzling hiss. Stumbled and fell back. Barked my heels
on the concrete.

Gee was awake and focused on me, his blueblueblue eyes
stabbing. *Something* billowed out and up and over me in
a wash of wet, steamy heat. Dark bloodred wings unfurled,
beat down. I curled as I dropped, falling. Saw a dark-sapphire
feathered beast with crimson breast and wings. Claws like
spear points, glinting at wingtips and feet. A splatter of liq-

uid flowers, perfume like rainbows hitting the ground. Sparks shooting up where the blossoms landed.

And he was gone. A raptor scree echoed into the night.

I landed on my butt, half rolling, half skidding across the concrete. My elbows took a bounce, ripping a layer of skin away. I rolled off the sidewalk into the street. And lay there, gasping. "Crap," I whispered, wincing at the ragged rips of pain. "Cah-*rap*."

I had never seen such a thing. Not in person. But I knew exactly where I had seen an image of one before. And Leo Pellissier had a lot of explaining to do. I eased to my feet and gathered up my stuff. Gee's blood had nearly dissipated, evaporating like pure alcohol rather than drying and leaving a residue of ruptured cells like, well, like blood. I found a patch larger than the others and dipped a finger into it. Sniffed. It didn't smell like human blood, but like pine and jasmine and heated copper. Big surprise. It was gone, evaporated, before I could figure out how to save any of it.

I limped to the house. Slammed back inside. Stared down Evangelina and Bruiser as I entered, throwing my sandals down in the foyer as I passed through and my weapons onto my bed. I went to the bathroom and turned on the shower, sticking my heels, then my arms from elbows to hands under the stream, cursing under my breath at the liquid's cleansing burn. I pulled out a first-aid kit and applied salve to the wounds, covering them with bandages. It would have to do until I could shift. Then, ignoring the two standing in my bedroom doorway, I opened my closet and yanked out my vamp-fighting clothes.

The stink of my anger and my blood and the burned smell of wax and pine coiled inside me with each breath. Ignoring the audience, I ripped off my blood splattered, torn pants and tossed them to the floor, not caring if I flashed an audience. I pulled on the silk long johns and slid into leather biker pants, the zipper ripping the silence. I stepped into socks and the butt-stomper boots. Opening the weapon safe in the closet, I began loading for vamp, sliding each vamp-killer into place, checking to see that each was snug, yet pulled freely. The knife used to stab through Gee's glamour had a nick in the blade a quarter inch deep, blackened as if by fire; the steel edge around it was shattered. I touched the blackened steel and it flaked away like ashes. It was useless. I could repair the blade, but I'd never trust it again. I could maybe replace the blade into the old hilt, but that would cost more than simply buying a new one. I hefted it into the garbage where it thumped hollowly, steel against plastic. I slid the M4's soft leather harness over my T-shirt. When it was comfortable, I reached into the safe and pulled out the soft velvet bag holding the vamp weapon Sabina had lent me. The priestess had asked for it back; I'd tried to return it once. Maybe she would be there this time, and I could ask the old vamp some questions about vamps and Mercy Blades and old grudges against Leo and Bruiser without getting my throat torn out. And maybe she knew something about weres, because sure as angels sing, every problem I was seeing started with the appearance of the weres, even before I knew they existed. I stuffed the velvet bag into the leather jacket's breast pocket.

"Jane?"

Fury blazed up in me. I whirled on Bruiser. "What? What do you want?" His mouth opened, confusion on his face. I let everything I was feeling rip through me. Heat flashed like lightning over my skin. I took a step toward him. "You know, don't you? What Gee is." Bruiser took a step back. "Tell me!" I hissed, Beast rising into my eyes. "You tell me what that thing is."

"Gee? Leo's Mercy Blade? I don't know, Jane."

"It's the same thing on the floor of Leo's foyer. I thought it was a phoenix rising, a heraldic emblem. But it isn't."

"Phoenix—no. The image in the foyer is an Anzu. A Sumerian storm god."

"A storm . . ." My voice trailed away, taking most of the anger with it. I backed away from Bruiser, never taking my eyes from him. I sniffed, smelling a trace of shock, but no dissembling, no stress pheromones in his sweat from telling a lie.

"Not the creator god," he said, "but a minor god, like the ones the Babylonians and the peoples of Canaan worshiped. A mythical creature who rides storm clouds, and who offers his loyalty to a person or family in return for a service, much like royal dispensation or a genie in a bottle. Some religious sects call them watchers, angelic beasts with a fondness for humans. They've been compared to dragons, but are much smaller and much more fierce, feathered, beaked, taloned raptors. But they aren't *real*. Why would you think that Girrard

DiMercy is an Anzu?" Bruiser's face was amused. He really didn't know.

I turned away and pulled on my leather jacket, buckled myself into enough weapons to start a one woman war, and left the house without another word, helmeting up and riding Bitsa out through the side garden entrance into the night. As always, the smells of the quarter were arresting, the combination like a gift to my Beastly half—food, people, vamps, sex, food, exhaust, lots of alcohol in its various forms. But mostly food. The now familiar aromas helped to settle Beast and let me think.

I shook off the last of the rage that had taken hold of me and was left with whirling questions. If Bruiser didn't know that Gee perhaps belonged to race of beings once worshipped as lesser gods, then, did Leo know? The MOC wasn't exactly forthcoming with info on his past. I had been snookered with the scattered details Gee had shared about how his parents, the Spaniard and the French woman had named him . . . Leo was French. Had an Anzu sworn fealty to the Pellissier family at some point the distant past? Or perhaps to vamps in general, treating vamps as members of one family? I'd believed everything Gee had said. I was supposed to be able to read body language— Okay, not applicable here. Anzu body language didn't seem to translate to human. As usual in my life, not knowing the answers to basic questions was dangerous. Hence this visit to Sabina, priestess of the Mithrans, one of the oldest vamps still kicking, the one in town who knew all the answers, even to questions I didn't know to ask.

My thoughts settling, I rode, letting the traffic pick the pace, the French Quarter packed with tourists and workers out for food, fun, and games.

As I wheeled between cars, I remembered the fractured moments when I had seen Gee transform. His feathers were blue and burgundy. The bird on Leo's foyer floor was burgundy without any blue. Gee's eyes were blue with a funky, oily shimmer that moved, like heat rising off asphalt. An effect of his magic, probably. And he was a lot smaller than the human he appeared to be when in his real form. A wingspan of twelve feet, body maybe three or four feet from beak to claws. I'd guess Gee weighed no more than sixty, maybe seventy pounds, just from the glance I had of his body.

The largest albatross had a wingspan as wide, but it weighed only twenty-six or twenty-seven pounds. Some Pterosaurs—prehistoric birdlike creatures—had wingspans up to forty feet and weighed up to two hundred fifty pounds, though I'd never seen anything that suggested they had true beaks or were feathered, but then, what did I know. Fossil discoveries were being made all the time. Maybe Gee was a prehistoric bird, though that conflicted with his comment about going home to heal. And where was home?

The weather was turning, with damp air blowing in off the gulf, sliding beneath a cooler layer of air from the north, or maybe it was the other way around and the cool air was underneath. Well, I now knew a storm god. Maybe I could ask him. A freaking feathered dragon.

I bent over the bike and roared my way out of the city. The night sky was completely overcast, a wet wind was scudding through the trees and gusting across the road, and the temps were now only in the mid-eighties. Cool for summer in New Orleans, not that I expected it to last, but it was better than the hot, wet hell of the past week.

By the time I got to the vamp graveyard I was cooled off and thinking again. Motor puttering loud, I sat outside the gates, boots on the street below me, and phoned Leo on his tracking-device-of-a-cell-phone. When he came to the phone, he spoke before I could introduce myself. "I attacked you when you fled. It was the action of an unchained. I am . . . sorry."

Leo had just apologized to me. I closed my mouth on what I had been about to say. Instead, I said. "Okaaaay. Apology accepted." A sharp silence hung in the air after my words. I figured that was enough of the niceties. "Let me in to the vamp graveyard. I need to see Sabina."

"Why?" That was Leo, no wasted words, no wasted emotion. Oh—unless it was to try to kill me. He'd wasted a lot on that.

"Open the gate or I'll just ride on through and you can deal with the dead bodies." Okay, maybe not so completely calmed down.

I could almost hear the laughter in Leo's voice, when he said, "And which dead bodies would that be, chère?" It sounded like sha, not cherie, the Louisiana version of the French endearment. And I didn't like Leo being endearing to me.

I gritted my teeth. "The enforcer-types I'll stake or shoot when they come to Sabina's rescue when the alarm goes off." I gunned the engine. "Now, Leo."

"Of course, Jane. Whatever you wish. Thirty seconds."

It was only after I hung up that I realized Leo had sounded like his old self. His old well-balanced, emotionally stable self, from before I killed his son's imposter and he got stuck in the *dolore*. And then feasted on Katie's dead blood. And then . . . Gee had fed Katie, who maybe fed Leo again—maybe when asking to become his heir—giving Leo some of Gee's blood? Vamp feeding arrangements were both gross and impossible to understand. I was getting woozy trying to figure it all out.

Leo being sane was a good thing, but no way did I think it was gonna be *all* good. There had to be another shoe to drop. After the last few days, I was likely to see a fashionista's closet full of falling stilettos.

When I figured my thirty seconds were up, I peeled out and swerved around the gate, into the cemetery and along the crushed-white-shell drive. It was dark, no security lights, not even a candle burning in the nonchapel where Sabina's sarcophagus lay, but I had better than average night vision after all the years I'd spent in Beast's skin and, even without the moon, I could see.

The mausoleums were white marble, each with a naked winged angel on top, also of carved stone, one mausoleum for each clan, except that Leo had killed off a few clans recently. The mausoleums were intact, repaired from one of my previous visits. Contact with me had been a bit rough on vamp real estate.

I swung the bike around and tightened my hand on the accelerator. And braked, dropping the bike into a low-angled skid when my eye caught sight of the angel on the Pellissier vault. I cut the engine, dropped the helmet, and walked away from Bitsa to see it better. It was too dark to be certain, but danged if the winged warrior didn't have Girrard's features. "Well, slap me silly," I muttered. "The guy is everywhere."

Before I got back to Bitsa, I heard a pop and whirled, grabbing for a stake and a vamp-killer, my heart thumping hard. Sabina was standing between two white buildings, wearing her nunnish white robes, her face serene, or as serene as an undead, blood-sucking monster can get. She wasn't vamped out, which was good, because my throat protector was lost to the wolves. "You did not request an audience."

"Cry me a river." The words slipped out before I could I stop them.

"I do not cry. You are impudent. Rude."

I blew out my irritation, hoping for an obsequious impulse somewhere inside so I could show proper deference. But there was nothing like that inside me right now. "So sue me."

Her head tilted to the side in that weird, reptilian thing they do. "Why would I wish to involve the legal system of this country?"

I figured modern snarky comments didn't translate well to a two-thousand-year-old vamp. "What do you want, little non-human?" she asked.

"I want you to tell me about the weres." When she didn't answer, I said, "You're an elder. Among my people, an elder is the keeper of knowledge, history, and the old stories, and they share that wisdom whenever they're asked."

"The Cursed of Artemis," she said, her mouth moving as if the words tasted bad. "Children's tales."

"Tales I haven't heard," I countered. When she didn't poof away or try to kill me, I dropped to the ground, sitting in the darkness, my back against a mausoleum wall. A misty rain began, as if condensing out of the heavy air and settling to the ground. I turned my face up to it. "I need to hear the stories, Sabina. Please." My housemother in the children's home where I grew up would be tickled with my manners.

Sabina ignored the rain, though her clothing was damp with it. "All myth is based upon some form of truth and history, though twisted and puffed up and hacked away. The tale of the Cursed of Artemis is no different." The priestess crossed her arms under her breasts and tucked her hands into her sleeves. It looked almost practiced, as if she wanted to appear human, aping human gestures. "Long before the Greeks named her Artemis, was Lolandes, the woman. I have often thought that her legend became confused with, and merged into, the earth goddess, who was common to all ancient tribal peoples. But Lolandes, renamed the Artemis of Grecian lore, was no goddess, but a powerful, long-lived mortal, one sometimes called a witch, though different from today's witches. She was the most powerful of her kind, in a time when women were revered, when political and religious power was passed through the matriarchal line. She was venerated for helping animals and humans in childbirth and for caring for wild animals."

Sabina turned her back against the stone wall, standing so close to me that the hem of her robes brushed my leather-clad knee. Beast nudged me to stand, not liking my submissive posture beneath the priestess, but I shoved her away. She went, giving me a huff of disgust.

"Lolandes once had a female bird as pet, a type of falcon, a fierce hunting bird. It was dedicated to her, never needing the jesses or the hood, and returned to her after each hunt, bringing Lolandes the choicest of kills from the hunting fields. The two were inseparable.

"One day at dusk, beneath a full moon, a wolf killed the bird, fighting over a doe they both had targeted. Lolandes cursed the wolf with a disease, similar to rabies, that affects mind and brain. And she took up the body of her bloodied pet and she mourned."

Sabina paused and I wanted her to hurry it up. But when you've lived for two thousand years, what's an hour or a decade or two? And I needed to hear the tale of the first weres, the Cursed of Artemis. So I schooled my mind to patience and my mouth to silence.

Rain collected on the skin of my face and beaded. The wind gusted hard, then soughed through the tops of nearby pines, needles and branches whispering. A hard blast of rain hit the earth nearby and died. The wind gusted again, stronger. Thunder boomed, far away.

Some minutes later, Sabina said, "The wolf ran into the woods. That night, it bit a civet, a lion, a dog, a snake, and other of Lolandes' predator animals, those she had cared for until now, transferring the curse of illness to each. The wolf hid by day. The next night, biting a gardener, he passed the curse of Lolandes to the humans. At the next full moon, the gardener changed into the form of a wolf and succumbed to bloodlust. Shortly thereafter other were-creatures began to appear, humans bitten by the cursed, forced to change by the light of the full moon. But the wolf was first. And the wolf's curse was greatest."

"No females who were bitten survived," I guessed.

"No. They did not. And Lolandes mourned her rash anger for the pain it had brought her animals and was ashamed that humans had been tainted with her curse. But it was too late to stop the change she had brought into the world. A curse cannot be undone.

"Lolandes studied and discovered a way, however, to minimize the damage to the human world, a partial cure that would allow the weres to bring over females and create families and societies, a therapy that would allow them to breed true. The cure"—she paused, as if searching for a word—"mutated the curse into one less easily transferred. She carried the cure to each of the were groups, all but the wolves. Them, she never forgave."

I'd taken a mythology course as an elective in high school, but I'd never heard this story. When I told Sabina that, she laughed, the sound dry as corn husks in the night. "So much has been lost," she said. "Yet, the story was told me by an old Roman scholar, one who claimed to have writings from the time of the Babylonians, long before the Greeks stole her name and story and made her a goddess. And it is true that the werewolves are the only moon-touched who carry the original taint, the original curse, unabated by Lolandes' cure."

It was a cure that effectively created new species, werespecies, human-animal hybrids that could reproduce true. I sat up suddenly, a thought shunting heat through my veins. *A falcon was hunting a doe?* Not likely. I made a leap of intuition, better known as a wild-haired guess.

Sabina must have heard my heart leap and race. She turned her face to me, her eyes focusing on my throat in the darkness. I froze, waiting, fingers on a vamp-killer at my hip. When she didn't move beyond the stare, I curled up a knee, one boot sole scraping on the shell path, an elbow braced on my knee. I pulled out the multifunctional cell and went online, checking the timelines of Sumer and Babylonia. "This female hunting bird," I said, redirecting her back to the subject matter rather than my pulse. "Could it have been an Anzu?"

Sabina shrugged and looked away. "I do not know if the cultures shared the Anzu."

According to the Internet, the kingdoms of Babylon and Sumer had overlapped in time. It was possible, if unlikely, that Lolandes'—or Artemis'—dead bird of prey had been an Anzu. One of which just happened to be hanging around Leo, the werewolves, and the were-cats, trying to bring the groups together. "Now wouldn't that be a handy dandy coincidence," I muttered. "Thank you, Sabina. I am, um . . . honored and . . .

humbled?" I drew on my Christian children's school manners. "Yeah. Humbled that you shared your story."

Sabina laughed low and turned her head to me again. I heard the slight snick of her fangs dropping into place, and because vamps can't feel amusement and go vampy at the same time, I knew it was deliberate, not a predator response to the pheromones of stunned reaction that escaped from my pores and sped my heart. I tilted my head up to hers. A smiling, ancient vamp, three-inch fangs exposed, is not a warm and fuzzy sight. Sabina disappeared as quickly as she had arrived, with a little pop of displaced air. Old vamps are fast enough to do that—move the air with a snap of sound.

I rehelmeted and cranked up Bitsa just in time to be hit with a blast of drenching rain. Bitsa is my dream bike; I love her like a part of me. But riding in the rain required changing gear into plasticized riding clothes over the leather. I pulled up to the chapel porch, rooted in Bitsa's saddlebags for the riding gear and a hand towel. Muttering under my breath about the heat and the stink of my own sweat, I dried off under her front porch and pulled the plastic pants and jacket over the leathers. The heat went up another ten degrees, steam-bath territory. As I dressed, my hand brushed the lump in my pocket, reminding me, and I draped the bag holding the sliver of the Blood Cross on the chapel door handle. It didn't seem like a smart place to leave it, but I wasn't taking it home again; I called out, telling the darkness what I had done and straddled Bitsa.

My headlight was thin and reedy, catching the raindrops as they slashed across the beam, creating more glare than visibility. Easing onto the dark-as-soot street I gave Bitsa some gas. Rain-riding was dangerous, especially at night, vision impaired by drops sluicing down the helmet faceplate, two tires speeding a lightweight vehicle with less traction than normal, water a slick layer on the road.

I took the roads slowly, back into the city as the rain slanted and the wind thrashed the earth. Microscopic droplets beat back up into the sky, broken from impact with the ground. Rain collected and ran, filling the ditches and bayous and every low place, ponding up in the streets.

Just before I got to the Mississippi River, I was stopped by the sight of a twelve-foot-long alligator, stretched across the street, jaw open, belly on the still-warm asphalt, taking a shower. I sat there, laughing at the sight, Bitsa growling beneath me. Beast shoved up into my consciousness, thinking, *Big teeth. Hard kill. Tough food. I like doe better.* Then she looked up at the rain and hissed. Disgusted with the gator and the weather, she curled up inside me, tucking her paws close and wrapping her stubby tail around her for warmth. Beast did *not* like rain.

I pulled out my camera and snapped a few shots of the gator, which took surprisingly well with the flash. Molly was gonna love this.

Back home, the house was dark. I stripped and hung the plastics and leathers up to dry in the shower, ate, and went online to find a huge zipped file from Reach, waiting in my e-mail box. He'd come through on a host of things, like the list of numbers Rick had called before his phone went dead. I recognized two numbers as belonging to police—Jodi and Sloan—but no others. None to me, for instance. Reach also sent a series of satellite photos of the vamp council headquarters for twenty-four hours before and during the vamp-and-were get-together. It was informative, not only because it showed that someone was willing to pay for satellite time to surveil the vamps but because the surveillance was paid for on the same local bank account that my retainer checks were drawn upon. Interesting. The vamps were paying good money to watch themselves.

And, more important, using Rick's phone, Reach had narrowed the possible hotels where Rick had been photographed kissing the wigged Safia down to two in East New Orleans. He couldn't rule out either, but Rick had been there for twenty-four hours before his phone died.

I input the addresses on my handy-dandy cell and got GPS directions on a city map and map app. I wanted to go in right now, guns blazing, and find him, but that would be stupid. It was raining, dark, and I hadn't reconnoitered either place. I might get Rick or myself killed.

I could call Sloan. Maybe the cops would go in, or maybe they'd just sit outside and watch the place to keep from blowing Rick's cover. There was no guessing with cops. I had more options than law enforcement officers. I could do things they couldn't. Lots of things they couldn't. But not if they were watching. So I didn't call them.

And that was when the real storm hit. All the rain and wind of the last few hours was only a prelude to the bona fide mama tempest, with gale force winds and rain that beat into the house like the entire Blue Man drum corp. No way was I going back out on Bitsa in this. And Beast didn't even hint that she wanted to shift. I fell asleep with the raging fury of nature like a lullaby in my ears.

CHAPTER 20

Đang. Brass Knuckles are Cool!

It was Sunday, and I left for church in plenty of time for the early service. I hadn't gone since Rick and I started dating, maybe because he was Roman Catholic and I was nondenominational, or maybe because I was sleeping with him without the benefit of a ring on my finger and guilt pricked me every time I thought about God. Guilt was one big drawback of religion, I thought sourly as Bitsa pootered along.

I got there at sunrise and parked under the tree in the little parking lot of the strip mall where the church rented space, set Bitsa's kickstand, pulled my Bible out of the saddlebag, and went inside, using the little ladies' room to change from riding jeans into a skirt. Not that anyone would have said anything about my jeans, even on Sunday morning, but I hadn't been brought up that way.

The church was empty and dim, though I could smell the preacher, an earnest, slender little guy who looked about twelve, so he was here someplace. I sat in the third row and closed my eyes, the Bible on my lap. I had a lot to repent of before I'd be clean enough inside to take the sacrament. And some of the things I'd done, like fighting, saying a few cusswords that had seemed appropriate at the time, and sleeping with Rick, I didn't really want to repent of, so I had some praying and thinking to do. I'd been brought up to be better than the person I had become. I knew my housemother never imagined, not in her wildest dreams, that I'd be a rogue vamp killer for hire, sleeping with a cop outside of wedlock, making out with a blood-servant in my shower, letting a witch live under my roof . . . Yeah. She'd be unhappy with me. I was unhappy with myself, especially the part about making out with Bruiser.

Light was diffuse in the small church, let in by high windows blocked by overgrown foliage, shrubs that had been left unpruned until they had grown into small trees. The building smelled of paint, dust, mice living in the walls, and the fainter scents of the previous worshippers. The muffled engines of cars going by was the only sound, even the mice were quiet.

Here was one place I could never hide from myself. Not "here in a church." But here inside, when I stopped and thought about God. I didn't think he'd be ticked off that I had begun to study my Cherokee heritage, even the more mystical aspects of it, which were a lot more like counseling than about religion. I didn't think he'd be ticked off that I had let a woman of a different species—a witch—lead me into meditation, despite all that "Suffer not a witch to live" stuff. I didn't think he'd be ticked off that I killed and ate things when I was Beast, or that I shifted. But the stuff with Bruiser in the shower. And sleeping with Rick. That kind of stuff I figured he'd be ticked off about, despite the fact that the Bible said all sins were equal, lying equal to murder, gossip equal to hating, a healthy roll in the hay equal to drinking one glass of bubbly too many. So it was the cultural part of it all, not the "What God thinks about it" part that was giving me trouble.

Tell that to my brain. Can you ask forgiveness for something you intend to continue to do if you get the chance? Smokers know they're going to smoke again. Hard drinkers know they're going to drink again. Did they ask for forgiveness? Was it a waste of breath? Did it amount to lying to God, another sin on top of any sins not being repented for? Something dark and guilty squirmed inside me, like a mass of blind snakes, cold and scaly and hissing softly.

I sat with my head down as the small early service crowd gathered, deliberately projecting a keep-away aura. And kept my eyes down through the service, not singing, not following along in the Scripture reading. Just listening to both the preacher and the silence in my heart. I had issues. I needed to address them. But later. After I solved this dead were-cat case. And found Rick. And decided what to do about Bruiser—who was being spelled by Evangelina. Would a spell have made me more attracted to Bruiser? Had the mad make-out session in the shower been spell-induced? Troubled, I passed the Lord's supper without partaking when it came around, and slipped out during the last prayer so I didn't have to talk to anyone.

I changed clothes in the parking lot, pulling the jeans up under the skirt and slipping the skirt off over them. And drove out of the strip mall lot just as the preacher opened the church door, no doubt looking for one of his flock who was clearly troubled.

I pulled up the map app of the hotels where Reach said Rick had been, and followed them to the east side of town. The first place I came to was the right hotel. It looked just like the pics I'd been given, and it smelled like sick, wet dogs. Like a kennel left unattended for weeks. Like dogs. Not cats. Werewolves, not were-cats. I parked and tucked my helmet under my arm, walking around the half-filled, cracked pavement lot, watching for a sentry and checking out the cars and trucks, trying for nonchalance. No new vehicles, nothing green, nothing high dollar. Most had bumper stickers proclaiming the owners supporters of legalized marijuana, promising themselves capable of lead-based self-defense, and advertising various brands of beer, vodka, or tequila. Only half were English, the rest were Spanish. I was really going to have to take a good Spanish class. High school was no help at all anymore.

I rounded the building. In the side lot, I spotted Rick's Kow-bike. Shock raced up my spine, stinging like fire ants. It was suddenly hard to breathe. The bike looked like it hadn't been moved in days, leaves and debris on the leather seat. He would never have left the bike here, outside, in last night's storm. Not if he was alive and uninjured.

Adrenaline poured into my bloodstream as I walked around the bike, but any lingering scents had been washed off in the deluge. Parked next to the bike on either side were pickup trucks, a rusty blue one and a rusty red one. And they smelled like werewolves.

Crap.

Trying to still the fury and fear in my bloodstream, trying to look less menacing than I felt, I walked along the row of hotel doors, sniffing. I smelled wolf, strong and fresh, and the scent of Rick, weaker, older. My heart skipped a painful beat. I stepped into the small hotel office, which stank of stale cigarettes, old beer, fresh marijuana, and air freshener strong enough to make me gag. Pulling up a pic of Rick on my cell, and a twenty out of a pocket, I slapped the bill down on the counter and held the cell out to the clerk even before he said hello. "Know this guy? Seen this guy? I'm not here to cause trouble." Leaving the bill on the counter, I thumbed open my PI license, tossed it beside the twenty, and added, "He's missing. Cops think he's dead."

The guy behind the counter was mid-twenties, stoned, lank-haired, with bloodshot eyes that stared at the money. He licked his lips like Pavlov's house pet before turning his eyes to the cell. He studied the picture a long moment before putting his fingertips on the bill and meeting my gaze. "I'd get fired if I told you he'd been staying with a girl and some other guys in rooms 114 and 115. So I can't tell you that." He picked up the twenty and put it in his pocket. "Sorry. And I can't tell you the rooms adjoin either."

I chuckled and said, "Hypothetically speaking, if someone busted in a door, and wanted to pay for it to avoid the cops being called, how much would that cost a girl?"

"Last time the repair bill was two hundred. But the cops got called."

I dropped two hundreds and a fifty on the counter. "Write me a receipt for a door for two seventy. No one sees it but my accountant and Uncle Sam at tax time."

The kid thought about it a moment, his brain on slow-mo. He scratched his butt while thinking, and finally nodded. "Make it an even three and you got a deal."

I added enough bills to make him happy, but kept my hand over them. "For this, you also turn off the security cameras for ten minutes. No one dies, no blood, no cops, no press."

"I'll leave it on just in case you get carried away and I have to cover my butt," he said, still scratching the object of his discourse, "but you can come back and steal it from me." He pointed at an old-fashioned VCR player under the counter. The kid might be stoned but he was still thinking. He gave me a receipt on a hotel letterhead, which had been photocopied on a machine in desperate need of toner. His signature was illegible and I was guessing it wasn't his, not that I cared. I'd be turning it over to Leo for reimbursement and to my accountant. A partial lie, another sin to add to my growing burden of them. I dropped an extra twenty on the counter to sweeten the pot. He said, "Business doing nice with you," and laughed as if he thought it was really funny. Stoner humor had always escaped me.

I walked to Bitsa, took out three handguns and belted two into a special holster at the small of my back. I checked the loads on them all, chambering silver shot rounds. I slid two knives into my waistband. I could have called for backup—either Derek Lee or the cops. I didn't. Rick's scent was fading. So I'd check the place out first. I did slide a pair of brass knuckles over my right fingers. I had never used brass knuckles, but right now, they felt good. I probably needed my leathers for protection, but I wasn't going back home to change.

I took a breath, studying the door locks. Settled my grip on the H&K 9 mil in my left fist, though I was a far better shot with my right. I'd be up close. Aiming wasn't essential. I'd need the power behind my right hook; I wanted to wound, not kill. I strode up to 114. Drawing up Beast, letting her flood my system. Unleashing just a bit of the fury boiling inside me.

I swiveled around and forward. Weight perfectly balanced with momentum. Lashed out, transferring power through torso, hip, thigh, knee, leg, foot. And kicked the door, my boot hitting just under the lock. The door jamb splintered. The door slammed open. Broke the security chain. Wood slivers and lock parts flew, catching the morning light. The door hit the back wall. The smell of werewolf hit me. I was inside before the two wolves in human form were half awake.

One went down at the foot of his bed with my boot heel imprinted on his jaw. The other one tried for a gun that I slapped away. Punched him in the face. I was pretty sure I broke his jaw and a few teeth. He was out cold, his remaining teeth not aligned right anymore. I looked at my fist. It didn't even hurt. Dang. Brass knuckles are cool!

Four seconds after I kicked in the door I was in the next room. Pivoted, weapon ready to fire at either door or window if needed. It was empty. It reeked of werewolf bitch, sickness, and sex. A lot of sex. Under that was the taint of Rick's blood. I broke into a hot sweat, but forced myself to stand and observe, taking everything in, with all my senses. Overlapping impressions bombarded me, visual and olfactory, the taste and texture of the air on my exposed skin.

The room was trashed, as if a pack of rabid dogs had torn it apart, dissecting the furniture into its component pieces, with only the bed still standing, though it was severely wounded. From the stink, the wolf-bitch had routinely bedded down and mated with all of the male weres in the nest of torn sheets and mattress stuffing. And with Rick, a lot.

Wolves mate for life, Beast thought at me. *Sick bitch.*

I scented old beef blood and saw a bowl filled with water in the corner, a bloody place on the carpet and a scrap of rancid meat against the wall where a were had eaten in wolf form.

The stink of were-bitch had a sickly smell, even to my human nose, as if I could sniff out the virus or bacteria that was making her crazy. It smelled stronger and more virulent than that running in the male werewolves' veins. The were-cats hadn't smelled like this. Sabina's old Roman scholar's info was starting to smell real likely.

The closet doors were missing. Female clothing hung on several hangers, the rest rumpled on the floor beneath the rod. The bathroom was neater than the rest of the place, maybe because it hadn't been used much. There were girl toiletries everywhere, spilled, dumped, half empty. The toilet lid was up, and an image of the were-bitch drinking from it made my lips curl with savage humor. A blond wig was half hidden under the counter.

Rick had been wooing a redhead in the photos, a girl I'd assumed was Safia. But by the stink of sex, he'd been with more than one were. If there was one wig there might be two. I turned slowly. Spotted a red wig, long tresses matted with crusted stuff I didn't want to examine. Fake prepackaged change of identity. I pulled it out with a toe and flipped it over to expose the mesh underside. A brunette hair was curled inside. I leaned in and took a whiff. Yeah. Were-bitch. At some point in his undercover investigation, Rick found the wolves. And ended up ... their prisoner?

Air moved through the open window on the back wall, and I went to it, unsurprised to see it broken out, blood on the shattered shards. I sniffed, parsing the pheromones. Rick's blood, by the smell; I could almost taste his fear. He'd tried to get away. He had gone undercover and found trouble. Rick was a prisoner, or had been. Beast growled deep inside me.

I went back to the bed. Rick's wallet and badge were under a pillow, on an undamaged spot of mattress. His blood was on the bed too. Rick wasn't undercover anymore.

Rage boiled through me, building pressure, needing an outlet it wasn't going to get. I needed to be analytical, methodical, not a raging maniac. But it was hard to breathe, my body felt clammy and cold in spite of the heat. I shoved down my reactions to the blood and semen and were-bitch scent, tamping the edges with cold, hard purpose.

Back in the room with the two naked wolves, one out cold, one in the middle of what looked like a very painful change, his human-shaped jaw crushed, I looked around. And smelled around. Marginally less ruined than the adjoining room, it was still a pigsty, littered with pizza boxes, beer bottles and cans, clothes everywhere. Inflatable mattresses, empty of air, were piled up in a corner as if tossed there when not needed. There was a pile of zip strips, the plastic handcuffs carried by law enforcement for securing subdued suspects quickly. To the side were several that had been cut off, the blood on most of them old and dried. The blood on one severed pair was fresher; it was Rick's blood.

I sniffed the strip carefully. There was no scent of death in the blood. Rick had been alive when he wore it. Maybe last night. Last night when I had elected not to go back out into the rain. My throat constricted. My chest burned with breath that throbbed and tore as it moved through me, harsh and strident in the small hotel room. A half sob, full of fury.

I opened the closet. Rick's bike jacket was on the floor. My eyes stung, dry and aching as I nudged the lapels open with a foot. His cell, the battery dead or the cell off, was beneath it. A handful of change was scattered there too. Nothing else.

I checked on the shifting were one last time, to see him lying on his side, fully wolfed out, panting raggedly, his paws running weakly like dogs' feet do in dreams. I walked to him on the filthy carpet, and his feet speeded up as he tried to pull them under him, panting in fear. I thumped him on the skull with the knucks, and said, "I'm not gonna kill you." He stilled, as if holding his breath. "The guy you were keeping here. Is he still alive?"

The wolf turned up golden brown eyes to me. He sniffed the air, scenting me as if to determine my species and purpose.

"You'll live even if the answer is no. But if you tell me yes, and I find out you lied, some marine pals of mine—the ones you met at the big coming-out party—and I, will track you down, and I'll hang your pelt on the wall of my house." I extended my fist and drew Beast up into my eyes, into my skin. Her pelt roiled just under the surface, coarse and spiky. When I spoke again, my voice dropped an octave. "But first, I'll play with you like a rabbit. I'll make you suffer. Got it?"

The wolf finally got his paws under him and scuttled onto the mattress against the headboard, his tail curled between his legs and under his belly, his head down and eyes rolled up, the whites showing under the irises. It was submissive behavior. He whined and nodded once, the human gesture looking all wrong on wolf.

"Is the guy alive?"

The wolf put his head down further, between his front paws. I tried again. "Was he alive the last time you saw him?"

Nod.

"Was that today? This morning?"

Nod. Nod.

Disgust and anger wormed through me. If I had skipped the church-and-guilt session I might have been here in time. *Maybe* . . . "Tap your paw. When did they leave?" Four taps later, I knew I had been sleeping, not guilting, when they left. *Four a.m. Why four a.m.?* "Were they in a car?" When he whined, I asked, "Car and a truck? Pickup truck?"

Two nods.

"Do you know where they were headed?"

The wolf hesitated this time, and I could see him thinking. I wondered if he thought like a human when he had a wolf brain or like a wolf. My own experience with shape changing might not be the same as weres'. Too bad we didn't have time to make nice and compare notes. Finally he nodded.

"*You* know he's a cop," I said. "*I* know he was here. Injured. Kept prisoner. He turns up dead, and got that way after this conversation, I'll remember you to the cops and to my buddies. Where were they going?" He looked puzzled and I said, "East of the river?" Head shake. "West of the river?" Nod.

That cut my search in half. My gut had been right so far today, so I asked, "Leo Pellissier's clan home?"

The wolf's eyes went wide in a thoroughly human reaction. Bingo. "At four in the morning?" I let disbelief color my tone. "When a vamp is most active?" When he ducked his head, indicating that I hadn't understood exactly right, I guessed, "To look the place over and plan for later?" He dipped his head into a half nod, half shake. I was warm, but not quite hot yet. Whatever the wolves had planned, I wasn't going to like it. "And they took Rick with them."

Again, I got the yes/no body language. His posture said it all. Total submission. And a tail-between-the-legs fear of me coming after him when I figured it out. Whatever the wolf was in his human form, in his doggy-shape, he was no alpha.

I glanced over at the other wolfman who was still sleeping the sleep of the beaten. His naked body covered most of the bed, and I recognized the big guy who had been smoking outside the biker bar when all this started. Fire Truck. He was no prettier naked than he had been fully clothed. I swiveled my gaze back to wolf-boy.

"The were-bitch. She has a use for the guy? A use that will keep him alive?"

The wolf slowly shook his head no, twice, his eyes on mine. His shoulders hunched at what he saw there, and his eyes flicked to the gun in my left fist.

"So, she's keeping him alive because she *likes* him?"

To my surprise, the wolf whined and nodded yes. My skin prickled as if my pelt rose. Hot fear slid though me as I made another wild-haired mental leap. From the way his nose twitched, and after the experience inside the bloodhound's body, I knew the wolf smelled my horror. "She's trying to turn him, isn't she?"

He nodded once. Without thought, I struck. Beast fast. Throwing my entire body into the punch. The brass knuckles hit him square in his nose. Throwing his head up and back on the follow-through. He pinwheeled off the bed. Into the wall. And slid down it to lie in a limp heap. I wanted to shoot him so bad it hurt. But I rolled the human-shaped wolf over and handcuffed his hands behind his back with his own zip strips, using three of the strips to make sure they held. I secured his feet, also, with several of the little units. Then I lifted his feet and attached them to his wrist cuffs with several more, effectively hog-tying him.

I did the same to the wolf on the floor, but if weres shifted using the same laws of physics as I did, it wasn't likely they would hold either guy.

Back in the office, there was a fresh stink of marijuana, coarse and prickly to my nose. I held my hand to the kid behind the counter and he removed the tape, placing it in my palm. But he didn't meet my eyes, his own sliding to the right. I smiled, knowing it wasn't a sweet smile. "If I find you made a copy or switched tapes, or anything else that comes close to breaking our agreement, I'll come back and take my three hundred plus bucks out of your hide."

Fingers shaking, he lifted a second tape from behind the counter and placed it in my hand. "Business doing nice with you," I said, quoting him. He didn't smile when I left.

In the parking lot I dug out my throwaway cell and punched in the number for the cop who had warned me that Rick was missing, Sloan Rosen. When he answered, I could tell he was at work, cop-shop noise in the background.

"You boys still missing a cop?" I asked, hoping they had recovered Rick, alive, since four a.m., and knowing Rosen would recognize my voice.

"Yes," he said, his tone conveying that he was in the presence of other cops, and holding a warning that told me to be careful what I said.

I gave the hotel name, address, and room numbers. "Rick LaFleur was there until four a.m. He was alive when he left, but the dogs he was investigating know he's a cop and I'm guessing they weren't happy about it. If you hurry, you'll find two trussed-up werewolves to question."

"Who is this?" Rosen asked. "How did you know about the cop?"

"Cute," I chuckled, knowing he was protecting both of us with the questions. "And while you're at it, let me suggest that a sheriff's deputy drop by Leo Pellissier's. One of the puppies told me the wolves reconnoitered the clan home of the MOC at four this morning." Sloan swore and I closed the cell, cutting the connection. I pulled out the battery, put them both in my pocket, and roared toward home.

My demeanor caused Evangelina and Bruiser to back away, their questions unasked. I shut my bedroom door and went online, pulling up city maps and vamp history and printing it all out so I could look over it one more time. I started at the front and went through everything, not reading, just looking, letting my mind take in it what it wanted. Midway through I saw the photo of a child, olive-skinned, dark-haired and dark-eyed. A pretty, young boy with short ringlets and a lace collar. I studied the photo. Something about the chin, the shape of the eyes, the mouth held in a tight, angry line, looked vaguely familiar. I flipped it over. On back, in the same cursive as the small sample of photocopied journal, was written *Terrence Sweets, 9 yrs*.

I kept on searching, knowing that *something* was here. If I just knew what to look for. Vamps didn't have conflicts that started today. They had conflicts with roots in the past. Sometimes way in the past. This one started back in the early 1900s, and because I hadn't figured it out yet, Rick might be dead. When I reached the end, I threw the pile of photos and photocopies onto the bed in disgust.

"*Think*," I whispered to myself. The cops had heard that were-cats were in town, parleying with Leo in the two weeks before the official announcement and weres came out of the furry closet. They sent Rick in to investigate. The wolves showed up and Safia somehow heard about them. Rick heard about the wolves from Safia and went to visit them too. So far so good.

After a day off in the mountains with me, he dove right back undercover—but something had changed in his absence. Ricky Bo had known there were problems when he got back to town, but for whatever reason, he couldn't call in official backup. So he'd taken a girl to breakfast at our favorite restaurant—Safia? The wolf-girl?—hoping I'd dig deeper. And I hadn't. I'd pouted. Working for Leo had done the rest. I'd ended up in the middle of fighting cats and dogs and left Rick out to dry.

Angry at myself, at Leo Pellissier, and at Rick, I reweaponed-up—not that I thought I'd need firepower until night, but, since I'd never been very good at walking softly, it might be smart to carry my big stick everywhere I went. Especially if there was a chance I might not make it back before nightfall. I dressed in my leathers, strapping the M4 to my back with the extended butt stock in place. I wouldn't be target shooting but the extra stability might be handy. The Benelli was loaded with seven hand-packed, silver fléchette rounds, 76 millimeter shell shot, six in the magazine, one in the chamber.

My braided hair I curled into a fighting queue, leaving nothing to grab during a down-and-dirty fight. I added three side-arms to my weaponry and magazines to my pockets. Lately, when I bought weapons, as many as possible used 9 millimeter ammo and interchangeable magazines. Handy in case a gun jammed. And all guns jammed eventually, no matter how well machined.

I added all my claws to sheaths, my favorite vamp-killer—the hilt hand-carved by Molly's husband Evan—under my left arm. I caught sight of myself in a mirror, my eyes glowing dark gold, my face pale and set.

A shadow on the wall at my back moved, the reflection of a branch at the window, pushed by the slow breeze outside, something I never noticed. But for an instant, it was a shadow on a cabin wall, moving with purpose. I heard again the slapslapslap of the *yunega's* body hitting my mother's. I felt my father's blood cooling on my face as I added more stripes, blood promising blood.

It was vengeance never satisfied, the empty place in my soul that justice should have filled was still dark and cold. If the wolves had killed Rick, I'd leave none of them alive. This time, the guilty would pay.

I turned slowly, watching in the mirror as my hands found each weapon, practicing the single-move drawing action, checking that each slid easily out of holster or knife sheath. I stared at the crosses I usually carried, leaving them on the hook in the closet. I wasn't hunting vamp. I wouldn't need them. But that wasn't why I left them there. I left them because I didn't deserve to wear them. I had never hunted thinking beings before, only insane vamps, mindless killing beasts with no hope of sanity.

Weres . . . Weres had human feelings, thoughts, hopes, and dreams. And it was likely I was going to kill some, deliberately, with malice and intent. Vengeance wasn't Christian. Vengeance was something darker. Older. Vengeance was bloodsworn. Blood promising blood.

I closed the closet. Dialed Derek Lee. He answered on the first ring. "Legs."

"If I need backup against wolves this evening, are you and your men available?"

"How much?" He meant how much would I pay him. And Reach had taken all my ready cash and then some.

"Free. Unless I can make Leo pay. The wolves have Rick LaFleur. He's hurt."

I heard the disgust like white noise breathing into the phone. "I'm in. I'll bring anyone else who'll come."

I ended the connection and headed out of town, gunning
Bitsa. I was going wolf hunting, and the best place to start was
the last place they had been—reconnoitering Leo's clan home
at four a.m. Maybe I could pick up a scent there. If nothing
else, I could tell Leo that Tyler had been framing Bruiser.

Midway across the river, I fished the cell phone out of my
pocket and tossed it over the barrier. Hence the name, throwaway cell, I thought with cold humor. Time to buy a new one.

New Orleans' infamous traffic was light as I sped toward Leo's
clan home, sweating in the day's wet heat, trying to breathe in
air that was mostly water. Last night's rain had evaporated
into the already steamy atmosphere, and I felt like I was
drowning with each breath, as much with worry over Rick as
with the high humidity.

I stopped on the west side of the river, at a little roadside
stand called Best's, that advertised on hand-lettered signs,
BEST BOUDIN BALLS 4 U, BEST BOUDIN IN LA., BEST C-FOOD, BEST
BOILED P-NUTS, and BEST GUMBO. The place looked like it had
been glued and nailed together with Katrina storm debris,
every board weathered, out of plumb, crooked, split, and
warped. But they had actually been nailed over a prefab body
to make the business look older than it was. Inside, Best's was
clean and neat, sparkling with white paint, and a nirvana of
fried and steamed scents. I bought a bag of boudin balls—
boudin being meat, most often pork, special spices, and rice
stuffed into pork casings, a kinder word than pork intestines.
Boudin was removed from the casings, shaped into baseball-
sized servings and fried in pork fat. Heart-attack-style food
for humans, comfort food for Beast.

I was antsy to get to Leo's, but hadn't bothered to eat before leaving the house for church. Fasting or guilt-tripping, not
sure which, but I'd used up all my available calories on the
wolves at the hotel. I was starting to shake. I ate six balls fast,
straddling Bitsa, ignoring the curious and worried small crowd
staring at my arsenal, and slurped down a two liter Coke, giving me the basic food groups: fats, protein, and carbs, delivered
with a caffeine/sugar kick. I stored the last six Cajun meatballs
in Bitsa's saddlebag, used the little individually wrapped wipe
that came in the greasy bag to clean up, and checked the time.
It was nearly three. The day was moving much slower than it
felt.

I kick-started Bitsa and gunned the bike out of the shell-covered lot, spinning small white shells into a long C-shaped trough as I turned toward Leo's once again. I had no plan. I was flying by the seat of my pants. The story of my life. All I knew for sure was that I'd park Bitsa downwind of the clan home and proceed in on foot to reconnoiter.

Most likely scenario was that the wolves would be gone, in which case I'd try to figure out which way they'd gone. Middle case scenario, I'd locate sentry wolves—watchdogs—left behind to survey the joint, probably from the distant tree line in wolf form. I'd take one of them. And make him tell me where Rick was. Then I'd call Derek Lee and his marines in to act as enforcers and backup while I freed Rick. Worst case scenario, the wolves would still be there, in which case I'd call Derek Lee and his marines in to act as enforcers and backup while I freed Rick. But that last state of affairs would be a lot more bloody. And a lot more dangerous.

I was two miles from Leo's, on a deserted stretch of secondary road with hayfields, pine tree forest, and scrub brush overtaking fallow fields to either side, when I caught a glimpse of brake lights in Bitsa's chrome. A car I had just passed slowed. Started a hard, fast, three-point turn in the middle of the road. I rounded a curve and decreased my speed, watching over my shoulder. When the car didn't catch up with me, I clutched, increased speed, and finished rounding the curve.

I saw the shapes first, leaping from a pickup truck, spreading out in a semicircle. Some low and horizontal—wolf-shaped. Some taller and vertical—man-shaped. That's when the smell hit me. *Werewolves.*

CHAPTER 21

Killing Teeth Tore Through . . . and Took Me by the Throat

I knew several things instantly, putting it all together in overlapping possibilities. There was no scent of Rick on the wolves. I'd been set up. The weres in the hotel had gotten loose and called their buddies. Or there had been an undetected wolf watching when I went in the hotel rooms. I hadn't sensed a sentry, but there might have been one. Or maybe the helpful clerk had placed a call when I left. However it happened, they'd been watching for me. And I wasn't getting out of this one without an ass whupping.

It was six to one, two humans, four oversized wolves, and a car full coming back this way for the second wave. The humans were the most deadly, despite the wolves having fangs and claws. The humans had guns; they took cover behind truck doors.

I had to get through this bunch. Fast. I aimed Bitsa between two wolf attackers. Pulled the M4 left-handed, clumsy. Needing the right on the accelerator. Thumbed off the safety and braced the butt stock against my forearm. I didn't need to ready the tactical shotgun for firing. It was built to be ready. I pointed it at the wolf on the left. Estimated he was forty feet away. Gunned the engine. Eating up the distance until I was close enough to fire. "Die, doggie," I muttered. And squeezed the trigger.

The firing concussion was muted by the riding helmet. The

weapon bucked. The hand-packed round hit the wolf in the ribs under his right front leg. The silver fléchettes exploded inside, ripping through and out in a spray of blood and gore. Not a direct hit, but good enough. I pointed the gun at the wolf beside him, much closer now. Braced the barrel on my right arm. Pulled the trigger. The first dogboy was still twisting and falling when his partner took the second round in the neck, dead on his feet. Not hard to do. Not hard to kill. Living with it later would be a bitch, though. Living was always harder than killing. A lot harder.

Threat level down by two. I took my first breath since gunning the engine, tasting burned powder and blood, hot on the air. I took out a wolfman next. Only feet away. Easy shot to the leg, showing beneath a car door. He fell, his mouth open, screaming; his gun spun in the air.

I was on them. Level with the semicircle of attackers. I tried to swivel the M4 as a human, hiding behind the wheel well, stood. But I was moving too fast to point and shoot. The gun boomed, kicked, and I missed by a mile. And felt the punch to my left side as I was hit. Beast slammed adrenaline into my system.

From the left a shadow loomed.

I tried to lift the M4 into firing position. My left arm wasn't working.

The shadow fell toward me. Dark body. Paws out. Vicious snarl I heard over the engine and the firing concussions. Before I could react, he hit. Claws against my helmet, scraping. Jaws brushing my nape. Hot, fetid breath.

His body hit my shoulder. Twisted me around on the bike seat. Slinging the shotgun toward him, but my hand wasn't working well enough to pull the trigger. My right foot slid off the footrest. My helmet was yanked to the side by claws, adding to the twisting torque. Then the axis of the wolf's leap left him behind.

Another wolf hit the front wheel. His paw disappeared into the wheel spokes. He screamed. Blood splattered. I kicked out, pushing on his body to face myself forward. His own weight pulled him from the bike. Bitsa recovered as if by herself, and roared ahead. Only speed saved me.

I was past them. But I was hurt. I had missed the second human, the shooter. Blood was running across my leg. Fast. And I couldn't catch my breath. I shrugged the M4 into a better posi-

tion on my lap and bent over the bike, roaring down the road.
Knowing I was leaving a blood trail a puppy could follow. I
had to get to Leo's to get help. My heart pounded, too hard,
too fast. Pain spread, wrapping around me like a silken web,
an unseen spider drawing the strands tighter. I wasn't going to
make it. I had too far to go.

Shift, Beast growled. *Now*.

I let off the accelerator and allowed the bike to slow, my
left hand barely holding on to the M4, unable to manage the
brake or clutch. Bitsa sputtered, the wrong gear for the loss
of speed. I turned off the road onto an overgrown track in
the scrub, an unused farm field entrance or hunting trail, and
bumped over the ruts. Thirty feet off the road, Bitsa died. I
braced with both feet on the ground and eased her down. And
the world tilted. Spun. I landed. My face in the dirt. I heard my
pained grunt. The light of day began to telescope down. Until
I could see only a sliver of a broken beer bottle in a clump of
spiked grass, the label weathered into a gray glob. I felt my
heart stutter.

Beast roared up over me. Filling my vision, her scream
echoing inside my head as her killing teeth tore through the
gray place and took me by the throat.

I panted. Little puffs of breath. Painpainpain beating with
heart. Tilted head and let helmet fall to ground. Swiveled ears
to hear, rotating both, searching for wolves. Pack hunters.
Only silence. No cars. No soft feet padding close. I fought pack
hunters once before, in hunger times. Killed many. But lost
hunting territory. Humans and pack killed all prey. Mountains
on fire killed rest. Did not want to fight pack again.

I sniffed breeze. Smelled rats, many. Stray cat. Smell of yellow jacket nest in ground, sound of buzzing nearby. Painful
stingers like big teeth. Manure from horses and cows. Smell
of chickens. Close. But no pack. Pack had dead to mourn. Was
safe for now.

Looked around. Huffed breath. Was lying in Jane blood
and Jane clothes, pelt sticky. Needed food inside Bitsa, for
shift. But Bitsa was on side, food underneath. Stupid Jane. I
pulled back paws from boots, paws and claws pushing on dead
cow skin. Stood, back paws inside more cow skin, front paws
inside Jane jacket. Jane guns and Jane claws of steel tangled in
cow. Pulled self out of stupid human clothes. Saw bullet drop

from side to ground and pawed it. *Ugly man guns.* Shook pelt free, hacked. Shook again, standing in sunlight, free of Jane except for her blood and her gold necklace. It bounced against my neck.

Still no wolves. I sniffed guns, holding head low to ground, inspecting big shotgun. Jane's favorite. Vampire killer. Now wolf killer. Better than killing teeth and claws. I huffed, disgusted, smelling fired gun. Stinks. But still better. Beast never killed three wolves in one day. Jane was good hunter.

I clamped on butt with teeth, far away from killing mouth of gun. Pulled into brush, out of sight of humans. Pulled rest of guns too. And Jane's clothes, filled with knives—Jane's claws. Left Jane's bike. Bigger than dead cow. Too hard to hide. I held head to air, sniffing. Turned in slow circle. Scent of water nearby, stagnant and full of crawly things, too small to hunt. Smell of animals and farm on slow wind. Chickens. Many chickens. Saliva flooded mouth at thought of chickens. White feathers tasted bad, but meat beneath tasted good. Blood tasted good. Hunger held on to belly like killing claws. Thirst squirmed like snake in belly. I moved into brush, padding toward smells. Good smells. Found water. Slurped water, frogs, wiggly things, drowned squirming snakes of thirst. Plopped beside little pool and groomed pelt, sticky with Jane's drying blood. But belly ached.

Changing from Jane to Beast, or Beast to Jane, was always hard. When dying, was harder still. When sun was up and moon was sleeping, was impossible to shift shape, unless death was near. When Beast was dying, death gave power to shape-change, no matter time of day or night. Jane understood. Skinwalker-magic. The magic of her kind.

But changing gave pain. Belly twisted in talons of predator called *hunger*. Pelt forgotten, rose and followed scent of food.

Trees thickened and branches weaved together in sky overhead. I padded faster, found tree with low limb and leaped, climbing high. Reaching with claws. Thick tail circling for balance. Caught bark and pushed/pulled up tree, shredding bark. Pine filled nose. Like Gee. Bird Gee. Reached limb and found balance on it. Looked down. Around. Found farm. Chicken farm. *Jane still asleep. Chickens are mine.*

I/Beast could count to five. There were many-more-than-five chickens in long chicken house. Two humans and two dogs in yard. Big truck full of many chickens in street. Human men moved cages of chickens from house to truck. Sound and smells all wrapped together, good chicken smells and stinky man smells and truck exhaust breath, and loud, ugly noises and good chicken noises. Dogs yapping. One raced in circles, chasing tail. Stupid dog.

Wind hid my scent, drawing it away. I crouched in brush to leave no prints, beside house full of chickens, unmoving, pelt hiding me. Waiting. Man dropped cages. More than five chickens got away, weak and sickly-looking, big bodies wobbling on weak legs. Making sounds of pain. Human let prey get away. Stupid humans.

Three chickens ran toward Beast. I rushed out of brush and grabbed chicken, killing teeth snapping around neck, jaws crunching down. Taste/smell of meat and blood, hot in mouth. Dropped chicken and snapped neck of second chicken. Grabbed both. Ran.

Bounded back into bushes. Raced away. Paws on animal path. Dogs barked and raced after. Humans shouted. I reached trees and raced up high into limbs. Fast, claws strong. Leaping, tail shifting, helping with stable landing, placed food in branches and leaped to ground. Hid. Dogs raced after. Two dogs. One big with big teeth. One small with stinky rotten teeth. Raced past. Noses to ground. Came back. Circled, circled. Never looked up. Stupid dogs.

Little dog with stinky rotten teeth stopped. Quivered. Nose off of ground. Snout aiming at me. I growled. Leaped, pushing off with back feet. Claws half sheathed, teeth showing. Swiped at dog. Hit his side with paw and saw him fly. Hit tree. I screamed and swiped at big dog. He yelped. Ran away. Tail tucked between legs. I screamed with victory. Trotted to dog beneath tree. Not dead. Claws half sheathed did not kill.

Batted him over. No blood. Breathing. I leaned close and huffed, learning his scent. Licked his body, harsh rasping tongue pulling on dog pelt. Licked his face and eyes, like kit, slow to move after birth. He stirred, whimpered. Good enough to make Jane happy. Jane liked dogs. Stupid pack hunters.

Tall in trees, far away, I ate chickens. Meat and bones and pulling sinew. Feathers slick with blood. Beaks pointy, crunched like small bone. Feet crunched, all bone and skin. Chicken gone. Licked snout. Found feathers stuck to muzzle. Settled to groom away dried Jane blood and fresh tasty chicken blood. Took nap in sun, high in tree. Free of Jane.

Woke and listened to forest. Bird, turkey, armadillo, possum, rats, rabbits. Watched hawk hunt, soaring overhead, diving toward prey. Watched sun drop toward end of sky. Groomed self again, removing last of Jane blood.

Jane woke to taste of her blood on my tongue, her mind slow. *Crap. What was that?*

Werewolves. I hacked in disgust. White feather blew from lips and floated on air. *Pack hunters. Jane killed three. Good hunter.*

But why? Jane raised up, trying to be alpha. *Werewolves out here . . . Before dusk. Crap, crap,* crap*! They were coming from Leo's! They already hit him. Maybe hours ago. I didn't smell Rick on the wolves. Did you smell Rick? We have to get to Leo's!*

No Rick-smell. Long walk. Hot day. I rose and dropped limb from limb to the ground. Went back to the puddle of water. Drank. Slowly. *I am alpha. Not Jane.*

Jane went silent, stuffing anger down in brain like paw on kit. *Pretty please?*

I hacked. *Long walk. Hot day.* And started toward Leo's den. Slowly.

Jane looked through Beast eyes at Leo's clan home. Watched barn, house, land all around house. Horses stood in center of field in tight circle. Prey animals, stomping, snorting. Shaking manes. Smell of fear on air. Smell of wolves strong, but not new. Not fresh.

Jane thought, *Why aren't there any people? Last time I was here, I must have seen ten people in the garden and barn. At least the sheriff's deputy is here.*

The deputy was standing on front porch, stick in hand, staring through open door. After long moment, he turned, went back to his car. Made punching motion and put cell phone to his ear. "Roul. Yeah. I see. You think you got her subdued? Can you keep her that way? Shit man, we weren't supposed to act until moonrise. Sun screws up the stasis spell. If this gets out before dark, when we can get back in— Yeah. Right. Okay." Deputy punched button on phone and got in car.

Started engine, low growl like cat, and drove slowly away, tires rolling over small rocks and shells. As car drew even, smelled werewolf stink.

Deputy was werewolf.

Yeah, Jane thought, surprised. *I recognize him from the biker's bar. And smart me, I told Sloan to send a deputy to Leo's. If the wolves got one of their own in as a cop, then they've been planning this return to Leo's territory for a long time, maybe just waiting for the opportunity.* She went silent inside of head. Worried.

I huffed and lay chin on paws, peering through tall grass. Smelled blood on air, strange blood. Like blood dropped on hot stone, vampire blood and pack blood, mixed. Scorched and burnt. And smell of magic. All coming through open front door.

I hunched shoulders and shuffled paws forward, through grass. Raised belly off ground and crouched toward house, through flowers, over shredded bark, moving slowly, like stalking, but no prey to pounce on. Moving toward Leo house and blood smell.

At bottom of front steps, smell of magic and blood grew stronger, smells flowing on air from open door of Leo house. *Big-cats do not hunt for prey in daylight. Dusk hunter. Night hunter. Dawn hunter. Best under pregnant moon, full and bright on ground. Not day hunter, to creep up man steps to man house to see inside.* But lifted paw and set it on bottom step. Pawpawpaw up steps fast, sheriff-deputy-wolf-smell beneath paws. Ready to leap from steps into bushes. But no need. No people moved. House was silent. Smell of blood and magic growing stronger.

Witch magic, Jane thought. *Which makes no freaking sense. Witches and vamps don't work together unless the negotiations are a lot further along than I thought. But then, nothing about vamps makes a lot of sense. Let me see inside.*

I padded to front door. Looked inside. White marble floor was splattered in blood. A young female lay on stone, eyes wide, one hand lifted up. Blood looked fresh, wet and new. Much blood. Female did not breathe. Heart did not beat. But she did not look dead and blue.

Not yet, Jane thought. *Nettie. She served me breakfast once. She helped me with the search of Tyler's room. She can't be twenty-five.*

Careful to avoid blood, I padded with hunter's crouch into house, stubby tip of tail jerking with Jane's worry. With fear of being in man house in Beast form. Walked across bird of prey in stone. *Leo's heraldic device,* Jane thought, studying bird. *Whether that thing is an Anzu or not, I don't know. But it isn't a phoenix. How could I have missed that?*

Inside foyer, in living room, found more bodies, looking dead, no breath. Many bleeding from bite marks. Not alive. But not dead. Afraid. Standing or sitting in small groups, looking at nothing, as if they had been herded into room like sheep.

Maids, enforcers, gardeners, grooms, the butler, and chef, Jane thought. *Stasis spells everywhere. The werewolves attacked, bit a bunch of them, and put stasis spells over it all. Spells they bought from a witch. But the deputy said the spell went wrong in the daylight. But . . . What do they want?*

To take over as alpha of city, I thought. *Working with Leo's enemies.*

Yeah. Okay. Power play. I get why they bit Leo's blood-servants. Turn them and take away his support system. But why kill Nettie?

Girl ran? Predators would chase; instinct for chasing. Girl fought? Predators would subdue. Kill may be accident. Or wolf-bitch, jealous. Like Jane with Ricky Bo. Heard sly tone in voice, hacked with laughter.

I'm not jealous.

I blew through nose and padded across room, around stasis spell, careful to avoid blood droplets. Into a corner where something gleamed. Metal. Silvery. Jane's chain-mail throat collar. It was mangled, torn by predator's killing teeth.

Jane stared, thinking. *They wanted someone to think I was part of all this.*

Pack hunters planned to make Leo think you are enemy. Make Leo think you turn against him. Jane was surprised. I snorted again. Sometimes Jane stupid.

Take it. And let's get out of here.

I lifted necklace in mouth and turned, tail swinging. Started from room. Heard click. Froze, dropped belly to ground. Useless move. No tall grass to hide behind. Belly-crawled to sound, to doors, like closet doors in Jane's house-den. Door was cracked open. Click inside.

Maybe more chickens. Maybe rabbits! Clicking inside. Unsheathed claws on right paw and caught door, silver collar dangling from jaw. Pushed it open with soft squeak of metal.

Sweet! Jane thought, pushing into front of brain, taking over as alpha. *Leo's security system.*

I stood on back legs and put front paws on desk. Lights blinked. Light box with picture showed Leo, his image fuzzy and reddish, like blood flowing in stream. He was awake and sitting on a bed, holding his arm close to his body. Blood was drying on his clothes, much, life-stealing blood. Spell over Leo's bed was red. A witch spell like one from Jane's Molly. *Hedge of thorns.*

The time stamp is moving forward. This is real-time, Jane thought. *Leo's in his lair, awake, and injured, bleeding. Behind a* hedge of thorns *spell. And what is that, in the corner?* It looked like part of a human hand, fisted. *His attacker is there with him, caught in a stasis spell. Which makes no sense because they passed me on the road and set up the ambush.*

As if he could hear Jane thoughts, Leo turned to the monitor camera and stared, his eyes ringed with pain like prey. I thought at Jane, *Protective spell, in his den. Evangelina gave it to him?* Cat eyes fell on small object on floor at Leo's feet, inside *hedge of thorns. Stake. Enemy attacked.*

And it's silver-tipped. Crap. *It's one of mine, one I lost at Booger's Scoot. Leo needs help, but I can't call for help in cat form. I can't shift until dusk, and we can't risk breaking the spells before dusk or Leo might just up and die. Again. Crap. This sucks.*

Beast is alpha. All day. In daylight. I turned and padded from house into yard, across sun-heated ground, into barn. Wolf smell was everywhere, thick carpet of it. I entered stall and dropped Jane collar in shadow near barn door. Drank from horse water in stall to remove metal taste from mouth. Smell of pregnant female horse everywhere, in water, in straw on floor of stall, old urine and dung strong. I sneezed to force dust and horse smell out of nose. *Pregnant horse would be much meat. Winter food to replace deer stolen by wolves.*

No! Jane thought. *No horses!*

I hacked and spotted hole in ceiling. Cave to sleep in. Leaped up wall, paws on railing, against window sill, pushed up into hole, front claws scrabbling, pulling body through. Moments later, was in darkness of hayloft and lay across pile of hay. Hungry again. Lay still, listening to mice. Too small to hunt. Only one mouthful crunch. Across barn, female cat hissed in warning, showing killing teeth, saying she would protect. Smell of kittens and milk showed reason. I yawned and lay head down.

Heat felt good. Closed eyes and slept.

Not long later, I woke. Dusk was near. Light like skin of fruit in sky. I was hungry. Barn was still silent but for horses below, milling and frightened. Scent of wolves and big-cat predator in their barn. *I could kill and eat horse.*

No! Jane thought.

Little horse. Baby horse.

No! Hey ... Wait. You could eat a horse. You're making a joke.

I hacked in amusement and padded to end of barn. Door for hay was latched closed. I unsheathed claws and caught latch with one claw. Let it fall. *Beast is smart. Good hunter.*

I pushed open door. Movement in tree line pulled eyes. Black shape. Spots showing beneath black coat. *Kemnebi.* The black were-leopard leaped over a downed tree, long, slender tail moving like tail of house cat, different from stubby Beast tail. His legs were short, his body long.

Graceful. Lissome, elegant. He's beautiful, Jane thought. *Almost as beautiful as you are.*

I chuffed, the sound nearly lost in the movement of horses below. But the leopard flicked his ears, swiveled his head. Found us in the gloom. His eyes were greener than Beast's, his skull larger, snout angled down.

He spun and jumped to the downed tree. Crouched. Stared at us, tail whipping. And he roared. Leopard roar, jungle cat roar, chuffing hollow sound. Beast pelt rose as air vibrated with his call. Horses milled below, snorting and stomping. One bugled. Barn shook as horse kicked wall. And Kem pushed away from tree, his body rotating, spinning, twisting in midarch. The scrub claimed him when he landed. I looked at ground fifteen feet below. And dropped down. Headed back to Bitsa. Jane could be alpha now. Next time big-cat was alpha in daytime, wanted to be in mountains, near loud stream. Sleep on sun-warmed rock. Hunt and eat deer. Better than chicken.

I came to lying on the dirt in my dried blood. I was starving, naked, and worried. I sat up and inspected myself, checking for new scars. And, yep, I had a new one. The bullet wound was an angry-looking, round, puckered, red hole under my left arm. The bullet had entered between my sixth and seventh ribs and punctured my left lung. And nicked a major vein or artery, to take me down so fast. The new scar was a handspan away from the other bullet scar on my chest, the one that had likely resulted in my shifting from Beast's cat form to human when I was twelve. I'd wandered out of the forest shortly thereafter and lived as human for a long time before I'd found my Beast form again.

I didn't scar much, except for life-threatening injuries, and most of those decreased in severity over time as I shifted back and forth from Beast to human. My throat, arms, and chest were ridged with scars from this gig, however. Working for the vamps was proving to be dangerous business.

I pulled my clothes out of the brush and shook them. My undies had been ruined by one of Beast's claws. My bra had a bullet hole in it and was so caked with dried blood that it flaked off when I shook it. My silk long johns were crusty with blood. I knew from experience that I'd never get the stains out. I couldn't make myself put them on. Ants had found their way into my leather pants, swarming the caked and clotted blood, and they didn't want to leave. I turned the pants inside out and beat them against a tree. Ditto my leather jacket, which had a bullet hole under the left arm, to complement the wolf-teeth rips in the elbow. All the leather gear would need work. As soon as the clothes were free of insect life, I dressed, commando style. I thought about putting on the church skirt still in the saddlebag, but combined with the butt-stomper boots and the bloody jacket it wouldn't look or work any better.

As I dressed, I had to wonder why no one had called in the peculiar situation at Leo's. Was the stasis spell strong enough to take all the blood-servants and -slaves over? Maybe it was combined with a keep-away spell. I wondered how much a spell like that might cost. But mostly, I was hungry. Ravenously hungry. And I remembered the boudin balls and the peanut bar—because chocolate would melt—the chips—for starting a fire, not that I needed one—and bottled water in the saddlebags. I ate everything and drank all the water, relieved myself, and dug out my GPS cell phone. I dialed Bruiser and he picked it up on the first ring.

"Why haven't you returned my calls!" he ground out. I could almost see his teeth gnash.

Been busy being ambushed, shot, shifting into a mountain lion, and taking a nap, didn't sound like a smart thing to say. And if Bruiser had access to the GPS tracking on the phone, he'd know I was lying if I said I'd lost the signal. "I was ambushed by some werewolves on the way to Leo's and got shot at. Furry little yappers are awful shots. All they got was a nick along my ribs. Get out here, and bring me a change of clothes, would you? Jeans, T-shirt, undies."

Bruiser swore softly and the anger dropped from his tone. "Pawing around in your lingerie drawer would sound interesting if you hadn't just said you'd been *shot*."

"It's not bad. Looks worse than it is." Which was a lie, though I looked okay right now; not like the shot had nearly killed me. "Anyway, I got away, and went in through the woods." I filled him in quickly about the scene in the clan home. "You need to get out here, because we'll need to call the cops."

"It will be dark soon. Leo and Tyler can handle it," he said. I could hear the faintest tang of bitterness in his words. Why should he help his former boss and his replacement?

"According to the security monitor, Leo is injured and Tyler"—I thought back to the people gathered inside—"isn't there. I think he's involved with all the problems. Involved as in responsible for. And responsible for framing you for murder."

"Sod it all," he cursed. "I'll be there, with our lawyer, in an hour."

"Bring me some food. A half dozen burgers. I'm hungry."

"A half—"

"And make it fast." I hit the END button and tucked away the cell. There was something very satisfying in ordering the MOC's prime blood-servant around. Remembering the bite marks on the blood-servants gathered in Leo's, I called Gee; left a message on his voice mail. "I know you've been trying to bring the wolves and the vamps together. But the wolves attacked Leo's today. He's hurt. He might need the Mercy Blade." I closed the cell. I didn't know if Gee was taking my calls, not after I'd accidentally stabbed him while trying to break his hide-me spell, but it was worth the shot.

I picked up Bitsa. She seemed little the worse for the bullet/claw/fang-based contretemps. Her paint was scarred and a wheel spoke was bent and coated with werewolf blood, but I could get that fixed with a little side trip to Bitsa's maker in Charlotte, North Carolina, when I went back to the mountains. For now, she was roadworthy and that was what counted.

I motored through the deepening dusk to Leo's. When I got there, the place was still shut down under the stasis spell, though the evening security lights had come on.

I down-clutched and rode through the twilight light into the azaleas, where I parked Bitsa and waited in the shadows for Bruiser.

CHAPTER 22

Dry Cleaning Bills Are Outrageous in My Line of Work

Bruiser didn't come alone. He had Evangelina in the car with him and a second car followed behind with two people in it, headlights casting bright beams across the drive and landscaping. They parked and all four got out, slamming doors. Two lawyer types were wearing suits, ties, and polished shoes. Bruiser and Evangelina were wearing jeans, boots, and white T-shirts, almost as if they had *planned* to look like the Bobbsey Twins. Something green and pointy twisted deep inside.

Keeping my bloody clothes out of the headlights' glare, I met them at the bottom of the steps, our shadows going in all directions depending on how the spotlights in the shrubbery hit us. Taking the bag full of hamburgers and the bag of my clothes from Bruiser, I rolled the food bag open as we climbed to the front door. The smell was greasy and wonderful and I tore into the first burger instantly, standing aside, chewing, as Bruiser leaned in through the open front door and flicked on a light. Stasis spells don't always stop electricity from working. Good to know.

Bruiser shook his head. Evangelina nodded to Nettie and said, "She's under a stasis spell." Well duh. But I kept that to myself. No need to antagonize the witch who was going to make it all go away without something exploding. She studied the room, seeing the spell from different angles. "The whole first floor is under a series of them, and they overlap like soap bubbles in a tub. This was not a cheap undertaking. Give me a minute to study it."

"Wait," I said, focusing on Evangelina and swallowing the bite I hadn't finished chewing. It stuck midway down but I talked around it. "Leo's under a *hedge of thorns*, a silver-tipped stake, one of mine, on the floor beside him, and he's bleeding." When I said it was one of mine, Bruiser turned at a slight angle to me, which freed up his right arm and positioned his body for an offensive strike. It was an unconscious move, but one that said he was primed for violence in defense of Leo. Which put me in my place, and said as much as anything where his loyalties lay. He might want to sleep with me, but he'd never put me or my needs in front of Leo. I could have told him that the stake was lost, but why bother? He should have figured that out for himself. I shoved my reaction to that down deep inside with all the other stuff I didn't want to look at too closely. "There's a hand showing at the edge of the security screen."

"You went inside?" one of the lawyers said. "What if you had set off the spell?"

I could see the edges of the spell, which no human could, but I wasn't about to say that. I made a slight eye roll. "But I didn't, did I? And it's a good thing I went, because I saw the security monitor with Leo bleeding and in danger. I have a feeling that his attacker is caught in a stasis spell only inches away. If you break the spells all at once and the *hedge* drops too, he can kill Leo before we can stop him, as weak as Leo is. And I got a good look at Leo's blood-servants and blood-slaves. Some are hurt. Some look like they have wolf bites. If we have paramedics and the proper emergency equipment ready when the spells go off, we can treat the injured. Maybe even save Nettie."

"I do not recommend calling the police until Leo is able to speak to this matter," one of the legal beagles said, his face shadows and planes in the porch lights.

"If you drop the spells and Nettie dies, when you could have saved her by doing it my way, are you willing to accept the legal and moral responsibility?" I asked. "Because if someone dies, I'll name you in a heartbeat, buddy."

"Patrick Sprouse, meet Jane Yellowrock." Surely I was imagining Bruiser's droll tone.

Neither of us replied to the introduction, but the lawyer's eyes trailed over my bloody clothes. "I was not suggesting that we allow the girl to die. However, Leo is wounded? And you are covered in blood. A great deal of blood."

"Dry cleaning bills are outrageous in my line of work," I said, going for flip and sarcastic. But I knew what he was really accusing me of. "I didn't set this up and I didn't attack Leo in his lair. The werewolves who set this up got off a lucky shot."

Bruiser gave me that half smile, but I could see his concern as he took in the amount of blood on my clothes. Patrick stuck out his chest and said, "My first responsibility is to Mr. Pellissier. If the girl is under the employ of—"

"It's Miss Yellowrock to you, lawyer-boy. And *the girl* a heartbeat away from dying in there has a name. It's Nettie. Now call for help. The only reason I didn't call the cops and paramedics already is to make sure somebody was here to handle the fallout."

Bruiser laughed as if he'd won a bet. "I shall call in some of Leo's scions to heal the less severely wounded, and bring healers and Sabina in to heal Nettie and Leo. But unless someone dies, there's no reason to contact law enforcement."

The lawyer nodded, his eyes on Bruiser. "I concur. Who would you suggest we bring in?"

Bruiser turned to me. "Describe the lair."

I understood what he was asking. Leo, as Master of the City, would have several lairs. "Pale gray walls, what looks like sterling silver or polished pewter poster bed, white sheets, except where his blood is, which is practically everywhere."

"He's here, then. That simplifies matters." Bruiser named three vamps and said he would go himself to pick up Sabina. I knew the priestess would have to be the one to heal Leo. Only one of the very old ones could heal a vamp from silver-poisoned wounds. "Do you have their contact information?" Bruiser asked the lawyers.

"Yes." The other lawyer, not worthy of introductions, perhaps, pulled out a cell phone and started punching numbers. I listened long enough to make sure he was calling vamps, and turned back to Bruiser. I didn't say thanks. You don't say thanks for doing the right thing. But I did give him a slight nod as I finished off my second hamburger and opened another. He eyed the fast food bag and shook his head. He and the witch sat on the top step side by side. The lawyers wandered back to their car, voices grumbling as they dialed vamps, grumbling about me, which made me smile.

Bruiser swiveled his head to me. "You do know how to make friends and influence people, Jane Yellowrock. I've said that to you before, but some sarcasm bears repeating."

"Yeah? Then let me influence you one more time. Send some people who are loyal to you to find Tyler and bring him in. He's in this up to his neck and sinking fast."

"Can you prove it?"

"Think so, yeah. Well enough to convince Leo. And I already informed NOPD."

Bruiser thought about that for a moment, maybe thinking that the hired help should have informed Leo and him before the cops. But he inclined his head in a brief bob, relief and thanks and something that looked like thwarted *need* on his face. "I'll call on the way to get Sabina and send a team for him."

"You can find him that fast?"

"If Tyler has his phone with him, yes," he said standing and moving down the stairs for his car parked below.

I thought about my cell and the GPS tracking device in it. "One more thing," I said. Bruiser paused. "The wolves who attacked Leo have Rick LaFleur and he's been hurt. If I can—"

"I have no idea where the wolves are. But if I hear something, I'll let you know. Before I call the police."

Yep, the hired help had been put in her place, but it wasn't like I could gripe about it when I was asking a favor. "Thanks."

The cars all pulled away, leaving me alone in the shadows with burgers and a bag of clean clothes. I rolled the bag's top closed and headed back to the barn to change. No need to advertise my bloody state if Leo's fanged henchmen were arriving. Old blood never turned a sane vamp on, smelling like death, like leftovers spoiled in the fridge, but the predator in them might want to take a closer look at my wounds. No need to give them a reason to make me defend myself.

As I approached the barn, the wind carried the reek of old blood before me and the barn emptied in a stampede of squeals and thrashing hooves, while barn cats of every size and description gathered, some twining around my ankles and jumping up on stall doors to get a better view. I was under no illusions that it was *me* that attracted them. It was the blood and the burger bag.

Inside, I stripped and sniffed myself. Though all my blood and the chicken blood had been groomed off me by Beast or flaked away when I shifted, wearing the clothes had left me stinky. I found a hose and drain in a grooming area and washed, the chill water hitting me with a shock. It must be well water, because my shower water never got this cold. It was almost as cold as mountain water. While I rinsed, I drank from the hose, feeling my tissues swell like a sponge as I rehydrated.

When I was cleaner, I dried off using two towels I found folded in a stack. They were clean but rough, smelling of detergent and only slightly of horse, which was a nice scent after my own old blood smell. I dressed in clean clothes, jeans and a tee. "Mine," I said to the cats, shoving them away from my food bag, and hearing an echo of Beast when she claimed things. Or people.

I shoved my feet into socks and the butt-stompers, and stuffed the stiff, bloody leathers into the small duffel. I wished for a brush, but made do with finger-combing the hip-length mass before braiding my hair and sticking stakes back into it. Dressed, I felt more secure, safer, though I knew better than most how little protection clothing really was. Last, I located the mangled silver collar that Beast had found at Leo's and hidden. "Dang," I murmured, turning it to the light as I made my way back to the house. It had defended me from multiple vamp-fang attacks and not been the worse for wear. Wolf fangs, backed up by powerful jaws, had ruined it. The pattern and some of the silver rings could be salvaged, but it wasn't going to be cheap.

Back at Bitsa, I placed the clothes and most of the weapons into the saddlebags, and reloaded the shotgun. I strapped it to the bike, knowing that if the cops did get called, I'd have to hide them. The M4 smelled freshly fired, and there was no good reason to have a fired weapon and bloody clothing at the scene of a bloodbath. For now, I strapped vamp-killers on each thigh and hip, and the one holster that wasn't bloody under my left arm. The strap rubbed uncomfortably on the tender skin of my recent wounds.

With as much accomplished as I could under the circumstances, I sat on the front steps of the house and nibbled the last burger, tossing bits of cheese and beef paddies to the cats that followed me from the barn. They were still milling around me when Bruiser and Evangelina, who seemed to be glued to his heels, got back, Sabina in the backseat. Three more cars pulled in within moments of one another, a human blood-servant/bodyguard/driver and a vamp in each. I recognized Innara, one of the coleaders of Clan Bouvier, and Koun and Hildebert, Leo's warrior scions, and noted that none of the vamps had been part of the conspiracy-whispering taking place at the vamp/were sleepover that had started all this. Bruiser had chosen well.

As they left their cars, doors slamming, I got to see what vamps wore in the their free time, when they weren't trying to kill me or attending a black-tie event. It was jeans for the guys and cotton pants and silk tank for Innara. Sabina was in her typical nunnish robes. She probably didn't own anything else. The bodyguards were dressed in jeans and jackets to hide the array of weapons each carried. We looked one another over, assessing danger levels, and decided we didn't have to react. I gave a little head bob to acknowledge them, and got one back from each, security personnel greetings, all business.

I gave a little head bow to Sabina, knowing that there was something more I should probably do to acknowledge her status, but I didn't know what it might be. She wasn't *my* priestess, after all. The vamps gathered around the open front door and breathed in, nostrils expanding and contracting as they scented, a weird, almost choreographed body movement, bizarre to observe on the non-breathers.

"Wolves," Hildebert said, his lips curling into a snarl. His fangs snapped down. I tensed, readying myself for a vamped-out rage, but his pupils didn't expand, his sclera didn't bleed scarlet. He was ticked off but in control. For now.

"Gone," Innara said. She bent and dipped her head, folding her body in a way that would have been distinctly uncomfortable for a human. It was creepy looking, like a lizard, her fingers outspread and her upper body whipping side to side. She took short sniffing breaths, following scent signatures. "For some time. I count ten or more. One was the woman. Her level of excitement is extreme. She is still in heat and smells"— Innara sniffed in little puffs of indrawn breath—"ill."

The others nodded as they drew in the air. "Twelve altogether," Koun said. "And the smell of magic is sharp and bright on the air. But what is that other scent?"

"Cat of some kind," Hildebert said.

"I saw Kemnebi when I got here," I said, to lead them away from thoughts of me, "in the tree line, hiding, watching. And there are barn cats. Maybe one of them, you know, got inside."

"Yes," Innara said. She looked at me under her lashes, assessing and suspicious. Which didn't make me happy at all. "Perhaps."

As soon as the vamps had sniffed their fill, the former—and surely soon-to-be again—prime blood-servant explained what they might expect to see immediately inside. He finished by saying, "I've sent Alejandro and Estavan for Bethany, but they may be some time convincing her to help us, and Evangelina doesn't think we can wait for the stasis spells to wear off, in case that triggers some other disaster.

"We can't see her wounds, but by the amount of blood Nettie has lost, she's close to death. I suggest that Koun be at her side when the stasis spell falls, as he has the most experience treating battlefield wounds. If she has to be brought over to save her, are you prepared for a youngling?"

Koun shrugged his massive shoulders. "If need be, I will take her. She has the signing of the paperwork and contracts?"

"Yes," Bruiser said, and I instantly wanted to get a look at the paperwork a blood-servant wannabe-scion signed just in case they got injured on the job. Talk about your worker's comp. "Sabina," he said, "you will need to be with me in Leo's lair."

My ears perked up. I wanted to see Leo's lair. But I also wanted to see what Koun did to heal Nettie. I wished I had a body for each soul, so I could be in two places at once. Deep inside, Beast snorted with amusement.

"Hildebert, according to Jane, it appears that the wolves bit some of the servants gathered in the formal room. We'll need to deal with the more serious injuries first. Then, when everyone is stable, we'll see if Bethany and Sabina are able to help them. Perhaps we can keep most of them from being infected by the were-contagion."

Hildebert said something guttural, but cussing is a universal language. I got the point.

"I called Gee. He can heal them of the bites if he gets the message in time."

Bruiser looked at me strangely and I got the feeling that he hadn't known that. "Jane, you will be with Sabina and me. When Evangelina drops the spell, you deal with Leo's opponent. Sabina will assist with Leo."

"And you?" I asked.

"I'll figure that out when Leo is stable." Bruiser turned his

attention to Evangelina. "Can you get us in place without setting off the stasis spells?"

"Jane can take you and the priestess in. I'll get the guys in."

Bruiser asked me, "Is there a stasis spell around the security console? I need to see the status monitor and make a few
adjustments."

"No," I said, sounding grumpy. "Just follow in my trail. If I
move left or right as if to avoid something, even if you can't
see anything, don't deviate. The spell covers every bit of blood
splatter, and there's a lot of it." Bruiser and Sabina close on
my trail, I stepped across the threshold and led the way across
the Anzu heraldic device to the security closet. "From here on
back I don't see any spells of any kind."

Bruiser opened the door to the console and a moment
later, he said, "Splendid. No one changed the passwords." He
clacked around on some keys and scanned a series of screens.
"You were right, Jane. Tyler's password is listed. He let them
in." Bruiser backed out of the narrow space, and indicated the
hallway.

"We'll take the stairs down and I'll call you when we're in
place," he said to Evangelina, who was still in the foyer, standing in front of Leo's huge warriors.

I hadn't known there *were* stairs down, but considering
the artificial hill this place was built on, it made sense. I followed them, Sabina's skirts swishing as she moved. I had noticed once before that her feet never made a sound, but her
starched skirts did. It was weird, but all vamps were eerie. The
old blood smell floated back from her as we walked, making
my stomach turn on the greasy burgers and boudin balls.

There were bloody prints and smears all over the kitchen,
most leading outside through a delivery door. The stairs were
behind the kitchen, in a narrow nook between a walk-in refrigerator and a butcher shop–sized cutting board. The only indication that something was there besides wall was a small entry
keypad. Bruiser pressed seven keys, placed his open hand on
the wall, and pushed. The wall opened inward soundlessly, the
stink of decomposing blood whooshing out, to reveal a dark
hallway. When Bruiser stepped in, the overhead light came on,
a motion detector at work, and revealed a steeply descending,
switchback stairway, a metal handrail on one side and slick
painted wall on the other.

Leo had made use of the interior space of the hillock under his house; the center of the mound had been hollowed out and reinforced. I spotted three security cameras and laser motion detectors. Not that they had done him any good, but it was hard to design a security plan for *any* eventuality. And I figured werewolf attack hadn't been high on the designers' minds.

We started down, Bruiser's and my boots clomping echoes off the bright walls. Blood, smelling of wolves and Leo, had dripped all over the stairs, smeared with paw and boot prints, all dry.

The door to Leo's lair was at the bottom, where Bruiser entered more numbers on another keypad. The door opened with a gust of air, a rotten blood and wet dog scent whooshing out along with a dull red light, to reveal the room. Leo's home-base lair was a small apartment consisting of a sitting area and a king-sized, four-poster, pewter bed with a headboard of curlicues and fleur-de-lis. And a lot of blood. The sheets and pillowcases were drenched in it. The rugs below were sloppy wet with it. And Leo was in the middle of it all, half lying on the mattress, his position changed from the first time I'd seen him. His bare right foot rested on a rug, his left on the mattress, and he was leaning back against a mound of bloody pillows wearing black pants and a once-white shirt. His face and body were slack, his skin so white he looked like a mannequin, waxy with death. His eyes were closed. And his chest was still, breathless, with that vamp undead-death thing.

My silver-tipped stake was at his feet, bloody and well-used.

Hedge of thorns encircled the bed, casting a reddish light over everything, giving Leo the only color he had, making the blood appear even more vibrant and deadly. But unlike the spell that protected my boulder garden, this one hadn't burned the rugs or walls and stopped short of the ceiling. And it seemed to provide an additional purpose than simply a last-ditch bolt-hole activated by the primary's blood. This one was a trap. Caught in the *hedge*, held a foot off the floor, was Girrard DiMercy.

CHAPTER 23

"Rock and Roll, Legs"

Gee was trapped in the spell like a moth in the strands of a spider's web, his body suspended above the floor, caught in a fighting posture. When we entered, his eyes swiveled our way. That, and breathing, assuming a storm god had to, were the only movements he could make. His swords lay on the bloody rugs, the edges coated with dried gore. But the blades were pointing away from Leo, and Gee's back was facing the bloody bed. Yet, the stake was on Leo's side of the *hedge*. "He was either defending Leo from attack," I said, "or running away when the *hedge* came up." And only Leo could tell us which.

Sabina shook her head slowly, her mantle rustling. "Little Leo, what have you done? Is there enough blood in all the world to heal you now?" Which did not sound good. She looked at Bruiser and addressed her comment to him. "Your master is close to death. When the spell falls, I can give him my blood, but I cannot restore him. He will need much blood. Much."

I stepped around Gee, observing him from every angle I could, looking for additional weapons; there were none that I could see. But there was a nasty gash on one arm, old and half healed. I had a feeling I might have given him that one when he was sitting outside my house. Because my guns were loaded with silver shot, and silver wouldn't kill an Anzu, I pulled two steel-edged vamp-killers and set my balance. Waiting.

Bruiser stepped to a wall phone, an old-fashioned one that had a dangly tangled cord. Our cells were useless underground. He dialed two digits, like on an intercom, and said, "Evie, we're ready down here. Send down ten blood-servants as soon as they're free of the spell and pronounced healthy. Leo's badly wounded. Yes." Phone to his ear, he nodded to Sabina and then looked at me. "Kill Gee if he resists." Into the phone he said, "Go." And hung up.

An instant later, everything fell. The *hedge* fell, the red light vanishing in a burst of white light. Sabina fell forward, toward the bed and Leo. And Gee fell to the floor.

He hit the bloody rugs like a broken marionette, air woofing out of him, ending in a grunt as I landed on him, one knee in his belly, a position I'd landed in a lot lately. He lay there, gasping, my knife at his throat, his eyes on mine. There was no evidence of fight in him. And no weapons that I could see.

"I did not wound my lord," he gasped. "I tried to protect him from the wolves." I sniffed carefully, parsing the disparate scents to their distinct origins. Under the reek of Leo's blood, I smelled Roul, another werewolf, and the were-bitch. And faintly, I scented Rick. He had been here, or someone wearing a lot of his blood had been here.

I chanced a quick look at the bed. Sabina was sitting on the mattress, one hand gently at Leo's lower back, one at his nape, holding him the way she might a small child. His lips were at her neck, sucking hard, his eyes closed and his face twisted as if with a great effort. It was bizarrely like watching a kid try to suck a thick milkshake through a straw, and I wanted to laugh, until I remembered who was handy to provide him a blood meal if he got well enough and violent enough to take one. My sense of humor was gonna be the death of me one day.

"Let me go to him," Gee said. "I can heal him."

"Not until Leo can tell us what happened here," Bruiser said, his voice tight, his gaze glued to Leo and Sabina. I glanced at the bed, seeing Sabina's skirts stained red, the white linen fabric wicking up the unclotted blood from the mattress.

Leo pulled from Sabina, his fangs still snapped down, his eyes vamped out. "Crap," I murmured. Where was the blood-servant cavalry from upstairs?

But Leo said, "Girrard, *mon ami*," and let loose a bunch of French I couldn't begin to follow, not with only my high school Spanish. Too weak to get up, Leo held out his hand.

"Let Gee up," Bruiser said. "Leo says Gee saved his life, and killed a werewolf to do it."

I looked at the blood on the floor and bed. Now the quantity made sense. I stood slowly and backed away, but I didn't put the blades up. Not yet.

Gee seemed to flow to his feet and across the room, to Leo. Sabina stepped back, the holes over her carotid artery closing as the vamp saliva constricted blood vessels and flesh. Though Leo had worked hard to suck her dry, she looked no worse for the wear. I had to wonder, as I always did, who she drank from. She had no scions and no blood-servants. None of the outclan did. But that was a mystery for another day.

Near midnight, all the blood upstairs had been cleaned up, and thanks to the healers and Gee, no one had died. Low level blood-servants and -slaves were hauling rugs and lugging the mattress up the switchback stairs from Leo's lair, stuffing linens into plastic bags to be burned. Higher level blood-servants were heading down the stairs to return minutes later, wobbly-kneed and drained. And I was watching everyone and everything, Gee at my side. "And once again, you're at the scene just in time to help avoid major problems," I murmured to Gee. "Fill me in?"

The Mercy Blade shrugged, a Gaelic-Frenchy shrug, all grace and delicacy. "I was watching the clan home to keep it safe, when the wolves struck the Master of the City. It was just before dawn, and I"—he placed a hand on his chest—"disrupted their plans. My presence and my small magics, trapped in the witch's *hedge of thorns*, kept my lord Leo alive until you came."

I nodded once, distracted, shunted to the sidelines. The sheriff and his were-deputy were sitting in Leo's office with Jodi Richoux and a governor's assistant. Yeah, I'd ratted out the deputy. He had known what his buddies had done and couldn't stay away. He had also taken the call, sent in by Sloan Rosen, to drop by the clan home to check things out. The betting bunch had laid odds the deputy would be fired and arrested, unless he accepted a plea bargain and told us where the wolves were holing up. It didn't look likely. The events of the night had now coincided with Jodi getting a judge to sign a warrant for Tyler Sullivan's room at the clan home. Only his room, nothing else. Any Louisiana judge knew not to rile the Master of the City.

Jodi had found the shells and the gun where I'd told her they were and an arrest warrant had been issued for Tyler Sullivan. I didn't envy whoever told Leo about the snake in his midst.

In the main room of the clan home, vamps loyal to Leo, and blood-servants loyal to their masters, had gathered. Katie was with Leo, giving him a feeding strong enough to finish his healing, and timely enough to guarantee she would be named his heir. The fangheads and walking blood-meals were all talking about it. And I guess it was exciting, if you lived and breathed fanghead politics—not that vamps lived or breathed.

For now, I'd had enough of vamps, weres, witches, ancient Sumerian gods, and even little green guys who liked to swim in fountains. I just wanted Rick, alive and well. I wanted to take him home, to my mountains, where we could be safe. Home to Beast's hunting territory.

But wishes were a waste of time. I'd broken my lease and had nowhere to live except for New Orleans. For now, I had a cheating boyfriend to find and save. If it wasn't already too late.

Unfortunately, I had no idea where to start.

Near two a.m., Bruiser found me sitting on the front steps in the shadows of the outside lights, feeding the last crumbs of burger to the barn cats. I was fighting sleep and depression in equal measure, and when he sat down next to me, I didn't look his way. Silence stretched between us.

I sniffed shallowly, detecting the smell of his blood, fresh and thin, and the scent signature of Leo, the trace chemicals telling me the MOC was out of danger. Low levels of toxic stress compounds meant Leo was fine, and the fact that Bruiser was alive beside me proved that Leo hadn't crashed and burned, which was a good thing. My job as Rogue Hunter would have meant that I'd have to stake Leo.

"Are you the new primo?" I asked finally. "Or maybe the re-primo?"

Bruiser chuckled tonelessly. "I suppose I am."

"Good. I need back into vamp HQ to look at the party tapes again. I need to go back to the beginning."

"Why?"

"Rick is still miss—" I stopped, breathed past the tears that flooded my eyes and constricted my throat. "Everything started with the party. That's as good a place as any to start looking."

Bruiser flipped open his cell phone and speed dialed a number. Thirty seconds later, I had total access to everything in vamp HQ, including the rooms I'd never been in. Yeah me! So why should I risk everything by telling Bruiser? I shouldn't. I stood, taking the steps to Bitsa in the azaleas. I stopped. Stared at the ground, hidden in the dark. I was gonna blow the top off Bruiser's can of worms. And I just knew it was gonna cost me, eventually. "You know Evangelina put a spell on you, don't you?"

Bruiser had stood when I did, but more slowly, and halted, half crouched, when I spoke. "Evie . . ." He stepped toward me and changed the question. "How do you know?"

"I can see it. She has a pinkish haze of magics all around her lately. And now so do you. It got to us"—I paused, glad of the dark to cover my blush—"in the shower. Be careful, Bruiser. Something's going on with *Evie*."

I kick-started Bitsa and eased her onto the drive. Only when I got to the street did I pause and helmet up and rearrange my gear. Then, exhausted and heartsore, I gunned the bike and headed back into the city.

"And you discovered this when?" I asked Wrassler.

"Not me. Not us. The cops found it the night after the were-cat died, when they were taking the office apart. Far as we know, till then, only Leo knew it was here. And he didn't tell."

Wrassler and I had entered through Leo's main office doorway, tearing down the crime-scene tape. Yeah, it might make the cops' jobs harder, but I didn't really care about that. I cared about stuff no one had told me, that might help me solve the murder and save Rick. Wrassler and I had talked things through until my head was spinning, but it was beginning to come together. The cops had found a second hidden entrance in Leo's office.

I'd gotten a good look at the first hidden passage. It was like something out of a horror movie, but without the lights or scary music: a stairway spiraling down to a narrow, lightless corridor between rooms to the outer wall. There, a lever opened a passage to the sidewalk, an egress if one was supernat-fast enough. The passageway smelled of were-cat, werewolf, vamp, dead fish, and cops. And Rick's blood, dried drops marked by crime-scene cones. If I had made nice-nice with Jodi, she might have told me there was blood, and I might have known early on that Rick was in trouble, but I'd been too busy to make better friends with the local cops.

The mixture of scents was confusing—the wolves and cats and vamps all in one hidden place. It seemed everyone knew about the passageway but me.

Now, we stood in front of the newest surprise—Leo's office's *second* hidden entrance. The passage had been found when the cops started taking out rugs and wall hangings splattered with crime-scene blood. It entered the office from behind the fireplace, the passageway eight feet high and twenty inches wide, leading to the next room, which had its own secret entrance—a private elevator. The tiny brass cage had access to hidden passages on every floor of vamp HQ, including the crawl space to the domes above the ballroom where the wolves had waited. The elevator smelled only of dead fish, were-blood, and Rick's blood. All the blood was old and dry, I guessed lost the night of Safia's murder. But the fishy smell . . . "I need to see the room the grindylow used," I said, not letting myself react to the blood smell or what it could mean.

"Okay by me. Little sucker trashed it. And now he's gone. No one's seen him in days."

The room set aside for visiting security was way more than trashed. It was wet, stinking of mold, ripped, and shredded. The grindy had let the tub overflow until the carpet was soaked, had shredded every piece of fabric and drenched the scraps, maybe trying to make himself a grindy den, a wet place like home. Days later, in the damp climate of Louisiana, untouched by anyone due to the visitor's status, mold had set in.

I knelt and studied the grindy's claw marks. The edges of the tears were smooth, not ragged, indicating razor sharp claws. I wouldn't want to fight the little sucker, not even if I had a cannon and way better armor. They were three clawed, like a sloth, the center one longer than the two beside. Just like the wound in Safia's throat, which was just weird. Why kill her here, not back in Africa?

Because she had been a good little girl until she met Rick?

The grindy's scent was definitely fishlike, but not any fish Beast had ever encountered. I drew up the bloodhound-memory of smells as I stood over Safia's body. I remembered fish. I had thought it was her supper. Stupid, to make a determination without evidence.

As far as I could tell, under the fish and mold smell, Rick hadn't been in the grindylow's rooms. I pulled the door shut and wandered back to the hidden elevator, hands in my jeans pockets. "Okay, how does this sound?" I said to Wrassler, who filled up the hallway behind me. "Rick infiltrated the Soniat Hotel, undercover, as a busboy or something, during the early, clandestine discussions with Leo and the Vampire Council. Safia met the cop. She was bored. Interested in a pretty boy."

Wrassler added to my narrative. "Somehow she knows about this passage. The night of the big bash, she arranges to get him inside HQ for some hanky-panky."

"Hanky-panky." I quashed my reaction to my words. This was a *job*. Not my heart breaking. "Okay. He's in, with her, coming up the passageway. Somehow, Rick is injured," though not badly, because I hadn't smelled his blood-scent over Safia's blood loss. "Tyler goes into the office, where he shouldn't be, catches them together. Safia is shot by Tyler to frame Leo and Bruiser. Tyler runs. Safia starts to shift. Then the grindy kills the person he was here to protect. Which makes no sense."

"Unless she'd tried to turn the cop," Wrassler said.

And the final piece fell into place. Kemnebi had said the grindylows *are . . . pets. Most of the time . . .* But he'd hesitated when he said *pets*. As if that description hadn't been his first choice. Pain gripped my stomach, burning. I said, "It all makes sense, like a woven scarf with all its knots, but only two pieces of string."

"Girly analogy."

I stuttered a laugh, surprised, but the laughter cleared my head. "Bite me. String one: Tyler wants revenge on Bruiser and Leo for something—I don't know what, so don't ask. He came over in the 1960s to work a frame, maybe something longstanding with the Marchands or the Rochefort clan in France, since he was working security for them. But for whatever reason, he had to abandon his plan. He's been waiting for a chance to finish it for years. Tyler comes back with the wedding party, starts his plan all over again, shoots Safia to set up Bruiser and Leo as murderers. Tyler runs, changes clothes, reappears in the ballroom in the middle of the fight. We never notice he's gone.

"String two," I said, "is all about the grindy. Kemnebi said grindylows 'are pets. Most of the time. Guardians, occasionally. Less often, the enforcers of were-law.' But what if they are the enforcers of were-law first, and pets second? And if Safia had bitten someone . . ." *Like Rick*. I stared hard at the carpet beneath my booted feet. "Say that . . . Safia tried to turn Rick. The grindy followed her to Leo's office, where she was bringing him in the night of the party. Grindy interrupted a struggle between Tyler, Safia, and Rick. Tyler shoots Safia and runs, Safia tries to change after being shot. And the grindy kills her for breaking were-law. Grindy grabs Rick, who's bleeding, maybe bitten. Or maybe he has to hurt Rick to subdue him. The grindy takes him through the secret passageway, into the elevator. Stashes him until . . . What? He gets away? The were-wolves find him?"

"Still has holes, but if the female weres knew each another, that might cinch up loose ends."

I must have looked confused because Wrassler said, "If the girls were gossiping behind Kemnebi's back or something, if they were sharing Rick, in the carnal sense, then there's the link between the girls that includes Rick."

I remembered the site at Beast's hunting grounds, the limb where the black cat had watched the wolves feeding.

"They knew each other," he said. "And, okay, maybe they were conspiring to bring the wolves into the worldwide were-fold. But maybe they were having sleepovers and eating s'mores. And the wolf-bitch stole Rick from her best cat-gal-pal."

The thought hurt, but I pushed it away. I could hurt later, after I saved Rick.

Our theory was more a leap of faith than logic, but it made sense. "Let's go over the security tapes, starting when the were-cats entered the compound. Maybe we'll spot something."

Wrassler picked up the house phone, dialed a number, gave instructions and hung up. "Come on, Legs. We got us a movie date."

Near dawn, Wrassler and I were so stoked on caffeine and stuffed with an early breakfast, we were shaky with the over-load. But we had our proof—video of the two were-females meeting in the street outside the hidden door to Leo's office and going inside together. It was clearly a planned meeting, between two people who were acquainted. "Roll footage number two again." I watched as the were-bitch let the wolves in, and later footage as Rick was carried out the hidden door, bleeding, over Fire Truck's shoulder, well after dawn on day two, the were-bitch urging him to speed, her hands on his back, her pack behind her. "If Leo had told us about the passageways we would have found Rick days ago," I said, hearing my misery. "The wolves had known the talks were taking place, just like the cops had. Seems like I was the only person in the city who didn't," I said.

"I didn't know," Wrassler said. But somehow that didn't help. He went on. "The female weres met, maybe at the hotel, liked one another, planned on some serious girl time, maybe, like I said, Safia thought the wolves deserved to be part of the negotiations. We might never know."

"The wolf-bitch gets in, lets her guys in later—not over the wall like we thought—using the secret passageways to get set up. And it all went to hell in a handbasket," I said, the words like ashes in my mouth. "Safia died. Rick ended up with the wolf-bitch." Hurt. Likely bitten by two different were species.

"It's complicated, but it works, especially if the cop knew the wolves were in town too, and was chatting up both females. If we hadn't concentrated on the party footage and had expanded the search criteria by twelve hours both ways, we'd a put it together days ago," he said, sounding disgruntled.

I pulled my phone and dialed Sloan Rosen. When he answered, I said, "One question. Was Rick introduced to the wolf-bitch by Safia? Before he *disappeared*?" I put emphasis on the last word, to tell him that I was working a hunch.

After a long moment Sloan said, "Yes." And ended the connection.

I figured that was all I was going to get out of my pals at NOPD. I cursed, short and sweet and swallowed down tears.

"Stacked deck, Legs. No blame to you— Wait. Stop," he said. "Who's that? That guy there?" Wrassler froze the feed on the shadowed form of a short man. Familiar, lean, ordinary-looking in every way.

Except I recognized him. Excitement shot through me like lightning. "Well, well, well. It's Booger, from Booger's Scoot. I wonder what ol' Booger knows about the wolves' den. You watch more footage. See if you can update our timeline of who was where and when. Make sure we're right in our thinking. Make sure we don't trip up anywhere. Then make a montage and send a linear timeline and the footage to Jodi Richoux. Tell her it's with Leo's compliments."

"Not yours?"

I shrugged. Jodi had kept me out of the loop, and now Rick might be dead. I hoped she choked on the evidence. I left the building into the gray dawn and powered up Bitsa for a trip back across the river to Booger's Scoot, hoping Booger could be *persuaded* to give me some info about Rick.

I motored past the biker bar in the dim light. Reconnoitering. And I discovered the weres. It was too dang easy.

They had come back here to lick their wounds. The were-bitch was up, standing in the fenced area, buck naked, under an outdoor shower, her face to the spray, her body, which I had thought deeply tanned, glistening in the pearly light, proving she was mixed race, that wonderful café au lait shade of so many mixed-race people. Her hair was black, falling below her shoulders, hugging her body like a wet veil. The smell of fresh sweat and recent sex floated to me on the wind, sickness and the reek of old blood and . . . My hands tightened on the handlebars. And I caught the scent of *Rick*.

He was alive. Fierce joy and fury slammed into me. Caught me up in killing claws. I broke into a hot sweat as adrenaline flooded my system. I could smell him on the woman's body as she washed away the sweat of the night. *Mine*, Beast hissed.

The woman turned, water sluicing down her form. And I finally got an unobstructed view of her face. "Magnolia Sweets," I whispered inside my helmet's faceplate. Terrance's mother. Leo's former prime blood-servant, whose son was sent to the Rochefort clan in the south of France when she disappeared. France, where Tyler Sullivan had come from, as part of the security detail for Amitee Marchand, who had been a blood-servant to the Rochefort clan. Old blood-servant loyalties ran deep. Deep enough to plot long and hard against Leo, and to use whatever people and resources she could find. Like Tyler, who lost his mother, position, power, and clan all in one day.

The last piece fell into place with an almost audible click in my mind. The familiar-looking child captured in the photograph was known to me. Tyler Sullivan was Terrance Sweets. Tyler had been trying to avenge himself and his mother—whom he thought was dead—on Leo and Bruiser for decades. Tyler was behind half of everything; Magnolia, insane from were-taint, and Safia were responsible for the other half. No wonder nothing had made sense. It was a two-pronged attack—or two threads weaving one tapestry, just as I had said.

A man stepped from a tent, out into the early light and looked up at the dawn sky. He wore loose cotton pants, and had a gun holster strapped to his bare chest. "Speak the devil's name and he appears," I murmured to myself. "Looks like Tyler and mommy dearest got reunited."

I wanted to roar in on Bitsa, guns blazing. I wanted to attack and set Rick free, but there were too many of them and not enough of me. They had beaten me here once before, and the sting of failure was still strong. If I wanted to get Rick out, I had to be smarter. A lot smarter.

I puttered on out of sight. Miles later, I came to a stop at a small graveyard, old, full of weathered, bird-stained monuments. Parked Bitsa, setting her kickstand. Forced my mind to feel nothing, think nothing. I drank a liter of water from Bitsa's saddlebags. Talked myself down from the killing rage. I needed to be cool. Smart. *Mine*, Beast hissed, digging into my psyche with her retractable claws.

I dialed three numbers: the first was a demand for reimbursement from Leo's prime blood-servant, enough to pay for backup and for Reach's services. Demanded, because all this was Leo's mess, after all. Payment was granted. The second was a call for backup from Derek Lee and his soldiers. It too was granted, now that money was no problem. The third was to Gee.

To his voice mail I said, as formally as I knew how, "Girrard DiMercy, Mercy Blade to Leo Pellissier, the Master of the City of New Orleans. I owe you this for saving my life the day we met. I know who the were-bitch is. I know why you saved her so many years ago. She was bitten by the wolves in the last vamp war, but unlike so many other females, she survived. And the Anzu feel, what? Responsible for the Cursed of Artemis? Some kind of misplaced guilt?

"Whatever it is, Magnolia Sweets, her grown son, and her werewolves have a human police officer held hostage. She's tried to turn him, with the help of her pack, against were-law, and according to their own law, there can be no mercy shown. I'm going into the compound, at the place where we first fought them, with paramilitary backup." I closed my eyes and breathed in. The air stung and tore and my eyes ached. "And if I find Rick dead, I'll kill them all myself."

The words felt strange on my tongue, coarse and raw, as if they sucked all the life out of me. The metallic tang of vengeance. Unable to say another word, I ended the call. Emptied another liter of water into my body, drinking it down. My tissues soaked it up, as if the rage and shame that were fighting inside me left my soul desiccated. "'Vengeance is mine; I will repay, saith the Lord,'" I whispered, the words familiar from Scripture. "But not this time, God. You had your chance."

I raised my bottle to the rising sun and poured several drops of water onto the earth. An offering. Turned to the south, poured another few drops. To the west, and then to the north, anointing the earth. Wishing it was blood I offered to the ancient Cherokee ways.

Tears burned my eyes, stinging like nettles. I sobbed once, all that I believed in like old, ashen pain. I drew on Beast's strength. She sank her claws into me, sharing her calm, her stalking patience. Her pelt was coarse and spiked just under my skin, raised in readiness. Her claws drew blood from my soul.

We hunt, she snarled. *The I/we of Beast.*

I calmed, her steadiness like a narcotic inside me. "We hunt," I agreed. I dialed vamp HQ and told Wrassler to wake Kemnebi and tell him what had happened and what we were about to do. If Rick was dead, I wanted vengeance, yeah, but maybe it could also be legal.

Half an hour later I got a call back. IAW had sanctioned a hunt and a bounty for each were-head we brought them, in human or wolf form. Jodi Richoux called to snarl at me about the were-hunt, demanding the cops be given the coordinates. I hung up on her. Which I'm sure pissed her off, as she called back four times before giving up.

And then, while prebattle adrenaline spurted into my bloodstream with every heartbeat, my hands checked the placement of every blade, inspected every firing weapon, made sure my ammo and extra magazines were secured but easy to pull. While I was examining the M4, Gee called me back. I stared at his number on the fancy cell screen. Fingers ice-cold in the morning heat, I picked up. "Gee."

"Do you understand why I have protected her for all these years?"

"Leo loved her. Leo hated weres. She was bitten in the vamp war. You tried to protect her from the curse, but on the first full moon, she went furry. So she packed up and left. Because of Artemis' curse, you went with her to be near her when she died. Only Leo's Maggie didn't die. She was one of few females who lived, if you can call being permanently in heat and insane living. And, loyalties divided, you stayed close to her."

"You know of the curse?" His voice was a whisper.

I could almost feel his shock through the cell phone, and smothered my reaction, which was pity, understanding, compassion. There was no room for those emotions in me today. "Sabina told me the story," I said. "You followed Magnolia back here, only to be drawn into Roul's plans to be an official part of the weres again, and into Tyler's revenge. Tell me, you little feathered creep. Did Tyler know about his mother still being alive?"

"No. He did not; not until he met her after the party. The digital footage you saw of him wasn't some human mating ritual, it was Tyler recognizing his mother. But learning she lived has not helped. He sees what she is, how she lives, and he blames Leo. Her insanity has made it worse for her son, not better. Hatred dies hard."

"You saved me from the were-taint when I was bitten. Why not Maggie?"

"I tried. By the time she confided in me, it was too late. There was too much contagion. All I could do was minimize the effect. And so she . . . lived. Though Maggie, my Sweet Magnolia, has, in truth, been dead for many years."

"Are you coming to help kill wolves today? Or to fight against us?"

"Neither. I have returned to Leo. I will tell him the truth. I will make my peace with him, and his blood will grow sweet again, his and his Mithrans'. They will suffer no more, and the Mercy Blade will abide with them once again.

"For me, you will put Magnolia out of her misery, like an injured wolf too damaged to survive. You will be . . . the Mercy Blade for the cursed. And I will be in your debt."

"Then, when I bring out Rick, I'll bring him to you."

"I will do what I can, little goddess." The call ended. And I was left, sitting on Bitsa in the heat, eyes gritty with fatigue, waiting for backup, to see that the sentence for breaking the most important were-law was carried out, according to their people's justice system. And to save Rick LaFleur. If I could.

I thought of the photos of Rick and the redhead. It was Maggie Sweets, wigged, in a saner moment, seducing Rick. Who may have already been infected and not thinking like himself. Rick, undercover, using his charm to go after the females. I blinked away tears.

Moments later, Derek Lee and his small army of mercenaries braked their panel van. The side panel door slid open and Derek grinned at me from the dark confines. I glanced over their gear and decided they had enough to win the small war I planned. Derek said, "Sit rep."

The situation report was brief. "Twelve foot chain link fence, only two exits, one on the front and one into the bar. Ten to fifteen werewolves still survive, if my count is right, likely in human form, likely hungover, and likely still asleep, in tents and a small cabin."

Derek handed me a pad and I sketched the site. "Bounty is ten thousand a head. Literally. PAW wants the heads. Rick LaFleur, an undercover cop, is with them, but may be infected with the were-taint, not thinking like himself. Him, we want alive. No children seen, no pets, no collateral damage permitted."

"Not good recon, Legs," Angel's Tit said.

"If I'd gone in closer, they would have smelled me."

"There is that," Vodka Sunrise said. "Noses on wolves gotta be better than bloodhound."

I wanted to argue that point, but it seemed silly.

Derek handed the sketch to the guys. "Rock and roll, Legs." The panel slid shut.

CHAPTER 24

Pick a Target. Aim. Shoot.

The Vodka boys parked a mile away and—except for the driver, V. Chi Chi, who was working a compact little device: com equipment, to coordinate the action—the soldiers filtered into the trees. I dropped my helmet into the van with a hollow thud and shook out my braids. Knotted them into a single queue. Pulled on fingerless gloves meant for firing. I was going to be the diversion that let them inside the compound. "Semper fi," Chi Chi said to me. I chuckled, and the sound came out like a growl. After that he didn't speak, but he shifted in his seat so he could watch me. Smart man.

At the appointed time, Chi Chi pointed a finger at me. I kick-started the bike and sat, feet on the earth. Revved her a few times, letting her snarl and Beast's scream merge, pound into my blood stream. The daylight grew crisp, sharp. The smells of the heated earth grew stronger, complex. Chi Chi said, "Go." And I gunned the engine. Shot forward. Head down, into the wind. I roared toward Booger's Scoot.

I drew Beast up, harder, stronger into my eyes, into my bloodstream, my reflexes. My heartbeat like war drums in my head. Racing to battle.

Booger's came into sight, bright in the morning sun. Bikes parked out front and inside the fenced compound. I downshifted in the parking lot and slewed to a sudden, sliding stop. White shells flew, catching the sun. Tumbling in the air. Time slowed, a gelatinous, thick constraint on the rest of the world, shackles I moved through like dark lightning.

I dropped Bitsa. Pulling the M4 and a silvered blade meant for throwing. Strode to the front door. Kicked. It slammed open. Splintered wood flying, hanging in the air, the door banging into the wall. Inside, the chain walls were already being lowered. Humans screamed and raced into corners like rats. I screamed the challenge of the *Puma concolor*.

And smelled Rick's blood. My eyes tracked the scent to a wolfman sitting at a table, trying to stand. Drawing a huge weapon. A .44 Magnum. I threw the blade. It pinwheeled slowly once. Hit him midchest. Just below the sternum. I pulled the H&K, raised it to the ceiling and fired.

After that everything was a jumble of death and blood as I moved through the bar, emptying the clip. Making my noisy distraction. Outside, in the compound, the sunlight was too bright, too glaring. The Vodka boys were already inside the fence, the wolf hunt and execution being carried out with military precision, methodical, precise, orderly. I had a vision of each of them, almost an overview. Behind cover. Pick a target. Aim. Shoot. Advance to cover. Pick a target. Aim. Shoot. Firing, taking down wolves and wolfmen. Mouth open, I scented for Rick.

I saw Booger fall, trying to shift into wolf. He died trying. Roul fell, his lovely hair flying. I saw Tyler fall, firing his small machine pistol, holes opening across his bare chest. The concussive sounds were deafening.

I followed my nose. Across the mat of sod. To the cabin in the center of the grassy yard.

Derek was at my left side when I reached it. My foot hitting the door so hard it splintered apart, sharp fragments flying. He was inside first, shouting "Clear!"

Rick lay on a cot, bound and gagged. Naked. Bloody. Half dead. And the were-bitch lay beside him, on the floor. Her throat freshly ripped out by three claw marks. I could smell the faint stench of fish beneath the smell of blood and feces. Fishy-smelling bayou water pooled at the bedside, mixing with the blood. The grindy had gotten to her first. The grindy had carried out were-law, first on his mistress, Safia, for biting Rick, and now on Safia's friend for the same crime. Nonhuman footprints, wet with water and blood, led out through a broken window. I was too shocked to even care. I knelt over Rick, my back to the room as Derek took Magnolia's head.

I pulled a knife and sliced through Rick's bonds. Lifted

him, his ragged breath hot on my neck. And carried him like a baby out of the cabin.

The van roared through the compound fencing, taking out an entire section of the chain link. One of the boys had cut enough away during my diversion so it wouldn't be a difficult feat. The van braked to a stop and the side door opened. I climbed inside, Derek with me. He slammed the sliding door. I sat on the floor. Holding Rick. "Go," I said. The word didn't sound remotely human.

Derek grunted, "Pellissier clan home." The van took off just as I smelled gasoline and saw a gout of fire through the windshield. The Vodka boys were burning the place. And I knew the bodies of the wolves would disappear, deep in a swamp somewhere.

We bumped horribly over the ground back into the street. Rick groaned, turned to the side and vomited. He was covered with bite marks, lacerations, cuts, his skin green and yellow and purpled with bruises old and new. And he stank of his own filth and sex and wolf and sickness. He was burning up with fever.

Derek opened a gallon of water and poured it over Rick, his blood and filth washing over me, sloshing to the floor. Somehow I had grabbed a sheet up with Rick, and I pulled it gently from under him and sopped his torso. Derek poured another gallon of water over him, washing him clean, which didn't seem like a standard battlefield medic task.

As if he knew what I was thinking Derek said, "I called vamp HQ. Asked the black leopard how to treat him. He said get as much blood and saliva off him as possible." Silent, movements economical, practiced, he tore into packets of medicated bandages and slapped them over the worst of the injuries, the bandages self-sealing. Four went on Rick's throat. More on his shoulders. And his groin. He rolled Rick over and applied some to his back, taking special care of a deep one over Rick's left kidney. Derek quickly ran out of the prepared bandages and started improvising. Opened packets of gauze, tape, antibiotic ointment, Cling Wrap, and applied more. I helped turn Rick and move his limbs, hearing Rick's breath hitch with pain and a wheeze from deep in his lungs.

My breath was hot and tight. My heart thundered in my ears. But as we worked, the Beast and battle chemicals leached out of my system. I touched Rick's face, his beard uneven and wet beneath my fingertips. His eyes were black, one swollen shut. His jaw was swollen on one side. The tattoos of the mountain lion and bobcat on his shoulder had been shredded as if chewed, and looked like ground meat, yet I could still make out tattooed blood droplets and both sets of big-cat eyes, the amber of the artwork almost seeming to glitter in the bloody mess.

When the worst of the bleeding had been contained, and the worst of the wounds covered, Derek handed me a bottle of water. "Here. See if you can get him to drink."

I shifted Rick gently and raised his head. His body burned where it touched me, his fever dangerously high. I held the bottle to his lips and dribbled a bit between them. They were chapped and swollen, split and bruised. A tear trailed down my cheek. It hurt to breathe past the ragged pain in my throat.

He swallowed. Again. And lifted a hand to bring the bottle closer. Latched onto it with his mouth and drank, hard and fast. Sucking it dry. Derek replaced it with another. Rick drained that one too and sighed as if it was the best thing he'd ever tasted.

He opened his one good eye. Blinked. Focused on me. His face was too beaten for me to read any emotion on it. Until he smiled. "Jane. Jane Yellowrock," he whispered. "I dreamed of you." His lips moved into what have been a smile. And he closed his eye.

Beside me, Derek was applying a blood pressure cuff, and checking Rick's vitals. I gathered Rick close and bent my head to his. "I dreamed of you too," I whispered into his ear. His smile widened. Only a hint. But I saw it.

Moments later, we pulled to a stop and Derek opened the van door. Rick in my arms, I stepped from the van and carried him up the front steps of the Pellissier clan home. Inside, standing on the mosaic of the Anzu, was Gee. Gee took Rick into his arms and sat down, right there on the floor. Blue magics spilled over Rick, hiding his naked, bruised and broken body in an indigo mist shot through with purplish, pink sparks.

Bruiser took me by the elbow and guided me through the house, silent, our footsteps the only sound, to a white marble bathroom. He removed my weapons, placing them carefully on a marble counter, gold flecks showing in the polished stone. He removed my leathers, undressing me like a baby. Unable to see for the tears that blinded me and dripped onto his head as he unlaced my battle boots, I let him. When I was naked, he pushed me under the steaming shower. And left me there. I cried. And screamed. And roared. And beat the walls with my fists.

I ended up head down over the toilet, retching until I was empty, clean, inside and out.

EPILOGUE

Two weeks had passed, and I still hadn't gotten the carnage out of my mind, my memory, my nightmares. I had thought I was used to the stink of slaughter, the screams, the cursing, the eardrum-blowing concussions. The stench of my own fear-sweat. The smell of the dead.

I'd been wrong. Nothing about that morning at Booger's Scoot had fit in with my past experience. Unlike my usual chase-'em-down-and-stake-'em method of hunting and killing rogue vamps, this had been a slaughter.

There were twelve werewolves in the fenced compound, most in human form. Within five minutes, all were dead. Maybe it had taken only two minutes. I hadn't checked the time. While the battle went on, it felt like it took forever. And only an instant. From the moment we got into the panel van, time had started breaking and stumbling as it tried to find its way back to normal. I still had nightmares; not of the battle, but of the time in the van, bandaging Rick's wounds. Holding him. I'd wake, crying, the feel of his fevered skin, his beard, fresh and intense in my memory.

I could have taken him to the hospital, and maybe I should have, but what could a doctor do? Treat his symptoms, not the contagion in his bloodstream. The world would have known he'd been bitten by werewolves. Repeatedly. If he went furry, he'd have been a prize to doctors and scientists. His life would never again have been his own.

So I'd left Rick there, with Gee curled up beside him on

the marble floor in the foyer, lying on the mosaic of the Anzu. Derek drove me home, me wearing Bruiser's sweat pants and hoodie, his scent trying to replace the scent of Rick's sickness in my nostrils. The Vodka boys brought Bitsa home later that day, cursing about the witchy locks that had burned them while getting her into the van.

My belief that I had been working two cases had been both right and wrong, though I managed to solve both of them. It had all been tied together, with Tyler and Maggie Sweets and the awful event that turned her were at the center, like a pole around which everything else swung.

The next morning, I had tried to visit Rick at Leo's, but he'd refused to see me. He'd sent word by Bruiser to keep away. And I'd left, hating the look of pity in Bruiser's eyes. Later that week, Bruiser called to tell me that Rick had left. Bruiser called. Not Rick. From him, I'd heard nothing, not a word, not a text, not an e-mail. Not even after the first night of the full moon, last night, which would have forced a shift on him, if he had the contagion. Bruiser told me some of what Rick had endured, things he'd learned from Gee DiMercy, the Mercy Blade, as the Anzu tried to heal him from the were-taint.

Rick went through hell at the hands, fangs, and claws of the wolves. Had suffered things that made him not want to see me. Guilt. Shame. Post-traumatic stress. Pure hell.

So . . . *Crap*. I was leaving.

Maybe it was all girly to leave an entire city and a really profitable job because of one man, but that was my plan. I hadn't told Bruiser or Leo yet. They thought I was just taking a few weeks off, heading back to the mountains to rest and visit with the Everheart sisters, who were justifiably worried about the changes in Evangelina, who had gone home, and wanted my input. The vamps would figure it out when I didn't come back. Or when I called Deon to ship my belongings home; they were boxed and ready to go, sitting on the floor of my closet with Maggie's trunk of belongings that I'd never bothered to open. What was the point? She was dead.

Tyler was dead too. Jodi and NOPD were not happy campers about the carnage at Booger's Scoot, but there wasn't much they could do about it until Congress settled whether weres were human, with equal rights under the law, or animals, and under control of local animal control officers. The battle had fueled the contentious legal debate between vamps and the U.S. government, but NOPD's problem was that no bodies had been found. No one could prove anyone was even dead. Stalemate. For now. No one had seen anything, heard anything, or knew anything. Derek's men were in the clear.

I hadn't burned any bridges. Not yet. For now, I was getting outta New Orleans. Away from the kinder and gentler Leo, who seemed to be around too often, his Mercy Blade at one side, his prime blood-servant at the other.

I locked the side gate. Pocketed the ornate key. Walked to Bitsa, parked out front of my freebie house, my Lucchese Western boots crunching on the asphalt. The light of the full moon glinted off the bike's chrome and artwork, the cougar claws that reached from the seat, along the gas tank, toward the front wheel, standing out in the dim light of midnight. The bike looked wicked good, even strapped down with bags and gear. Even damaged by wolf attack. I checked to see that Angie Baby's new doll was safely strapped to the bike in its shipping box and wouldn't tumble to the highway.

I straddled Bitsa and rose up, ready to kick-start her. I heard the sound. The motor of a bike, revving high. Heading this way. I froze. Listening. And slowly, so slowly, swung my leg back over the bike. Pulled off the helmet. And stood there, the wind in my face. Waiting.

The bike downshifted, making a turn onto my street, half a block down. The red Kow-bike puttering to a stop in the middle of the street. Rick put his feet down, bracing himself, his head and face hidden by the helmet and face shield. For a long moment, he watched me.

And then his scent reached me. And my Beast rose up hard and fast, holding me still.

Pelt roiled beneath my skin, so hard that my flesh ached and burned, as if I would shift where I stood. And I remembered Rick's blood-scent in the elevator at Leo's. He'd been injured early, hidden, carried out by the wolves. But it was Safia that the grindy had killed first. Safia, who conspired with the wolves behind her lover's back. Safia, who slept with Rick and bit Rick, long before Magnolia Sweets got to him. It was Safia who first broke were-law. And because she broke were-law, she was dead. The wolves were dead.

And Rick had been infected with the were contagion.

Big-cat, Beast thought. *I/we smell black leopard. Big-cat.*

ABOUT THE AUTHOR

Faith Hunter was born in Louisiana and raised all over the South. She fell in love with reading in fifth grade, and best loved science fiction, fantasy, and gothic mystery. She decided to become a writer in high school, when a teacher told her she had talent. Now she writes full-time, works in a laboratory full-time (for the benefits), tries to keep house, and is a workaholic with a passion for travel, jewelry making, kayaking, writing, and writers. She and her husband love to RV, and travel to white-water rivers all over the Southeast. For more, including a list of her books, see www.faithhunter.net.

ALSO AVAILABLE IN THE
JANE YELLOWROCK SERIES

FROM

Faith Hunter

BLOOD CROSS
A Jane Yellowrock Novel

The vampire council has hired skinwalker
Jane Yellowrock to hunt and kill one of their
own who has broken sacred ancient rules—but
Jane quickly realizes that in a community that is
thousands of years old, loyalties run deep...

Available wherever books are sold or at
penguin.com

Faith Hunter

BLOODRING
A Rogue Mage Novel

In a near-future world, seraphs and demons
fight a never-ending battle. But a new species of
mage has arisen. Thorn St. Croix is no ordinary
"neomage." Nearly driven insane by her powers,
she has escaped the confines of the Enclaves and
now lives among humans. When her ex-husband
is kidnapped, Thorn must risk revealing her true
identity to save him.

<u>Also Available</u>
Seraphs
Host

Available wherever books are sold or at
penguin.com

THE ULTIMATE IN
SCIENCE FICTION AND FANTASY!

From magical tales of distant worlds to stories of
technological advances beyond the grasp of man, Penguin has
everything you need to stretch your imagination to its limits.

penguin.com

ACE

Get the latest information on favorites like
William Gibson, T.A. Barron, Brian Jacques,
Ursula K. Le Guin, Sharon Shinn, Charlaine Harris,
Patricia Briggs, and Marjorie M. Liu,
as well as updates on the best new authors.

ROC

Escape with Jim Butcher, Harry Turtledove, Anne Bishop,
S.M. Stirling, Simon R. Green, E.E. Knight, Kat Richardson,
Rachel Caine, and many others—plus news on the
latest and hottest in science fiction and fantasy.

DAW

Patrick Rothfuss, Mercedes Lackey, Kristen Britain,
Tanya Huff, Tad Williams, C.J. Cherryh, and many more—
DAW has something to satisfy the cravings of any
science fiction and fantasy lover.
Also visit dawbooks.com.

*Get the best of science fiction and fantasy
at your fingertips!*